ARTIFICIAL

INTELLIGENCE:
HOW MACHINES THINK
F. DAVID PEAT

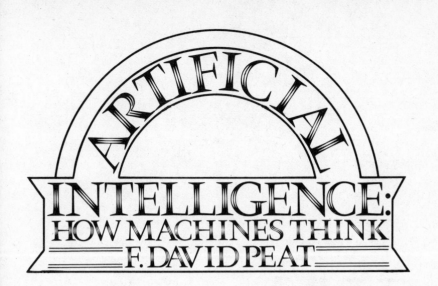

ARTIFICIAL INTELLIGENCE:
HOW MACHINES THINK
F. DAVID PEAT

A BAEN BOOK

ARTIFICIAL INTELLIGENCE: HOW MACHINES THINK

A Baen Book

Baen Enterprises
8-10 W. 36th Street
New York, N.Y. 10018

First printing, January 1985

ISBN: 0-671-55933-8

Cover art by Robert Tinney

Printed in the United States of America

Distributed by
SIMON & SCHUSTER
MASS MERCHANDISE SALES COMPANY
1230 Avenue of the Americas
New York, N.Y. 10020

CONTENTS

CHAPTER 1
Evolution of a Thinking Machine

Can a machine think? Is a computer aware of its own existence? Will the twenty-first century see the evolution of a silicon-based intelligence that is parallel to our own? There are scientists and engineers who believe that, given the present trends in research, such advances are not only possible but inevitable. Others, however, are critical of these visions and claim that computers work in ways that are qualitatively different from those of living brains and that they are forever doomed to remain machines that can at best mimic but never generate true thought.

Within this book we shall explore the various ways in which artificial intelligence (AI) researchers are designing computer systems that exhibit, or at least simulate, different aspects of intelligent behavior. We shall meet computers that are able to learn about the world around them and use that knowledge to solve practical problems. We shall meet computers that can function as well as any human expert in making a complex diagnosis, computers that can write simple stories and understand newspaper reports, computers that are developing the rudiments of vision, and computers that can talk and understand human speech. We shall also meet intelligent robots that work in factories, on the ocean bed, and in outer space. Finally, we shall take an imaginative leap into the future and consider where these trends are leading us and what will be the nature of a twenty-first century in which artificial intelligence has become a reality and our own carbon-based intelligences have become linked to silicon-based intelligences in a new phase of evolution.

But before we can discuss all these issues we need some form of historical orientation and perspective for the artificial intelligence research of the 1980s. We must discover where this new technology came from and how its concepts and theories were created. The answers are not easy to give for there is no single thread spelling out "artificial intelligence" that stretches back into our intellectual history. Suppose for a moment that this book was about physics rather than intelligent computers and that in place of expert systems, robots and machine vision were quarks and black holes. The task of tracing such a history would be far simpler since modern physics is the product of revolutions in relativity and quantum theory that took place in the first decades of this century and, in turn, these revolutions had their place in a discipline that stretches right back to Newton and Galileo. The scientists who work in these fields would have all begun their careers with formal training in physics and mathematics before entering an area of specialization. There are only a few twists and turns in the story of physics, a few changes of direction and a handful of surprises. By contrast, artificial intelligence has a very varied history. Individual research workers may have a background in physics, mathematics, linguistics, engineering, neurosciences, psychology, physiology, or some other discipline. Artificial intelligence is a field that crosses boundaries and embraces the approaches and insights of a host of different fields.

The origins of artificial intelligence form a web of interwoven strands some of which represent intellectual achieve-

2

ments such as advances in symbolic logic, cybernetics, and theories of the brain and perception; others are concerned with technological matters such as computer design and discoveries in microelectronics. In addition there are the various goals and motivations of artificial intelligence research and, to discover some of these, it is necessary to go back over 2,000 years to the Greeks and Chinese with their legends of living statues and mechanical objects that perfectly simulated the movements of living animals. Within Chapter 7, on robots, we shall hear more about these myths and in particular of the Golem that was brought to life in sixteenth century Prague by Rabbi Loew, a man who many AI researchers feel to be their spiritual ancestor.

An additional motivation for AI research is the need to know how the human brain works and what is the nature of mind. While the conventional approach to this problem comes from psychology and the neurosciences, it is also possible to simulate various aspects of human thought by means of an electronic machine and to explore the similarities and essential differences between the processes of the computer and those of the human brain.

For this first chapter we shall confine ourselves to a single thread that is common to all AI research and development; the computer itself. Although the electronic computer was developed as recently as the 1940s the desire to automate computations both for scientific and commercial reasons goes back much further. The Babylonians and early Chinese were convinced of the need to keep records of their business transactions and were involved in early attempts at invoicing and bookkeeping. During the same general historical period the science of astronomy was born and, in several areas of the world, priests and scientists made careful observations and kept meticulous records of eclipses and the movements of heavenly bodies. Commerce and astronomy both called for a systematic symbolic representation of quantative features like weights, prices, times, and positions and this led to the development of number systems and the codification of simple laws of arithmetic. In a sense the first system for writing down an addition is the ancestor of an artificial intelligence computer for it is a way of mechanizing thought, it is a system which when carried out according to a given set of rules will always produce the correct results. The very first arithmetic both freed the mind for other, more interesting contemplations, and sowed the seeds of a future slave labor of the intellect.

The keeping of accurate astronomical records eventually led to the creation of calendars and later to accurate clocks. These calendars were both the distillation of a large mass of observational data about the heavens and devices for performing calculations. With the aid of a calendar a priest can predict important religious festivals, an astronomer can pinpoint the time of an eclipse, and a farmer will know when to plant and harvest his crops. Probably most famous of these calenders were produced in South and Central America by the Mayas, Aztecs, and Incas. They are essentially algorithms and devices for calculating events in the future: the Mayan device, for example, consisted of two intermeshing cycles of 260 and 365 days which together produced the greater cycle of 18,900 days. This calender could be used not only to predict the familiar seasons and lunar phases but also the cycles of the planet Venus.

Islam produced the astrolabe, an instrument which could be used to calculate degrees of latitude by observing the elevation of certain heavenly bodies. The astrolabe gave local time in Mecca with reference to any point in the hemisphere and could therefore be used to perform acts of navigation. These early devices used a simple system of interlocking wheels and cycles to mirror the movements of the heavens and were actually simulating the arithmetic transformations represented in these mechanical movements. In a very real sense the mechanical calendars and astrolabes are ancestors of our modern computers and represent another step in the mechanization and automation of reason.

While astronomy and navigation were developing, the whole

field of commerce was also blossoming. An extreme example can be found in the office and counting house of Victorian London where rows of clerks sat on high stools hard at work with their ledgers. Some were employed to count the day's takings and enter them into a book. Others spent their hours adding columns of figures and copying the results from one book to another. In addition, some of these human calculators made copperplate duplicates of company correspondence, bills, and invoices. Thus, by the nineteenth century the arithmetic of commerce had become a labor-intensive business that cried out for mechanization. If the industrial revolution had automated the work of the human hand then why could it not do the same with the human brain?

Even two centuries earlier this problem had been well appreciated and, faced with his father's income tax accounts, the young Blaise Pascal invented a machine to perform repeated operations of addition. Fifty years later Wilhelm Leibnitz went a stage further with his Stepped Reckoner which could not only add but could multiply, divide, and extract square roots. To Leibnitz must also go the credit for realizing that the operations of the computer could be simplified if it were to use binary digits in place of the more familiar base ten system. Over the next two hundred years mechanical calculators continued to be constructed but were generally too costly and required engineering too precise to be mass produced for use in offices and counting houses. The Mount Everest of all those machines was developed towards the end of the nineteenth century and was motivated not by the demands of commercial arithmetic but from the need to produce accurate mathematical tables.

In the eighteenth and nineteenth centuries scientists and engineers had begun to produce mathematical tables that could be used for accurate navigation, to calculate angles and ranges of artillery, and to help in difficult scientific calculations. Some of these tables survived into our own schooldays and the reader may remember the book of logrithms, exponentials, trigonometric functions, and square roots that has today been replaced by the pocket calculator. With the help of these tables, engineers, navigators, artillery men, and scientists could speed up and simplify certain aspects of their calculations. Mathematical tables were certainly a great help but their major drawback was that someone had to calculate them to begin with. Take for example a single page from those school logrithms; it contains 10 columns and 60 rows, 600 entries in all. For a single page alone, therefore, 600 entries must be computed by hand and each to an accuracy of seven, nine, or even thirteen places of decimals. While the individual calculations were not particularly sophisticated they were by no means trivial, in terms of the labor involved, and were often farmed out to country clerics as a means of supplementing their incomes. It is not particularly surprising that at times, errors crept into these calculations and were not spotted in a subsequent check. It is not too difficult to make a slip in a calculation or to incorrectly copy down a set of figures from one notebook to the next. So the various mathematical and engineering tables that were produced in the nineteenth century tended to be marred by errors which at times could lead to disastrous results when it came to calculating the elevation of a gun or determining a position at sea.

For their part scientists in the nineteenth century were also faced with the task of performing long and arduous calculations by hand and even with the assistance of mathematical tables their tasks could be forbidding, particularly when mathematical tables contained the occasional error. Some of these calculations required many days of intellectual hard labor. For example, one outstanding problem occurred in astronomy when Newton's laws were applied to a system containing more than two bodies. The calculation of the motion of only three bodies under their mutual gravitational attraction could take a scientist months and months of hard labor, working several hours each day and carefully transcribing the results of each day's calculation from book to book. Tasks like these persisted even into the twentieth century. In 1930, for example, E. A. Hylleraas applied the newly discovered quantum theory to a problem analogous to that of the astronomer's three-body problem, in this case the motion of two electrons and one nucleus to form the helium atom. Hylleraas's task was assisted by a mechanical desk calculator, the updated version of Leibnitz's Stepped Reckoner, but nevertheless the computations took many weeks of work and were hailed as something of a triumph when they were published.

Hylleraas's calculation has an interesting sequel which very clearly demonstrates the problems that could arise when calculations were performed by hand. Following Hylleraas's publication of the energy of the helium, the spectroscopist G. Herzberg performed very accurate experimental measurements that turned out to be in conflict with Hylleraas's theoretical result. For a time there was a flurry of speculation; was quantum theory incorrect, had an error crept into the experimental measurement? In the end Herzberg and S. Chandrasekhar decided to perform a calculation of their own, which turned out to agree with the experiment. The original error, it later turned out, had crept in when Hylleraas was copying down figures from one page of his notebook to the next. A later attempt to calculate the energy of the helium atom using a supposedly more accurate approach was also found to contain a similar error of transcription (the controversies were finally resolved by using electronic computers). It is ironic that the calculations that Hylleraas labored over can now be set as an exercise that a physics student, seated at a computer terminal, can work out, program, and solve in an afternoon.

As with physics, calculations in commerce, engineering, ballistics, navigation, and science were becoming increasingly labor intensive and there was clearly a great need to discover some method of automating and speeding up their performance. Mathematical tables had gone some way towards speeding up the process yet the tables themselves had to be calculated by hand and were therefore prone to human error. It was the vision of Charles Babbage that a mechanical device could be designed to calculate these tables in an automatic way and even print the results. But as it turned out, Babbage's dream was a century in advance of the technology available to him and had to wait for the advent of modern electronic circuitry until it could finally be achieved.

I would like to introduce the story of Charles Babbage and his Calculating Engine with a personal anecdote. In 1955, shortly after starting my university studies I ran into an interesting gentleman who was known to my father as "old Mr. Babbage." One day we happened to sit together on a bus traveling into town and Mr. Babbage began to tell me about his grandfather who had invented the automatic cigarette machine. He explained how he had been a remarkable inventor, mathematician, and entrepreneur who, unfortunately, had never made a fortune. In passing, he also mentioned that his grandfather had built a computer and that he still possessed many of the notebooks and drawings referring to that project. While I could believe in a nineteenth-century cigarette machine, a computer seemed a little farfetched and, to my eternal regret, I never followed up the story and asked to see the notebooks. It was only two years later, when I met my first computer, DEUCE, that I realized the significance of the name Babbage. The grandfather of "old Mr. Babbage" could conceivably have been Charles Babbage himself, but was more probably his son, Henry Babbage who indeed completed the building of the Calculating Engine.

Charles Babbage was born in 1792 and distinguished himself early in life as a mathematician. He was elected a Fellow of the Royal Society and in turn helped to found the Royal Astronomical and Royal Statistical Societies. He appears to have had varied interests, for in addition to his numerous inventions, he also aided in the creation of the modern postal system. But it is for his invention of the computer that Charles Babbage will be remembered. Realizing that transmitting the mathematical tables from the computations to the typeset pages was laborous and error-prone, Babbage set about designing a mechanical device which would perform the calculations and then print the results directly. In 1823 he obtained official support and began work on his Difference Engine which was to compute various mathematical functions by a technique known as the method of differences. But the project, like others that were to follow, proved too costly so in 1834 Babbage attempted a new design called a Calculating Engine. This machine was like nothing that had gone before, for where Leibnitz's Stepped Reckoner required a human operator to set up each operation step by step, Babbage's engine was controlled by a program. Babbage had been struck by the complicated patterns that could be woven into a carpet on a Jacquard loom, controlled by punched cards. Babbage's Calculating Engine was to weave a pattern of numbers instead of a pattern of threads and for each type of calculation a punched card was produced. As the calculation proceeded, the program was read from the cards and in this way the engine was able to carry out a wide variety of tasks. This concept of a computer program also allowed the results of one stage of the calculation to be used as data for the next and, like any modern computer, Babbage's machine could loop, branch, and use the result of one stage to modify the next.

The Calculating Engine was divided into several sections; the "Store" where up to 1000 numbers could be stored, the "Mill" where the number crunching took place and calculations could be made to 20 decimal places, and input and printing sections.

But to supervise the manufactur of this engine was a considerable task and Babbage's energies and finances appear to have run out before work had progressed very far. Babbage put on another spurt in 1857 but realized that the engineering skills his drawings demanded simply did not exist. The whole philosophy of a uniform set of engineering standards had not been thought about in Babbage's time and he continually had to urge his craftsmen to catch up with his specifications.

As it turned out Babbage did not live to see the completion of his Calculating Engine but while the device did not exist in practice its abstract concept certainly excited interest. One of the most enthusiastic of his followers was Augusta Ada, Lady Lovelace, daughter of Lord Byron. Lady Lovelace was a prodigous mathematician who immediately grasped the essence of Babbage's design and after pressing him for details wrote an article on the Calculating Engine. She is also said to have written programs for Babbage's engine and recently a new computer language has been christened Ada in honor of the first computer programmer. Lady Lovelace must also have given some thought to the possibility of artificial intelligence, for in her paper on the Calculating Engine, she addressed the question of whether a mechanical calculator could be said to think.

Towards the end of his life Babbage attempted yet again to finish his engine by concentrating on a simpler design. He died in 1871 and his work was continued by his son Henry Babbage right into the first years of this century. It is clear that Charles Babbage truly anticipated the programmable computer but the technology he required simply did not exist in his time and computers could not become a practical possibility until mechanical devices were replaced by electronic circuits.

Towards the end of the nineteenth century and during the early decades of the twentieth, a number of other mechanical devices were constructed to aid in special calculations, for example, to produce tide tables and carry out differentiations.

One of the last of the pre-electronic computers was built in 1936 by Howard Aiken of Harvard University in partnership with IBM. Aiken did not use cogs and wheels for the Harvard Mark I but eletromagnetic relays from standard business machines. The computer itself was 50 feet long and 8 feet high and performed its arithmetic operations in sequences that were controlled by a punched paper tape. At the same time, in Germany, the relatively unknown Konrad Zuse was working on a different type of computer which used electric circuits. Zuse's work was performed in isolation and, terminated after World War II, had no real influence on the later course of events.

The birth of the modern computer lay in a marriage between the new technology of vacuum tube circuits and the intellectual mobilization of a world war. If World War II could produce the effort necessary for building an atomic bomb it could also construct an electronic computer, for what could be achieved by Babbage's cogs or Aiken's electromagnetic relays could be done far faster by an electronic circuit. Electronic engineers knew that their vacuum tube circuits could be made to switch, add inputs together, and simulate simple logical operations so all that was needed was the necessary financing and a proper design in order to build a calculator that would work at electronic speeds. In the United States the impetus came from the need to produce accurate bombing tables and in England it came from the problem of cracking enemy codes.

Intelligence gathering has always been a prime factor in wartime strategic planning. Under Queen Elizabeth I, Lord Walsingham organized a network of intelligence agents who were also skilled in cracking codes. Major spying networks were also created by Cardinal Richelieu and Frederick the Great. In modern warfare considerable intelligence can be obtained by intercepting the enemy's radio messages and then decoding them.

The British scored a major victory near the start of World War II by obtaining a German *Enigma* cypher machine. However, the problem of decyphering enemy messages still took a considerable amount of computational skill and time for this reason some of Britain's top mathematical minds, including Alan Turing, were assembled in great secrecy at Bletchley Park.

It was clear to Turing that effective cypher cracking depended on having a fast automatic calculating device and that meant building one that used electronic circuits. Turing had already spent some time thinking about the design of a computer and had even held some conversations with the mathematician and physicist John von Neumann in the United States.

Turing and others developed a design and by 1940 an early version was being put together. In 1943 COLOSSUS was busy cracking the German codes. It was a special-purpose machine that worked using two rolls of punched paper tape, the holes in the tape corresponding to binary digits that were converted into electrical pulses within the machine. Even during the war Turing saw that more general computers could be applied to a wide variety of problems. In the immediate postwar years he therefore moved to the United Kingdom's National Physical Laboratory where he worked on ACE, named in deference to Babbage's machine (Automatic Computing Engine).

Meanwhile in the United States the demand for accurate bombing tables had led to the development of an electronic computer at the University of Pennsylvania. ENIAC (Electronic Numerical Integrator and Calculator) was built by J. P. Eckert and J. W. Mauchy with help from John von Neumann during the design phase. Von Neumann is one of the great intellectual giants of the twentieth century. Born in Budapest he trained both as a mathematician and chemical engineer. His early contributions were to mathematics and the emerging quantum theory and he went on to publish important work in almost every field of physics. In 1944 he coauthored *Theory of Games and Economic Behaviour* with Oskar Morgenstern, a book which introduced the concept of the "no-win" situation. During World War II von Neumann was involved, along with many other top United States scientists, on the design of the atomic bomb. It was while working at Los Alamos that he became convinced of the importance of a high-speed computing device; not only would such a machine have important military applications but it could also be used to solve many of the outstandingly difficult problems of theoretical physics.

Von Neumann therefore collaborated on the design of ENIAC which was completed in 1946, but even as this machine was being constructed von Neumann was working on a faster and more advanced design. His conceptions were partly guided by reference to the architecture of the human nervous system, or rather by the way its processes are carried out. These ideas were later expressed in his book *The Computer and the Brain* (1958). Like Turing in England, von Neumann saw the importance of a machine that could solve general problems, simply by changing its program. The early computers such as COLOSSUS and ENIAC had been built for specific tasks and when variations in the program were required, they were achieved by manually changing the wiring of an external board. Von Neumann is generally credited with recognizing the importance of a program that could be stored internally in the computer as a series of digits in the system's memory.

Following ENIAC came EDVAC, BINAC, and UNIVAC (which was produced for the United States Department of Census). All these early machines, as with the more advanced ones of our present day, conformed to the basic design first set down by von Neumann. It is only in the 1980s that computer specialists are contemplating radically different approaches, using parallel processing, which they term non–von Neumann machines. The postwar revolution in computers came about not through an innovation in theory or design but from advances in technology, for the vacuum tube gave way to the transistor (invented in 1947) and, in turn, to whole arrays of transistor circuits that could be placed on a microchip. This advance enabled computers to be constructed that were much faster and could pack more memory and processing power into a given space.

The early vacuum tube computers were dinosaurs of the computer world and like these early reptiles, rapidly became extinct as the result of their size and slowness. I can well remember my first encounter with one of them, DEUCE, the commercial version of Turing's ACE, when I was a student

13

at Liverpool University in the late 1950s. Although inferior in its abilities to one of today's briefcase-sized microcomputers, DEUCE occupied a room all to itself; in fact, one could open a door in its back and walk inside its arithmetic unit. DEUCE was distributed all over the room, its short-term memory, for example, took the form of mushroom-shaped protrusions from the floor which contained its mercury delay lines, and on days when the sun shone too hard in the room these mushrooms would heat up and the machine would become confused.

Programming DEUCE was a major task in itself since each digit of the program had to be punched, hole by hole, into a Hollerith card so that even the shortest program took many hours to set down. The problem I was working on was that of three competing chemical reactions and involved the solution of simultaneous differential equations. It proved too much for DEUCE and the machine could only work on the problem in easy stages, spewing out the results, stage by stage in the form of punched paper tape which was then fed in as data for the next.

Yet for all its size and slowness DEUCE had a personality of its own. Seated before its flashing lights one could almost believe that it had emotions, that it could become offended by rough treatment. On occasion it seemed to forget what it was doing and would wander off in its programmed world generating absurd strings of numbers. On others some fear deeply buried in its subconscious would be activated and its alarm bell would ring furiously, giving the operator the guilty feeling that he had performed a violation on its electronic person.

But DEUCE was doomed, for transistorized circuits at a fraction of the size and cost were to replace tubes so that faster and more powerful computers could be produced. It was a combination of transistors, improvements in memories, and better circuit design that produced the computer revolution of the 1960s for it brought these machines within the price range of most businesses, which could then use them to work out payrolls and invoices. In addition, no self-respecting university was complete without one. Von Neumann had been right, the outstanding problems of physics, engineering, and chemistry were to fall before the power of the electronic computer. For example, I continued my theoretical research at a time when research groups all over the world were applying quantum theory to work out the structure of atoms and molecules using calculations that would have been impossible a decade earlier.

For a time I remained on the outside of this mainstream of research but in the 1960s found occasion, again, to seek the help of a computer. The machine I worked on was an IBM 1620 and it represented a welcome improvement over DEUCE but was still painfully slow by today's standards. I had been working on a theory that required some computing power to test it out. In the case of the IBM 1620 this meant tens of hours of computing and armed with a flask of tea I would sit up all night and feed the problem into the machine. A year later an IBM 360 was installed and my problem was reduced from hours of computing time to minutes but it still required some very careful programming to avoid overloading the memory.

This was also the era of timesharing, in which a single computer could be switched between a large number of tasks. Since human reaction times are vastly slower than those of the computer and even mechanical inputs and outputs are something of a bottleneck, the logical solution was to have a whole series of inputs and outputs. While the computer was working on one problem another part of its brain would be receiving the data on a quite different problem. In a timesharing computer a whole series of terminals is distributed around an office or university campus and the computer's attention is constantly switched from one job to another. Since the human operators need time to digest the output presented to them and to physically type in new instructions the computer can be working on someone else's problem during this delay.

The 1970s also saw the introduction of the cheap and portable microprocessor or personal computer. Microprocessors have had a revolutionary impact in terms of home computers and TV games but they are also making important contributions to robotics and artificial intelligence. Where once a robot had to be directly connected to a mainframe computer it is now possible to build its brain directly into an arm or some other part. But the timesharing computer and the microprocessor of the 1980s are soon going to look as antiquated as DEUCE looks today, for scientists are now working on a supercomputer with ultrafast superconducting circuits and a massive memory and beyond that lies the optical computer that uses laser light in place of electric circuits.

The computer began its life in the minds of scientists like Pascal, Leibnitz, and Babbage as a device that would take the labor out of numerical calculations. The electronic computers that were produced from the designs of men like Turing and von Neumann did exactly this and magnificently so but they could also do something more than mere mathematical manipulations; they could work with the abstract symbols of logic and they could operate with words of the English language. In short, they could do some of the things that we associate with intelligent thought. So while the majority of scientists continued to use computers to perform difficult and elaborate calculations, and the business world installed them to reduce the labor of bookkeeping, a few thinkers saw that these new machines had the potential to simulate the operations of human thought and in this way the new science of artificial intelligence was born.

The ways in which symbolic logic, electronic networks, and modern computers can be used to simulate the operations of thought are discussed in the next chapter. The present chapter concludes with a very brief overview of how computers work.

Computer Architecture

It is not really necessary to understand the design of a

computer in order to appreciate the issues of artificial intelligence. For example, in laboratories all over the world scientists and engineers are attempting to devise improved circuitry and memory systems which work faster and occupy an even smaller space, yet none of this substantially affects the basic principles of artificial intelligence beyond making it possible to carry out more complex tasks in a shorter amount of time.

The computers we have met in this chapter are the sort of machines found in the home, office, and AI laboratories and are more properly termed digital computers for they operate by electronically manipulating binary digits. There are also analog computers which are used only for certain specialized tasks in scientific or engineering projects. Analog computers work in a very different way from digital machines. They can electronically simulate some complex physical process but do not concern us in this book.

Like Babbage's computing engine the modern digital computer consists of a central processing unit control, memory, and input/output devices which are described below.

Input/Output

The input and output, as the name suggests, are the means for extracting information from the computer and putting data in. There are a host of different input devices used in AI research; obvious ones like punched cards, punched tape, magnetic tape, floppy and rigid disks, keyboards, light pens, touch-sensitive wheels, joysticks, and tablets and more subtle ones such as TV cameras for vision, microphones for speech recognition, robot arms, and various sensors. In addition there are remote links using telephone lines, satellites, and one day possibly input will come direct from the human brain itself. In all these devices an incoming signal is processed electronically and converted into a series of binary pulses that can be understood by the computer.

As to output, there are screens, printers, magnetic and paper tape, punched cards, and synthetic speech, as well as electronic signals to robotic arms and to a host of other electronic and electrical devices. For the home computer user the input and output are used for telling the computer about the problem and then getting the answer out. But when it comes to artificial intelligence, input and output act as senses to the outer world, ways in which the computer can reach out and touch, learn about and respond to the world around it.

Central Processing Unit

The central processing unit or CPU is the cerebral cortex of the computer for it is here that all its arithmetic and logical operations are carried out. It is often difficult to realize that all the complex and sophisticated things that a computer carries out can ultimately be reduced to the movement of binary electrical pulses within the CPU. The reason for this will be explored in Chapter 2 but briefly it is because even the most sophisticated of mathematics can be represented as a sequence of arithmetic operations and the processes of logic can similarly be reduced to binary arithmetic. But some of these operations require an enormous number of elementary calculations to be performed so the computer's abilities stand or fall on the speed with which its central processing unit can carry out these simple calculations. This speed is determined by two things: the speed with which a single addition can be performed, and the time it takes to send a number or electronic pulse from one location in the processor to another. This latter speed is limited by the velocity of light, since electronic pulses in a computer can never travel faster than light. So the CPU must be made as small as possible if it is to maintain a high speed and this means advances in design and solid state electronics. The electronic advances in CPU design are discussed later in Chapter 8.

Even with the very fastest of CPUs, that will be produced in the superconducting computers of the future, the central processing unit is something of a bottleneck since all the data in the computer has to flow through this unit and it can only do one thing at a time. Even with modern time sharing computers in which the machine rapidly switches between a number of different problems the CPU can only carry out a single train of thought at any given instant. The human brain, by contrast, can think of many different things at once and at the same time can control a variety of processes within the body. The solution is to have the computer do several things simultaneously and carry out its different thought processes in parallel. A major breakthrough in computers will occur when the single CPU is replaced by a large number of units all working in parallel on different aspects of the same problem. Such computers are already being used as prototypes by the artificial intelligence community and are called non–von Neumann machines. Some of them use from five to a few hundred processing units to carry out their parallel processing with additional units to control the overall flow of data and information. One plan calls for the interconnection of a million microprocessors to produce a radically different type of computer which may evolve a form of intelligence out of this "society of minds."

Control

The computer also needs some method of controlling the sequences of arithmetic and logical operations that are carried out in the CPU and, if several users are working on the machine, of switching from problem to problem. In Babbage's machine this control was achieved by using a string of punched cards and in the first electronic computer a punched paper tape was used. Today programs are entered into the machine and then stored electronically where they exert their control over the flow and sequence of computing operations.

In addition, modern computers do not come into the world in total ignorance—but like human babies, they possess many inborn abilities. Before a modern computer is programmed for a particular task it already possesses a great deal of control and procedural knowledge that has been built into its semiconductor chips. For example, there are sets of special mathematical functions which need to be used over and over again, there are programs for debugging errors and there are interpreters for the various programming languages themselves—BASIC, FORTRAN, Ada, LISP and a host of others. If a computer is not preconditioned to accept a particular programming language then it has absolutely no idea what to do when the instruction GO TO or PRINT is typed in.

Memory

A modern computer has to remember a great deal: the program that is fed into it, the raw data used in that program, and the intermediate results that are generated while the program is running. Like the human brain the computer has two sorts of memories, long term and short term. That is, things it needs to remember over long periods of time and things it can afford to forget when it is switched off at night. The long-term memory is stored magnetically on a disk or tape; in older computers punched cards and magnetic drums were also used. Even a computer program or data written down by hand or printed in a book is a form of long-term memory.

While long-term memory systems have enormous capacity for storing millions of facts, they tend to be rather slow in operation. In using a floppy disk for example the computer first has to trace the location on the disk where the particular information is stored, then it reads these magnetic fluctuations, converts them into digits, and moves those digits to storage areas in the computer's short-term memory.

While long-term memory is located in one of the peripherals that are connected to the computer, short-term memory is stored in the computer itself or in some unit attached to it by a bus capable of transmitting information at very high speed. The short-term memory generally takes the form of magnetic fluctuations recorded on a solid state device. These memories are very fast but limited in overall capacity.

The computer's basic currency is the binary numbers, 0 and 1. Of course these numbers are not actually present in its circuits as such but in an abstract form as an electrical pulse or the absence of a pulse so that a string of pulses and gaps corresponds to a string of binary digits such as 00101101. A single binary number is called a "bit" of information; computers however prefer to move around their binary numbers in units that are, say, eight bits long, such as 01111001, 11000011, and so on, called "bytes." Roughly speaking, the 0 and 1 bits are the letters of the two-letter computer alphabet and the eight-letter bytes are its basic words.

Bytes are stored and retrieved in the computer memory in an analogous way to envelopes in pigeon holes. Each pigeon hole has an address, so when a piece of data is stored in the memory, it is electronically "written" or recorded at a particular address. Later when this data is required it is retrieved or "read" from the same address in the computer memory. Since the computer can go directly to any short-term memory address and read its content, and does not, like a mailman, have to walk up the road until it finds the correct address, the system is called RAM or random access memory. By contrast the data recorded on the cassette of your home computer can not be accessed at any random point but must be read in sequence.

Some of the control systems of a computer, such as debugging programs, the rules of the programming languages, and certain special functions are permanently recorded in the computer memory even when it is switched off. This means that while the contents of these particular addresses can always be "read" by the computer no new messages can be put into that particular slot. Such memory locations are called ROM or read only memory.

Programming Languages

The very first computers were difficult to program for they

had to be instructed to carry out even the simplest operation using a numerical code. It wasn't good enough to type in "1 + 2 = ." The programmer had to instruct the computer to store the number 1 at a particular address and the number 2 at some other address. Then the number in one address had to be read and added to the number read from some other address and the result stored in a further memory location, all programmed in terms of numerically coded instructions.

A major development was a computer language that allowed computer engineers to program the machine using symbols that were a little closer to conventional mathematics. This program was then interpreted to the computer by means of a compiler and assembler program which first interpreted its symbols and then converted these symbols into strings of numbers that could be used directly by the machine.

Today a variety of compilers, interpreters, and assemblers are designed into the computer and stored in its permanent memory so that the user can use more or less any language he takes a fancy to. The businessman may use COBOL, the schoolchild will learn BASIC or LOGO, the scientist will use FORTRAN, and the artificial intelligence worker LISP. But these are just a few of the programming languages available and for each one there are local variants or dialects.

One of the important goals of AI research is to develop programming languages that are identical to the type of languages we use in everyday life. For example a doctor consulting a computer diagnosis system would prefer to ask his questions in normal English, or French or whatever language he naturally speaks, provided that it is also dosed with a liberal number of technical terms. A shop floor engineer who programs an industrial robot would like to use the same terms and specifications that he employs when talking to a machinist on the shop floor machine. A scientist will prefer to work directly with equations and diagrams.

These various languages are known as "high level languages" and they operate within the computer much as a chain of command works in an office. Suppose, for example, the chairman calls in his assistant one day and says, "It's time we had a nice glossy company report to satisfy the shareholders, you know what to do." The chairman has used a high level language which is then interpreted by his assistant who calls in the head of the design and writing sections and explains in more detailed terms what is needed. The directors then hold meetings with the heads of groups responsible for layout, photography, research, writing, and so on. Finally a number of individual workers deal with the details of their task. So instructions in a high level language pass down the various levels of a hierarchy, being interpreted and amplified the lower they go. The chairman does not need or want to know how the report is actually put together, the assistant does not need to know how a design it set up, the designer does not bother about the cameraman's lighting arrangements, and the cameraman does not concern himself with the chemical composition of the developing bath. As one moves from a high to a low level, details are filled in by individual workers.

In a similar way instructions that are given to an AI computer using some high level language may look like normal spoken English, but are then translated into a more detailed programming language, then into strings of symbols, and finally into sequences of digits that can be executed by the computer. Low level instructions operate much faster in the computer so it is of considerable advantage to have higher level languages interpreted directly onto a microchip when the computer is manufactured. This is called "hard wiring" language. In addition, certain artificial intelligence systems, such as vision or speech synthesis systems which have been developed over years of research will eventually be hard wired onto a single chip to produce a cheap and rapid system in place of the expensive computer prototype.

In less than 40 years the computer has developed from the first, crude vacuum tube device that was capable of performing only a limited number of operations in response to an external punched tape program into the fast, compact computers of today. And even today's computers are beginning to make way to even more advanced machines that will be capable of parallel processing and performing hundreds or thousands of millions of instructions each second. But these computers are still glorified calculating engines, electronic extensions of Leibnitz's Stepped Reckoner. To give them the power of thought and intelligent behavior requires another step, once which involves the manipulation of symbols in logic and natural language. As to how this can take place we will learn in the next chapter.

CHAPTER 2
Thought and Logic

Artificial intelligence (AI) is the study of the ways in which computers can duplicate or simulate certain functions of the human intelligence. One generally accepted definition of the field reads: Artificial intelligence is concerned with understanding the principles of intelligence and building working models of human intelligent behavior. So the science of artificial intelligence can be approached from two directions: from computers and their programs and from psychology and the neurosciences. Knowledge of human behavior and brain structure can help in the design of an AI system, likewise the study of AI systems can give clues as to how humans may process the information around them. In each area of AI there are a few research workers who take extreme positions; some, for example, attempt an exact simulation of processes in the brain, others concentrate upon a particular problem to be solved and believe that the computer should evolve its own efficient approaches which may be very different in principle from those of the human brain. In the chapters that follow we shall find examples where computers can work faster and more effectively than humans at certain tasks and others, like vision and language understanding, in which human skills are exceptionally difficult to duplicate.

The previous chapter was concerned with the computer and its evolution, the present chapter will therefore concentrate upon human thought. But we shall not be so much concerned here with questions of neuropsychology and brain structure, as with the overall way in which information is processed and with the structure of thought. Even this question is a staggering one for it has remained unsolved since the beginning of time. Indeed to ask, "What is the nature of thought?" is to pose one of the deepest questions that can be voiced.

Before we plunge into the mechanisms of thought it is salutory to being more gently by asking what it is that the brain actually does. A moment's reflection will show that this brain of ours is far more than an organ located in the head that sits and thinks. To begin with the brain controls the unconscious processes of the body such as respiration, blood pressure, heart beat, muscle tone, and a host of other processes, all of which indicates that there is no hard and fast division between the brain and the rest of the body. In its operations the brain merges into the whole nervous system and into the flows and fluctuations of hormones and neurotransmitters that are part of the body's general chemistry.

Many actions taken by the brain seem to be quite distinct from those of thought. For example, the brain filters the information that bombards the senses. Its extensions, the eyes, are involved in seeing. Hearing, speech, and movement of the limbs also involve processes that cannot properly be called "thinking." Even the act of "seeing" the solution to a problem or the connection between two ideas seem to lie outside the normal movement of thought. So there are a great many brain activities that could not properly be called "thought." And as to thought itself? It appears to be composed of a whole complex of processes, many of which lie outside the present domain of AI research. Although we may not be able to pin down thought, it is familiar to all of us. Thought is that constant internal movement of the mind, that buzz that occurs as we try to solve a problem, give a lecture, remember a vacation, or simply day dream. Thought seems to be ubiquitous to human life for it even takes place during sleep in the form of dreams. But a dream itself is an interesting clue to the nature of thought because its contents and flow generally appear to be absurd and illogical and so different from that of our waking thought. Is this truly so? Some introspection will indicate that much of our thought has the flowing nature of the dream and it is only when we discipline ourselves to write or speak in a rational manner that the order of "logical thought" is present.

It is easy to fool ourselves into believing that our thought is always rational and logical yet introspection demonstrates how thought so often proceeds by association and conditioning. There are thoughts that are sparked off by an image, a taste, an odor, by other thoughts, and by words that are heard or voiced internally. It is particularly easy to observe the flurry of thought that is generated by a word; simply repeat to yourself a word like "death," "love," or "heat" and observe the sequence of thoughts that it generates. What order does this sequence obey and where is its logic? Poets and painters have explored the rules of thought and made use of these associations. They indicate to us how rich is the movement of thought and how little of it is concerned with what we take as a rational ordering. A single example of the cinema may suffice to make this point. The filmmaker takes great care with his lighting and camera angles to produce exactly the images he needs. These visual images are then edited into a flowing sequence that tells a coherent story. There is a very definite grammar to film, a stringent set of rules which if violated will be immediately spotted by the viewer. But are these the rules of ordinary logic or are they related to some other way in which human thought is ordered?

27

Within the realm of thought there are a great many subtle movements each of which has its own ordering and grammar. Some of these orderings are clear and have been made explicit to us, others are felt untuitively or only dimly perceived. Yet our western civilization has conditioned us to think of thought in terms of language and, in particular, of grammatical and logical rules of construction. This prejudice has permeated much research in AI so the reader must exercise caution for when computers are designed to simulate human thought they are only imitating a very narrow range of behavior.

Intelligent and logical thought is generally associated with activities such as problem solving and rational argument. However, when it comes to our own daily life most of us are aware of the rarity of a rational, ordered approach. When we assess personal risk or safety in our diet, habits, driving a car, or thinking about national defense and nuclear power plants, most of us solve these problems in very "illogicial" ways. Illogical they may be, yet there is a surprising consensus of agreement on many of these issues. Many arguments and disputes involve moves and strategies that lie outside the normal rules of formal logic yet are well understood by the participants. A child may, for example, employ the "demonstration by repetition," in which the same point is made over and over again, and quarreling parents may use the "demonstration by intensity" in which one shouts louder than the other or employs greater emotional force. The familiar "argument by generalization" is used by bigots all over the world to justify their prejudices as in "I can't work with redheads, my last secretary was always throwing tantrums and she was redheaded." Then there is the masterly "argument by deflection and irrelevance" as in, "Well, if I can't go there tonight, how come you went last week?"

So even when we agree to confine our attention to those modes of thought used in an argument and debate we immediately find that what most people use as a convention is very different from the logic of the ancient Greeks. The above examples all violate the laws of traditional logic yet they are nonetheless rules for thought and, moreover, rules that are agreed upon by the participants of arguments. It is even possible to arrive at conclusions and a consensus of opinion by proceeding in this way. In what follows we shall be dealing with the laws of thought and of logic that began with the classical Greek philosophers but we must always bear in mind that this is only one of many conventions for ordering thought within a society.*

Accepting these limitations on thought and on rational thought in particular, we can pass on to the logic of the Greeks. One of the great advances in logic begins with Aristotle who formulated the syllogism, a formal argument that enables the philosopher to arrive at a true conclusion based on certain premises. For example, given that "All men are mortal" and that "Socrates is a man," it is possible to deduce that "Socrates is mortal." Syllogisms are essentially the shapes of arguments and can be written down to look a little like the proof of a mathematical theorem except that in place of algebriac symbols or numbers there is language:

Major premise: All men are rational.
Minor premise: Some animals are men.
Conclusion: Therefore, some animals are rational.

Compare this overall shape of one of Aristotle's syllogisms to a deduction in mathematics:

Given that: $x + y = 7$
And $y = 2$
Therefore $x = 5$

Just as in mathematics there are correct and incorrect answers so it is with the syllogisms of logic. For example the above syllogism enables us to deduce that "some animals are rational" but not that "all animals are rational" or that "all animals are men." One does not have to go out into the world and observe animals and men to discover that

---

*It is only when we come to the last chapter that we shall explore ways in which computers may be able to move beyond "logical thought."

these deductions are false but simply to follow the rules of a syllogism, given that its major and minor premise are true.

The syllogisms that Aristotle set down are a collection of various ways in which deductions can be made from a series of facts about the world. But the syllogisms themselves are not so much about facts or nature as about the structure of language and its rational or logical use. An examination of the syllogism given above indicates, for example, that the basic shape of the proof is unchanged if we substitute the word "Greeks" for "men" or "bipeds" for "rational." Indeed, a whole range of substitutions are possible which preserve the basic form of each syllogism:

Major premise: All dogs are four legged.
Minor premise: Some pets are dogs.
Conclusion: Therefore some pets are four legged.

Indeed, we can go further and do something that the Greeks had never thought of, we can substitute symbols for words:

Major premise: All X are Y.
Minor premise: Some Z are X.
Conclusion: Therefore some Z are Y.

Here X, Y, and Z can stand for anything we choose and provided that the minor and major premises make sense then the conclusion must be true. Hence Aristotle's logic begins to look a little like school algebra, or rather school algebra and the logic of language may both have a common underpinning in thought.

The syllogisms of Aristotle are composed of propositions which contain nouns (men, Greeks, Socrates . . .), quantifiers (some, all, one . . .) and predicates (is a philosopher, are mortal, lives, is dead . . .) and form part of a wider field called predicate logic. In addition, Greek philosophers also discussed the logical ordering of hypothetical propositions of the form: "If . . . then. . . ."

"If the sun shines then we shall go to the beach."
"If we go to the beach then I shall pack a picnic."
Conclusion: "The sun is shining therefore I shall pack
        a picnic."

Although propositional logic is simpler than predicate logic it is enormously powerful in the things it can do. And just as with predicate logic one can perform a variety of substitutions in propositional logic:

If p then q

If p then r

Therefore: If p then r; when p, q, and r stand for phrases. Another deduction in the propositional calculus is

If p then q

If not-p then r

Therefore if not-q then r.

The above propositions all look rather simple but it is possible to substitute whole propositions for the variables p, q, and r and through a process of concatenation and nesting to develop some very elaborate arguments based simply on the axioms of propositional logic.

The study of logic went into something of an eclipse during the first centuries after Christ but in the middle ages it was taken up again by Arabic and Christian scholars until it was soon considered an essential element in the education of every learned man. In the seventeenth century Leibnitz, whose Stepped Reckoner was discussed in the previous chapter, attempted to put logic in a very special position. Leibnitz proposed that philosophers should devote all their energies to the construction of a *Characteristica Universalis* or universal language for philosophy.

Leibnitz realized that philosophical arguments often get bogged down by language itself and the ambiguities and confusions that it can produce. The answer therefore lay in the construction of a new, artificial language, a symbolic form that would be totally free of ambiguity and would represent thought in a way that was as rational and orderly as mathematics. In order to arrive at philosophical truths or to solve disputations, philosophers would simply have to agree on certain basic assumptions and then sit down to compute theorems about the world, basic truths that would be arrived at in a totally logical manner. The whole process of philosophy would therefore become automatic and fool-proof.

The suggestion that all the controversies of philosophy could be automatically resolved in a symbolic language of thought was particularly attractive and several philosophers returned to it in the two centuries that followed. Bertrand Russell and Alfred North Whitehead, for example, attempted to found the entire reasoning of mathematics on the logic of propositions and published their work in the famous *Principia Mathematicia*. This was followed by the *Tractatus Logico-Philosophicus* written by Russell's student Ludwig Wittgenstein. But in later life the same Wittgenstein was to demonstrate the futility of Leibnitz's program by showing that any language rich enough to contain the subtleties of human thought must of necessity be filled with ambiguity and subject to a variety of different uses. Wittgenstein showed that there is no simple, direct correspondence between statements in language and events in the real world and wherever logic is used as a mirror or image of the world certain essential features will be lost. What can be said in an absolutely logical way tends to be rather superficial and does not encompass the great artistic and ethical debates of humankind.

But leaving aside Leibnitz's desire for the automation of philosophical argument, he did suggest that traditional logic could be written down in symbolic form and these symbols then manipulated just like the formulae of mathematics. Leibnitz did not, in fact, publish his work on symbolic logic. Bertrand Russell in his *History of Western Philosophy* suggests that if Leibnitz's work had been generally known it would have advanced the subject by 150 years. In the hands of logicians, mathematicians, and philosophers of the nineteenth and twentieth century this program was completed. Agustus De Morgan, mathematics tutor to Augusta Ada, Lady Lovelace, whom we met in the Chapter 1, began to cast the propositional and predicate logics in symbolic form so that logical arguments now looked like pages from a mathematics book. In the early twentieth century several logicians argued that symbolic logic, now called the propositional calculus and the predicate calculus, was logically prior to mathematics and it should therefore be possible to base the whole of mathematics upon the foundations of a handful of axioms in logic.

In making this transition from a logic based in language to one using mathematical symbols, a particularly significant contribution was made by George Boole. Boole was born in 1815, the son of a Lincoln tradesman, and taught himself mathematics to the point where he was making significant contributions to the subject. Boole also took an interest in the various forms of logic and, contemporary with De Morgan, argued that it was more properly a branch of mathematics than of philosophy. His major work in this field was contained in his book, *An Investigation into the Laws of Thought, on which are Founded the Mathematical Theories of Logic and Probabilities.*

Boole's approach to logic was to divide the world into two classes and to define operations that could be performed on these classes. The classes could be called p and q, 0 and 1, yes and no, "and" and "or." In fact, the whole process of his logic took the form of operating on strings of 0s and 1s and this, although it may not appear so on the surface, was equivalent to the propositional calculus.

Suddenly something very powerful has taken place in this journey from the syllogisms of Aristotle. We began with the ways in which the Greeks could order rational thought by means of proofs or logical patterns in language. We showed how these patterns could also be expressed using the symbols of algebra to produce a symbolic calculus. Now Boole has demonstrated that this symbolic calculus is equivalent to the manipulation of strings of 0s and 1s, in other words to the operations of a binary arithmetic. But this same binary arithmetic had already been chosen by Leibnitz as the natural language to be used by calculating machines. In a series of steps the laws of thought have to be cast in a form exactly suited for automatic computing. By working with binary arithmetic, a computer is also performing logical operations which can ultimately be translated into the rational arguments of a language.

The story now enters the twentieth century and the world of computers, but before we reach that era it is necessary to pause and add yet another word of caution about the importance of symbolic logic and Boole's laws of thought. We have already pointed out that thought is only one of the brain's many activities and logic is only one way in which thought can be ordered. What we have explored in the preceding pages is one form of that logic which has its origins in the Greek language and culture. But there are other forms of logic, that originate in China and India, for example. These two cultures have deep and subtle philosophies which evolve according to laws of argument and development which are not always identical to those of the West. Although the logics of the East may not be as well codified they nonetheless exist and have an honorable tradition. The Hindu philosophers, for example, will arrive at their conclusions often by means of negations and arguments involving "that which is not." In Zen philosophy solutions to knotty problems are arrived at by very different routes from those of Western logic. To ask:

"What was your face before your parents were born?"
or
"What is the sound of one hand clapping?"

is to expose the impotence of Greek logic in the face of certain problems. Friends of mine who have lived with various groups of North American Indians and have studied their languages tell me that they too have different processes for arriving at general conclusions and for deciding on a course of action. Some of these processes are similar to those of traditional logic but others work in different ways. This whole topic of the laws of thought in different cultures and the changes that take place between childhood and adulthood is well worth serious study and may reveal some interesting conclusions about the nature of thought and its evolution.

Even within our Western tradition not everyone agrees with the exclusive position of the Boolean laws of thought. There are philosophers and logicians, for example, who have developed multivalued logics, variants on the traditional categories of true and false which may include "fuzzy" concepts, ambiguities, and intermediate states of truth. But these are still variations upon a traditional theme, possibly a more interesting approach is that of Günther Grassmann, a contemporary of De Morgan and Boole. Grassman, along with his two contemporaries, believed that the true subject of mathematics was the process of human thought, but unlike De Morgan and Boole, he did not visualize this thought in terms of traditional logic. Grassmann established an algebra in which the flow of thought was to be reflected, with each thought containing its opposite and thoughts having other thoughts enfolded within them. As it turned out, Grassmann's ideas did not prove immediately popular and discouraged by this lack of attention, the mathematician turned to Sanskrit. When Grassmann's algebra was eventually taken up it was not because of its supposed connection with thought but for its intrinsic qualities as a branch of mathematics. It is only within the 1980s that Grassmann's original ideas have been reexamined by physicists Basil Hiley and David Bohm. Hiley and Bohm have been using Grassmann algebras in a proposed unified theory of relativity and quantum mechanics but have also speculated on how the algebra may be used to represent certain processes of thought which Bohm calls the "holomovement" or the "implicate order." It is possible that ideas like these may one day have importance for artificial intelligence so we shall explore them in greater depth in Chapter 9.

To return to symbolic logic and Boolean algebra, we have seen how these abstract systems can be used to represent the logical operations of thought but as to why this should be so is something of a mystery. Why should it be that the arithmetic operations of binary numbers have anything to do with the electrochemical processes of the human brain? The connection is a mystifying one and had to wait until the twentieth century for clarification.

In 1937 a graduate student at M.I.T., Claude Shannon carried out a mathematical investigation of electrical circuits containing switches and relays. The results which were expressed in his master's thesis contained some interesting implications for AI research. Shannon reasoned that switches and relays can only be in one of two states, on or off. Hence a circuit containing switches and relays, no matter how complex it is, is ultimately composed out of various combinations of two-state systems. In other words the behavior of such circuits can be described using the logic of two-state systems and this logic is exactly that described by George Boole in his laws of thought.

Hence Shannon was able to show that complex electrical circuits could be described in terms of Boolean algebra and binary arithmetic, and conversely that this arithmetic and algebra could also be simulated by such circuits. Shannon's thesis therefore provided a rigorous justification for Leibnitz's insight that binary arithmetic was the natural language for a calculating machine.

The next phase of the story involves a neurophysiologist, Warren S. McCulloch and a mathematician, Walter Pitts. McCulloch had been for some time interested in the structure of the brain. The problem was, however, that this organ is immensely complicated both in its structure and behavior so it is a major difficulty simply deciding where to begin and what to study. McCulloch and Pitts settled on a much simpler problem than the brain itself and concentrated on a collection of neurons or nerve cells which they attempted to represent mathematically. Each neuron consists of a cell body (which contains the nucleus) and long fibers called axions. At the end of each axion there are a series of fine dendrites which make physical contact with neighboring neurons. When a given nerve cell fires, electrical signals pass

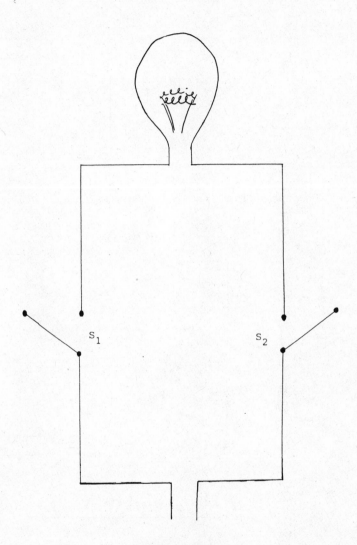

Figure 2-1
Logical operations can be represented by means of electrical circuits containing switches. Here the logical operation "and" is simulated. The lamp lights when switches S_1 *and* S_2 are on.

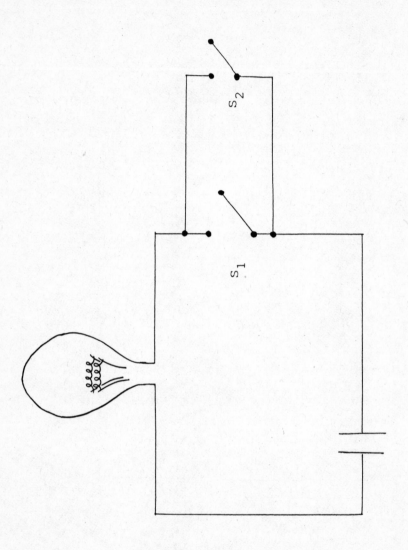

An "or" circuit in which the lamp is lit provided switches S_1 *or* S_2 are on.

along the axion and trigger chemical processes in the dendrites which in turn may trigger a neighboring neuron to fire in reponse. Hence a collection of neurons is a little like a complex interconnected electrical circuit in which a given disturbance can spread out through the entire system.

It is now known that the brain's neurons are quite complicated in their behavior, there electrical responses are what is known as nonlinear and involve complex chemical interconnections as well as electrical processes, but in the early 1940s this information was not as well defined and McCulloch and Pitts felt justified in making some simplifying assumptions. It appeared, for example, that the strength of a signal between one neuron and the next was unimportant and what really mattered was if that particular neuron fired or not. Hence, McCulloch and Pitts considered neurons as having only two states, firing and not firing, and in that way influenced the other neurons around them. In short, a set of interconnected nerves were electrically similar to circuits containing switches or relays which had earlier been described by Shannon. In their paper, "A Logical Calculus of the Ideas Imminent in Nervous Activity," the two scientists advanced the theory that nerves in the brain acted like electrical switches and their combined action could therefore be described both by the propositional calculus and Boolean algebra. While Shannon and the philosophers of symbolic logic had shown how electrical circuits could imitate the laws of thought, McCulloch and Pitts had shown that the brain itself could be simulated by electrical circuits and described in terms of Boolean logic. The circle was complete, from the Greek laws of thought to Boolean logic and the behavior of electrical circuits and from the human brain to switching circuits described in Boolean terms. According to this grand argument it should indeed be possible to simulate some aspects of human thought using an electronic computer that operates according to binary arithmetic and the processes of the propositional calculus.

Another pathway towards this twentieth century mechanization of the mind resulted from the new topics of cybernetics and information theory. The idea that feedback can control the performance of a machine by monitoring its output and feeding back this information into the input had been understood since the industrial revolution. Machines were fitted with spinning governors to regulate their speed; when the machine ran too quickly these governors would spin out further, act to cut off steam entering the machine, and slow down its performance. In this way, feedback could be used to establish an ideal speed which the machine would then hunt for by constantly monitoring its output and using it to modify its performance.

Each house with central heating possesses a feedback device called a thermostat. The temperature of the room is set to an ideal value and the thermostat constantly monitors room temperature to detect deviations from this ideal. If the temperature drops too much then this information is fed back to the furnace which increases its output; when the temperature rises too much this information is again fed back to shut off the furnace. This form of feedback is present in mammals who also have internal thermostats which enable them to regulate their internal body temperature irrespective of external conditions.

During wartime studies of anti-aircraft gunners it was noticed how a skilled gunner would aim his weapon, not directly at the target, but at the position the enemy plane would occupy by the time his shells reached it. The gunner was actually planning for events in the future, he was anticipating events and using a mechanism of "feedforward" to control his behavior.

So the ideas of feedback and feedforward appeared to apply across the board, to machines, to electrical circuits, to the nervous systems of animals, and to processes in human brains. In 1943, the same year as McCulloch and Pitts published on neural networks, Norbert Wiener and Arturo Rosenblueth published their "Behaviour, Purpose and Teleology" and five years later Wiener published his famous book *Cybernetics*. In addition to becoming a Boolean network of relays and switches the human brain was also a cybernetic machine whose goal oriented, purposeful behaviour could be explained in terms of the mathematics of feedback and feedforward. In 1943 Claude Shannon also extended his earlier work on networks into the science of information theory. His *A Mathematical Theory of Communication* gave rise for yet another metaphor for the brain in which "bits" of information picked up by the sense organs are processed by the central nervous system.

By the end of the 1940s, with the first electronic computers in operation, scientists had already pursued the analogies between the brain and the computer in terms of cybernetics, information processing, the electrical properties of neurons, and the operations of Boolean algebra and symbolic logic. The door was therefore open into the new field of artificial intelligence. Indeed, Alan Turing was already speculating on the possibilities of machine intelligence and a number of scientists had begun work on learning networks. Since, according to McCulloch and Pitts, the brain can be mathematically modeled in terms of a network of Boolean switches, why not try this in practice and build a pseudo-brain out of electrical circuits? The most ambitious of these projects was named the Perceptron and, constructed at Cornell University, it consisted of a randomly wired electrical network connected to a series of photocells. The idea behind the perceptron was when simple geometric shapes were presented to the photocells they would give rise to electrical signals that propogated into the network. By stimulating the photocells over and over again it was hoped that some form of learning and pattern recognition would take place within the Perceptron. Indeed some scientists believed that if such networks were made large enough they would spontaneously develop intelligent behavior. Unfortunately, the Perceptron and other networks like it never performed as their inventors intended, they were far too simple ever to imitate the human brain and scientists soon learned that results could not be won in such an easy way. However, within the last few years a new generation of networks have been constructed which have more complex behavior and appear to exhibit some of the characteristics of learning; we shall learn more about them in Chapters 8 and 9.

In the decade that followed the invention of the electronic computer, tubes gave way to transistors and the computer was used in science, commerce, government, and for military applications. Computers were used to solve the sort of problems that would have taken human mathematicians years to solve and could replace whole companies of clerks and office workers. The new computers were number crunchers par excellence. However, despite the sudden enthusiasm for the computer's power to perform millions of calculations in a second, a handful of scientists had decided to follow in the footsteps of Shannon, von Neumann, Turing, McCulloch, and other pioneers. In England a small group met informally at the laboratory of the neuroscientist W. Grey Walter. Grey Walter himself was experimenting on a series of electrical turtles, not particularly complex objects in themselves but exhibiting some very interesting behavior. The battery-powered turtles contained a simple electronic circuit, photo cell, flashing lights, and wheels. These electronic animals would respond to their own flashing light in a mirror, herd together, retreat after being kicked, and go back to their hutches as their batteries ran down. Another member of the British group, W. Ross Ashby published his "Design for a Brain" in 1948 and constructed a device that would stabilize itself against fluctuations in the external environment.

In the United States several scientists were exploring the possibilities of teaching the new computers to play games. Checkers and chess certainly involve some intellectual effort on the part of the players and if a computer could play a skillful game then there would be some reason to say that it could think. Another approach was taken by Alan Newell and Herbert Simon who were designing a computer system that would solve problems in mathematical logic. By the mid-1950s there were a number of attempts to simulate intelligent thought by means of a computer or some other electronic device like a network or electronic turtle. It was in 1956 that the topic began to crystallize as a definite discipline of its own and finally acquired the title of artificial intelligence.

The Dartmouth College Conference

In the mid-1950s Claude Shannon, along with Marvin Minsky from M.I.T. and John McCarthy from Dartmouth College, approached the Rockefeller Foundation and suggested that it should fund a gathering of scientists who had a common interest in the potential of computers for simulating human intelligence. The foundation responded in a favorable way and in the summer of 1956 several of the top U.S. researchers assembled at Dartmouth College to discuss the future of what was now called artificial intelligence. It was as a result of this meeting that artificial intelligence became recognized as a study in its own right with a well-defined goal.

What was perhaps most striking about the Dartmouth Conference was the way in which it gave rise to a remarkable series of goals and claims for the future of AI research. As it turned out the magnitude of some of these claims was ultimately to backfire on the community as a whole. For example, predictions were made that by 1970 a computer would become a grandmaster at chess, discover significant mathematical theorems, compose music of classical quality, understand spoken language, and provide language translations. Specific research projects were also initiated at Dartmouth. These included:

A complex system of artificial neurons that would begin to function like an artificial brain.
A robot that would build up an internal picture of its environment.
A computer program to derive the theorems of the *Principia Mathematica*.

43

A model of the brain's visual cortex.
A chess playing grandmaster that would provide significant insights into the nature of human intelligence.

As it turned out all these problems proved to be exceptionally more difficult than anyone had anticipated at the time and most of the projects and predictions failed to materialize. Computers did indeed play chess at a high level but not until the 1970s. They were able to prove mathematical theorems, they did make some strides in understanding language and in developing vision processing but only after considerable research work had taken place. The failure of the Dartmouth Conference predictions to materialize led to a backlash on the part of granting agencies and university departments. Although the major university and industrial laboratories continued to pursue the goals of AI research, many of the smaller groups suffered from lack of funding and such projects as machine translation were virtually eclipsed for a time. It is only now, when artificial intelligence can boast definite achievements and Western governments are boosting their funding under the threat of the Japanese fifth generation computer, that AI research is again moving into high gear.

In the chapters that follow we shall explore several achievements and frontiers of AI research. Some of these areas are concerned with understanding the ways in which the human brain works and with simulating intelligent thought. Others have more immediate and utilitarian ends, such as the design of efficient translation machines, expert systems, and intelligent robots. In the final chapters of this book we shall enter some more speculative areas and return to the question of the human brain and the future of silicon-based intelligences.

CHAPTER 3
Solving Problems and Searching for Solutions

In the previous chapter we saw that computers can not only perform calculations and work with numbers but they can manipulate the symbols of logic as well. It is a small additional step from the manipulation of symbols to the solving of logical problems, and at this point the computer is definitely doing something that is close to the operation of a human brain. Problem solving is one of our most human characteristics. Indeed it is so much a part of our everyday life that if we don't have a problem before us then we tend to invent one as a form of recreation and fun. As we shall see this same problem solving has also become one of the most important fields of AI research.

When one thinks about problems in general it is difficult to know where to begin; there are so many of them. There are the sort of problems that look like problems and these include brain teasers in the newspaper, income tax forms, the end game in chess, and mathematical questions in a child's homework. These feel like problems because they force us to think and even to sit up at night with a cup of coffee and a pad of paper to scribble on. But there are also problems that feel more like acts of planning and organization. For example, there is a certain amount of problem solving in planning a day in town and drawing up a list of stores and articles that are to be purchased. Planning and drawing up timetables can range in complexity from deciding on an evening's entertainment to scheduling a factory for the production of a new airliner. There is also a whole class of problems which don't feel like problems at all, partly because they don't seem to make us think and in addition their outcomes don't look like what we normally call solutions. For example, has the act of picking up a pencil from a table anything to do with problem solving? Or listening to music or catching a baseball? But when we explore the processing involved by the central nervous system or attempts to duplicate these actions by a robot, then we realize that these are very complex problems indeed. Finally, at some time in our lives we find ourselves facing problems with a capital P. They generally involve our emotions and many revolve around divorce, office jealousy, children's behavior or the possibility of nuclear war. With the exception of this final most overwhelming class of problems, all the others are the food of AI research and applications. Curiously enough we shall discover that some things that are trivial for us to do, like catching a ball or recognizing a face, are immensely difficult problems for the computer while others, like performing an expert medical diagnosis, can be rapidly carried out by the same machine.

A major activity of artificial intelligence is concerned with problems and their efficient solution; the motivation for research in this field arises from a number of different goals. To begin with there are a host of industrial, scientific, and social problems that the human race would like some help in solving; these include problems that at present can only be solved by a limited number of human experts or by whole teams of thinkers. In addition to the need for solutions to socially significant problems we would also like computers to solve problems so that we can examine the psychology of the problem-solving process itself and see to what extent it resembles our own approaches and in this way come to a deeper understanding of our minds. Finally, there are problems that the computer must solve for itself if it is to function more efficiently. If robots are going to behave in an intelligent way they must first be capable of learning about their environment and then acting on that knowledge. As we shall see, the issue of a machine's intervention with the world invites some of the most difficult problem solving of all; problems that our human brains have resolved through thousands of millions of years of evolution.

Let us begin, however, with the first type of problem, the sort that gives our carbon-based brains a headache: brain teasers, mathematical problems, and games of skill. The first question that may strike us is that if computers can perform many million calculations per second and store enormous quantities of information, then why do they not automatically become chess grandmasters and at the same time take over from the mathematicians in solving the outstanding mathematical problems of the twentieth century? To see why this has not yet taken place and why true problem solving requires the application of symbol manipulation and computer intelligence, let us consider two examples that have been left to us by the seventeenth century mathematician Pierre de Fermat.

Fermat was one of the leading mathematicians of the seventeenth century, an amateur who made great strides in establishing the theory of numbers and anticipated analytic geometry. He was not particularly interested in publishing his mathematical results so much of his work was not discovered until after his death. In the case of his analytical geometry for example, the credit for the creation of this branch of mathematics therefore went to Descartes and is today called Cartesian geometry.

Fermat was particularly interested in numbers, their properties, and in the sort of theorems he could prove about

47

them. He was intrigued, for example, by prime numbers, those numbers like 3, 5, 7, 11, 13, and so on that cannot be exactly divided by any number other than themselves and 1. 12, for example, can be divided exactly by 1, 2, 3, 4, 6, and 12, but 11 cannot be divided by anything other than 1 and itself. The Greeks had been able to prove that the prime numbers go on forever and that there is no highest prime number. Mathematicians in the seventeenth century were interested to what extent there is a logic or pattern to the way in which prime numbers keep popping up amongst the natural numbers. For example, are there large gaps between high prime numbers or do they sometimes bunch together? And what about prime pairs, pairs of prime numbers that are separated by just one even number, like (11, 13) and (17, 19)? Are these prime pairs even distributed and do they go on forever or at some very high prime pair, do they simply stop?

In researching these prime numbers Fermat constructed a number of theorems such as if p is a prime number and n is any positive integer, then, $n^p - n$ is divisible by p (try it!) and the conjecture that $2^{2^n} + 1$ is prime, which he mentioned in a letter to Pascal. The problem with Fermat's mathematical work was that he tended to "see" these theorems using a profound mathematical intuition but did not go as far as to bother to prove them. The suggestion that $2^{2^n} + 1$ was prime was a very interesting one because if it were true then it would enable mathematicians to generate very large prime numbers automatically. But was this indeed a theorem or simply a conjection? In other words, could the result be rigorously proved or were there exceptions to the rule? Now mathematicians happen to favor analytic proofs that are *always* true, irrespective of a value for n, but isn't this also the sort of theorem we could also test on a computer?

Is the number $2^x + 1$ always prime where $x = 2^n$ and n is an integer? All one has to do is to program this on a home computer. Let $x = 2^n$ and substitute for x in $2^x + 1$ and test the result by dividing by all the numbers 1 to $2^x + 1$. (A moment's thought will tell you that in fact you don't have to divide by *all* numbers since $2^x + 1$ is an odd number and can only have odd divisors starting with 3 and going up to ... we'll leave that as a brain teaser for the reader.) At first the results come out pretty quickly; for $n = 1, 2, 3$, your home computer will generate the answers 3, 17, 257, test them, and discover they are indeed prime. But as n grows the prime numbers themselves rapidly increase in value and the computer must now pause first for a second or two, and then for a minute while it works out if the number is prime or not. By the time it reaches $n = 5$ it is generating the number $2^{2^5} + 1$, that is $2^{25} + 1$ which equals 4,294,967,297, a fairly large number and brute force divisions to check that it is prime are going to take some time. But the problem is still within your capacity at home and if you are willing to think about it and spend some time polishing the program, you may want to try $n = 6$ and even 7!

But, in fact, the answer is already known. Euler showed that $2^{2^5} + 1$ is not prime, but divisible by 641, and he did this in the eighteenth century long before electronic computers! So where big numbers are concerned the computer may not always be the best answer, particularly when human mathematicians can employ their intuition to discover a more ingenious solution.

Another number problem is called Fermat's Last Theorem and states that there are no natural numbers x, y, and z that satisfy the equation.

$$x^n + y^n = z^n$$

where n is an integer greater than 2. In the case of $n = 2$ we, of course, have solutions, for this is just the algebriac expression of pythagorean theorem of geometry.

$$x^2 + y^2 = z^2$$

But is it obvious that the general equation has no solution for *any* value of n greater than 2? And if so, how can it be proved? In 1637 Fermat wrote in the margin of a book he was reading, "I have discovered a truly remarkable proof but this margin is too small to contain it." Fermat died and later the reference to this "proof" was discovered, and for the last three hundred years the world's top mathematicians have tried to prove Fermat's Last Theorem, or at least try to find a single exception that will show that the theorem can't be true. In fact, the mathematicians worked without success. Indeed, one famous mathematician had a set of preprinted replies made containing the sentence "Your proof of Fermat's Last Theorem contains an error in line. . . ." He had so many manuscripts containing new attempts at a proof, sent to him, each one making a mathematical error during a new and complicated proof that he simply filled out the number of the line in which the slip or error had been made and sent it back to his hopeful colleague.

If human mathematicians can't solve the problem, what about the computer? $x^n + y^n = z^n$ is a very simple equation to set down. Choose a value of n and test the equation by brute force to discover if there is an exception and it does indeed have a solution for some value of x, y, and z. When that is done then step up the value of n and try again.

Such a program can easily be written as an exercise by the reader. You can do it on your home computer, it will run all day, and the next day, all year and right on into your retirement. It may go on running well into the twenty-first century. At some point it may stop and announce that an exception to the Theorem has been discovered, on the other hand it could continue past the era of parallel supercomputers, into the era of symbiosis between human and silicon brains, it could still be working away when humans had left earth to journey to the distant stars. But, by that time, it may well have become a museum curiosity since a human, or human/silicon mathematician would have discovered a very elegant symbolic proof or counterproof to Fermat's Last Theorem.

The first lesson to learn about computer problem solving is that brute force must be tempered with intelligence for while computers can churn out several million, and will soon perform a billion, calculations in a second the world of mathematics can churn out even vaster numbers in a blink of the imagination. There are of course times when brute force solutions cannot be avoided. There are problems in mathematics and engineering that have no single analytic solution, yet an answer must nevertheless be obtained. The answer therefore is to use some system of approximations which is brought as close as possible to the desired solution by sheer brute force computing. Then there are problems that can first be simplified, classified, and otherwise simplified using the computer. A good example of this is the solution to the four-color map problem which was finally solved by human mathematics but only after considerable help was given by a computer. (The four-color problem was one of the outstanding problems in mathematics and asked what was the minimum number of colors that are needed to produce an arbitary map such that no adjacent defined areas have the same color.)

When it comes to general problem solving in mathematics, it is clear that unless the computer's approach is refined by some measure of intelligence and it is able to manipulate ideas and symbols rather than numbers, then its brute force is simply not going to work. But if mathematics requires the development of artificial intelligence for the effective solutions to problems then what about games and to begin with, a really simple game like tic tac toe? With tic tac toe there seems to be no reason why a computer shouldn't be a grandmaster. All it has to do is evaluate every possible move, together with each reply and the possible counters to those replies and so on until it has discovered every possible game. Hence, as soon as the human player has made his move the computer will know exactly which moves to make that will eventually force a win or a draw.

How can this computation be done in practice? The tic tac toe board is a 3 × 3 set of squares chalked on the blackboard or drawn on a piece of paper. If the computer takes the first move it will place its X in one of these nine different squares. The human, in reply must place his O in one of the eight remaining squares; thus, there are 9 × 8 possibilities in all for the first two moves. The computer counters by placing its X in one of the seven remaining squares. In order to think this far ahead the computer would have to examine 9 × 8 × 7 different moves. And to cover every possibility by the time the board is filled with Xs and Os, the computer would have to take into account 9 × 8 × 7 × 6 × 5 × 4 × 3 × 2 or 9! different possibilities, which works out at 362,880. So for tic tac toe there is no reason why a brute force computer should not be world champion: calculating a few hundred thousand moves is the sort of thing the computer can do in a fraction of a second. In this case brute force is invincible. But suppose that the human, tired of being beaten, decides to increase the size of the board by one row and one column. The 4 × 4 board now has 16 squares in all and the computer must evaluate 16! possibilities. Simply by increasing the row and column by one square the computer is faced now with 2×10^{13} possible moves to examine, that is 20 million million, which is going to take a conventional computer around a month to work out. As for a 5 × 5 board the number of moves is 1.5×10^{25} or 15 million million million million. The poor computer is stuck again. And if it wants to progress from tic tac toe to chess, well there are more than 10^{120} possible combinations of moves in a conventional game for a brute force computer to contend with. The only solution for a brute force chess move seems to be to replace every atom in the earth, the solar system, our galaxy and the entire universe by the fastest electronic computer, divide up the problem between them and keep going until the universe ends. There still won't be sufficient time.

These various examples are really an excuse to play a few games with numbers. One could go on selecting other examples where the number of possibilities can increase astronomically, yet humans are still able to deal with these situations. A bright child who has lost a few games of tic tac toe soon discovers how to win. The tactic is to occupy a corner box on his first move and a central box on the second. If this is done then he is bound to win. His opponent, however, will try to occupy the central box on his move and so force his opponent into a draw. The smart child does not need to know about all possible combinations but simply uses a few principles (rules) to win the game.

As soon as the computer is fed with these rules it can forget about its brute force searching method and win or draw its games using a far smaller number of calculations. So a computer that understands the overall principles of a game or problem has an enormous advantage over a brute force machine. Indeed, as it plays a skillful game of tic tac toe the computer begins to look as if it were thinking. An obvious leap forward would be to allow the computer to learn the strategy directly by playing the game rather than having a human program supply it with rules for winning.

When it comes to a game like chess, the strategy for winning is far more complex, even for humans. The world's most brilliant mathematicians may not make the top rank of chess players for although good chess certainly depends upon reasoning power and the ability to plan ahead, it also involves a great deal of experience and study of classical games of the past. For example, a good player doesn't make his first moves by thinking out all possible combinations but moves according to a recipe of opening strategies. He does not plan his middle game by exploring every move in depth but gives his attention only to certain patterns and pieces. He may, for example, focus on the center of the board, concentrate on the most important of his pieces, and make use of tactical moves, like forks.

In the case of tic tac toe only a few simple rules are needed to program a grandmaster computer. But when it comes to chess the knowledge required includes general rules, tactics, information on standard moves, openings and classical games, together with rules of thumb for evaluating particular situations. The problem of writing such a program for a computer has risen from the sort of thing that could be done by an amateur at home to a major research project. We shall return to the problem of designing a chess playing computer later in this chapter. For the present we shall concentrate upon a prior difficulty that is common to all these problems, that of searching for a particular solution amongst a large number of possible alternatives.

Search

The examples drawn from games and mathematics all involved the search for an ideal or winning solution among a very large number of possibilities. This situation is common to so much AI research from vision to language understanding. To understand how a search is carried out let us consider a particularly simple example, that of the knight in a story who must make a number of choices. Our knight rides in a dark wood and comes to a fork in the road, he decides to take the right hand path, and rides on until he comes to a castle. At the entrance to the castle the knight must chose between two doors, he opens one, enters the castle and discovers a box containing two keys. The knight picks up one of the keys and continues on through the castle. At each juncture in the story the knight must choose between two alternatives, one will take him further into the castle until he finds his princess, the other may lead to his death, his incarceration, or to him getting lost. Only if he makes a series of correct choices will he finally reach his goal.

The knight's journey can be represented symbolically by means of a graph.

The knight chooses between two paths: path A leads him deeper into the forest and to dead ends and other paths, only path B leads to the castle. Of the two doors, door C leads the knight into the dungeons and to his doom, door D leads into the room containing the two keys E and F. The graph could be continued for several more steps but it is simple to see that at each level of the graph more and more alternatives

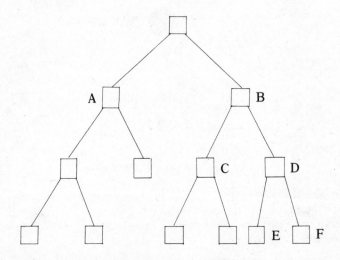

The knight's journey through the forest and into the castle can be represented using a tree graph.

are revealed. If the knight were to choose between three or four alternatives then the complexity of the graph would grow even faster.

Graphs like these are called tree graphs and are common to many different problems found in AI research. For example a tree graph can be used to represent the moves in checkers: Corresponding to each of white's moves, black has a series of countermoves and to each of these white, in his turn can choose between a further series of moves. Graphs like these all have the characteristics of becoming more complex as they move from root to crown, for at each level more and more possibilities are opened up.

Graphs can be useful in visualizing a problem, in showing interconnections and in establishing some sort of strategy to solve a problem. What is immediately clear is that as the number of levels increases the total number of combinations

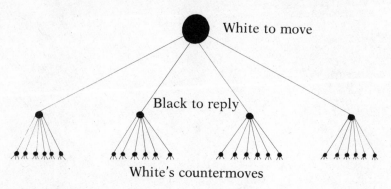

F. David Peat

White to move

Black to reply

White's countermoves

The various moves in a game of checkers can be represented by a tree graph. Even in this simplified version it is clear that the number of possible moves grows rapidly as one moves along the tree from root to crown.

---

rapidly becomes astronomically large. This rapid increase in the number of possibilities to be explored is termed the *combinatorial explosion,* and represents one of the major barriers to effective problem solving. It is a barrier than can only be avoided by employing some clever strategies and a measure of artificial intelligence in designing the computer system.

Graphs can also be thought of as mirroring the process of problem solving. Each circle or node in the graph represents some state of affairs of the problem, for example, the arrangement of pieces on a chess board, a step in the mathematical proof or the orientation of a robot's limbs. The lines connecting each node, called *arcs,* represent the legal moves that can be made in a game, the movements of a robotic limb, or the operations of logic. So the application of a rule or the movement of a piece takes the problem from one node to another along an arc. The problem is presented at the top of the graph and the lines representing the various maneuvers, manipulations, and applications of rules. The circles or nodes represent intermediate states on the way to

56

a solution and one hopes that somewhere within that tree graph will be a node that represents the final state and solution to the problem. Solving a problem is therefore equivalent to doing a tree Search, that is, looking through all the nodes of the tree for the solution and then connecting it, branch by branch to the root node at the beginning.

Tree graphs can represent such problems as proving theorems in logic, planning a day's shopping, analyzing the structure of an English sentence, representing the hierarchial structure of an office organization, moving a robot's arm, playing a game, making a medical diagnosis, working out the structure of a molecule, or scheduling the machine shop of a factory. Some graphs, like tree graphs, are fairly simple but others are more complex with nodes not only connected from above and below but also horizontally.

In solving problems there are times when one reasons forwards through a graph from root to crown and at other times when one reasons backwards. For example, suppose there is something wrong with your car and in order to make a diagnosis you try to reason backwards from the symptom to the cause. Similarly, in logic you try to prove a theorem by reasoning backwards from the proposition to one of the axioms of the system. In this backward reasoning

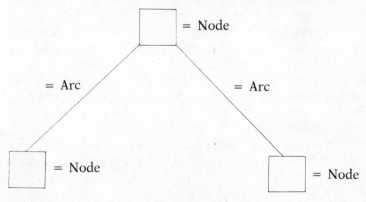

The basic elements in a tree graph.

we begin at one of the twigs and try to reason backwards or downwards towards the root node, for this reason the procedure is called a *top down search*.

The *bottom up search* occurs when you try reason forwards and try to work out the implications of something; for example, given that a particular part of a nuclear power plant has failed you can try to work out what will be the various results, that is, arrive at the twigs that branch out from that particular root. This bottom up solution searching or forward reasoning is also used in games like chess when one tries to work out the implications of a particular move.

In the chapters that follow many of the problems, in logic, games, expert systems, vision, language understanding, and robots, involve graph searches in order to find a given solution. It is clear therefore that some overall strategy and control to a graph search is a key issue in the development of AI systems. If a computer is left to itself then its brute force approach may take far too long to search through all the branches and twigs for an appropriate solution. One of the important ways in which artificial intelligence can be used is to speed up a tree graph search by employing some appropriate strategy.

The simplest approach is to decide between a breadth first or a depth first search. If one guesses that a workable solution can be found in very few moves, then the best strategy is to search horizontally, layer by layer, using a breadth first search. However, in a game of chess, it will be many moves before checkmate results. What is needed is to pick out an appropriate branch and then search it in great depth, ignoring the other branches for the time being.

Depth or breadth first searches, top up or bottom down searching are only the first steps in problem solving. The really interesting work is found when we begin to explore individual systems and approaches which enable the computer to find its way to a solution through the most complex graphs.

Logic Theorist and General Problem Solver
Right in time for the famous 1956 Dartmouth Conference

on artificial intelligence, Allen Newell, J. C. Shaw and Herbert Simon were able to present the output from Logic Theorist, one of the world's first problem solving programs; a system that had been designed to prove theorems in mathematical logic.

Herbert Simon, who was to receive the 1978 Nobel Prize for Economics, had originally been interested in the way human organizations worked and the various approaches their members took to solving the problems. Working with Allen Newell at the RAND Corporation he realized that computers could be used to explore the mathematical models that were based on his theories of problem solving. At first Simon decided to look at the problems encountered in chess and in manipulating logical symbols but eventually focused his energies on theorems in Russell and Whiteheads's *Principia Mathematica*. This book, which concerns the foundation of mathematics, begins with five theorems of the propositional calculus. It includes a rule of substitution in which any variable, p say, can be replaced by a proper combination of variables, for example, $(p \lor q)$. In this way more complex expressions can be built up by successive substitutions. Beginning with these axioms it is possible to derive various theorems in logic simply by applying the rules of procedure. Likewise, if one is given a possible theorem, its validity can be proved simply by working backwards to one of the axioms. If the process can be completed then the theorem is true but if a gap occurs in the logical connection then the theorem is invalid. The whole process is quite automatic, given a set of symbols and the rules for manipulating them.

Simon and Newell realized that proving theorems in logic was exactly the sort of problem solving that a computer could carry out and enlisted the help of J. C. Shaw to develop the necessary program. The resulting system (Logic Theorist) employed a breadth first search for its proofs but otherwise used brute force. (Later the researchers added some modifications such as selecting particular branches first for an in depth search and rejecting others as being too complicated.) But the fact remained that Logic Theorist was indeed able to prove theorems in logic. It operated with symbols that could stand for words or concepts rather than simply manipulating numbers and in one case it discovered a more economical proof than had been originally spotted by Whitehead and Russell.

Nevertheless the system placed too much reliance on brute force and the group therefore decided to build some more intelligent behavior into it. To begin with, Logic Theorist had been designed to solve a specific problem, but what the Simon's research group was after was an approach for solving more general problems. The result, General Problem Solver, was designed to use some universal approaches common to many problems so that the same general program could be applied from case to case without the need for major rewriting. But, of course, General Problem Solver had to do better than carry out a blind search, it had to take the whole nature of problem solving into consideration and use some of the approaches that humans themselves employ.

Psychologists had already carried out research on the ways in which humans solve problems by having volunteers voice their thoughts while working on various problems. The psychologists would then collect these transcripts together, read through them, and attempt to decypher exactly what had been going on. Simon and Newell followed the same plan and asked their colleagues to solve a series of problems while speaking out loud and articulate the various moves they made. The results showed that as humans work on problems they not only keep an eye on the present status of the problem but also on the goal they are trying to reach. So their reasoning is both backwards and forwards at the same time.

This approach, called *means-ends* reasoning, was therefore built into the General Problem Solver which was designed to solve problems not only in logic but in chess and in those crypto arithmetic puzzles where letters stand for numbers. The General Problem Solver (GPS) employed its control and

---

LOGIC THEORIST

Logic Theorist was designed to solve problems in symbolic logic and derive theorems from Russell and Whitehead's *Principia Mathematica*. The axioms of the logical system are:

1.　$(p \vee p) \supset p$
2.　$p \supset (q \vee p)$
3.　$(p \vee q) \supset (q \vee p)$
4.　$[p \vee (q \vee r)] \supset [q \vee (p \vee r)]$
5.　$(p \supset q) \supset [(r \vee p) \supset (r \vee q)]$

Two rules of inference are used:
Substitution: Any variable can be replaced by a valid expression, for example "p" can be replaced by "(p ∨ q)."
Replacement: The connective $\supset$ can be placed via its definition so "p ∨ q" becomes "⁷p ∨ q." (⁷ is the symbol for negation.)
Using the axioms and rules of inference Logic Theorist was able to prove such theorems as:

$(p \supset {}^{7}p) \supset {}^{7}p$
${}^{7}(p \vee q) \supset p$
$[p \vee (q \vee r)] \supset [(p \vee q) \vee r]$

---

supervision in a general way without bothering about the details of individual problems. As far as the control was concerned, letter puzzles or statements in logic were simply an abstract string of symbols. The various operations of the system (moves in the puzzle, logic, or chess) were first classified and then ordered as to what they could achieve. In addition, the differences between the present state of the game or puzzle and its goal were also evaluated and an operator chosen that would reduce this difference. So GPS operated not in a blind way by exploring all paths but by selectively reducing the differences between the present state and its goal. A further refinement was to classify degrees of difficulty and give them orders of priority so that the computer would first resolve a really hard part of the problem rather than simply remove the first differences it came across.

GPS proved to be a considerable success and paved the way for a whole series of problem solving offspring that are found today in many AI systems. But in 1957 when Newell, Shaw, and Simon began working on their General Problem Solver they were not so much interested in producing the world's best automatic problem solver as in gaining insights into the strategies that can be used in the face of a problem and in comparing the ways in which computers and humans work towards a solution. With GPS up and running it was now possible to compare a computer and a human as they worked on the same problem. In a series of such tests, remarkable agreement was found between the two approaches. If computers did not "think" then at least they went through many of the same moves as humans did. There were of course some differences in approach, humans needed to go back from time to time and refresh their memories and on occasion would backtrack from the final goal rather than working forward. On the GPS side the system tended to be long winded in the way it solved problems and on occasion would get trapped in dead ends.

An interesting development of the basic General Problem Solver design came about in 1971 with the building of SHAKEY the Robot. We will meet SHAKEY in Chapter 7; it was one of the first intelligent robots and was constructed by Stanford Research Institute to move in a world of rooms, doors, and boxes. SHAKEY was supplied with a camera eye to spy out his world and wheels and a motor to move around with. Given a task of, say, pushing two boxes together in a particular room, SHAKEY would find his way to the correct door, go through it, into the room and locate the appropriate boxes. The way in which SHAKEY could see its world and move around in it are discussed in Chapter 7. They do not so much concern us here as the way in which the robot solved the logistical problems involved in finding its way to a goal and executing its required task. Various computer systems took care of SHAKEY'S vision and movement and left its brain free to consider the problem solving aspects of moving through a maze of rooms, boxes, and doors. Considered in the abstract, this problem of reaching a goal is little different from proving a theorem in logic or reaching checkmate in chess. There were a number of moves open to the robot such as GOTODOOR (DOOR 12), GOTHRUDOOR (DOOR 12, ROOM 2), GOTOB (BOX 1) and so on which when decided upon could then be passed on to other parts of the control system to execute. The problem solving aspects came in choosing the correct sequence of moves, say GOTODOOR (DOOR 12) rather than GOTODOOR (DOOR 23) and using them in the correct sequence. Just as with other problems in which a tree graph is involved, there is only one sequence of arcs and nodes that leads to the goal and this sequence must be discovered by an intelligent search.

The problem faced by SHAKEY can also be thought of as a series of moves based on preconditions. For example, to execute GOTHRUDOOR (DOOR 12, ROOM 2); that is, to go through the door that connects rooms 1 and 2 and enter room 2; the robot must be in room 1 to begin with. Suppose the robot happens to be in room 3, then to execute GOTHRU-DOOR (DOOR 12, ROOM 2) it must first meet the precondition of being in room 1, that is it must first carry out a series of moves involving other doors and rooms.

SHAKEY was at first controlled by a descendent of the General Problem Solver called STRIPS, which used a means-ends analysis to minimize the differences between current and goal states. The system worked well enough but like GPS, STRIPS tended to be long winded and not particularly intelligent when it to came to priorities. For example, the system would evaluate a complicated series of moves only to discover that some vital precondition had not been met. STRIPS was rather like the person who goes on a camping trip and unpacks his stove and food only to find that he's left his matches at home. In the case of STRIPS the system would then have to backtrack right to the beginning and start again working along another branch of the problem.

The solution was to produce a more sophisticated version of STRIPS, called ABSTRIPS, which first classified the nature of the problem in an hierarchical fashion. In everyday planning we humans tend to concentrate on the important things first and leave details for later. If we are going on a picnic we make sure we have the stove, matches, and a can opener before we bother about individual cans of food or whether the bread should be white or whole wheat. Similarly ABSTRIPS was given a list of critical preconditions which had to be met before a problem could be solved. Once these preconditions were satisfied the system would then give its attention to details. If the system did make a mistake by not meeting some preconditions, then rather than having to go back to the root node of its problem graph it would only have to backtrack through one level. By arranging tasks in an order of priority ABSTRIPS was able to cut down the search time from over 5 minutes as was the case with STRIPS to 30 seconds.

Problems solvers have now been developed for a wide variety of problems including playing games, solving mathematical problems, supervising the tasks of robots, designing computer programs, determining the structures of molecules, and working out various schedules and plans. Many of these systems began in the laboratory as research projects used to explore the potential of artificial intelligence but more recently some of them have been adapted specifically for utilitarian ends; for example, MOLGEN assists scientists in planning molecular genetics experiments. Another series of problem solvers which should have considerable commercial application are those that work out scheduling for a large factory. Scheduling is a particularly difficult problem to solve since it often involves a type of planning in which a very large series of subgoals must be achieved in a particular order and demands a leap forward from the strategy of STRIPS and ABSTRIPS.

Suppose that you decide to redecorate your home. Following the example of ABSTRIPS you can begin by making a list of priorities, or subgoals which are critical to the goal of redecoration. These include painting the ceiling, papering the walls, and varnishing the floors. At other levels of this hierarchy there are preconditions to these subgoals such as stripping off old wallpaper, filling in cracks in the ceiling, buying paint, cleaning brushes, and so on. A system like ABSTRIPS will order these various preconditions so that the subgoal of papering the wall can be carried out with all the prior steps in the hierarchy of moves accounted for. But suppose these particular steps are given to some robot of the future which carries out the task. The robot carries out all instructions and carefully repapers the wall. But the first thing one realizes is that with the walls repapered the robot is going to have a considerable problem to paint the ceiling. For as the ceiling subgoal is being achieved, paint will drip on the new wallpaper. Hence, decorating a house contains a series of self-contained subgoals which can frustrate each other if they are not carried out in the correct order.

Decorating a house is rather a trivial example for humans because it is quite familiar to our experience and there are a relatively small number of interacting subgoals. But what about building an aircraft in which there are a large number of subgoals which can be independently met? In a system with 20 subgoals, for example, there are around 3 million different orders in which they can be achieved!

With a small number of subgoals a problem solving system can try to work out the consequences of all possible combinations but as the number of subgoals mount it reaches exactly the same combinatorial explosion that has dogged problem solving all along. There are simply too many possibilities for the computer to explore and problem solving systems must adopt approximations, rules of thumb, and other subterfuges to help them towards a solution.

Despite all the work that is being carried out on problem solving systems, none of them yet exhibits the flexibility and ingenuity of a human. Psychologists continue to explore human problem solving by having volunteers speak their thoughts out loud as they work on a particular task. They find that humans tend to make guesses, break rules, and use all manner of ingenious tricks to arrive at a solution. One study, carried out by Barbara and Fredrick Hayes-Roth for the RAND Corporation, exposed what the psychologists called "opportunist problem solving." Volunteers were given a map of a small town, showing shops, cinemas, car parks, and so on, together with a shopping list and asked to plan for a day in town. The task did not simply consist of going from store to store for there were constraints as to time and location. For example, some stores were close to others, some goals, like going to the cinema, could only be achieved at a particular time of day and others, like carrying around fresh vegetables or ice cream, had the more subtle constraint that one should not leave fresh produce in a car for a long period.

On the one hand, humans were able to think logically and assess priorities, work out the scheduling problem of visiting a number of shops at different locations and attempt to satisfy constraints of time; on the other they were also flexible and dynamic, they considered problems in a multidirectional way and were not necessarily bound by their priorities. For example, if the achievement of a high priority task required the shopper to be in a particular part of town they would then take advantage of their proximity to another shop which had a low priority and in this way achieve an extra task "free." While a well designed computer problem solver can work effectively and efficiently in analyzing subgoals into hierarchies and priorities it simply does not take advantage of a short cut when it is gratuitiously presented. Humans, by contrast, are opportunistic in the way they solve problems and will grasp at every advantage that is offered them. Computers still have a long way to go if they are to outsmart humans in problem solving.

Game Playing

Armed with some knowledge about what problem solving systems can achieve, it is now time to return to the game of chess. The idea that a computer would be able to play an intelligent game of chess has long fascinated the artificial intelligence community and is certainly intriguing to the general public. Chess is such a human game and seems to exert our intellectual capacity to the extreme that the possibility that a computer could beat us must have seemed fairly remote back in the 1940s. We have already seen how the number of possibilities represented in a tree graph can increase rapidly and in the case of chess, the speed of this increase is truly phenomenal. In the average state of play a player is faced with some 30 possible legal moves when his turn comes. By the time the game is over each player will have taken around 40 turns so the number of different combinations of possible moves is 10^{120}, an incredibly large number, far bigger the sort of numbers that are met in atomic physics or astronomy. It is clear that when it comes to chess, the computer cannot rely on brute force alone but must make its move in a finite time without knowing for certain if that move is a necessary part of a winning strategy.

The idea of a chess playing machine predates even the first electronic computers. Some of the automata of the eighteenth and nineteenth centuries were constructed to play chess or at least to produce the mechanical actions necessary to move a piece from one position to another on the board. One of the most famous of these was built by von Kempelen and traveled all over Europe beating the rich and aristocratic at chess. The impressive performance of this machine was somewhat diminished when it was discovered that a human dwarf was concealed inside and worked the mechanism. Charles Babbage also considered building a version of his Analytic Engine that would play chess and perform at exhibitions to raise funds for his other projects.

The idea of mechanical and electromagnetic devices that could solve chess programs was pursued right into the first decades of the twentieth century until their limited potential gave way to that of the electronic computer. It appears that nearly every pioneer in the field of computer design and artificial intelligence, beginning with Konrad Zuse and Alan Turing, had at some time or other considered the possibilities of a computer chess player, and as early as 1950 Claude Shannon wrote an article for *Scientific American* on computer chess. By the time of the Dartmouth Conference many different individuals were working on chess playing programs, either as a hobby or a matter of serious research and the prediction was made that a computer would soon be playing grandmaster level chess.

One of the earliest of the successful game playing programs did not involve chess itself but checkers, which is considerably simpler although still a challenging game for humans. As early as 1947 Arthur Samuel was thinking about a checker program for the newly invented computers. As he analyzed the game itself, Samuel discovered how difficult it was to extract information from the recognized experts in the game and how, on occasion, an expert does not always perform in the way he claims to act. Later in the 1970s as AI researchers began to construct *expert systems* for solving problems in chemistry, medicine, and geological surveying, they would discover exactly the same difficulty when working with human experts.

Samuel pressed on and constantly refined his program to the point where, early in the 1960s, it was playing checkers at a master's level. But chess proved to be a far more difficult game to play. It was only in 1967 that the first computer was allowed to play at a chess tournament and, in 1968 David Levy, an international master, made a £500 bet that no chess program would beat him within 10 years. The bet was not lost, but by the summer of 1978 a computer was certainly able to give Levy a good game. Four years earlier the Russian KAISSA program had triumphed at the first world computer chess championship, but in 1978 an earlier version of Northwestern Universities Chess 4.7 that had played against Levy was able to beat the hitherto superior Russian program. So by the end of the 1970s, although the computer was not a grandmaster, it could certainly give a good game to class B players and occasionally produce brilliant flashes of play.

With the emergence of much faster computers, Levy decided to renew his challenge and increase the wager $6,000. In 1984 the champion program Cray Blitz, played on a Cray X-MP computer, met Levy in London for a four-game match. After winning all games, Levy felt that the possibility of a computer beating a world champion chess player was even more remote than he had previously thought. He argued that most research was being directed along the wrong lines and that program designers should make a closer study of how human chessmasters think. However, Robert Hyatt, a leading scientist on the Cray Blitz program, is pinning his hopes on the forthcoming Cray 2 computer, which will be capable of examining a hundred thousand positions per second. In a standard tournament, the computer will explore all possible permutations to adapt a depth of four complete moves and, where more interesting positions are concerned, up to twenty moves ahead.

Since so many different teams have worked on chess programs there is no single accepted method of design. Some rely heavily upon knowledge gained from classical games of the past and on the tactics of various theorists, others exploit the computer's power to search through a vast number of possible moves while employing a variety of heuristics and rules of thumb to avoid a combinatorial explosion.

Many of the more successful chess programs make use of an approach first suggested by Shannon for searching through a complex graph without getting trapped in a combinatorial explosion. Shannon's tactic was to search to a fixed depth, say four moves ahead, and then evaluate the potential of each of the terminal positions on the graphs, that is the various possible states of the board. Once the best positions had been evaluated, the program could then borrow from von Neumann's game theory and adopt a minimax procedure to ensure that its move would place it in the most commanding procedure.

The method of evaluating different states of the game was no simple matter and drew upon all the rules and lore of chess; for example a position that gave control over the center of the board is preferred, powerful pieces should be placed in commanding positions, the king should not be in danger, and the value of one's pieces should exceed those of one's opponents. In most cases the method of evaluation is programmed into the computer but more interesting computer plays will evolve when the computer is allowed to make its own evaluations based on its experience and hence improve its skill with the more games it plays.

But even a strategy of limited search followed by an evaluation could not hope to produce a reasonable chess player. As a depth of four or even six moves can take considerable computing time but it is still not sufficient to expose the interesting possibilities and a position that looks very favorable may be reversed a couple more moves ahead. Chess masters when they play are able to ignore whole series of moves, take in the general pattern of the game, and then follow a particularly favorable path as deep as 10 to 20 moves ahead.

The original strategy was therefore modified to keep on searching in those cases where the terminal position looked fluid, or a piece was being threatened. When this search was completed and all terminal ends had been evaluated the computer would then carry out a secondary search on the most promising move and confirm this choice to a much greater depth. In addition, at the start of a search, particular moves were ordered into the most promising ones which were then searched first while potentially disastrous moves were ignored altogether. One way of doing this was not only to give the computer explicit instructions but to have it remember moves that were bad ones in the past and then look for analogous moves which could also be rejected in future.

There are a whole series of variations within this general chess playing scheme. One approach is due to Alex Bernstein who produced one of the earliest chess playing programs. His approach is not so much to carry out a search of possible moves but to select goals and pick only those moves that lead towards a particular goal. The goals themselves come from traditional chess practice and involve developing particular pieces, gaining control over the center of the board and so on. Another approach that avoids a search, particularly at the start of the game, is to use textbook moves. A whole series of ideal moves is stored in the computer's memory which then selects particular moves that seem appropriate in a given situation. This particular approach can be generally used in problem solving by working out a series of scripts or plans appropriate for typical situations. When the computer is faced with a particular situation, it searches through its library for a plan which best fits the case and then applies it. We shall see in Chapter 5 how this approach has been applied to the various problems associated with language understanding.

Work on chess raises one very important issue which turns up again and again with AI research: if a computer can challenge a chess master to a satisfying game of chess then must we admit that the computer is intelligent? I imagine that at the start of this chapter you would probably have agreed. Chess is a game of the intellect, it involves strategy and cunning, the ability to plan many moves ahead, and take advantage of any breaks shown by an opponent. Skill in chess is much praised in our society; one only has to think of the drama of the Bobby Fischer/Boris Spasky matches to realize this. So if a computer can participate as an equal partner in this kind of table game are we not forced to acknowledge its intelligence and ability to think as we do when we play chess?

On the other hand by the end of this chapter we have also learned just what this entails: it is the operation of a complex set of rules, supplied by the program for carrying out searches and evaluating moves. Now it is certainly no longer true that the program instructed the computer what to do move by move, rather it established some general rules of procedure. We can now ask — can play which takes place in response to a large set of rules truly be called thinking or is it simply a highly complex and sophisticated extension of automatic, mechanical activity?

If you feel that the computer does not really think then you imply we human beings function in totally different ways and that when we play chess or solve problems, we operate in superior ways to the computer. But do we? We must postpone further discussion of this question until Chapter 9. For the present let us be aware of a trend in AI research. It is generally true that AI workers will set a particular goal for a computer system, such as a grandmaster level at chess, and say that when a computer reaches this level then it must truly be judged as intelligent. But as that goal is approached people begin to reexamine the task and say that what they once thought of as intelligent human behavior does not appear all that intelligent any more—possibly they were fooled in the first place and such a task is mechanical after all. This has led some cynics to define true artificial intelligence as any task which a computer is not yet able to do.

In the field of artificial intelligence things move quickly and what was once a piece of frontier research that challenged the largest computers of the time is now available to anyone who is willing to pay a few dollars for a chess playing game. Thanks to computer chip technology it is now possible to hard wire an elaborate computer chess program onto a silicon chip, or series of chips, for a few cents. This proliferation of cheap chess playing units also gives some idea of the potential and the speed with which AI devices can be adopted. For once a computer system has been debugged and developed it can rapidly be converted from a large university computer into microprocessor form. When it comes to AI applications, it is not a matter of waiting for years while prototypes are developed and factories tooled up for production, the move from laboratory bench to the shop window is extremely rapid and need only be a matter of months. This transfer is also accompanied by a price reduction from hundreds of thousands of dollars to just a few dollars. Indeed, the piece of plastic that enclosed an AI device may cost more than the electronic hardware itself.

In the first years of the 1980s AI is only just getting started but as research moves into high gear it is possible that a whole series of throwaway applications will be reaching us from coffee cups that talk to us over breakfast to intelligent automobiles.

But before we finally leave the business of problem solving here is a problem for you, the reader, to play with. Rearrange the following letters

FEERFLSCNEERE

to form a familiar word. We shall return to this puzzle and how it may be solved in the final section of the book. For the moment you, the reader, can play with it. It is not a particularly difficult problem so you may like to observe yourself solving it and consider the types of moves you make. You may also wish to program your home computer. One approach is to generate all possible permutations of the 13 letters. How many possible combinations are there? Is there a way of cutting down this number and speeding up the search? How do you recognize if a word is impossible in English or when it is beginning to look right? Does your computer program work in the same way as you do when you try to solve the problem? Towards the end of this book we will return to the whole business of problem solving and reexamine the assumption we have used and the possibilities for the future of artificial intelligence.

CHAPTER 4
Expert Systems

In the first three chapters we explored the emerging history of artificial intelligence and the first applications of computers to problem solving and the game of chess. Now it is time to jump forward to the present day and an AI application that is generating considerable excitement amongst doctors, engineers, businessmen, and industrialists because of its enormous implications, the expert system.

Imagine the following scenario: it is late at night and a child is crying in pain. The worried mother dials an emergency medical number and pours out her concern to the doctor at the other end of the line. As the doctor listens he begins to examine his files to find out about the child's medical history. He asks the mother several questions and suggests that she should bring her child to the emergency wing of the local hospital. As soon as the child arrives at the hospital a series of tests are ordered by the doctor, who, as the results come in, makes his diagnosis and suggests a course of treatment.

The hero of this story is, as you may have guessed, not a

human doctor but a computer, an expert medical system. But does that make our scenario a piece of science fiction? Not at all, for if we leave aside the computer doctor's abilities to conduct a spoken conversation over the telephone (the limitations on this use of natural language are discussed in Chapter 5), then everything else is not only possible but has already taken place. Expert systems exist that can perform as well as or even better than a human specialist in diagnosing a large range of diseases of the body. For several years other expert systems have been in routine use by scientists to help them determine the structure of complex molecules, design experiments, and assist in mathematical calculations. Expert systems are currently being used to prospect for minerals, trace faults in machines, custom design computers, help in the scheduling of factories, search through very large databases, and assist in education. Expert systems have already saved individual companies millions of dollars and new systems are being designed all the time. By the time you read this book systems will be being tested for use by lawyers, accountants, travel agents, and a host of other professionals. The 1980s are very probably going to be the era of the expert system and by the end of the decade it is possible that each of us will telephone an expert system whenever we need to obtain advice and information on a range of technical, legal, or medical topics.

The first of the expert systems grew out of the collaboration of Edward A. Feigenbaum, a computer expert, and Joshua Lederberg, a professor of genetics. Lederberg had been awarded the 1958 Nobel Prize in medicine as a result of his work on the genetics of bacteria and in addition to this valuable research, he had also become interested in the potential of computers to assist scientists in their research. While to some extent physics is a "clean" subject involving fairly clear-cut experiments and interpretations, other subjects like biology and organic chemistry involve experiments and analyses which produce large masses of data, all of which requires careful sifting and interpretation. Lederberg

GUS: A Computerized Travel Consultant

Client: I want to go to San Diego May 28
GUS: What time do you want to leave?
Client: I must be in San Diego before 10 am.
GUS: Would you like PSA flight 102 that arrives at 9:15 am?
Client: What is the next flight?
GUS: Air California flight 310 that leaves at 8:30 am and arrives at 10:00 am.
Client: I'll take the first one.
GUS: In what name should I make a reservation?
Client: Dan Bobrow.
GUS: I have confirmed the following flight: PSA flight 102 on Wednesday, May 28 from San Jose to San Diego which leaves at 7:30 am and arrives at 9:15 am. What date do you want to return on?
Client: On Friday in the evening.
GUS: Would you like the flight that leaves at 7:45 pm?
Client: That's fine.
GUS: I have confirmed the following flight: PSA flight 307 on Friday, May 30 from San Diego to San Jose which leaves at 7:45 pm and arrives at 9:30 pm. Thank you for calling. Goodby.

Note that GUS must make a number of inferences about his client's statements such as "the first one," "on Friday," and about his departure time on May 28th.

was convinced that computers, with their capacity for storing and searching through collections of data, would be invaluable in assisting scientists. He decided, therefore, to concentrate on the problems involved in determining molecular structures.

Feigenbaum for his part had begun as a graduate student of Herbert Simon with whom he worked on a learning system called EPAM. His training was in the cognitive sciences but, like Lederberg, he too was interested in the ways in which humans construct hypotheses and build intellectual models based on data and observations about the world. So, when in 1965 Feigenbaum moved to Stanford University, it was natural that he should discuss his ideas with Lederberg who was by that time Director of the Kennedy Laboratories of Molecular Medicine.

The problem they focused on was suggested by Lederberg and involved determining the structure of an organic molecule based on spectroscopic data. The expert system they designed to do this was called DENDRAL.

Organic molecules are a little like those structures one can build with a children's erector set. Starting with a few simple components it is possible to fit them together in a number of different ways and in this fashion produce a very large number of different complex structures. It is the property of a carbon atom that up to four other atoms can bond to it to form a stable molecule. For example:

$$
\begin{array}{ccc}
\text{H} & \text{H} & \text{Cl} \\
\vert & \vert & \vert \\
\text{H-C-H} \text{ methane,} & \text{H-C-Cl} \text{ chloroform,} & \text{Cl-C-Cl} \text{ carbon} \\
\vert & \vert & \vert \\
\text{H} & \text{Cl} & \text{Cl}
\end{array}
$$

$$
\begin{array}{c}
\text{H H} \\
\vert \ \vert \\
\text{tetrachloride, H-C-C-OH ethanol (drinking alcohol),} \\
\vert \ \vert \\
\text{H H}
\end{array}
$$

$$
\begin{array}{c}
\text{H} \\
\vert \\
\text{H-C-C-OOH acetic acid (vinegar).} \\
\vert \\
\text{H}
\end{array}
$$

In turn, these units can act as building blocks, units in the organic Lego set, which lock together to form much longer molecules containing hundreds or thousands of carbon atoms. Since each given unit can link to very many neighbors and in several generic ways, the number of possible products is very large. In fact, the production of organic molecules is very like the growth of a problem graph with the consequent combinational explosion in the number of possible different molecules.

In view of the complexity and vast number of organic compounds it is a major problem for the organic chemist to identify and determine the structure of any new compound he comes across in a chemical reaction. Simply analyzing the compound and discovering how many carbon, hydrogen, nitrogen, and other atoms it contains is not enough, for the same number of atoms can be combined in different orders and geometries to form a large variety of different structures. To pin down a particular organic molecule the chemist has to determine its actual geometry; in other words, which atom bonds to which and at what angle. Data on these bond angles and bond lengths can be gained from various types of spectroscopy which can also tell the chemist which basic groups or subcollections of atoms form the building blocks of the larger molecule.

Determining a molecular structure is therefore quite different from solving a problem in logic. It is not simply a matter of setting down a few rules and then working out the results. Logic is certainly needed but the number of possible configurations could be too large so that in real life, chemists must take short cuts by constructing hypotheses, and using their experience of similar problems to generate rules of thumb, good guesses, and other forms of expert systems. It became clear to Feigenbaum, Lederberg, and Carl Djeraisse, a physical chemist who was now working with them, that it was not sufficient to give the computer the laws of chemistry and allow it to proceed in a step by step logical way. Rather, it had to be supplied with the sort of general knowledge and expert guesswork that humans use in simplifying and solving problems.

In this way the first expert system was conceived and the Stanford team began to question organic chemists on the ways in which they used data from the mass spectrograph to build up a picture of a molecule's structure. But it was here, as they tried to build up a picture of how human experts work, that they ran into a similar problem to that met by Arthur Samuel as he was building his checkers playing program. Human experts are not always clear as to how they do things. They tend to forget some of the moves they make, oversimplify others, leave out important exceptions to a rule, and may even perform in quite different ways from what they had actually described. This problem of extracting human expert knowledge was to prove the bottleneck in the development of DENDRAL and is still a major difficulty in building today's expert systems.

DENDRAL was designed to use a combination of rules about the ways in which organic groups can bond, together with general knowledge, heuristics, and expert chemist's "tricks" for interpreting the data from mass spectrometry experiments. The system was running in 1968 and by 1976 DENDRAL was updated with COGEN and REACT, expert systems that are today used routinely in laboratories all over the world. Another variant is Meta-DENDRAL which circumvents the problem of extracting knowledge and rules from human experts by evolving rules of its own which can then be fed to update the DENDRAL program.

While the Stanford group were improving their first DENDRAL system, another group, at M.I.T., was independently working on an expert system of their own. Carl Engleman, William Martin, and Joel Moses decided to concentrate upon mathematical problems as their area for exploitation and in 1968 worked out the design for MACYSMA. The system would ultimately carry out a large number of different mathematical operations: 600 in all from differentiation, integration, algebra, solution of systems of equations, to generating series and dealing with vectors and matrices. Today MACYSMA is extensively used by mathematicians, scientists, and engineers who gain access to it by calling up a central computer in Massachusetts via the ARPANET computer network.

But why should scientists and mathematicians need an expert system like MACYSMA? If mathematics is a logical study then would not a problem solving system of the type discussed in Chapter 3 do just as well? The answer is that while the sort of arithmetic one uses at school is fairly automatic and could be performed by a problem solving program, higher mathematics is something very different. Suppose a mathematician wishes to solve a differential equation, he must first discover the general type of equation which is done by exploring its mathematical shape. When he has classified the overall type, he must now cast it in some standard form ready for solution by performing a number of transformations and variable substitutions. Finally with this done he will choose a particular method of solution for that standard form. Some of these steps are fairly well defined but others will involve some ingenuity on the part of the mathematician and he will call on tricks of the trade and a knowledge of short cuts that comes from long experience. Hence working with a difficult piece of mathematics is not simply a matter of applying standard rules but involves the intuition, guesswork, heuristics, and the general knowledge of a mathematical expert. This is exactly what an expert system is designed to do and provided the motive for developing MACYSMA.

Throughout the 1970s the basic MACYSMA system continued to be improved. Eventually the systems' ability became so extensive that it was necessary to design a computer primer to MACYSMA which also explained how MACYSMA carried out certain of its operations. An extension of this explainer program is ADVISOR which acts as a professional consultant for users of the MACYSMA system. A possible future modification of MACYSMA would be to give it even greater powers in solving problems. At present the system works by tackling individual mathematical difficulties as they arise. That is, it performs integrations, solves equations, and multiplies vectors on request but it does not know what all these variables and equations actually stand for. For example, a mathematician will recognize $\nabla^2 V = 0$ as a partial differential equation of the second order while a physicist will recognize it as Laplace's equation for motion in a fluid, or an electrostatic field, or wave motions or even the flow of heat. The equation can be used to describe many different systems in engineering and physics but the actual physical conditions involved will guide the physicist in seeking solutions and making approximations.

Therefore, for many applications it may be of advantage for MACYSMA to understand what the equation represents and the actual meaning of its symbolic manipulations. Given an overall concept of the particular problem in physics or engineering and an outline of the user's plan for solving it, the computer system could then make suggestions, point out possible pitfalls, and perform some of the calculations on its own initiative.

A Map of Knowledge

DENDRAL and MACYSMA are examples of the earliest expert systems to be built. But how were they, and the systems that came after them, designed and built? To understand the general principles of an expert system, think what happens if your automobile breaks down on a very cold night in a deserted spot and you telephone for a human expert, a motor mechanic. Left to yourself, you may poke about in the engine and come across the fault by chance or good luck. But when the experienced mechanic arrives he begins to make a full diagnosis in a more systematic fashion. The key to the mechanic's success is that he has created in his head an abstract map of the automobile and all its functions. This map is, to some extent, independent of a particular make of car. This mental map is also supplemented

82

by a large amount of knowledge about spark plugs, carburetors, fuel pumps, and other parts of the car plus the particular quirks of individual car models and rules of thumb about the way various faults manifest themselves.

In the simplest cases, a human expert's internal knowledge can be arranged like a tree graph that enables a particular fault to be traced from a given set of symptoms. But, as we shall see, the richness of his expertise and what distinguishes him from the amateur with a handbook is the extent of the general knowledge he has gained from experience. The mechanic's mental graph will have two major branches labeled fuel and electrical. If the plugs produce a good healthy spark when the engine is turned over, then the mechanic knows that the electrical branch is functioning and he will therefore direct his attention to the fuel supply and discover if a healthy supply of air and gasoline is reaching the cylinders. However, if the plugs do not spark and the battery is well charged, the mechanic must trace his way along the abstract tree branch that leads from battery to plugs through the distributor, ignition coil, and leads.

By performing a search of his internal knowledge tree and asking a question at each node, the mechanic is able to proceed from symptoms to the cause. The various questions he asks during this search could be written in the form of the propositional calculus; as "If . . . then . . ." statements.

"If (there is no spark) then (investigate the electrical system)."

"If (there is a good spark) then (investigate the fuel system)."

"If (no mixture is entering the cylinders) then (investigate the carburetor)."

"If (no gasoline is entering the carburetor) then (investigate the fuel pump)."

"If (the fuel pump is working) then (investigate the connecting line from the gas tank)."

or on another twig of the branch

"If (gasoline enters the carburetor and no mixture reaches the cylinder) then (investigate the carburetor's needle valve)."

"If (gasoline enters the fuel pump and no gasoline leaves) then (investigate the fuel pump)."

Finally a twig is reached and the mechanic finds that the fuel line is blocked, most probably it is frozen. Other tree branches would have led to other diagnoses, a dirty needle valve in the carburetor, a cracked distributor cap, a dirty lead from the battery. The search along that abstract tree that represents the car's functioning is sufficient to lead the mechanic to a particular part of the engine which he suspects of malfunctioning.

But up to now the mechanic has operated in a totally logical fashion by searching through a knowledge tree using a set of "If . . . then . . ." rules. However, in practice, a good mechanic can speed up the search by calling upon his experience and judgment. For example, the mechanic may ask how the car came to stall or failed to start and this may give him a valuable clue as to the probable cause of the trouble. He may also glance at the fuel gauge to ensure that the car has not run out of gas and if the day is particularly cold, he may at once suspect the frozen fuel line and may check by disconnecting the line to the fuel pump. The mechanic may also take into account the make and age of the car and recalling common problems found in those models, he will immediately jump to a particular node within the search tree and make a simple test.

So the human expert uses a variety of approaches, some of them purely logical like tracing back the fuel supply from the cylinders to the gas tank, some based on experience like checking first to see if the gas tank is full, while others involve rules of thumb and general knowledge about particular cars. It is this complex process of diagnosis that the expert computer system sets out to duplicate. It is clear that while the system must involve some form of problem solving, its capacities must be even wider to embrace all manner of general knowledge and rules of thumb. Expert systems therefore involve a great deal of artificial intelligence and represent a particularly important practical advance in the field.

What is particularly interesting in the case of our mechanic he may not be consciously aware of the complex interaction between logical procedure, rules of thumb, general and specific knowledge, intuition, and guesswork. Certainly all this knowledge was never taught to him in any systematic way, rather it was absorbed over his apprenticeship and through subsequent years of work with new knowledge and experience constantly being added to the old and supplementing, changing, or replacing it. So what a human expert knows about his field is very special and very complex and, in the sense that it has taken many years of experience to gather together, it is also very valuable. This is of course why one has to pay such a high price for expert advice and diagnoses.

Human expertise is found in many areas; engineering, medicine, law, science, and so on; indeed, in any field in which there is a combination of law, rules, exceptions, intuition, and long experience is needed. In the case of the average engineer, doctor, or lawyer there are many such professionals who share this knowledge but when it comes to a medical specialist in a particular field of disorders or, a specialist in computer design, there there will be so few such experts in the world that their knowledge is particularly valuable and, unfortunately, concentrated in only a few companies or cities in the world. Clearly, it would be worth spending considerable time and money to produce a computer system that could work as well as a real expert in his chosen area.

Schlumberger Ltd. is a 5 billion dollar corporation that has become involved in artificial intelligence research for this very reason. The company is in the business of oil field exploitation and development, a field that involves the interpretation of drilling data by highly trained engineers. The faster and more accurate this interpretation can be done, the better the company is able to make rapid decisions on which areas to develop and where to drill for gas and oil. Hence, the accurate and rapid interpretation of what is called logging data is crucial to the Schlumberger existence. But there are simply not enough highly trained and experienced experts to go round and to train new ones means taking a highly paid engineer away from his job. The solution, as Schlumberger sees it, is to develop computer clones, expert systems which can be developed and reproduced at the fraction of the cost of employing or training a human being. The company has already began spending over $5 million a year on its AI research and sees this as critical to its expansion by the end of the 1980s.

Another company to realize the benefits of an expert system is the Digital Equipment Corporation (DEC) which manufactures the VAX line of computers. Each time a new computer is ordered it has to be assembled to the customer's particular requirements. The activities of the customer may suggest a given combination of basic modules, and these in turn have to be assembled within the confines of a particular location. By the time the engineer arrives on the scene he has to unpack and assemble the machine by sifting through and interpreting a mass of diagrams and drawings in which each part has to be exactly placed and each cable and interconnection has to be of exactly the right length and make the proper mating. With so many parts to interconnect it is very easy to make errors. The answer for DEC was to spend $2 million on the development of an expert system which instructs the engineer in every step of the operation from which box to unpack first to the order in which particular pieces are to be interconnected. This system alone is said to have saved the company some $10 million. DEC is now working on an expert system which will design individual packages for customers and can be used by the salesman who must take into account individual requirements and come up with a series of best solutions and prices to show his customer.

The design, sale, and use of expert systems is already a valuable and rapidly expanding business. Several major U.S. corporations are producing expert systems for their own in-house use and are also thinking about developing expert systems to sell to their customers. AI researchers who specialize in this work are under constant bombardment with offers of highly paid positions and consultancies from a variety of firms and scientists are already working on a generation of expert systems that will be used to build other expert systems.

Designing an Expert System

When an AI team sets out to design an expert system its members, called *knowledge engineers*, must first select an appropriate area to investigate. Clearly the field should be ripe for exploitation in that it contains only a few highly paid human experts and it is therefore cost effective for the team to spend its time and money in developing a computer system. The field must also represent a compromise in that its diagnoses are neither too loose in their methodology nor too rule bound. If answers and diagnoses can be made by the rigorous application of a small number of rules or laws then the whole process could be done by a more simple problem solving system. What distinguishes the expert system field is that in addition to rules, the diagnoses call for general and specific knowledge, tricks of the trade, exceptions, reasonable guesses, and reasoning from partial knowledge. On the other hand this whole process cannot be too loose or it will be beyond the capabilities of present day expert systems and too difficult for knowledge engineers to program.

Once the field has been identified the knowledge engineer will then spend time with the human experts and try to gain an overall picture of how they work, what rules are involved, and the principles that guide them. As we have already seen, this process is the real bottleneck in constructing an expert system. A human expert generally believes that his task is more simple and methodical than it really is and he, therefore, tends to forget about special cases, exceptions, and the unique ways in which certain rules must be used. So the knowledge engineer must be constantly aware of the fact that the data he works with is incomplete and will have to be updated as the system evolves. Indeed, this openness is true of the whole field of human expertise in general; actual situations will change, new experts will come along, new cases will be discovered and therefore even when an expert system is up and running it will be necessary to continually update it and to take account of new trends in the particular field.

All this means that the knowledge engineers have to construct their expert system in a very flexible way, so that knowledge can constantly be added without having to rewrite the whole program. Even the user of a home computer knows the problems that can crop up when he wants to modify a game or some other program he has written. The actual change may be simple but it may have an effect on some other part of the program or the display and adding further modification has the effect of opening the proverbial can of worms. The answer, as any good home programmer knows, is to work in a modular way, make the program "transparent," and distribute the various processes between subroutines, reserving the program itself for overall control. In a similar way an expert system must be designed to grow in an incremental fashion and to use its knowledge in modular packages. But this also involves a payoff in the way in which knowledge is itself represented and stored in the computer and the special way in which computer searches are made.

The first expert systems, like DENDRAL and MACSYMA, were time consuming and expensive to produce and involved something like 50 man-years of work each. But today's complex systems take only a tenth of this time and simple improvements may a few take man-weeks or -months. One of the ways in which the building of a knowledge system can be speeded up is in the way the engineers work with the human expert. In the early stages of their interaction a prototype of the system is built which is used to solve a variety of scenarios. As the expert observes the system in operation he becomes aware of its over-simplifications and errors and begins to refine the procedure by adding more rules of thumb and guidelines. In this way the knowledge engineer, human expert, and the expert system work hand in hand on the development phase. But the bottleneck of human interaction still remains and future research is being directed towards expert systems that design and build other expert systems and systems that have the built-in capacity to learn, profit from their mistakes, attempt new procedures, and constantly reexamine and restructure their knowledge bases.

Current expert systems have generally been developed through a knowledge team's interaction with a single human expert; for example a doctor, geologist, or computer designer. However, this does voice the problem that in first capitalizing on and then cloning a particular expert's knowledge, the expert system is proliferating a single person's point of view. The expert system, therefore, is in danger of becoming a tsar of knowledge in a particular area and a final court of appeal. However, in the human arena for each considered opinion of every acknowledged expert, one can always find a dissenting voice. This oppenness of opinion to further debate is a healthy aspect of knowledge and one which must one day find its way to the area of expert systems.

While the knowledge engineer is gathering human knowledge he is also thinking about how it will be symbolically represented and stored in the computer. He must also decide upon an overall control system for directing the flow of knowledge during problem solving and on a way of applying the rules and knowledge to specific problems. Finally, there must be some method for humans to interact with the expert system since it is designed for practical use by noncomputer experts. This interaction should preferably be in normal English or some other everyday language but containing the required technical words and formulas if necessary.

We shall leave the question of the interface between the user and the computer until Chapter 5 where we discuss natural language systems and computer speech since in many systems this is simply a matter of adding on a language module called a *natural language front end* to the expert system. For the present, we will concentrate on the other major problems faced by the knowledge engineer, that is, how to represent the knowledge and how to use it. We shall see that this issue of knowledge representation extends beyond expert systems and touches every major area of AI research.

Knowledge Representation

Although the concept may appear obvious to the layman, the idea that knowledge could be of significance in AI systems came as something of a revelation to the AI community itself. Throughout the 1960s researchers tackled a range of projects including machine translation, vision, language understanding, and problem solving. In the main, their approach was to discover various rules and procedures that could be applied automatically to a given problem. For example, in translating a text from Russian into English, the various rules of grammar were supplied along with a Russian-English dictionary. In exploring machine vision a series of transformations and processes were used to extract data and thereby recognize an object picked up by a television camera. But all these problems turned out to be far more difficult than scientists had expected and in several areas progress was slow or appeared to have reached a barrier. In the case of machine translation, for example, continuing research produced only minimal improvements in the speed and accuracy of translations and this caused several leading researchers to despair that computers would ever make good translations.

A major problem arose with the problem of ambiguity that is inherent in all languages. Simply knowing the grammar of a language and having a good dictionary will never resolve the ambiguity inherent in ordinary sentences. Yet humans are able to deal with ambiguities in a very successful way, they understand the general context in which they occur and they have considerable knowledge about the world to draw on. Throughout the 1970s, AI researchers began to realize that what had been missing from all their earlier approaches was the use of general world knowledge. Humans can solve problems, understand language, and recognize the world around them because they already have a great deal of built-in knowledge about how the world works, what particular objects do and are used for, how people act, and so on. As soon as this combination of general and specific knowledge was added to the computer's system a number of problems suddenly appeared to be solvable. In a sense, the computer systems designed in the 1960s were like newborn babies who were asked to make sophisticated responses to the world, yet had never been given the chance to explore, reach out and touch the world, and assimilate all its tastes and textures by stuffing them in its mouth. So today general and specific knowledge has become a key issue for artificial intelligence, not only in building expert systems but in many other fields of applications.

But what is this "knowledge" that must be supplied to computers? It is clearly more than a collection of facts or a database. Take for example the knowledge that is printed in a book; it may be a table of chemical compounds or a list of physical properties. By itself this data does nothing; it simply sits on the page. Give the book a good kick and knowledge will still not spring into being, the pages do nothing; it can solve no problem and make no deduction. Facts and data only go to work for us when we set them moving by establishing relationships, laws of deduction, and rules of procedures for using these facts. Therefore, the building of a knowledge base requires not only a symbolic representation

91

of facts but, in addition, the rules for manipulating and ordering these facts.

No present day computer can be given a knowledge base that is anywhere near as complete and complex as the one we hold in our own heads. The "world" a computer knows about must therefore be tailored to suit a particular range of problems; internal medicine in the case of a particular expert system, objects found in a room in the case of a vision system, the actions of humans in a story for a limited language system. These miniworlds contain several different forms of knowledge; for example, there will be a whole range of facts about objects and people. There will also be knowledge about the way things work or act, there will be knowledge about events, there may also be information about motivations and goals and emotions and beliefs. Finally, there will be knowledge about knowledge itself—meta knowledge, a subject which we shall return to later. Current knowledge bases, and in consequence, expert systems, are all somewhat similar in that they find it difficult to handle different forms of knowledge within the same system. Knowledge about facts, for example, calls for a different way of storing and manipulating the data than knowledge about how things work and it is a major problem to mix different representations within the same system.

The first decision that must be made when a knowledge engineer sets up the knowledge base is how to represent the collection of facts and data he has accumulated. Existing computer languages, symbolic logic, and the language of mathematics have the advantage of being precise with each term well defined. However, these artificial languages do not possess much richness and are unable to deal with shades of meaning and the sort of subtleties that a natural language is ideally adapted to express. But on the other hand, the ability to use a natural language lies beyond the capacity of present computer systems simply because its very richness embraces such things as ambiguity and context dependent meaning which are too complicated for computer programs to handle in any natural way. The answer to knowledge representation therefore is to develop new languages that combine the flexibility and capacity of natural languages with the precision of mathematics, logic, and programming languages.

But how exactly is knowledge to be represented and manipulated? We have met one approach already in Chapter 2, the logic of propositional and predicate calculus.

"All nitrate salts are soluble in water."

"Silver chloride is insoluble in water."

"If hydrochloric acid is added to a solution of silver nitrate, then a precipitate will form."

are not only statements in the propositional and predicate logic but exactly the sort of sentences one would expect to find in a book on chemical analysis. Some forms of technical knowledge, therefore, fall very well into the mold of logic. A number of individual facts can be stored together and by applying the rules of logic, it is possible to make extensive deductions by automatically linking together tens or hundreds of these elementary facts.

Logic bases, therefore, have the advantage of having the capability to make powerful deductions which the user knows must automatically be true. Hence, for some AI uses, logic bases are heaven sent and ideal for the task. But for others, they have serious disadvantages. For example, how is a logic base to operate if knowledge is incomplete, if certain judgments are based on beliefs, metaphors, and analogies, or if things are only true within certain contexts, or at given times? In such cases a representation using logic is inappropriate and difficult to handle.

An alternative approach is to use knowledge in the form of relationships. John may be the husband of Mary, the father of David, own a car, have a social insurance number, and be employed by Arthur. Beginning with a particular object or person, one can string together a vast network of relationships.

So knowledge networks have the advantage of explicitly representing the natural interconnections of data that has been gathered. Deductions can be made by starting from a particular object or relationship and then allowing its effect to spread through the network or by observing the way different parts of a network match up in the patterns of their relationships.

While logic had been around long before the invention of the computers, networks were first designed at the end of the 1960s and developed during the last decade. As with logic representation they are suited to certain types of knowledge and have the same disadvantages when it comes to dealing with beliefs and time ordering. In addition, the essential binary nature of their relationships makes it difficult to deal with the ideas of classes (all, some, at least one). And, unlike logic representations, their deductions are not always automatically correct but must be verified.

A system that is a little closer to the heuristics and rules of thumb used in human knowledge is called a *procedural representation*. A procedural representation is a little like the answer one is generally given to the question "What is a spiral staircase?" After grappling with words, the interrogated person often resorts to a spiraling movement of his hands so the knowledge about a spiral is expressed by an action, or a procedure. The same thing happens if one points to part of a machine and asks, "What does that do?" A scientist may answer in terms of concepts and descriptions while an engineer may reply by actually showing how the thing works. So some knowledge can be expressed in terms of procedures or miniprograms that execute a few steps to simulate a process or relationship. For example, the area of a carpet can be expressed as the procedure "length × breadth." The weight of water in a swimming pool can be expressed by the sequence (length × breadth × height × density). Parts of speech can also be expressed in terms of the ways they function in a sentence. A big advantage of this procedural approach is that the way the knowledge is represented and stored is intimately tied up in the way it is used. Procedures are both knowledge representation *and* use.

Another representation that on the surface looks similar to procedural representation makes use of what are called *rules of production*. The representation is very close to the way people carry things out and use their knowledge in practice. As they are written, the rules may recall the propositional calculus but they are not so static as those of logic.

"If the dial goes above 100 THEN you must push that lever."

"If the dial goes above 100 AND the red light comes on THEN you must switch into the second circuit."

This sort of knowledge representation is, therefore, close to the way in which experts explain how they operate and the ways in which things work. This is a clear advantage when it comes to building an expert system that gives explanations for what it does.

Procedural and production systems are fairly new approaches that have only evolved during the last decade. Production rules are quite attractive when it comes to building expert systems but, as with any other representation system, they also have disadvantages. In their case deductions are not always made in the most efficient way, and overall control of the flow of data logic is not as smooth as it might be.

Rules of procedure and production are not the only ways in which data can be represented and manipulated. Another approach is to use menus and scenarios in the form of frames and scripts, these are discussed in Chapter 5 on language. Ideally an expert system would contain many different forms of knowledge representation and rules of inference and deductions each appropriate to the particular facts and data. However, such a design is very complicated and lies beyond the capacity of most current computers and knowledge engineers. It is a point that we will explore towards the end of this chapter.

Once a knowledge representation is chosen and a human expert is cooperating with the knowledge engineer, the project can go to completion. The goal is to produce a system that will function as well as any human expert and, given that the computer can rapidly explore a much larger number of possibilities, the system may even function at a higher level than the original human expert. The final system employs all the human's experience, knowledge, rules, and heuristics and uses a deduction system to arrive at a diagnosis and give advice. The design itself will be modular to enable the system to be constantly improved and updated. But the expert system is not necessarily complete even at this point. To begin with, the doctor or engineer or scientist who consults an expert system may wish to know how it arrived at its diagnoses or its justification for taking a particular step. In its simplest form this explanation consists of a recapitulation of all the moves made by the expert system during its deductions. But these steps may contain far too much detail and their logic may be quite different from that generally used by human experts. A good expert system will therefore have to have an interpreter that recapitulates the steps taken during a diagnosis and then converts them into an explanation appropriate for humans to follow.

Growing with Knowledge

In any given field of human expertise, knowledge, approaches, and techniques are constantly changing so, left to itself an expert system will gradually become out of date. Current systems are therefore updated by their knowledge engineers from time to time but the ideal solution would be a system that constantly learns, updates itself, and corrects its mistakes. A scientist or doctor spends part of each day reading the latest journals and reports about his subject. Will it be possible one day to construct expert systems that operate in the same way by scanning the latest data banks in their topics?

Learning, however, is not simply the accumulation of new facts. In human terms, additional knowledge often causes us to examine and reconstruct what we already know. A single new fact may cause us to throw away what has become outdated and make new patterns out of the rest. So learning is a process of assimilation and integration rather than a bottomless sack into which we throw new data. Clearly the future of expert systems and artificial intelligence in general depends upon being able to develop systems that will spontaneously learn about the world around them.

In updating an expert system one runs into another major problem, that of limits to the size of a knowledge base. At present expert systems are limited by the number of facts they contain. An expert system can perform as well as any human expert in a given restricted domain but outside that domain, the system is more hopeless than a newborn baby. As it reaches its limits, the system continues to offer its diagnoses with the same confidence as before, yet now these diagnoses are either unreliable or stark nonsense. One answer to this problem would be to take a number of different expert systems that have been created, each in related but overlapping areas and combine them into a single super expert system that contains hundreds of thousands of facts. Unfortunately, no one yet knows how to construct and manage such large databases. Expert systems seem to have reached a limit to any further increase in the size of their knowledge bases and researchers feel that a definite quantum leap in performance will only be possible if this barrier is broken. Researchers have various suggestions as to how this should be done. One approach is to question the conventional wisdom that a computer program should be "transparent," with the control of the program very clearly displayed and separated from the things it controls. Some scientists are now arguing that human thinking does not work like this and that human knowledge is intimately tied up with the way it is used. Knowledge engineers should be prepared to let go of the simplicity and clarity of control in favor of systems that use several different forms of knowledge representations that are intertwined with rules of procedure and deduction, something that sounds a little closer to a human brain.

An issue that is related to these questions of explanation and database size is that of dealing with meta-knowledge or knowing about knowledge. We humans not only know things but we also know that we know them. We can not only solve problems but we can also observe ourselves solving them, we can reflect on the approaches we use and then act in new ways. As we work out a brain teaser, we also explore the way in which we work and in turn, we observe the thought processes we employ to explore that exploration. By contrast the computer mechanically applies its rules and procedures to move around its facts and knowledge which lead to deductions. The expert system does not think about the fact that it is thinking; it does not observe and improve its own operations.

Suppose one were to ask a human expert, a mathematician, "Can you solve this differential equation?" There are several answers that the mathematician could give and each would involve the world of meta-knowledge, that is knowing about what he knew. The mathematician may say "Yes" and write down the solution. Or he may say "Yes" but take no further action. The latter answer means "Yes, I *know* that I know how to solve this equation. I recognize its general form and I know all the mathematical moves that I would have to make. But the actual processes would take too long and I'm busy at the moment." Or the mathematician may say, in a tentative way, "Yes," meaning, "I think I know how to solve it. I can certainly recognize what to do in a general sort of way but I've forgotten some of the transformations I'd have to use. Possibly they'll come back to me when I get down to it." Or, he may say, "No. But I do know the general theory about differential equations and I know which book to go to and that will give me the specific information I'd need to learn in order to solve it." Or, he may say, "No. It's not my specialty. I recognize the problem and know that it's beyond me. I know I've got very poor intuition in this area but I do know that this is a particularly difficult equation to solve so even if I were to read a textbook, it wouldn't help me very much."

So the mathematician knows what he knows and what he needs to know and how to use all this knowledge to solve a problem or to gain some new knowledge and understanding. He can think about a problem and then think about the whole structure of a particular problem solving procedure. He can also think about the knowledge we will use in solving that problem. Now this general ability is exactly what a computer system requires to enable it to handle large amouts of data and to direct its own problem solving capacities in a more effective way. A computer may be supplied with all manner of heuristics, strategies, and other techniques for exploring a knowledge tree or a problem tree, but the individual steps are still carried out in a mechanical fashion. But suppose that the computer could monitor and analyze its own actions. Suppose that it recognized when it was behaving productively and when it was simply engaged on a wild goose chase down the branch of some problem tree. Suppose that it even began to question the effectiveness of its original design! A major breakthrough in expert systems and AI applications will come about when research workers are able to deal with this dual movement between knowledge and meta-knowledge.

Another advance in expert systems will come about when they are able to use their powers of reason in more flexible and efficient ways. Deductions that make use of logic, networks of relations, or any of the other approaches we have learned about can be very powerful but they are not the only ways in which humans reason. Humans also employ metaphors and analogies, they work with abstractions, and they use intuition and guesswork. While a logical system may be superior to a human in making deductions within a closed and regular system, it may be hopeless in those areas where knowledge is incomplete and where what is known may involve probable rather than absolute truths. Expert systems of the future are going to have to use more flexible approaches both to knowing and to reasoning.

Of course, it could be objected that computers must evolve their own ways of solving problems and these need not always be modeled along human lines. This is indeed true; for example, one approach to robotic vision systems involves a mathematical modeling that is vastly different to anything a human does. But on the other hand when it comes to expert systems, since they are designed to act as consultants and colleagues to humans, their reasoning processes should not be altogether alien to our own.

Expert Systems

At the start of this chapter we met two of the earliest expert systems to be designed, DENDRAL and MACYSMA. They were soon followed by other expert systems for use in science and medicine. CRYSALIS, built by Feigenbaum and his colleagues, is another approach to determining molecular structures, but this time using electron density maps. These maps tell scientists where electrons are spending most of their time in a molecule but do not give any information as to the actual atoms and how they are arranged. Interpreting an electron density map is a little like being given a map of population density in a city block and using it to determine where houses, stores, and sidewalks are located. CRYSALIS is fairly sophisticated in its approach since it makes some attempt to deal with the problem of using different types of knowledge and initiating the opportunistic ways in which scientists solve these structure problems.

Expert systems which are already assisting scientists include systems like MOLGEN, SYNCHEM, and LHASA which help chemists design their experiments. SYN and EL are used in electronics work, and PROSPECTOR helps geologists in mineral exploration. PROSPECTOR was developed at Stanford Research Institute and has already paid for itself by discovering a mineral deposit in the United States. Its success is likely to precipitate the development of similar systems of commercial importance. PROSPECTOR operates by digesting information from human geologists on features of the terrain and following this, it then attempts to match the data against a series of geological models in its data banks. The system next enters into a dialogue with the geologist and asks for specific information which helps to pin down the exact model. A particularly interesting aspect of PROSPECTOR is the way in which it works with probalistic reasoning and ends by suggesting the most likely geological model of the area. In 1982 PROSPECTOR was used to search for molybdenum deposits in Washington state and located a find worth in the neighborhood of $100 million.

At the start of this chapter we gave the example of a computer doctor and it is in this area of computer assisted medicine where expert systems will soon be making an important social contribution. Medical diagnosis is an ideal area for exploitation by expert systems. It is constantly in demand and of considerable humanitarian importance. Acknowledged experts exist in each particular medical field but they are always in short supply, particularly in less industrialized nations. In addition, the whole procedure of a medical diagnosis lends itself well to expert system design. A doctor is taught to carry out a regular and systematic set of moves yet the information he looks for and his process of deduction can be quite subtle and involves recognizing the shape or pattern of a disorder. Indeed, diagnosis it is far closer to the way we recognize a face in a photograph than the way we prove a theorem in mathematics. In addition, the computer may be superior to the doctor when it comes to retaining a whole library of information on drugs, their side effects, and the complications of prescribing more than one drug in combination. In place of a single pill per day the computer may be able to prescribe an exact dose that varies over the course of the disease and is matched to the patient's body weight. A computer doctor may also be faster and more competent in those aspects of diagnosis that involve interaction with other medical computers, such as those used in automated laboratory analysis and interpretation of images from CAT or NMR scans. On the other hand, one should not be blind to its disadvantages. Medicine is a profoundly human occupation in which the relationship between doctor and patient can contribute significantly to the cure. It is possible that expert systems could become yet another branch of the technology that stands between the doctor and the patient and produces a sense of distance and remoteness. On the other hand, if expert medical systems act as consultants and assistants to doctors and free them to interact in a more direct way with their patients, then they will be welcomed by doctors and patients alike.

In the future one could also envision systems that contain files on patient histories and conduct preliminary interviews directly with the patient before referring them to the appropriate doctor or clinic. These could act as filtering systems that pass the real problems on to an appropriate doctor and themselves offer treatment for minor illnesses.

In current systems, the doctor interacts with the expert consultant using a dialogue in which the doctor offers his findings and the computer then requests additional information on past medical history and the results of tests. Some of this knowledge will be inexact or based on beliefs, assumptions, and experience such as the doctor's, "It looks to me very like. . . ." Statements like these can be digested by the computer if they are first converted into sentences of the form "On a scale from zero to 9 I would place the severity of this symptom at 3." Since medical diagnoses often contain opinions and judgments, a representation in terms of logic or networks is generally less appropriate than one using frames or production rules.

There are now several expert systems that have been developed for different medical diagnoses and treatments, most of which are being used in hospitals as experiments. For example, an expert system is used with a number of patients and compared with human diagnoses, the results are then analyzed by a medical team. Some systems like PUFF (for pulmonary disorders) however have already passed the testing stage and are assisting doctors in many hospitals.

MYCIN was one of the early successful systems and was designed to give advice on the diagnosis and treatment of infectious diseases in smaller hospitals where a specialist may not always be on call. It is not unusual for an infection to manifest itself after surgery. The tests necessary to track down the bacteria responsible may take many hours or even days to complete, so the doctor is sometimes forced to start treatment with incomplete knowledge. MYCIN was constructed to act in a similar way and talk over the patient's condition with the doctor. At the end of the consultation MYCIN then suggests which diseases are probably present and the drug and therapy of choice along with two alternatives. Another expert system that prescribes a drug is M.I.T.'s Digitalis Therapy Advisor which combines a mathematical model of the action of digitalis within the body along with information on the individual patient. The aim of conventional digitalis therapy is to very carefully balance the dosage to control the heart's rythym while at the same time avoiding toxic side effects. In its initial tests the system performed well and generally agreed with the prescriptions of professionals, but in some cases the treatment of the attending physician was judged superior. This issue of the effectiveness of an expert system in the workplace is an important one. Some expert systems have now been well tested in the laboratory and under experimental conditions but there is always the concern that these systems will not work as well under more general conditions. The RI system developed for use on VAX computer systems showed a 90 percent accuracy in the laboratory but only 60 percent when first used in the field. The problem was not so much the expert system but in the way engineers were using it. It

A Dialogue with MYCIN

MYCIN: Patient's name (first-last):
DOCTOR: Fred Smith
MYCIN: Sex:
DOCTOR: Male
MYCIN: Age:
DOCTOR: 55
MYCIN: Have you been able to obtain posi-
          tive cultures from a site at which
          Fred Smith has an infection:
DOCTOR: Yes
MYCIN: What is the infection?
DOCTOR: Primary-bacteremia

MYCIN goes on to ask the doctor some specific questions about the specimen and the tests
that were performed on it and then MYCIN
gives its diagnosis

MYCIN: My therapy recommendation will be
          based on the following probable in-
          fection(s) and potential causative
          organism(s):
          INFECTION-1 is PRIMARY BAC-
          TEREMIA
          <Item 1> The identity of ORGA-
          NISM-1 may be PSEUDOMONAS-
          AERUGINOSA
          <Item 2>. The identity of OR-
          GANISM-1 may be KLEBSIELLA-
          PNEUMONIAE
          <Item 3> The identity of ORGA-
          NISM-1 may be E.COLI
          <Item 4> The identity of ORGA-
          NISM-1 may be BACTERIODES-
          FRAGILIS

<Item 5> The identity of ORGA-NISM-1 may be PROTEUS NON-MIRABILIS

DOCTOR: On a scale of 0 to 4, where higher numbers indicate increasing severity, how would you rate Fred Smith's degree of sickness?

DOCTOR: 3

MYCIN: Does Fred Smith have a clinically significant allergic reaction to any antimicrobial agent:

DOCTOR: NO

MYCIN: Fred Smith's weight in kilograms (or <number> POUNDS):

DOCTOR: 70

MYCIN: (Rec 1) My preferred therapy recommendation is as follows:

In order to cover for items <1 2 3 5 6>:

Give: GENTAMICIN

Dose: 119 mg (1.7 mg/kg) q8h IV (or IM) for 10 days

Comments: Modify dose in renal failure

In order to cover for item <4>:

Give: CLINDAMYCIN

Dose: 595 mg (8.5 mg/kg) q6h IV (or IM) for 14 days

Comments: If diarrhea or other GI symptoms develop, patient should be evaluated for possible PSEUDO-MEMBRANOUS COLITIS.

Do you wish to see the next-choice therapy?

continued

DOCTOR: Yes

MYCIN continues to suggest alternative therapies. If MYCIN has been extended with TIERESIAS the doctor can continue his conversation and press the system for details.

COMPUTER: Is the patient's illness with ORGANISM-1 a hospital-acquired infection?

DOCTOR: WHY? (i.e., WHY is it important to determine whether the infection with ORGANISM-1 was acquired while the patient was hospitalized?)

COMPUTER: This will aid in determining the category of ORGANISM-1. It has already been established that
(1.1) the gram stain of ORGANISM-1 is gramneg, and
(1.2) the morphology of ORGANISM-1 is rod, and
(1.3) the aerobicity of ORGANISM-1 is facultative
Therefore, if
(1.4) the infection with ORGANISM-1 was not acquired while the patient was hospitalized
then
there is strongly suggestive evidence (.8) that the category of ORGANISM-1 is enterobacteriacae.
Also:
there is weakly suggestive evidence (.1) that the identity of ORGANISM-1 is PSEUDOMONAS-AERUGINOSA (RULE 27)

DOCTOR: How 1.3? (I.e., HOW was it established that the aerobicity of ORGANISM-1 is facultative?)

COMPUTER: The following was used:
(3.1) RULE 27 indicated there is strongly suggestive evidence (.8) that the aerobicity of ORGANISM-1 is facultative.
(3.2) RULE 27 indicated that there is weakly suggestive evidence (.2) that the aerobicity of ORGANISM-1 is anerobic.
Since this gave a cumulative CF of (.8) for facultative, and (.2) for anerobic, it has been established that the aerobicity of ORGANISM-1 is facultative.

turned out that they were not fully understanding how it worked and were feeding it incorrect data. But the system itself must take part of the blame. Expert systems are designed to be used by people with no experience of computers and the system must therefore be foolproof in general use.

INTERNIST was designed at the University of Pittsburgh to make diagnoses in internal medicine. The original motivation of the research was not only to provide a computer expert but also to study ways in which human doctors make hypotheses and arrived at their diagnoses. INTERNIST is probably the largest of all expert systems and contains 100,000 pieces of information.

Early in the 1980s the system could diagnose over 500 diseases, which is some three quarters of such known diseases. Its performance was good and it is possible that by the time this book is read that an updated version of INTERNIST may be in regular use in many hospitals.

One of the major sources of expert systems is Stanford University's Heuristic Programming Project (HPP) which first developed DENDRAL back in 1965. The project currently employs 70 faculty, graduate students, and staff with Edward Feigenbaum as one of its senior research workers. Projects include MRS, an expert system that will reason about its own problem solving activities, explain its actions, and accept advice from its user, MRS is part of a long-range project that is investigating the nature of expert systems and contains a control structure and a meta level which is used to describe the system's goals and actions and contains its own knowledge representation.

Humans are able to project their thoughts so that they become double-edged swords; not only are they about the world outside but they are the subjects of other thoughts which can then contemplate them. This movement between level and meta-level is superbly done by the human brain and, in the case of computers, appears critical to their future development. Stanford's MRS is not only able to solve problems but to treat its own problem solving abilities as an object for examination. Hence MRS has representations in which a statement can be something that is executed by the system as it solves a problem or it may be something about other statements and the way they are executed. With this flexibility MRS has already been used as a tool in the construction of other expert systems.

EURISKO is a learning system that gathers data, notices regularities, formulates hypotheses, designs as it carries out experiments, develops heuristics which help it to avoid blind alleys of reasoning, extends its knowledge representation, and focuses on important concepts. The system has been applied in such diverse areas as VLSI design, ship building, programming, and oil spill clean-up.

Additional HPP projects include ONCOCIN which gives advice on cancer therapy; DART which understands how computers are structured and the things they do and uses this knowledge to diagnose equipment failures; KBVLSI which

Explaining and Justifying

Expert systems should explain their actions and justify their deductions. Digitalis Advisor explains how it checked for Thyroid function:

I CHECKED SENSITIVITY DUE TO THYROID-FUNCTION BY EXECUTING THE FOLLOWING STEPS:

1. I ASKED THE USER THE STATUS OF MYXEDEMA. THE USER RESPONDED THAT THE STATUS OF MYXEDEMA WAS PRESENT.

2. SINCE THE STATUS OF MYXEDEMA WAS PRESENT I DID THE FOLLOWING:

2.1 I ADDED MYXEDEMA TO THE PRESENT AND CORRECTABLE CONDITIONS. THE PRESENT AND CORRECTABLE CONDITIONS THEN BECAME MYXEDEMA.

2.2 I REMOVED MYXEDEMA FROM THE DEGRADABLE CONDITIONS. THE DEGRADABLE CONDITIONS THEN BECAME HYPOKALEMIA, HYPOXEMIA, CARDIOMYOPATHIER-MI, AND POTENTIAL POTASSIUM LOSS DUE TO DIURETICS.

2.3 I SET THE FACTOR OF REDUCTION DUE TO MYXEDEMA TO 0.67. THE FACTOR OF REDUCTION DUE TO MYXEDEMA WAS PREVIOUSLY UNDETERMINED.

2.4 I ADDED MYXEDEMA TO THE REASONS OF REDUCTION. THE REASONS OF REDUCTION THEN BECAME MYXEDEMA.

continued

The system can also justify its questions and actions:

COMPUTER: Please enter the value of serum-k.
USER: Why?
COMPUTER: The system is anticipating digitalis toxicity. Decreased serum-k causes increased automacity, which may cause a change to ventricular fibrillation. Increased digitalis also causes increased automavity. Thus, if the system observes decreased serum-k, it reduces the dose of digitalis due to decreased serum-k.

---

is concerned with the nature of the design process and, in particular, the design of integrated circuits; GUIDON 2 which uses NEOMYCIN as its knowledge base and acts as an intelligent tutor in the teaching of diagnosis; PRX which explores the way in which new knowledge can be automatically acquired from a large database and when used with part of the database of the American Rheumatism Association it successfully identified new knowledge that had not been previously confirmed in its data base; and AGE is a project to design a software laboratory for knowledge-based programs. In addition to these individual projects the Stanford group continue to explore new approaches to problem solving and the design of knowledge bases.

The expert systems mentioned above represent only a handful of those that are currently being tested or are under development in science and medicine. Another large area for exploitation is in the field of education where expert systems can be combined with computer assisted learning to provide a teaching machine that gives individual attention to each student and tailors the course exactly for his requirements.

SCHOLAR

Scholar is an expert tutoring system and gives its geography lesson along the following lines:

SCHOLAR: What is the language of Argentina?
STUDENT: Probably Spanish.
SCHOLAR: Very good.
Approximately what is the area of Argentina?
STUDENT: Tell me something about Peru.
SCHOLAR: Peru is a country.
It is located in South America.
The capital of Peru is Lima.
Now answer the question you didn't answer before.
STUDENT: The area of Argentina is 1,100,000 square miles.
SCHOLAR: Approximately true, but a more exact value is 1,200,000. The eastern bordering country of Peru is—.
STUDENT: Catholicism.
SCHOLAR: Wrong. Catholicism is not a country but a religion. The correct answer is: Brazil.
Where is Peru?
And so on.

This system will match its pace to that of the student, it will monitor his progress, and select the correct range of questions for him to try out. Information will be vastly superior to current text-based question and answering systems and will use voice, music, film, slides, animation, and video, all stored in the computer's memory. A particularly exciting possibility is the use of full color, three-dimensional simulation in which the student feels that he is actually operating a nuclear power plant or carrying out a complex chemical synthesis. Of course, this simulation is *not* the real thing since the world is far richer and more complex than any simulation and we learn to interact with it in so many different ways. Nevertheless, a computer experiment or a full color simulation can be a valuable exercise when combined with experiments, events, and visits.

One could also imagine an encyclopedia taking the form of an expert system. One problem with looking up things in a reference library is that we already have to know something about the topic in order to ask the right questions. In addition, one wants an answer that gives the right amount of detail and at the correct level. Reference books can't talk back to us but an expert system may be able to deal with our vague and partially formed questions and tailor the answers to our requirements and educational backgrounds.

The impact of computers in general in education is a vast one and lies far beyond the scope of this book. Seymour Papert has discussed one aspect of this in his book *Mindstorms: Children, Computers and Powerful Ideas* (Basic Books, NY, 1980). Papert began his computer work with Marvin Minsky at M.I.T. by developing the theory of the Perceptron, that early attempt to build electronic learning circuits. He then moved into the field of education and developed the LOGO language. PAPERT's idea is that given a computer and an appropriately designed language, young children can engage in a stimulating and rich form of learning by doing.

The whole field of computer assisted learning is controversial in that it touches on the future restructuring of the schools and the educational system. A computer that is brought into the classroom is not simply another tool but something that can have a profound effect on the way things are taught and the social interaction that takes place between children and the teacher. There are many arguments in favor of and against the way computers are presently being used in schools and parents would do well to familiarize themselves with what is going on in their own school boards and become involved in decisions that are being made on their behalf. It should be borne in mind, however, that the future may already be beyond our control since, through video games, children have claimed the computer as their own and the gap is already widening between these children and their parents and teachers.

Video games themselves will take great strides forward when powered by expert systems. Players will receive a wide range of sensory feedback and will be able to play against a skillful and intelligent opponent who monitors a series of games and selects the strategy, simulations, and approach that the player enjoys most. Expert systems will also be used in offices, shops, and shopping centers, garages and other maintenance areas, real estate and law offices, by accountants, banks, engineers, and many other professionals.

Expert systems will also be increasingly developed for warfare. They will be employed in intelligence gathering and modern weapon systems. Possibly most frightening of all, they will be designed to conduct nuclear war. If the event of a nuclear war, decisions must be taken far faster than any human is capable of making. A survey of strategic defense by Tom Mangold in the British magazine, *The Listener* (Sept. 8, 1983) suggested that after launch, the enemy missiles that are identified by orbiting satellite must be attacked and destroyed within 250 seconds and those that survive would have to be destroyed by a second, laser-based line of defense before the missile reenters the atmosphere. But such missiles will throw off a large amount of chaff and decoys to confuse defensive measures. The only solution lies in supercomputers operating at a billion to a trillion calculations per second, and expert systems that are able to identify enemy warheads, develop defensive tactics, and execute them. As Dr. Robert Cooper, head of DARPA, says, "We want systems that can act alone, can plan, strategize, employ resources, and do the things that human beings normally do in a more leisurely paced engagement." The conclusion seems obvious that, whatever the politicans may say, they are planning for a war that will be conducted between computers alone. Two silicon-based intelligences will play their games of superchess using carbon-based pawns and then destroy the board.

But let us pass on to systems that are involved in producing the next generation of expert systems. TEIRESIAS is a system developed by R. Davis that is designed to serve the MYCIN medical system. This system makes use of the distinction between knowledge and meta-knowledge. For example, a human expert can use TEIRESIAS to communicate with MYCIN and discovering what it is doing, in turn TEIRESIAS will act as a tutor to improve the computer expert system.

TEIRESIAS asks leading questions of the human expert, digests his replies, and then begins to modify MYCIN's database. The expert may, for example, believe that MYCIN has made an error or misdiagnosis. In the normal course of events it would take a knowledge engineer some considerable time to track down the problem but with TEIRESIAS's help the human doctor can follow MYCIN's logic, call for explanations at particular points, and finally track down the error. A system like TEIRESIAS has enormous implications, for if expert systems are to be accepted by professionals and members of the public who have no background in computer programming and have no particular desire to spend the time to learn, then the expert system must function entirely in the domain of conversational English. At times a human may be satisfied to enter into a dialogue with the computer system on its own terms and receive its diagnoses and advice. But at others, the user may need to question the system in greater detail, he may wish to supplement its knowledge, or he may disagree with its diagnoses and want to debate its interpretations. In these cases, there has to be some way of examining what the system does and interpreting its operations. This involves understanding the structure of the knowledge within a computer and following how this knowledge is used to solve particular problems. In other words what is needed is an expert system that works in the domain of meta-knowledge. Ideally, a meta-knowledge system like **TEIRESIAS** should be quite general, a *front end* that could be added to many other expert systems provided only that these expert systems use the same general knowledge structure for this knowledge.

Another important class of expert systems are those which understand about computer programming and can assist human programmers in working with very complex systems. Expert systems, for example, have already reached a high level of complexity in their programming as have other AI systems. But many of them are already too big for a single human programmer to understand and therefore an attempt to modify them usually leads to disaster since it becomes increasingly difficult to understand how a modification will affect the entire program. For example, a simple change in one part of the program could have unpredictable repercussions in another.

The long term goal of this research is to have a computer write its own programs. For example, humans would explain the overall problem and goals in general terms and then leave it to the computer to create the necessary program. In terms of expert systems the logical extension would be to have a meta system that holds extended dialogues with human experts and then proceeds to design and program the expert system by itself. Such an approach involves a great deal of intelligence, knowledge, and understanding and lies far beyond the capabilities of any existing system. But already there are computer systems that represent the first tentative steps towards this goal. For example, there are systems that help a programmer by keeping track of his bookkeeping, make a note of various indices and addresses used, act as text editors, and edit the program.

For example Programmer's Apprentice, an expert system which while not acting at the level of a full automatic programmer assist the human programmer and cuts down the complexity of his tasks. Developed at M.I.T., the system can understand an abstract plan of what the program is trying to do. In addition, it knows about many of the commonly used concepts in programming and how they work.

Programmer's Apprentice works in a cooperative way with the human programmer. Not only does it understand what could be called the "surface" of the program, that is, the particular code of instructions used, but it has an understanding of how the program itself works. As the program develops, the human and the expert system "talk" to each other. The Apprentice builds up a picture of how data will flow through various parts of the program when it's operational, and how this flow is to be controlled, it realizes that certain parts of the program depend upon other parts, and what are the particular subgoals of each of these parts. As the writing proceeds and the complexity of the program increases, the human programmer will begin to lean heavily on his computer assistant. Assuming that a front end has been added to enable the two colleagues to talk to each other in English the conversation could go something like this.

HUMAN: I want to change the way I worked on that part of the program we worked on yesterday. I want to do the listings in a different way.

COMPUTER: Okay. What you propose is going to affect some of the other parts of the program.
HUMAN: Which ones?
COMPUTER: Backtrack, Occupation, Field.
HUMAN: What's the problem with Field?

The computer explains exactly what will happen and together the two program writers begin to revise the program accordingly.

HUMAN: Okay. We'll do it like you suggest.
COMPUTER: Okay. But now the special tests you added to "Occupation" are no longer necessary.

HUMAN: Get rid of them.
APPRENTICE: Okay. By the way you must also write some
                new code for a section in Backtrack. Do you
                want to see it?

The Programmer's Apprentice is also particularly valuable in updating and expanding the program because it can keep track of all the logical interdependencies in a complex flow of data and control. What is interesting about this whole process is that by the time the program is complete it will no longer be clear which parts were written by a human and which by computer. In a limited sense the computer has taken the first step towards programming itself.

Programmer's Apprentice has already been used at M.I.T. to help in the implementation of a new program editor. Work on its development continues under Dr. Charles Rich and Dr. Richard C. Waters who expect the expertise of the system to grow. However, the dream of a fully automated programming computer still remains in the future.

Another move at the frontier of expert system design involves the whole structuring of an expert system. As we have clearly seen, present day expert systems begin with a collection of rules, facts, and codified experience which is then represented according to some abstract scheme. Some critics have observed that the way all this knowledge is structured inside the computer has very little relationship to the structure of the actual system it is supposed to refer to. Possibly if the expert system is designed to reflect the logical connections that exist with the underlying systems, or the physical laws that describe it, then knowledge engineers could gain new insights into how to control the problem of expanding search spaces and how to expand a knowledge base beyond its present size.

In the example of the car mechanic who we met near the start of this chapter, his mental map of an automobile bears little relationship to an actual car and its engine. But if we were to make a schematic picture of the car's electrical system, or the fuel system, by showing all the interconnections between the various black boxes like distributor, battery, spark plugs and such, then this would begin to look closer to the mechanic's mental map. In fact, a mechanic's internal image of the faults that can develop in an automobile is quite similar to a topological map showing the various interconnections within an engine.

The example of an automobile engine was used for illustrative purposes (although I would not be surprised if automobiles have developed microchip expert diagnostic systems for use within their latest models), but when one comes to electrical circuitry, however, you find a field which has already spawned several expert systems. In building an electrical device the actual *shape* of the circuit does not so much matter as the interconnectios. In mathematical terms it is its *topology* that counts and not its *geometry*. It is possible to create an expert system for dealing with electrical circuits in which the topology of the system's knowledge flow reflects the topology of the circuitry itself. At M.I.T. work is proceeding on systems in which underlying interconnections and physical laws are used as a guide to the ways in which knowledge systems are ordered. Such systems may, for example, be supplied with diagrams of a particular circuit and then use that diagram to cut down the search space that the computer must explore or speed up the search itself by relating its strategy to the actual structure and laws of the real system. Already groups at M.I.T. and Stanford are exploring such an approach in relation to diagnosing malfunctions in computers. The next stage would be attempting to extend this approach to medical systems and relate the knowledge structure of an expert system to the actual structure and interconnections of body organs, the circulation and nervous systems, metabolic pathways, and the equations of biochemistry.

The exploitation of expert systems has only just begun, yet scientists are already working at the frontier to develop the next generation of expert systems. A 1982 survey conducted

SOPHIE

SOPHIE is an expert teaching system which understands circuit design and servicing.

SOPHIE: The piece of equipment you are studying is a regulated power supply. Would you like to start with a faulty instrument that needs fixing?

STUDENT: Yes.

SOPHIE: The instrument has a fault and its present control setting is: (Here SOPHIE supplies data on currents, voltages, and variable resistances.)

STUDENT: What is the output?

SOPHIE: The output voltage is 11.7 volts.

STUDENT: What is it in a working instrument?

SOPHIE: In a working circuit the output voltage is 19.9 volts.

STUDENT: What is the voltage between R8 and Q1?

SOPHIE: The voltage at N1 is 47.6 volts.

STUDENT: What is the base-emitter voltage of the voltage limiting transistor:

SOPHIE: = base
The base-emitter voltage of Q5 is −.037 millivolts.

STUDENT: What about for the current limiting transistor?

SOPHIE: The base-emitter voltage of Q6 is 0.349 volts.

STUDENT: What should it be?

SOPHIE: . . . 0.593 volts.

STUDENT: Replace Q6.

Table 1

EXPERT SYSTEMS

The following, taken from a 1982 U.S. Department of Commerce report, lists expert systems according to their functions. By the time this book is published it will probably be out of date.

Function	Domain	System	Institution
Diagnosis	Medicine	PIP	M.I.T.
	"	CASNET	Rutgers
	"	INTERNIST	U. of Pittsburgh
	"	MYCIN	Stanford
	"	PUFF	"
	Computer faults	DART	Stanford/IBM
Data analysis and interpretation	Geology	DIPMETER ADVISOR	M.I.T./Schlumberger
	Chemistry	DENDRAL	Stanford
	Chemistry	GA1	"
	Geology	PROSPECTOR	SRI
	Protein crystallography	CRYSALTS	Stanford
Analysis	Electrical circuits	EL	M.I.T.
	Symbolic mathematics	MACSYMA	M.I.T.
	Mechanics problems	MECHO	Edinburgh
	Naval Task Force threat analysis	TECH	Rand/NOSC
Design	Computer System Configurations	R1	Carnegie-Mellon U.
	Automatic programming	PECOS	Yale
	Circuit synthesis	SYN	M.I.T.
	Chemical synthesis	SYNCHEM	SUNY/Stonybrook

Application area	Program	Task	Institution
Planning	SECHS	Chemical synthesis	U. of Cal. Santa Cruz
	NOAH	Robotics	SRI
	ABSTRIPS	"	SRI
	DEVISER	Planetary Flybys	JPL
	OP-PLANNER	Errand planning	Rand
	MOLGEN	Molecular genetics	Stanford
Learning from experience	METADENDRAL	Chemistry	Stanford
Concept formation	AM	Mathematics	Carnegie-Mellon U.
Signal interpretation	HEARSAY II	Speech understanding	Carnegie-Mellon U.
	HARPY	"	"
	SU/X	Machine acoustics	Stanford U.
	HASP	Ocean surveillance	System Controls Inc.
Monitoring	VM	Patient respiration	Stanford
Use advisor	SACON	Structural analysis computer program	Stanford
Computer Aided instruction	SOPHIE	Electronic troubleshooting	B.B.N.
	GUIDON	Medical diagnosis	Stanford
Knowledge acquisition	TEIRESIAS	Medical diagnosis	Stanford
	EXPERT	Medical consultation	Rutgers
	KAS	Geology	SRI
Expert system construction	ROSIE		Rand
	AGE		Stanford
	HEARSAY III		USC/ISI
	EMYCIN		Stanford
	OPS 5		Carnegie-Mellon U.
Image understanding	VISIONS		U. of Mass.
	ACRONYM		Stanford

for NASA listed the industries and govern concerns that have moved into the field of expert system research. (See Table 1.) That same report also lists some 45 *major* expert systems and does not include the many other systems that are either under development or are variants of these main systems. By 1990 it predicts that expert systems will begin to construct themselves in cooperation with human experts and by the year 2000, they will develop in a semispontaneous fashion using knowledge based on technical papers and textbooks in each particular area. As with other areas of electronics and computer development, these systems are going to get cheaper and will soon become available to all.

And what will their social impact be? That is impossible to predict. Society is an open system with an internal structure that is so rich and complex that any perturbation has an incalculable effect. A major innovation can be absorbed by society and produce very little effect; on the other hand even a minor change can totally transform in the way people relate to each other.

Expert medical systems may well alleviate the pressures that are placed on our medical resources and raise the general health by producing rapid and accurate diagnoses; in the future we may phone our computer doctor once a month and have it run a rapid check on us by means of a few sensors hooked up to our telephone. The implications for the office and factory are equally far reaching. One application that I will particularly value is the predigestion of the world's data. It is often said that more knowledge is being produced each decade than in the whole of human history and that more scientists are alive than have ever lived before. But it is equally true that there are more second-rate scientists alive today than have ever lived and that more second-rate research is being published! And as for all this accumulated knowledge? Well, it is not really knowledge, it is data, facts, the raw material spewed out by tens of thousands of laboratories, universities, commentators, and committees. By itself this data is of little use, it is now beyond human

EXPERT SYSTEMS: WHO ARE DESIGNING THEM

A 1982 U.S. Survey indicates that, outside the universities, the following agencies are engaged in expert system design.

Non-Profit
SRI
RAND
JPL

Government
NRL AI Lab, Washington, DC
NOSC, San Diego, CA

Industrial
Fairchild
Schlumberger
Machine Intelligence Corp., Sunnyvale, CA
Xerox PARC
Texas Instruments
Teknowledge, Palo Alto, CA
DEC
Bell Labs
IntelliGenetics, Palo Alto, CA
TRW
BBN
IBM
Hewlett Packard, Palo Alto, CA
Martin Marietta, Denver, CO
Hughes
AMOCO
JAYCOR, Alexandria, VA
AIDS, Mt. View, CA
Systems Control, Inc., Palo Alto, CA

capacity to digest it all, for it comes out faster than any one human could hope to read. And here is where the expert system could really help mankind; it could digest all this data, all the scientific and social and psychological and economic research, all the government reports, all the committee minutes, and everything else that finds its way into print. It could digest it and extract the nuggets, the occasional flash of gold, the pieces of knowledge that could be useful to us, the rest could be excreted into electronic oblivion. But possibly that task lies way beyond an expert system of the twenty-first century!

CHAPTER 5
Natural Language Systems

Of all the research that is discussed in this book, it is when we come to the study of natural language that we face some of the most exciting and far-reaching questions about the nature of intelligence and the ways in which the human mind functions. Language is ubiquitous and without it our social and private lives would be impossible, so naturally we insist that our computers should master it too. We use language for thinking and for socializing, we play with language and we plan with it, we use it to cement our social institutions and to confirm our inner selves; we can never escape from language. Indeed, its power is so pervasive that we take language and our ability to use it for granted. Even a three-year-old child can rapidly acquire proficiency in its language and understand sentences it has never heard before.

Natural languages are rich in ambiguity and allusion and serve us in a host of very different occupations; hunting, making love, negotiating, arguing, resolving philosophic issues, telling stories, giving directions, asking questions, resolving doubts, buying cabbages and anything that we humans choose

125

to do. These natural languages are very different from such things as "the language of the bees," programming languages, or the "language of mathematics," none of which have the same richness, subtlety and power to handle metaphor, meaning, and poetry or serve in the various activities we engage in.

In their quest to give language to the computer, the AI community finds itself confronting the same questions about the nature of mind and intelligence that are being asked by philosophers, psychologists, linguists, neuroscientists, sociologists, and anthropologists and by Greek philosophers over two thousand years ago. Language is so intimately tied to the way we think and to the structure of our brains that it is improbable that the answers to these questions will be solved in the near future.

Language has a universal quality. No matter how far one travels to isolated tribes or primitive people, or how far back one moves in recorded history, human beings always speak fully formed languages. To the lay person these languages may appear very different, one from the other, yet to the linguist they have so many similarities that language is considered to have a universal quality. A simple way of appreciating this universality of language is the fact that a human baby, taken from one culture and set down in another is always able to learn the new language. Language has been taken as that special ability that distinguishes us from the animals. Indeed, if we ask whether animals, like the dolphin or chimp, could have a consciousness then we usually pose the question in terms of language: are the dolphin's clicks a form of language, is the chimp's sign language a true language? In his book *Linguistics* (Penguin Books, London, 1971) David Crystal goes as far as to say:

It is impossible to conceive of a rational being, or a society, without implying the existence of a language. Language and thinking are so closely related that any study of the former is bound to be a contribution to our understanding of the human mind.

In the early days of computer design, Alan Turing faced the question, "Can machines think?" and decided that the answer lay in a machine's ability to use language. The Turing Test he devised was based on the Imitation Game, a parlor game he had invented. In the Imitation Game, a man and a woman sit in separate rooms and the player tries to determine which is which by asking them questions. To avoid any additional clues all the questions and answers take the form of typewritten messages.

At first sight Turing's game looks simple, the player has only to ask "Are you a man?" and the game is over. But here comes the trick. One of the players, the man for example, is given the goal of beating the questioner and can answer in any way he likes. The other, the woman, will help the questioner by telling the truth. So to the question "Are you a man?" the woman may answer "No, I'm not" and the man may write "Oh, take no notice of him, he's lying. I am the woman!" Direct questions will not help very much and the player must become involved in more subtle uses of language if he is to guess which is which.

And the Turing Test? Well, after playing the game for a time with a man and woman we now replace the man with a computer and continue as before. This time the player has to determine which is machine and which human. The goal of the machine is to beat the player. Turing's contention was that once a computer can play the Imitation Game as well as any human then it must be judged as intelligent.

In the long term, the ability of a computer to use human language may shed some light on the nature of thought and machine intelligence. But even in the short term there are some very important goals to be met. If computers are to be used to their greatest potential then they must be user friendly, so that we can interact with them on human terms and without having to learn programming languages. In the future, the computer's ability to interact with people using natural language will become an increasingly important feature. Databases and expert systems, for example, will be consulted in everyday language, without the need to use a programming language or phrase questions in a formalized or restricted way. Moreover, such systems will be able to engage in extended conversation as the user cross-questions the computer about a particular reply and asks for further information, explanations, or justifications. Computers will read texts, business reports and newspaper articles, extract significant details, make comparisons, reorganize their data banks, and prepare reports of their own and translate manuals and business letters between a variety of languages. Complex machinery will be controlled by computers that, like HAL in the film "2001," respond to the human voice and give verbal status reports, warnings, and instructions.

Origins

In the 1930s, before the first computers were built, scientists discussed on the possibility of machines that would deal with natural language and automatic translation. Ten years later, in 1943, the world's first electronic computer COLOSSUS was created to assist the British in cracking German codes. As an offshoot of such wartime work Warren Weaver (coauthor with Claude L. Shannon of the seminal book *The Mathematical Theory of Communication*, University of Illinois Press, 1949) was struck by the similarity between code cracking and decyphering the meaning of a sentence in a foreign language. In 1949 Weaver circulated a paper entitled "Translation" in which he suggested that the new computers could be used to solve the "world-wide translation problem."

By the mid-1960s, the more general issues of natural language understanding had begun to excite interest. Language processing had received a considerable boost both through the development of high level programming languages such as LISP and from the research of the M.I.T. linguist Noam Chomsky. Conversation systems, such as ELIZA, that relied upon key words in a text and used pattern matching excited considerable interest, even though their understanding of

128

the sentences they dealt with was minimal. In the early 1970s more sophisticated information retrieval and language processing systems such as LUNAR and SHRDLU were built and were followed by systems that could produce summaries of stories as they arrived over the news service, carry out simple conversations, and answer questions about texts they were given. Today research on natural language is devoted to understanding more extended texts and general attempts to improve natural language processing.

Overview

Like Merlin, King Arthur's wizard, computer natural language systems appear in a variety of disguises. Indeed, there are probably as many different natural language systems as there are research projects. Some systems are designed to serve as front ends add on to existing computer systems so that they can interact with a user using natural language. Others are built to act as question answering systems or to understand and précis texts. In each case the individual system will reflect the particular assumption and theories about language that are held by its designers.

In the face of such variety, generalizations are difficult but, roughly speaking, natural language systems consist of three parts. Firstly, something to analyze the typed input in terms of sentence structure, word meaning, overall concepts, and so on.

The second part of the system comprises a formal representation of the knowledge, information, and meaning conveyed in the text. In addition it may make inferences, deductions, comparisons, summaries, and generate the answers to questions.

Finally, there is the output that takes the answers, deductions, or précis and converts them from a symbolic representation into sentences in natural language. This part of the system deals both with expression or meaning and with generating sentences that are grammatically correct.

In the sections which follow we shall see how individual

systems work in practice and explain their limitations and successes. To begin, let us look at the first part of a language understanding system, the text analyzer, which breaks down sentences and paragraphs into their component meanings.

Text Analysis: Semantics Versus Syntax

Historically, the first attempts at analyzing a text and uncovering its meaning relied heavily upon the internal structure of the individual sentences and used *parsers*, or sentence analyzers, that were programmed using the rules of grammar. The reason for the reliance on syntax is not difficult to understand. Suppose that you are alone in a foreign country and discover a message in your hotel room. With the aid of a dictionary you begin to look up each word only to be given a list of possible meanings and variations. Soon the message is transformed into a collection of possible words but in no particular order. It is at this point you realize that the grammar and word order of the language hold an important clue as to how sentences are put together.

The study of this sentence structure is known in linguistics as syntax, and fortunately was put on a scientific basis by Noam Chomsky in the late 1950s at exactly the right time for those in the AI community who had begun to work in language understanding.

Chomsky distinguished between what he called the "surface structure" of a sentence, the subject of traditional grammar, and its deeper structure which carries the meaning. For example, sentences with very different surface structures, he argued, can have an identical structure at a deeper level. "John closed the door" has, according to Chomsky, the same deep structure as "The door was closed by John" and in consequence, the same meaning. Chomsky showed how sentences could by analyzed to expose their deeper structure by meaning of transformations and how one sentence could be changed into another without affecting its meaning.

Chomsky's approach had an even deeper implication for he asserted that these processes of analysis and transformation were the same as those carried out by the brain itself. According to Chomsky, each time we speak, deep linguistic structures are generated within the brain, which in turn lead to the surface structures consisting of strings of words. Finally, these word strings are transformed into the phonemes of speech.

Chomsky argued that the process of generating deep structures, applying transformation, and producing speech was something innate and passed on genetically. Children, therefore, do not so much "learn" a language as acquire proficiency in the use of a language with a particular surface syntax such as English, French, Russian, and so on because the deeper rules of language generation and structure are already present from birth within their brains.

Chomsky's ideas (which have only been given the briefest of outlines above) naturally excited the attention of the AI community, for, if the brain's proficiency with language lies in a set of genetically inherited rules and transformations, then these same rules could be programmed into a computer.

The sentence, "This student will program the computer" consists of a noun phrase (NP) "This student," and a verb phrase (VP), "will program the computer." The latter VP can be split into a verb "will program" and a noun phrase "the computer." The whole thing is easily displayed using a derivation tree.

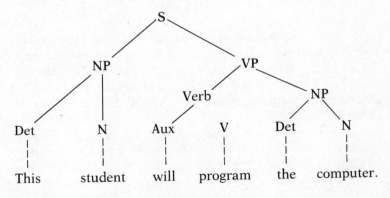

And this tree begins to look like exactly the sort of thing that a computer loves to handle! In the above simple sentence, we see the movement from the deep structure onto the surface structure. When one analyzes more complex sentences the power of the method becomes even more apparent.

Chomsky's approach emphasizes the way the brain, or the computer for that matter, can *generate* sentences. The process can be presented mechanically in terms of *rewrite rules*. In the series below, the rule is that one should proceed from level to level each time rewriting the term on the left by the string of symbols on the right.

S	$\longrightarrow$	NP.VP
VP	$\longrightarrow$	Verb. NP
NP	$\longrightarrow$	Det. N
Verb	$\longrightarrow$	Aux. V
Det	$\longrightarrow$	this, . . . , the
N	$\longrightarrow$	student, program, . . .
Aux	$\longrightarrow$	will, . . .
V	$\longrightarrow$	program, . . .

Of course, to generate more complicated sentences a more extensive derivation tree is needed, but no matter how deep the structure, once we finally reach the surface we always find nouns, verbs, and so on. The final rewrite rule tells us that these elementary objects can be rewritten using words of the English language.

The real power of Chomsky's generative grammar lies in its *transformation rules* that enable us to generate one surface structure from the other while leaving the meaning intact. For example, the rule

$(VP_1\text{-}Aux\text{-}V\text{-}NP_2)$ $(NP_2\text{-}Aux + be + en\text{-}V\text{-}ly\text{-}NP_1)$

relates the active to the passive voice and transforms

"This student will program the computer."
into

"The computer will be programmed by this student."

The Chomskian approach was a godsend to the AI community. According to theory all they had to do was provide a computer with a generative grammar and allow it to generate text or analyze incoming sentences for their deep structures. Parsing and text generation could take place in two phases; one to expose the deep structure corresponding to each surface sentence and the other to relate the deep structure to its meaning. In addition, automatic translations could be produced by analyzing a surface sentence for its deeper structure and then moving from this deep structure into the surface structure of some other language.

However, the results were not always a total success. A computer programmed with the necessary vocabulary, rewrite rules, and transformations could churn out thousands and tens of thousands of sentences. Most of these were well formed and made perfect sense but some of them were pure nonsense and not the sort of thing that a native speaker would ever produce. It was clear to linguists that Chomsky's system needed modification. In 1965, Chomsky himself published "Aspects of the Theory of Syntax" in which he introduced elements of semantics (word meanings) at deeper levels of his grammar. Other researchers have attempted to constrain Chomsky's rules to avoid meaningless sentences and have added rules of their own.

As things stand, Chomsky's theory does not give a complete account of the nature and generation of language. It certainly stimulated some very important research in linguistics and natural language processing and its insights were valuable.

Most computer language systems owe a debt to the theory but it cannot be the final word. Since Chomsky's first work, other linguists have devised alternative accounts of how language is generated and the underlying nature of its structure. In turn AI researchers have adopted and modified these ideas and made use of them to parse or generate sentences.

Case Grammars

Those readers who struggled to learn Latin may recall the extent to which various cases dominated the language. A noun, for example, can take a slightly different form depending on its function within the sentence, for example, whether it is in the nominative, accusative, genitive, dative, ablative, or vocative case. Cases tend to be less important in modern European languages but still play a role in Russian and German. Some linguists refer to these as surface cases and, by analogy to Chomsky, suggest that a deep case structure exists for the whole sentence.

This deep structure consists of a small number (in one theory nine) of cases and a limited number of relationships between them. In this way it is possible to analyze a large number of sentences and expose their underlying structure of case relationships. Case grammars are related to the idea of *semantic networks* and have also been adopted into AI research.

Discourse Analysis

A radically different approach to Chomsky's is concerned with the way language is used and the function it has within social communication. Discourse analysis gives attention to why we choose a particular sentence form in a given situation and the use we make of that sentence. Its "systemic grammar" employs networks which express the various options open to a speaker when he faces the meaning potential of his language. Discourse analysis and systemic grammar have found their way into AI programs and probably the most famous example of their use is in Winograd's SHRDLU system which we shall meet later in this chapter.

Semantic Grammars

When it comes to very restricted situations there may be no need to program all the rules and transformations of grammar and a simpler system may suffice. Take for example a computer that has to deal with airline bookings. Rather than analyze all possible sentences into the familiar categories of noun, verb, and so on, it would be more appropriate to make the analysis using categories of destination, flight, flight-time, and so on.

Provided the application is sufficiently limited, it will be possible to construct a grammar based on a few concepts and the relationships that exist between them. The rewrite rules for this grammar take the form of substitutions of words for concepts and categories. For example, the computer could rewrite "airline" by "British Airways," "Delta," or "Air Canada."

Parsing

When someone asks a question of a computer using natural language the computer must first understand what has been said before it can generate an appropriate answer. Similarly when a piece of text is presented to the computer it must be able to extract a meaning, recognize what is significant in the text, and how that particular information will modify the computer's general knowledge about the world.

The first step in working with natural language is therefore to *parse* or analyze the incoming sentences. Guided by the rules of a grammar discussed above, the computer breaks apart each sentence and determines how it works. For example, the computer may discover through syntactic analysis that someone or something performs an action upon a particular object. If a Chomskian grammar is used, for example, the sentence is broken down to expose its deep structure and at that level it becomes possible to determine its meaning.

During or following the step of syntactic analysis a further process is, of course, needed before meaning can fully be pinned down. This takes the form of semantic analysis, looking up the meanings of words in an internal dictionary. At some point around this step in the parsing, the computer may also begin to build up a symbolic representation of what the sentence means using, for example, a semantic network or one of the other representations we met in Chapter 4 on expert systems. The system may also begin to use the syntactic structure and word meanings to make new inferences or to create links with its data banks and in this way begin to generate natural language replies.

As with other AI projects the building of a good parser involves a trade-off between a number of demands and requirements. For some purposes it may be quite acceptable to have answers generated in simple English, provided that the meanings are clear. For others, the parser must be able to generate sentences of higher quality. Some systems may work with deep linguistic structures while others produce results based on transformations of the original surface form.

Parsing itself is a time-consuming business which can involve the computer in a large amount of backtracking. Take, for example, the sentence,

"John said that the green can be watered as soon as it has been mowed."

As the computer scans along the line it is faced with the problem of determining if "green" is an adjective or noun and then with the problem of "can." Is "can" a noun or a verb? A human hearing that sentence would have no such problem, the intonation and the slight pause between "green" and "can" would prevent any ambiguity arising. But the computer parser must make a hypothesis: that "green" is an adjective, for example, and test it out by attempting to parse the sentence. At some point towards the end of the line it will discover the error, backtrack, choose "green" as a noun and begin again with this new hypothesis. Clearly, when many cases of ambiguity arise in a text the process will involve a great deal of computing time.

One way out of the backtracking problem is to attempt some form of parallel processing in which several alternatives are simultaneously explored. Another is to use heuristic rules that, for example, make use of world knowledge about common actions and events or present lists of the most probably choices. But in parsing a sentence there is no univerally agreed way of proceeding, no accepted body of wisdom of how humans do and computers should parse a sentence. No wonder there is such a proliferation of systems!

No matter how well a parser is designed there comes a point where computers simply cannot deal with an English sentence. Take, for example, the sentence,

"The police were instructed to stop drinking after midnight."

Who was to stop drinking? The police or people in bars?

"They went to visit the old men and women."

Who was old? The men or the men *and* women?

There are many other examples:

"Visiting relatives can be a nuisance."
"He said he was coming today."
"The child is drawing a cart."

When it comes to dealing with ambiguity, humans don't generally have major problems. The computer, however, is often at a total loss in deciding how it should treat words with multiple meanings and in working with the more subtle forms of ambiguity.

"Disambiguating" as the AI community terms it, has become a major problem in language understanding. One way of removing ambiguity and determining meaning is to provide the computer with some general knowledge about the world. A computer that knew about farming and about writing would be able to clarity potential ambiguity in

"The farmer herded his sheep into the pen."

Clearly, that has nothing to do with a fountain pen. But what about

"The farmer decided to buy a new pen."

That ambiguity can only be clarified by reading on and discovering if the farmer is standing in a stationery store, a field, or is in the middle of writing a letter.

Uncovering the meaning of a sentence therefore depends very strongly on general knowledge about the world, on how people act, and the sort of situations they find themselves in and about objects and the functions they perform. Meaning also depends upon the overall context of a passage and upon the wider context in which that text occurs.

It is clear that by itself a parser does not always have sufficient power to extract all the meaning from an extended text and the AI community therefore has additional problems to resolve, those of representing world knowledge and using it to resolve the problems of context dependent meanings. But, provided these problems have been solved, the computer can go on to make précis, answer questions, and generate replies.

Inference and Text Generation

To some extent text generation is the reverse of text analysis, for the computer attempts to transform an internal message into one in written or spoken English. One procedure is to first map the abstract symbolic computer representation onto deep linguistic structures and use these to generate sentences that have the correct surface structure of the natural language in question. Such a program is far from simple and, as with text analysis and parsing, its success ultimately depends upon the computer's ability to understand the meanings of words and sentences it deals with. Actual systems exhibit a large range of performance. A précis-making system may be fed with the sentences:

"The man rides a bicycle. The man is tall. A bicycle is a vehicle with wheels."

and generate

"The tall man rides the vehicle with wheels."

At this simple level the system is good at syntax but need only have the most superficial knowledge about what the sentences mean. A more advanced system, however, can deal with an incoming text like:

"John saw Mary wrestling with a bottle at the liquor bar. He went over to help her with it. He drew the cork and they drank champagne together."

and generate

"John saw Mary wrestling with a bottle at the liquor bar. John went over to help her with it before he drew the cork. John and Mary together drank the champagne."

This example indicates that the computer has some sense of who are the actors within this drama, what they do, and how their various actions have consequences. So good text generation must also involve some understanding of semantics and the general knowledge of how the world evolves.

Current research proceeding in many areas aims at improving the generation of meaning to attempts at extended dialogue and rules for the stylistics of how humans speak and the various goals that influence the way they construct their sentences.

Some Milestones in Natural Language Processing

This section will explore how various research workers and designers have combined the approaches of syntax, sematics, concept analysis, and text generation, and used them to construct natural language systems. Restricted by the computer memories available and slow processing speeds, the first natural language systems could not make full use of semantic and syntactic possibilities. One alternative was to store a small number of sentence *templates* in the computer and match these against incoming data. For example, by matching an incoming sentence against the template

"How many ____x____ does ____y____ have?"

or

"What is the ____x____ of ____y____ ?"

would trigger an appropriate reply which made use of words "X" and "Y" extracted from the incoming question. An additional approach was to identify key words, significant in that particular domain of discourse and use them as keys to initiate a given response.

Possibly the most famous of these early systems was ELIZA, created by Joseph Weizenbaum in 1966. Named after Eliza Doolittle in Shaw's "Pygmalion," the system was programmed to carry out a connected conversation with a human seated at a keyboard. ELIZA was designed to accept a variety of scripts or contexts for these conversations, and depending

ELIZA

Joseph Weizenbaum's ELIZA program could simulate the conversational skills of a Rogerian therapist by recognizing keywords and transforming a patient's statements into questions. Here ELIZA is in the middle of a session with a young woman.

WOMAN: Men are all alike.

ELIZA: In what way?

WOMAN: They are always bugging us about something or other.

ELIZA: Can you think of a specific example?

WOMAN: Well, my boyfriend made me come here.

ELIZA: Your boyfriend made you come here?

WOMAN: He says I am depressed much of the time.

ELIZA: I am sorry to hear you are depressed.

WOMAN: It's true. I am unhappy.

ELIZA: Do you think that coming here will help you to be happy?

WOMAN: I need some help, that much seems certain.

ELIZA: What would it mean to you if you got some help?

WOMAN: Perhaps I could learn to get along with my family.

ELIZA: Tell me more about your family.

WOMAN: My mother takes care of me.

ELIZA: Who else in your family takes care of you.

WOMAN: My father.

ELIZA: Your father.

WOMAN: You are like my father in some ways.

continued

ELIZA:	What resemblance do you see?
WOMAN:	You are not very aggressive but I think you don't want me to notice that.
ELIZA:	What makes you think I am not very aggressive?
WOMAN:	You don't argue with me.
ELIZA:	Why do you think I don't argue with you?
WOMAN:	You are afraid of me.
ELIZA:	Does it please you to believe I am afraid of you?
WOMAN:	My father is afraid of everybody.
ELIZA:	What else comes to mind when you think of your father?
WOMAN:	Bullies.
ELIZA:	Does that have anything to do with the fact that your boyfriend made you come here?

upon the particular context or script, ELIZA was supplied with different keywords, sentence templates, and conditioned replies. Possibly the most famous of these scripts was designed to disguise ELIZA as a psychiatrist of the Rogerian school. The illustration gives a sample of the sort of conversations ELIZA could carry out.

In books like *Becoming a Person*, Carl Rogers has expounded a "client-centered" approach to counseling in which the doctor makes no attempt to impose a psychological model or set of values on his patient but simply encourages the patient's own natural growth towards health. Part of Roger's technique is to listen to the patient talk about his or her problems and intervene only to encourage further explanation or to ask for elaboration of a particular point. Rogerian sessions, therefore, proceed under the patient's direction but with subtle and gentle cues given by the doctor.

Weizenbaum's computer program follows the Rogerian model by, for example, replying to the patient's statement with an encouraging

"Please go on."

or using a template to turn a statement into a question.

PATIENT: I'm worried about my job.
DOCTOR: You're worried about your job?

In addition, the computer is on the look out for certain key words such as "dream," "mother," "father," and "wife" which may trigger a more assertive response.

PATIENT: It all happened after I'd seen my father.
DOCTOR: Tell me more about your father.

The possessive "my" triggers the computer to store a particular phrase or word for later use. Following several neutral statements on the part of the patient the computer doctor is programmed to revive this phrase and insert it in a template such as

"Earlier you said that you were worried about your health."

or

"Could that have anything to do with your job?"

By combining these various mechanical responses ELIZA was able to give the illusion of carrying out an extended conversation. The computer, however, had only the sketchiest understanding of syntax and no understanding of what the conversation meant. Nevertheless, some people who talked to ELIZA really felt that they were conversing with a sympathetic doctor and began to pour out their feelings. In some cases volunteers who had worked with the system asked Weizenbaum if they could consult with the computer in private as they felt that it really understood their problems. One psychiatrist went so far as to suggest that an expanded version should be used in mental hospitals and other psychiatric institutions to enable a large number of people to consult the "doctor."

Weizenbaum was shocked at the emotional reaction generated by his rather simplistic "doctor" program. He concluded that the "delusional thinking" employed by people when they interacted with ELIZA showed just how little the general public understood the workings of computers. In his book *Computer Power and Human Reasoning*, he used the example of ELIZA to make critical comments on the whole race for artificial intelligence.

Weizenbaum's misgivings did not, however, deter Dr. Kenneth Colby, a psychiatrist, who had originally worked on the development of ELIZA. Colby went on to develop a related program called PARRY which simulates the replies of a psychiatric patient. Colby's sytem opened the interesting possibility of having two computers talk to each other, one as doctor and the other as patient.

With the improvements in computer and natural language processing, other researchers have returned to ELIZA and PARRY, augmented and improved their design, added elements of discourse analysis and extended the data base of keywords and structured replies. The results of ELIZA and PARRY's offspring are said to be particularly impressive in the ways they appear to handle language and engage in conversations with humans.

ELIZA has certainly taught the AI community several lessons. For example, given a user-friendly approach, people can have very positive reactions to computers, even to the point of becoming emotionally involved. It is often said that people are critical of computers because they don't understand how they work. But this is probably not the full story;

after all, how many of us know how a microwave oven works and did our grandparents really understand the principles of the steam engine? It is more probable that the dislike of computers stems from the fact that people are forced to adopt complicated ways of interacting with them: learning programming languages, posing questions in artificial ways, and so on. But given a machine that can be addressed in normal English and which replies in ordinary sentences the user's reaction may be more open.

Another lesson ELIZA teaches is that an ingenious program can go a long way toward simulating human behavior. ELIZA's knowledge of syntax may have been crude and its understanding of language nonexistent but it certainly did what it was programmed to do and created the illusion of a human conversationalist. It shows that a good AI system does not always require the most elaborate, general solution to the job at hand.

Finally, readers, struck by the fact that human beings were fooled into believing that they were talking to an intelligent being, will wonder about the implications. At first sight it does appear that ELIZA has in some sense passed Turing's test. People conversed with the computer and felt that they were speaking to a sympathetic and understanding being. Yet with only a little ingenuity it is possible to expose ELIZA for the mindless, mechanical agent it is. The reason that ELIZA appeared so human is that we are naturally polite and sensitive to unwritten conventions. We agree to be bound by informal rules of conversation, not to probe each other's motives too deeply, not to ask leading questions of a stranger, and to accept self-effacement at its face value. In addition, humans forget that so much of what passes for conversation is simply mechanical response and structured replies to conventional keywords. Two Englishmen meeting at the bus stop will often conduct a conversation using keywords and template replies.

MAN 1:   Doesn't look too good.

MAN 2:   Shocking.
MAN 1:   Looks like we're in for a wet weekend too.
MAN 2:   Worse than last year.
MAN 1:   D'you see the match?
MAN 2:   Did you?
MAN 1:   They want to get rid of that center forward.
MAN 2:   That's right.

ELIZA, in fact, reminds us that humans are willing to indulge in highly structured conversations based upon conditional responses and how they will accept the convention of the "psychiatrist" and not question his motives or press him with a leading question. Under the correct conditions and with an advanced version of ELIZA it may be perfectly possible to fool human beings.

LUNAR AND SHRDLU

Other early approaches went beyond templates and attempted to represent language by means of the propositions of logic. By making deductions within a logical network, it was possible to generate answers to simple questions which could then be translated into English sentences. By the 1970s attempts were being made to construct more advanced systems in which semantic considerations were integrated directly into syntactic analysis. For example LUNAR, build by William Woods, was designed to help geologists evaluate data about rocks brought back from the moon. Questions were translated into a formal logic-based language where they could then be used to make queries of a datebase. LUNAR contained a vocabulary of some 3,500 words and was confined to the type of questions and sentence constructions that geologists tended to ask.

SHRDLU had an even more restricted world—a collection of colored cubes and pyramids resting on a table top. The only goals within this world were to stack certain blocks on top of others. Of course, to achieve such a goal the computer needed an internal model of the table, where the particular

---

SHRDLU

A conversation with SHRDLU can take place as follows:

USER: How many blocks are not in the box?
SHRDLU: Four of them.
USER: Is at least one of them narrower than the one that I told you to pick up?
SHRDLU: Yes, the red cube.
USER: Can the table pick up blocks?
SHRDLU: No.
USER: Can a pyramid be supported by a pyramid?
SHRDLU: I don't know.
USER: Will you please stack up both of the red blocks and either a green cube or a pyramid?
SHRDLU: OK
          (Performs the action.)
USER: Had you touched any pyramid before you put the green one on the little cube?
SHRDLU: Yes, the green one.
USER: When did you pick it?
SHRDLU: When I was stacking up the red cube, a large red block, and a large green cube.
USER: Why?
SHRDLU: To get rid of it?
USER: Why did you do that?
SHRDLU: To clear off the red cube.

---

blocks were located and if, for example, the top of one block needed to be cleared before another block was placed on top.

There was one further restriction on SHRDLU, the block world did not in fact exist as real blocks on a real table but as a model within the computer itself.

SHRDLU was written as a Ph. D. research project by Terry Winograd from M.I.T. using the LISP language. It combined the rules of syntax and semantics all within the same program and while ELIZA operated in a purely mechanical way, generating stereotypical sentences in response to key stimulii, SHRDLU always understood what it was doing. Within the limited world of colored blocks SHRDLU was eminently successful. In response to a request to stack one block on another, the system would consider the state of its world, work out a plan of action, and then carry it out. After completing its task SHRDLU would answer questions about what it had done, the way it had moved the block, and how particular blocks had been stacked with respect to others. Not only could SHRDLU carry out a conversation using simple sentences but it appeared to understand questions put to it and generate the appropriate answers. By restricting SHRDLU's world Winograd had removed the problem of ambiguity which haunts natural language processing.

Nevertheless, some researchers feel that SHRDLU's achievement is illusionary and that once an attempt is made to extend the block world the whole system falls apart. They argue that by restricting the computer's world in such an extreme fashion Winograd has created a totally artificial situation. Since so little happens within the block world it is always possible to render all its processes explicit. But such a representation could never apply to in a real situation, nor could the various elements of language processing such as inference and understanding be integrated together in such a convenient way. In addition, since the block world was so limited in the range of events that could take place the more subtle uses of English would never be required. In other words, SHRDLU appeared to so successful simply because complex sentences were never needed. Nevertheless, Winograd had given yet another example of how useful AI programs can be, provided one is willing to work within limited domains.

MARGIE, SAM, AND PAM

LUNAR and SHRDLU were created in the early 1970s. By the middle of that decade Roger Schank and his colleagues

---

BORIS

BORIS, developed at Yale University, is a successor to SAM and PAM and can make inferences from the stories it has read.

Processing Paragraph 1

Richard hadn't heard from his college roommate Paul for years. Richard had borrowed money from Paul which was never paid back. But now he had no idea where to find his old friend. When a letter finally arrived from San Francisco, Richard was anxious to find out how Paul was.

After reading the paragraph BORIS answers questions put to him by a user.

USER: Who is Paul?
BORIS: Richard's friend.
USER: Did Richard want to see Paul?
BORIS: Yes, Richard wanted to know how Paul was.
USER: Had Paul helped Richard.
BORIS: Yes, Paul lent money to Richard.
USER: Why didn't Richard pay Paul back?
BORIS: Richard did not know where Paul was.
USER: How did Richard feel when the letter appeared?
BORIS: Richard felt glad because Paul and he were friends.

---

at Yale University were working on a new generation of natural language systems whose emphasis was upon language comprehension. MARGIE used what Schank called "conceptual dependency," an idea related in some ways to the older concept of an *interlinguia* in which different surface forms can carry the same meaning. MARGIE represented meaning in terms of a small number of *semantic primitives*, elementary actions and states used to establish the relationships between concepts in the sentence.

MARGIE could analyze concepts in a text and then, using a semantic net, carry out a limited number of inferences. The result was to generate new sentences that paraphrased the input while preserving the meaning.

INPUT: John killed Mary by choking her.
OUTPUT: John strangled Mary. John choked Mary and she died because she was unable to breathe.

SAM and PAM were extensions of MARGIE in that they sought wider contexts for the meaning of a text. Schank introduced the ideas of "goals," "themes," "plans," and "scripts" in an attempt to come to grips with this problem of meaning. Schank believes that we all employ a large number of scripts to help us understand situations and stories. Each script provides a context for understanding in terms of the sort of situations and activities a person may encounter, for example visiting a restaurant, going to the doctor, or making a transaction at a bank. MARGIE, SAM, and PAM are just particular examples of the work of the Yale group and illustrate the wider problem of understanding more extended texts and dialogues.

LIFER, however, was specifically designed as a commercial system, a front end to be added on to various computer systems and provide input and output in natural language. Designed by Garry Hendrix in 1977, LIFER translates natural language input into an *application language*, which is a particular subset of the English language appropriate to the particular task in hand. Depending on which computer system LIFER is to serve, a particular restricted language is defined and its rules written down. LIFER has been used, for example, to provide natural language access to expert systems, databases, and such systems as HAWKEYE, a system which combines aerial photographs, maps, and generic descriptions to obtain descriptions of land surfaces.

While LIFER is somewhat limited in the range of sentences it can deal with, it has certainly proved its usefulness in providing a user friendly front-end to a variety of complex computer systems.

Connected Conversations

There is little point in designing a smart computer unless the user can also talk to it. Computers in the near future will be capable of receiving instructions, giving answers, and holding more extended conversations with humans using natural language. Systems like ELIZA can of course engage in extended conversations, but since the system has no comprehension of what it is saying, its abilities are far too limited to serve as a question answering system for the computers of the future.

However, another system contemporary with ELIZA was capable of answering simple questions put to it in English. LUNAR, contempory with ELIZA, had a 3,500-word dictionary and rules for semantics and syntax. It could generate replies to questions like

1. What is the average concentration of aluminum in high ALKALI ROCKS?
2. Which samples contain P205?
3. Give me the modal analyses of P 205 in these samples.
4. Give me EU determinations in samples which contain ILM

By calling the above questions "simple," I will probably have lost the sympathy of readers who are not particularly familiar with modal analyses and EU determinations. It is true that LUNAR is something of a wizard when it comes to rocks and their chemistry but as regards English comprehension the system is far less sophisticated. While the questions above may refer to quite complicated concepts they are all phrased in simple English and involve direct, factual requests to a database. None of them uses an elaborate construction, subtle tenses, or contains an ambiguity of sense or vocabulary. Equally important, each question can be answered in isolation without any reference to what has been asked or answered earlier in the conversation.

So when it comes to simple, direct questions, with a restricted vocabulary and involving uncomplicated English sentences, a system like LUNAR fits the bill. But full computer conversation demands something far more sophisticated. Not only must the system be able to handle parsing and text generation, have access to a database and to general world knowledge, but it must also be able to build up a general picture of the conversation it is currently engaged in. A computer that carries out a connected conversation must continually make a representation of all the questions that have been put to it, and the answers it gave, and use this representation when asked to give the reason for a particular reply.

Current conversation systems are able to deal with questions like

Which U.S. electronics manufacturing company's profits were higher than average in 1984?

All that is required is a parser to uncover the meaning of the sentence, some method of relating that meaning to a database, and finally a text generator to produce the answer which, in this case, will consist of a list of company names. But suppose the executive who asked the question now scans the list and types in:

"What did they make?"

This simple question, so casually produced, contains two land mines for any question answering system, the words

QUESTION ANSWERING SYSTEMS

Commercial systems can handle conversations like this:

Q: Give me the after tax profit of every oil company for every year from 1970 to 1980.

A: I only have figures up to 1981.
Do you want to see them?

Q: Yes.

Research projects are working on machines that will hold conversations like this:

Q: Give me the amount of stock issued by Ontario corporations in 1979 and 1980.

A: Do you want the totals by company or by overall?

Q: Totals per company, by name and year.

A:
COMPANY	YEAR	STOCK VALUE
....	....	......
....	....	......

Q: In 1982, what directors sat on the boards of the two most profitable companies?

A: None.
There were no profitable companies in 1982

The following conversation is beyond current systems:

Q: How many directors sit on more than eight boards?

A: 3

Q: Which three?

A: B. Blue, G. Green, M. Mouse.

Q: How many did Green have?

A: 10

Q: How many seats did the Ontarians have?

continued

A: 18
Q: What companies had average income of more
than $25 million between 1970 and 1980?
A: ABC Widget, Pentland House, ...
Q: I want to see the income.
A: *COMPANY*   *AVE INCOME.*

"they" and "make." To understand what "they" refers to,
the system must have some memory of what it has just been
doing. It must have some awareness of the previous question
and an answer it generated. Suppose it can do this, it will
for example understand that "they" refers to U.S. electronics
manufacturing companies who made higher than average
profits in 1983, or more simply "they" refers to names in the
list that it earlier typed out.

But what will it do with the word "make"? The word
could refer to profits or products. How is the ambiguity to
be resolved? The system could take a number of strategies,
depending on how it has been programmed. It could ask:

"Do you mean 'make' in the sense of profits or products?"

Or it may be designed to operate within a limited domain in
which "make" has only one sense, or which uses heuristic
rules to define a most probable meaning for given words. On
the other hand the system could call on its memory of the
previous question and recognize the key word "profits." An
even more sophisticated machine may be able to recognize
the general plan or "drift" of the conversation of which we
have seen only two questions, and realize that it has been
about various manufacturer's products. Therefore, in spite of
the reference to profits in the preceding sentence, the system
will stay with the overall context and list various electronic
products.

Commercial conversation systems are somewhat limited

in their ability to handle ambiguities, complex sentence constructions, and to maintain a record of the overall context of a particular conversation. Nevertheless, they represent an enormous improvement over the more machine oriented ways we have traditionally talked to computers. What office manager would be willing to type

SELECT NAME FROM EMP. DEPT WHERE (DEPT. DNAME = 'SALES' OR DEPT. NAME = 'ACCOUNTING') AND EMP. DEPT # = DEPT. DEPT #)

when he could simply ask,

WHO WORKS IN THE SALES AND ACCOUNTING DE-PARTMENTS?

INTELLECT is probably the best known commercial system that can answer these simple kinds of questions. It was developed by AIC, the Artificial Intelligence Corporation of Waltham, MA, to allow middle management to interrogate a company's database without having to learn the ins and outs of computer programming and rules for extracting information. INTELLECT can handle questions like

HOW DO THE AVERAGE EARNINGS OF SALESMEN IN NEW YORK COMPARE WITH THOSE IN CHICAGO?

HOW MANY SALES PEOPLE IN NEW YORK ARE OVER QUOTA?

HOW MANY OF THEM ARE MANAGERS OR SUPER-VISORS?

THEIR NAMES?

The system is purchased as a front-end which is added to a company's existing computer system. It is essentially a

---

INTELLECT

INTELLECT is a commercial natural language front end produced by the Artificial Intelligence Corporation of Waltham, Massachusetts.

INTELLECT: AIC's INTELLECT IS NOW READY FOR YOUR QUESTIONS PLEASE ENTER YOUR NAME

USER: AIC's INTELLECT DEMONSTRA-TION.

INTELLECT: PLEASE ENTER YOUR FIRST REQUEST

USER: GIVE ME THE NUMBER OF EM-PLOYEES IN CLERICAL

INTELLECT: ANSWER: 56
NEXT REQUEST

USER: PLEASE REPORT THE SALARY OF CLERCL PEOPLE IN THE WEST AND SOUTH.

INTELLECT: I'M NOT FAMILIAR WITH THE WORD "CLERCL".
IF IT'S A WORD YOU EXPECT TO FIND IN THE DATABASE HIT THE ENTER KEY.
OTHERWISE EITHER FIX ITS SPELLING OR ENTER A SYNO-NYM FOR IT.

USER: CLERICAL

INTELLECT: ANNUAL
SALARY LAST NAME
$30,000 DRISKILL
$31,000 WHITE
$32,000 SAGERT
NEXT REQUEST

USER: OF THE CLERICAL PEOPLE,

WHO LIVES IN CALIFORNIA
INTELLECT: LAST NAME
                 ATTENDONE
                 KIRKWOOD
                 NEXT REQUEST.
USER: HOW MANY COOKS ARE
                 THERE?
INTELLECT: YOUR REQUEST IS AMBIGUOUS
                 TO ME. DO YOU WANT
                 1): LAST NAME = COOK.
                 2): JOB TITLE = COOK.
                 PLEASE ENTER THE NUMBER
                 OF THE INTERPRETATION YOU
                 INTENDED.
USER: 2
INTELLECT: ANSWER: 1
                 NEXT REQUEST.
USER: TO BE OR NOT TO BE, THAT
                 IS THE QUESTION.
INTELLECT: SORRY, I DON'T UNDERSTAND.
                 NEXT REQUEST.
USER: BYE.
INTELLECT: THANK YOU FOR USING AIC's
                 INTELLECT.
                 GOODBY.

    The conversation has been somewhat condensed, as have INTELLECT's replies.

---

system for interpreting and answering questions in English and for its world knowledge, it makes use of data in each company's data banks. As part of the installation, AIC's engineers create a lexicon which is unique to the particular problem in hand, for example using a company's slang, acronyms, and unusual words that are relevant to that company's operations.

Early in 1983 INTELLECT was being sold to some 500 companies and its applications ranged from questioning commercial-loan portfolios in a bank and sales and production of polymers and resins to queries about which cars met environment rules.

Understanding an Extended Text

The language systems we have met up to now can parse sentences and extract their meaning, they can even carry out limited conversations. But what of a computer's ability to understand more extended texts or to engage in a long conversation? Will computers ever be able to understand reports, speeches, technical papers, and stories, or even hold a debate with a human opponent? We know that in games like chess the computer is able to deal with both the logic of immediate moves and some long-term strategy, but will it be able to understand the strategy of a politician's speech or complex meanings in the scene of a play?

The problems of understanding an extended text are particularly intriguing and touch on the way humans recognize situations, store information, make plans and represent the world around them. To get some idea of how complicated these processes can be, think about what happens when you read the following sentence:

Tom entered as the words were spoken, with a radiant smile upon his face; and rubbing his hands, more from a sense of delight than because he was cold (for he had been running fast), sat down in his warm corner again, and was as happy as—as only TOM Pinch could be.

In terms of computer comprehension we have already met the problems of parsing and we understand how important is world knowledge about rooms, hands, people, and so on. We have briefly met the notion of a script which outlines what people do in typical situations. But the sentence above is far richer than all of this, as anyone who has reached Chapter 12 in Dickens's *Martin Chuzzlewit* will realize.

Supposing you have never read the book, what can you learn from the sentence? That Tom has come back into a room, that he is cold, and that he is happy? We can also deduce that someone in the room has been talking but we don't know who it is or if anyone else is in the room, or why Tom has been running, or why he is so radiant or even the reason he left the room in the first place. Not only are we ignorant of all these things, and of the character and role of Tom Pinch, but, moreover, we are not clear which of these questions is going to be important and which will be irrelevant. Not only are we ignorant about the sentence but we don't even know what we are supposed to know!

The interesting point about the things we need to know as we read a story is the curious way in which they are encoded by the reader. Suppose for example that one had read the previous paragraph in *Martin Chuzzlewit*. It contains the answer as to who has uttered the words as Tom entered the room. But one would have to read the whole chapter to discover why Tom is happy. And what of Tom's character? This is revealed way back in Chapter 2, or at least the first description of Tom Pinch can be found there, for each time he appears we add something to our knowledge about him and to his role in the book.

So within the reader's understanding of that particular sentence is enfolded, in a very complex way, all manner of facts and feelings, images and attitudes that have already been generated by his reading of the book. In addition to this is his anticipation of what may happen as he reads on, his emotional identification with the various characters and the tension between his hopes for Tom's future and his suspicions of what could befall him.

So as we read we must encode information contained in a variety of ways, some explicit and some implicit. And as we read we are constantly reassessing all that has gone before, anticipating what we need to remember and what we can afford to forget. Not only do we understand things and then store them in some complex unknown way but we are constantly revisiting them in our mind and reassessing them as we read on in the story.

It is clear that when we read a book something incredibly subtle is going on, and that reading involves emotion, memory, and intellect. It is an ongoing activity, constantly revising, anticipating, and comparing. Clearly it is not a simple matter of making a literal record of what has happened, for much of what has happened may be irrelevant, while other parts may only become important as one enters further into the book or are to be understood in a poetic way. In fact, information must be selected, enfolded and encoded in very subtle ways.

Such a level of performance is far beyond the largest and fastest computers. It is beyond them because we have no real idea of the internal processes that take place when we read a novel, or indeed when we watch a film, or recall an evening we spent with friends. However, no one really expects a computer to understand the novels of Charles Dickens or indeed to write novels of its own. We, therefore, should start with a more modest task. FRUMP was designed in the late 1970s by Gerald Francis de Jong as a Yale University thesis project. The aim of the system was to understand and make précis of stories as they came in over the UPI wire service. FRUMP will never be able to understand the novels of Charles Dickens but it could certainly go further than comprehension at the level of single sentences.

FRUMP was able to make sense of the news stories it read because it was provided with general knowledge about the sort of things that happen in car accidents, earthquakes, diplomatic visits, and so on. De Jong called these knowledge outlines *sketchy scripts* to distinguish them from the more complete scripts that were used in systems like SAM. The trouble with more comprehensive scripts is that they take too much computer time to scan. De Jong, however, argued that since one tends to skim over news items, all that is needed is a rough outline of a stylized situation. Armed with this sketchy script, FRUMP is led to expect certain situations and look for the major actors and consequences.

But how can FRUMP begin to read an article before it has selected a script? Here the format of the news story is of great help. Most good reporters will give the main outlines of their story within the first few sentences. FRUMP therefore reads the opening paragraph and if it cannot then select a script it rejects the story as beyond its comprehension. In those cases when a particular script is chosen, FRUMP begins to scan the story with the aid of its script assistant. However, as further scanning of the story continues, it is possible that some new twist will occur and FRUMP therefore has the capacity to call on more scripts.

Unlike earlier systems FRUMP does not work by mechanically reading every word of the text in order, rather it scans rapidly ignoring some sentences and jumping back to others. The system consists of two parts or modules: a *substantiator* which actually does the reading and a *predictor* which controls the scanning and predicts the overall idea of what may happen next in the story.

Suppose for example that the news item appears to be about a kidnapping and the relevant scripts chosen. *Predictor* will therefore expect to read about a ransom note, a victim, and a large sum of money, it therefore asks substantiator to look for the victim's name. Substantiator scans the text, parts at a time, and sends this information back to predictor who then asks about the ransom note. But supposing that substantiator can find no information in the story about a kidnapping victim. Possibly predictor has made an error, possibly the story isn't about a kidnapping at all but about a robbery. The system will then attempt to fit a different script. Once predictor's anticipations are satisfied the scanning stops and FRUMP prints out a summary in English, French, Spanish, Russian, and Chinese. The whole process takes under half a minute and since UPI stories only arrive, on average, every five to seven minutes, the system can produce its multilingual précis in real time.

The system De Jong operated in 1979 contained some 48 scripts and could handle a limited number of stories that came in over the news service. It turned out that about half of the wire service stories were written in such a way that a script would be of little use in deciphering them. Out of the remaining 50 percent not all of them were about events described in FRUMP's scripts or FRUMP was deceived by the first sentences and select the wrong script. In consequence it missed the point of the story, drew incorrect conclusions, or correlated unrelated events. FRUMP'S average success rate was therefore poor, only 5 percent of stories coming over the wire service were processed correctly. This average could have been raised with a larger library of scripts which would not have slowed the system significantly.

De Jong, now at Illinois, is working on improvements on story comprehension. In one approach the computer is provided with general world knowledge which it improves as it continues to read stories. In place of scripts, *schema* are used which are continually updated. Faced with a new situation, the computer makes use of its general knowledge about people's goals and behavior and how the world works, learns from that particular story, and then attempts to generalize it. For example, when it is presented with a story about kidnapping and extortion it makes use of its knowledge about theft, bargaining, and human goals and attempts to construct schema for "kidnaping" and "extortion." As further stories are read the system notes similarities and differences and further refines these new schema. SAM and PAM make use of such devices as extended scripts, plans, themes, and goals which relate to the various situations characters may find themselves in and the actions they carry out. The suggestion is that humans employ these primitives when they read and understand a story. Our internal scripts enable us to antici-

FRUMP

UPI Story March 26, 1979
INPUT:
   JERUSALEM (UPI)   A BOMB EXPLODED IN
THE WALLED OLD CITY OF JERUSALEM MON-
DAY JUST ABOUT THE SAME TIME THE LEAD-
ERS OF EGYPT AND ISRAEL SIGNED A PEACE
TREATY IN WASHINGTON.
   A POLICE SPOKESWOMAN SAID THERE
WERE "SOME" CASUALTIES BUT NO FUR-
THER DETAILS WERE IMMEDIATELY AVAIL-
ABLE.
   THE BOMBING CAME DESPITE INCREASED
SECURITY PRECAUTIONS BY ISRAELI ARMY
TROOPS AND BORDER GUARDS AGAINST POS-
SIBLE ATTACKS BY ARABS OPPOSED TO THE
TREATY.
   BUT ARABS IN THE WEST BANK AND GAZA
STRIP DECLARED MONDAY A DAY OF MOURN-
ING, SHUTTING THEIR SHOPS FROM NABLUS
TO GAZA TO PROTEST WHAT THEY SEE AS A
BETRAYAL OF THEIR CAUSE.

SELECTED SKETCHY SCRIPT $ AGREE
CPU TIME FOR UNDERSTANDING = 2763 MIL-
LISECONDS

ENGLISH SUMMARY:
   EGYPT AND ISRAEL HAVE AGREED TO A
TREATY
Here FRUMP misses the point of the story because it does not have the appropriate sketchy
script. With a new script added FRUMP can make
a second attempt at understanding the UPI story.
                                    continued

SELECTED SKETCHY SCRIPT: $EXPLOSION
CPU TIME FOR UNDERSTANDING = 5250 MILLISECONDS
ENGLISH SUMMARY:
  AN EXPLOSION IN JERUSLAEM HAS IN-JURED SEVERAL PEOPLE.

FRUMP

UPI Story November 17, 1978
INPUT:
MOSCOW (UPI) SOVIET PRESIDENT LEONID BREZHNEV TOLD A GROUP VISITING U.S. SENATORS FRIDAY THAT THE SOVIET UNION HAD ONCE "TESTED BUT NEVER STARTED PRODUCTION" OF A NEUTRON BOMB. BUT ONE SENATOR SAID HE DID NOT CONSIDER THE STATEMENT "A SERIOUS MATTER."
  SEN. SAM NUNN, D-GA, WHO ATTENDED THE SESSION WITH BREZHNEV, COMMENTED ON THE NEUTRON BOMB STATEMENT TO REPORTERS AFTERWARD:
  "THE WHOLE THING ABOUT WHETHER THEY TESTED ONE AND WHETHER THEY MIGHT HAVE THE CAPABILITY OF ONE IS NOT A VERY IMPORTANT FACTOR. IN SOME WAYS I WOULD FEEL MORE COMFORTABLE IF THE SOVIETS HAD NEUTRON WEAPONS RATHER THAN THE MONSTER THEY CALL TACTICAL NUCLEAR WEAPONS."
  NEUTRON BOMBS WOULD BE USED LO-CALLY FOR DEFENSE, PRIMARILY AGAINST A TANK ATTACK, AND ARE NOT CONSIDERED LONG-RANGE STRATEGIC WEAPONS.

SEN, ABRAHAM RIBICOFF, R-CONN, HEAD OF THE AMERICAN DELEGATION, SAID THE 65-MINUTE SESSION WITH BREZHNEV WAS A 90-DEGREE SHIFT FROM THE SHARP EXCHANGES BETWEEN THE SENATORS AND SOVIET PREMIER ALEXEI KOSYGIN ON THURSDAY.

SELECTED SKETCHY SCRIPT $COMMENT
CPU TIME FOR UNDERSTANDING = 9351 MILLISECONDS
ENGLISH SUMMARY:
    LEONID BREZHNEV TOLD THE UNITED STATES THAT RUSSIA HAS TESTED A BOMB.

pate what comes next and to look for certain actions, and as we read we constantly make guesses and using hypotheses to help us understand what we read.

Suppose a character in a story walks into a restaurant. We immediately anticipate that he will sit at a table, be visited by the waiter, order a meal, eat it, and pay for his food before he leaves. For SAM, this sort of information is contained in a script:

Players: customer, server, cashier
Props: restaurant, table, menu, food, check, payment, tip
Events: 1   customer goes to restaurant
           2   customer goes to table
           3   server brings menu
           4   customer orders food
           5   server brings food
           6   customer eats food
           7   server brings check
           8   customer leaves tip for server
           9   customer gives payment to cashier
          10   customer leaves restaurant

Header: Event 1
Main
Concept: Event 6

Note that the script header "customer goes to restaurant" is both an event in the script and a way of identifying the script itself. Sentence 6 is important because it contains the main concept of the whole script, the goal of the customer who first walks into the restaurant.

Guided by such scripts SAM will parse and match sentences in a story with those in the script. It will also make use of the script to fill in any missing information as the following examples shows.

Original story:

John went to a restaurant. He sat down. He got mad. He left.

Computer paraphrase:

John was hungry. He decided to go to a resturant. He went to one. He sat down in a chair. A waiter did not go to the table. John became upset. He decided he was going to leave the restaurant. He left it.

This paraphrase, which is generated in English, Chinese, Russian, Dutch, and Spanish, extracted meaning from the simple story and expanded this information to fill in the missing gaps. SAM's inference that John left the restaurant because he did not get served may not be correct but it is a good guess.

PAM, who followed SAM, made use of more general semantic primitives called themes and goals. SAM's scripts are fairly specific and could, for example, represent one of several ways of fulfilling a goal. If John were hungry he could indeed go into a restaurant, but he could also go to a grocery store, purchase food, then return home to cook it. So a

Generic RESTAURANT Frame
  Specialization of: Business-Establishment
  Types:
    range: (Cafeteria, Seat-yourself, Wait-To-Be-Seated)
    default: Wait-To-Be-Seated.
    if-needed: IF plastic-orange-counter THEN Fast-Food,
               IF stack-of-trays THEN Cafeteria,
               IF wait-for-waitress-sign or reservations-made
                   THEN Wait-To-Be-Seated,
               OTHERWISE Seat-Yourself.
  Location:
    range: an ADDRESS
    if-needed: (Look at MENU)
  Name:
    if-needed: (Look at the MENU)
  Food-Style:
    range: (Burgers, Chinese, American, Seafood, French)
    default: American
    if-added: (Update Alternatives of Restaurant)
  Times-Of-Operation:
    range: a Time-Of-Day
    default: open evenings except Mondays
  Payment-Form:
    range: (Cash, CreditCard, Check, Washing-Dishes-Script)
  Event Sequence:
    default: Eat-at-Restaurant Script
  Alternatives:
    range: all restaurants with same FoodStyle

continued

> if-needed: (Find all Restaurants with same FoodStyle)
>
> . . . .
>
> With the aid of this script the computer can deal with knowledge about restaurants and go on to the following script:
>
> EAT-AT-RESTAURANT script
>
> Props: (Restaurant, Monday, Food, Menu, Tables, Chairs)
>
> Roles: (Hungry-Persons, Wait-Persons, Chef-Persons)
>
> Points-of-View: Hungry-Persons
>
> Time-Of-Occurence: (Time-Of-Operation of Restaurant)
>
> Place-Of-Occurence: (Location of Restaurant)
>
> Event-Sequence:
>
>   first: Enter-Restaurant Script
>
>   then: if(Wait-To-Be-Seated-Sigh or Reservations)
>
>   then Get-Maitre-de's-Attention Script
>
>   then: Please-Be-Seated Script
>
>   then: Order-Food-Script
>
>   then: Eat-Food-Script unless (Long-Wait) when
>
> Exit-Restaurant-Angry Script
>
>   then: if (Food-Quality was better than Palatable) then Compliments-To-The-Chef Script
>
>   then: Pay-For-It-Script
>
>   finally: Leave-Restaurant Script

character's goals tend to be more general as is the notion of a story's theme.

All these approaches go some way towards a machine's understanding of very simple story, but a disadvantage of

CYRUS

CYRUS, developed at Yale University, uses heuristic rules to help it answer questions in an intelligent way. Its knowledge base is built up from information passed on to it from FRUMP and deals with the lives of former Secretaries of State Cyrus Vance and Edmund Muskie. In the following dialog CYRUS answers questions about Cyrus Vance:

USER: When was the last time you were in Egypt?
CYRUS: On Dec. 10, 1978.
USER: Why did you go there?
CYRUS: To negotiate the Camp David accords.
USER: Who did you talk to there?
CYRUS: With Anwar Sadat.
USER: Has your wife ever met Mrs. Begin?
CYRUS: Yes, most recently at a state dinner in Israel in Jan. 1980.
USER: Who have you discussed SALT with?
CYRUS: Carter, Brezhnev, Gromyko, other American and Russian diplomats, and Mustafa Khalil.

the approach, is the amount of computing time needed to work with a script, plan, or frame. As additional scripts are added to the system to enable it to treat more cases then the processing time begins to slow down appreciably. This is one of the reasons that De Jong decided to work with more restricted sketchy scripts and avoid parsing the whole text.

For example, systems may possess many scripts and a wide range of goals and plans, they may deal with more subtle and longer stories. However, it is not clear if this will produce a major breakthrough in comprehension, or simply a step by step improvement with each step becoming more difficult to achieve.

Some researchers feel that the major problems of text understanding still remain to be solved and that a breakthrough will only come from human insight rather than from improvements in computing power. The problems connected with language and text understanding are indeed difficult ones and the best that the AI community can do at present is to analyze and clarify the problems involved and attempt to gain insight into the various approaches humans use towards the understanding of texts. The Yale group has been particularly active in this field, making hypotheses as to how humans read and understand stories and attempting to correlate their insights with recent results from psychology; however, not all AI researchers agree with the group's approach and the hypotheses that it generates.

One particular approach of the Yale group has been to investigate the sort of questions we asked earlier in connection with reading a passage from Dickens. These questions have been discussed, to some extent, by psychologists but a great deal of work remains to be done before we have a full theory of story comprehension. The Yale group made use of this earlier research plus some insights of their own to come up with several factors which, they felt, would have to be built into a future story understanding system.

While FRUMP, SAM, and PAM have moved beyond the level of understanding single sentences to the comprehension of a full paragraph, but they are still a long way from dealing with stories, reports, and extended conversations. Some researchers are attempting to extend the idea of syntax from the domain of a single sentence to an entire story. Others are using discourse analysis to uncover the structure of conversations and determine the goals and attitudes of the speakers and the point of what they are saying.

At Yale University the AI group is looking at the various ways in which stories hang together and produce a feeling of continuity. Once these various rules and structures have been isolated then it becomes possible to program them into a computer for full story comprehension. Take for example the rule of causality:

The boulder rolled down the mountain.
The hut in the valley was crushed.
Next day we read that many people were killed.

This makes perfect sense even though there are considerable jumps between each sentence, from a boulder to a hut to an undefined "we" on the following day. Our knowledge about the way the world works and the causal relationship between events allows us to fill in the missing links. But suppose we break that causal link with:

The car would not start.
The hut in the valley was crushed.
Next day we read that many people bought ice cream.

Each sentence makes as much sense as those in the previous example, yet taken together the whole passage feels absurd. Clearly causality is an important structure that must be built into any story and it is, therefore, one form of structure that could be searched and then represented by a computer.

Another story structure involves a series of goals:

He wanted to pass the examination.
He spent each evening at the library.

This is easy to understand, but substitute the word "bar" for "library" and we are brought up short in our reading. The continuity of sense can be further distorted by substituting "I" for "he" or changing the tense in the last sentence. This distortion indicates that a common time frame, location, and a character's point of view all help to give coherence to a story.

Roger Schank at Yale suggests that various clues are activated very early in the reading of a story and help us continue with the reading, anticipate some outcomes and ignore others. They also make us observant to exceptions or unusual events which we then attempt to integrate into our general body of knowledge about the story.

In addition to these clues there are longer range structures which cause paragraphs to hang together, connect into stories or chapters, and involve plot, character development, subplot, and so on. All these could be programmed as structure elements into a story-reading computer.

Language understanding has pushed artificial intelligence to its limit and produced systems that make only modest inroads in solving the many general problems involved. Language understanding begins with semantics and the internal structure of a sentence and extends this with semantics for individual word meanings and general knowledge to uncover the ambiguities inherent in all natural language. Even with single sentences the most advanced systems still make mistakes. Extended conversation systems must understand the general flow of a conversation, its overall context, the different points made, and the goals and motives of the speakers. Understanding of simple paragraphs may require a range of scripts for typical situations and recognition of the various clues for continuity in a story. The comprehension of a more extended text is far beyond even the most advanced systems and requires an enormous general knowledge about the world and the people in it. It requires the ability to understand character and place, plots and goals, moods and emotions, and to encode and understand the meaning of a story in a variety of different ways.

If we are to revive the Turing test then it must be in this wider context of understanding a novel or an extended conversation between friends. No computer or computer system can remotely approach such a capability and it is clear that it will have to make a significant advance before it is judged as "intelligent."

Machine Translation

Translation is a world-wide business that is both expensive and labor intensive. In a bilingual country like Canada every notice, form, and pamphlet that the federal government produces must be printed in both official languages. Companies that do business between Quebec and other provinces have to face the problems of translation which extend to all their correspondence and to bilingual text that is printed on packages and advertisements. In Canada alone the cost of this translation was $76,758,000 (Can. $) in 1982–1983. Multiply the Canadian experience by that of the European community and the cost and labor of translation becomes immense.

Computers that could handle even a percentage of this translation work would be of immense importance. However, despite the possible financial rewards this field had not been very actively pursued until recently. Possibly this is because the United States, the traditional leader in the computer field, has never had to face the issue of requiring translation on a massive basis. The problem is more acute for the Japanese who have made machine translation a significant part of their fifth generation computer thrust.

The earliest approaches at translation involved looking up every word in an internal dictionary choosing a meaning in the target language and then arranging all the target words according to the particular word order of the language in question. The technique was particularly crude and foundered on the obvious problem of ambiguity. Words in a language can have a variety of meanings and can even function in different ways, for example as verbs or nouns. Simply by looking up the meaning of a word in a dictionary does not resolve these ambiguities.

Warren Weaver, a pioneer in computer translation, introduced the idea of a *window* in a sentence and suggested that, to resolve the ambiguity of a particular word the computer would need to know what came before and after it. The bigger the window, Weaver argued, the easier it would be to clear up an ambiguity. But a very wide window would also slow down the speed of a translation so Weaver suggested that a fixed window size should be chosen so that 95 percent of words would be translated correctly 98 percent of the time.

Research on machine translation was therefore directed to setting up internal dictionaries in computers and dealing with the problems of identifying a word when its ending changes with the case. The early translations themselves were never good enough to see the light of day but had to be read over by a human translator, cleaned up, and edited.

In the 1950s there was, however, some pressure within the United States to produce a good translation system. The motive came from the desire to translate Russian documents, particularly papers in scientific and engineering journals. Some of the world's top physicists were working in Russia and scientists in the West were anxious to know what was going on. Translators in the early 1950s just could not keep pace and many senior scientists taught themselves Russian simply so that they could read what their contemporaries behind the Iron Curtain were working on. So if Russian translation had to be performed by some of the top scientific minds in the West, clearly an automatic translation approach would be of immense value. A. G. Oettinger had already attempted a Russian-English machine translation program but it floundered over the problems of ambiguity and the multiple meaning of words. The absurdities that can occur during machine translation can be graphically illustrated by taking an English sentence, translating it into Russian and back into English again. A much quoted example consists of the biblical question "The spirit is willing but the flesh is weak" which came back as "The wine is agreeable but the meat is spoiled." This example has been quoted in many books about computers and, it makes the computer look ridiculous and allows people who feel threatened by these machines to feel superior. "If a computer can be that stupid," they think, "then I've got nothing to worry about. I would never make a mistake like that." And of course, they are correct, the computer totally misunderstood the sentence and, while it make a brave attempt at translation it produced what in earlier days was known as a "schoolboy howler."

But this is exactly the point: the mistranslation is indeed a "schoolboy howler." It is just the sort of thing that a school child would produce, who did not recognize the biblical style of the sentence and was confused by the words "spirit," "weak," and "flesh." After all, within the sentence itself there are insufficient clues as to the meanings of the words. One either has to make a reasonable guess, using the most probably meanings of the words which taken together makes sense, or to make use of some additional knowledge and recognize that the passage is in an earlier version of English.

Really, that particular sentence was an unfair and extreme example for the poor computer. But even with more commonplace examples the automatic translation machines showed no hope of approaching human competence. Their translations were poor, and with hard work on the part of their programmers the systems could be only marginally improved. And Yehoshua Bar-Hillel, one of the pioneers in the field, despaired that computers would ever be able to approach the abilities of humans in making translations and using language.

In the previous chapter we have seen how complex are the processes of understanding a language and a text. Now we have the added difficulty of translation which itself contains so many unanswered questions that it is no wonder the early computer systems had their problems. Leaving out computers all together, the whole problem of translation itself continues to excite debate. For centuries people have questioned if true translation is ever possible. Can a translation, no matter how great, ever convey the totality of a work or does it concentrate on revealing only certain aspects? Suppose that the language we speak determines, to some extent, the way we think and the view we have of ourselves and the world. Does this mean that there are some, subtle things that can never be properly translated? Or is language universal and does there exist some *interlingua*, some representation of meaning that lies below language and can its statements be expressed in any surface language?

Machine translation therefore appears to be yet another of those tasks we demand from computers without full understanding how we ourselves perform and in which we expect AI researchers to forge ahead without having first resolved some very important questions of principle.

Of course, no one expects computers to go as far as translating novels, Greek verse, drama, or the subtleties of human conversations. Their real task is to translate more pedestrian prose of technical papers and reports. But even in these cases, their performance was so poor that in 1968 a report of the Automatic Language Processing Advisory Committee of the United States National Research Council, suggested that there was no immediate prospect that computers would be able to translate general scientific texts. Following this report, funding for automatic translation fell off and the topic moved into a form of limbo. Machine translation became a dirty word amongst linguists and was generally ignored.

While machine translation was in eclipse, work on natural language processing and knowledge representation was making great strides and some researchers felt that since computer language systems had improved, the conditions were right to make another attempt at machine translation. Today, we are seeing the result of that second wave of interest and, in the light we are seeing the result of that second wave of interest and, in the light of the Japanese fifth generation project, some countries feel that it is worthwhile putting money into research and development of an automatic translation program.

Rather than attempting to build a universal translator

MOPTRANS

MOPTRANS, developed at Yale University, reads and translates newspaper stories about terrorism. Given the following story: in Spanish:

> La policia reliza intensas diligencias para capturar a un presunto maniatico sexual que dio meurte a golpes y a punaladas a una mujer de 55 anos, informaron fuentes allegadas a la investigacion.

MOPTRANS parses the story and generates the following English translation:

> The police are searching for a sex maniac because he killed a 55-year-old woman.

A human translator produced the following version;

> Police are searching for a presumed sex maniac who beat and stabbed to death a 55-year-old woman.

---

many researchers today feel that it is more important to tailor their systems to particular tasks. For some purposes, it may be quite acceptable to obtain a very rapid and rough translation rather than an expensive and time-consuming one that is more accurate. For other tasks, the computer can act as a translation assistant which looks up words and automatically prepares some parts of the text. Finally if report writers are willing to produce their text in a restricted form, then computers systems can be quite successful in producing translations in a variety of languages.

One of the modern approaches to translation began with Yorick Wilks' system at Edinburgh University. Wilks suggested that the understanding needed in computer translation is less comprehensive than that required by a system that has to understand text or answer questions. For example, while a computer that translates between two languages must resolve ambiguities it need not explore the logical implications of statements or make deductions about facts contained in these sentences.

The Wilks' computer system first analyses the input text into substrings of words whose meanings are then converted into a formal semantic representation. The philosophy of this approach is very close to that of an *interlingua* and assumes some representation of meaning that lies outside ordinary language. In this case the *interlingua* is constructed out of formulas of basic elements which deal with the sort of actions and states that humans are concerned with. World knowledge is therefore intimately built into the formal representation itself and is not some additional module to be referred to by a text analyzer.

Finally once the meaning representation is complete it is translated into French using a text generation system. In this way acceptable French translations are produced from fairly short paragraphs of English text.

An alternative approach to translation comes from the TAUM group in Montreal, Canada. TAUM was formed in 1965 by of linguists, translators, and computer scientists associated with the University of Montreal. The group rejected the full *interlingua* approach in favor of what they called "pivot languages." They suggested that sentences in a given language can be analyzed semantically and syntactically into a deeper linguistic structure unique to that particular language, called a pivot language. In TAUM applications, English sentences are first analyzed and represented in pivot English. Next, with the aid of an internal dictionary and transformation rules the pivot English is translated into pivot French and finally, sentences in normal French are generated out of pivot French.

The TAUM group also decided to work with restricted language systems rather than more general tests. Each time a scientist writes a technical paper he unconsciously adopts the convention of his colleagues and uses restricted sentence constructions, a limited range of tenses, and a specialized vocabulary. The style, vocabulary, and approach will be very different from that used by a sports writer, an economist, a lawyer, or a political commentator. Professions and groups all use language in specialized and restricted ways. Linguists call these systems sublanguages since, while they are all part of a natural language they do not use its full range of expressions and potential. The syntax of a sublanguage is conveniently restricted; meanings of words are generally unambiguous. And sublanguages do not generally use metaphors, images, analogies, multiple adjectives, and poetic expressions.

By restricting their attention to sublanguages the TAUM group felt that they could make headway in producing working translations of English text. The system divided the processing into analysis into pivot languages, transformations between pivot languages and expression into a target language. The system was also versatile. Unlike other systems its internal dictionary is not intimately tied up with the whole system and it is possible, therefore, to move from one sublanguage to another without major disruption of the system and translate into some language other then French.

TAUM was first used on a large scale to translate weather reports and, in the course of its operation, generated some 2.5 million words per year with only 15 percent of sentences requiring revisions. As TAUM-AVIATION, the system was adapted to the translation of maintenance manuals. This system proved more difficult to produce, since the vocabulary and syntax was larger and, as a commercial venture it floundered on the actual cost of translation. In early 1983 the cost of human translation in Canada was $0.145 (Can.)

per word. At first sight TAUM looked highly competitive at
$0.083 per word but when the cost of a human supervisor to
check and revise the text was added, TAUM's price rose to
$0.183 per word.

Another example of translation between sublanguages was
the computer translation between Russian and English of
technical manuals used in the Apollo-Soyuz project. Several
companies use a commercial translation system to help prepare multiple language versions of their manuals. The trick
is to have a human do part of the work by writing the
original text with the machine limitations in mind, using
restricted sentences, and carefully avoiding ambiguities.

Translation looks as if it will become a developing field in
the next few years. The economic pressures to produce a
good computer translation system are high and if advances
in natural language processing are added to prototype translation systems the final result may look more attractive.
While human translation costs continue to rise, the cost
effectiveness of a computer translator will fall until a break-
even point is reached at which a given product (the computer or the computer plus human editor) can deliver at a
more economic cost.

Machine Speech

In many cities an automatic voice at the other end of the
phone informs the caller how long it will be before a bus
arrives at his local stop and if there will be delays due to
traffic. In Japan a bank's computer can carry out transactions with its customers over the telephone. In some U.S.
stores the salesperson does not need to punch items into the
cash register but simply calls them out. At a hospital a child
with cerebral palsy presses a symbol on a board and, for the
first time in its life, hears its thoughts translated into speech.
It is possible that, by the time you read this book an entire
high quality synthetic speech system will be produced on a
single chip, and no home will be complete without its talking
coffee cup.

Speech synthesis is one of those branches of artificial intelligence that has rapidly passed from research to reality and a host of commercial possibilities. Speech synthesis is both an end in itself and also one step on the way to giving a computer full conversational power. At some time in the future we may indeed have a computer like HAL in the film "2001: A Space Odyssey," that can discuss problems with its human colleagues, listen to their difficulties, and suggest solutions.

But present-day speech units are a long way from HAL's naturalistic voice production and operate in a variety of different ways. The design of an automated voice bus timetable, for example, requires only a limited number of phrases which, when strung together, will produce sentences.

"OC Transpo. Schedule for stop 6743. Route 5 in. Experiencing short delays due to traffic. Buses normally arrive at 9 and 19 minutes. Thank you."

At different times of the day and under different traffic conditions, this recording will produce alternative messages but it is easy to spot how they are constructed out of a series of numbers and stock phrases.

"(Stock phrase: "OC Transpo. Schedule for stop") + (select and voice particular bus stop number) + (stock phrase: "Route") + (select and voice route number) + (optional stock messages concerning weather or traffic conditions) + (select and voice times of the next two buses) + (stock phrase "Thank you").

The sentence and all its variations is generated by selecting and stringing together a handful of prerecorded stock phrases and numbers and the whole system can easily be programmed on a microprocessor. For applications in which the vocabulary and range of expression is limited, prerecorded human speech is used. The individual phrases are then electronically processed to compress the information they contain, without compromising their quality and stored in a permanent memory along with their computer addresses. In order to generate corrected speech the message is expressed as a string of addresses referring to appropriate words and phrases which are then selected from memory and played in sequence. The whole system can be stored on an integrated circuit (IC) chip. The results can be fairly successful but certainly not as flexible as true human speech. The problem is that each word or phrase is recorded in a neutral context and when strung together, they generate a sentence which, while it sounds human, does not carry the necessary intonation or inflections. In short, the synthetic speech sounds too mechanical to be real.

One step closer to true synthetic speech is to generate everything electronically without using prerecorded speech. The naturalness of synthetic speech depends upon the amount of computing power available and on the particular algorithms employed in generating the computer voice. At the simplest microprocessor level, a sentence generated within the computer, or input via a keyboard, is analyzed, word by word, into sound elements called *phonemes*. Just as written words are created by stringing letters together, so spoken words result from the combination of phonemes. All the speech synthesizer has to do, therefore, is to analyze words into their phonemes, string the phonemes together with suitable pauses between words and sentences, and convert the result into acoustic signals. The result is true synthetic speech, electronically generated.

But this process isn't as straightforward as it sounds. Just as parsing a sentence involves difficulties over ambiguity or varied possible meanings of a given word, so synthetic speech encounters the problems of the different phoneme representation of various words. As any foreign student of English knows, the language is full of multiple rules, irregularities, and exceptions. Take the "ou" sound. Is it to be pronounced as in "cough" or "bough" or "dough"? Is "ow" pronounced as in "low" or "now"? And "oo" is pronounced differently in "book" and in "cool." So it is not simply a matter of converting letter groups into phonemes; there are a whole series of complicated rules needed to generate the correct electronic pronunciation. Add to this the problem of accenting words, depending on their meaning as in

re' cord   or   rec ord'

or

sub ject'   and   sub' ject

Even with the help of all these pronounciation rules computer speech, at a microprocessor level, is not particularly good. Individual words may be comprehensible, but sentences can give trouble, particularly if they are long ones.

To obtain realistic speech, far more computing power is needed than a microprocessor chip can provide. Human speech is not simply composed of a string of words and pauses but has a music and flow of its own. The way each word is inflected depends upon its significance and meaning in the sentence, words can be prolonged and shortened and the silences between words can be messages themselves. Each sentence in human speech is given its life by variations in tone, pitch, intensity, intonation, and even dialect. At present, only experimental systems can begin to approach the complexity of human speech and their products still sound artificial. Part of the problem is that psychologists do not fully understand the various unconscious processes human beings employ when they speak.

One aim of speech synthesis research is to produce a good quality system that can be transferred onto a single chip and mass produced at very low cost. Another is to employ all the power of a mainframe computer in order to produce something that closely approximates human speech. This latter goal, however, also raises a number of social questions. What, for example, should be the sex of a computer's voice, should it be male or female? Some people have argued that to give computers masculine voices is to perpetrate that association between masculinity, technology, and authority. Others have speculated on how our attitude will alter towards the same computer if its voice changes from male to female. And what will our reaction be if, during a telephone conversation, we realize that the voice at the other end is not human but synthetic? Will we feel anger, suspicion, or fear? Will we feel that we have been deliberately deceived by a machine? Will we admire the power of the computer or feel dwarfed by it? Will the simple addition of a human voice to the computer add to the illusion that a computer can actually think and possess a personality of its own?

Computer engineers have always assumed that a computer that can talk back to humans will be truly user friendly but some sociologists have their doubts and wonder if humans would prefer their machines to be more clearly fallible and mechanical.

Speech Understanding

To complete our HAL of the future, a computer that fully understands language and can converse with humans will have to understand speech. We humans have a marvelous ability to deal with human speech. We can hold a conversation with a friend at a noisy cocktail party while many people are speaking at once, yet if we hear our name spoken across the room we are suddenly able to "plug in" to another voice and, through the noise, gain some idea of what it is saying. Likewise, we are able to follow a conversation over a faulty telephone line and make sense even when parts of the words are obscured by static.

When we think of this amazing power of the human ear and brain then we realize what an incredibly difficult task we are setting for the computer. Oscillations of air pressure produced by a human voice, reflected and absorbed by a room, combined with oscillations from other humans all reach the human ear and are decoded into speech and into meaning as fast as the utterances take place. How on earth could we ever hope to build a computer capable of doing such a task?

But on the other hand the stakes are big, and voice activated computers and machinery are important goals of the future. To begin with we can talk much faster than we can type, we don't have to be trained to talk, we don't have to sit down at a special desk to talk, talking comes easily and naturally to us. We can talk while we perform other tasks, like driving a car, an airplane, examining a piece of machinery, drinking coffee, or pacing about in an office.

The possibilities of voice-activated systems are endless and already there are commercial systems, available at reasonable costs, that respond to spoken instruction. One example is the store cash register which responds as the salesperson calls out the names of articles and prices. Such a system is not really a true connected speech understanding system but, instead, identifies only individual words spoken by a particular individual. It works in the following way. Incoming sound is picked up by a microphone and electronically processed into digitized signals, much as the sound of an orchestra is processed in a digital recording. The digital signal is then compared with templates stored in the computer's electronic dictionary of some 100 commonly used words.

Even at this level, the word recognition system must be "trained" by each particular speaker. At the start of the day the user will repeat key words to the machine so that it learns to identify that voice and accent with, say, 95 percent accuracy. If some other user comes along the system would probably not be able to recognize many of the words he or she uttered unless it is "retrained." Another difficulty with such systems is the problem of background sounds and distortions introduced by different microphones which can interfere with matching of incoming signals.

To go from single word recognition to understanding connected speech is a considerable leap and it is not difficult to appreciate the reason why. Consider the following sentence, it consists of individual words that are strung together with gaps between them. Even if you do not understand the meaning of individual words, like nopal or garron, you have no difficulty in recognizing the words or in reading the sentence aloud. But suppose you were to record the sentence and then play back what you had read? You would find that it does not consist of a simple string of words. To begin with, there are gaps of silence between certain words, while others run into each other so that if that sentence had been in a foreign language, you would have trouble in discovering where one word ended and another began. As people speak, they "swallow" parts of words, drop consonants, and pronounce words in ways that depend on their position or significance in a sentence. The problem of word recognition in connected speech is, therefore, far more difficult than recognition with single, isolated words.

However, humans are evolutionarily adapted to deal with connected speech even when it is spoken in a noisy forest or across a bad telephone line. We are able to perform so well because we anticipate what is being said; if we lose or misunderstand an individual word we are able to fill in the gap almost without noticing it. Clearly, if a computer is going to be able to understand ordinary human speech then it will have to use all its knowledge about syntax, semantics, the topic of conversation, and the attitude and background of the speaker.

Connected speech systems must therefore operate in both a top down and bottom up way. Their recognition of individual words will help them to discover what the conversation is about and in turn enable them to make hypotheses about what will be said next and guide the recognition of individual words. When it comes to bottom up processing, there is no point in trying to begin with individual words since it is not clear where one word ends and another begins. In addition, the end of a word may be lost and swallowed by the speaker. The system therefore works by attempting to match incoming digital signals with templates consisting of sound units, called allophones. (Some systems also use the syllable as the basic sound symbol.)

Once the allophones have been identified, they are then combined together in an attempt to produce a particular word. In practice the computer will never be 100 percent certain that an incoming sound can be identified with a given word; it may sound a bit like another word, or it may be a combination of two words run together. The best it can do is identify several possibilities and allocate a "score" to each of them.

Given that some words in the speech have been identified, the system applies its various rules of syntax, semantics, stress, intonation, and so on to help it interpret additional words. It also uses its general knowledge to suggest the most probable statement or reply to a question. The HEARSAY system, for example, developed at Carnegie-Mellon University, was designed to play chess with a human opponent. Knowing about the state of the game enables HEARSAY to anticipate a range of next moves that are spoken by the human. This greatly limits the number of possible words and statements that the system needed to untangle in the incoming speech. HEARSAY also employed its rules and knowledge in a modular way so that they acted like a committee that judges incoming information and throws out suggestions which are then written down on a blackboard until a consensus can be reached.

Once such a process of anticipation is begun, it influences the processing of the next word. Anticipations act to guide the decoding of words and each decoded word, in turn, enables new anticipations to be made more accurate. Of course, it is a major headache to control and coordinate the whole process and to prevent a combinatorial explosion taking place as the system searches through too many possibilities. Another difficulty, in designing a system which works cooperatively from the top and bottom, is how to begin the whole process. One approach is to start with the first two or three words in the sentence and then use these to help construct anticipations. Another is to scan the incoming sound rapidly and pick out words that are easily and positively identified; these stand out like islands in the otherwise unintelligible sound and can be used as signposts from which further processing can be controlled.

An idea of how important the rules and anticipations are in speech understanding is given by HARPY, a system developed at Carnegie-Mellon which makes use of search networks. HARPY is 97 percent successful in identifying words but it is only 42 percent accurate when it comes to identifying individual sound elements. In fact, the system's general knowledge about language is used to fill in the gaps, just like humans do. This process can be more dramatically shown by selective switching on some of the rules. If syntax rules are added to the system, it improves its accuracy by 25 percent, and with semantics a further 25 percent improvement is found.

A major impetus to move ahead with speech understanding came from DARPA, the U.S. Department of Defense's Advanced Research Projects Agency. In 1971 DARPA began funding a major five-year research project known as SUR (speech understanding research). Work was carried out at a number of locations including SRI, Bolt, Beranek and Newman Inc., and Carnegie-Mellon University. The aim of the project was to produce a system that could understand connected speech, operating with less than 10 percent error and in some limited domain which used around 1,000 words. At the beginning of this project no system could recognize connected speech and individual word recognition systems only had vocabularies of less than 100 words. By 1976 several systems, which came some way toward meeting these criteria, were operating successfully.

From Carnegie-Mellon University came HARPY, which could identify some 184 sentences with about 5 percent error, work with five different speakers, and was used to answer questions from a database. Other DARPA funded systems included HEARSAY-I that could understand spoken commands in chess and HEARSAY-II used for document retrieval.

Today, systems are being developed by IBM, Sperry Univac, and Bell as well as at several university AI centers. In addition, commercial systems can be purchased in a range of prices from individual word recognizers to suit the pocket of the amateur to Nippon Electric's $80,000 (in 1983) connected speech recognizer. These commercial systems at present do not perform quite as well as the top level DARPA projects but will probably improve rapidly as they compete for the world market.

CHAPTER 6
Computers That Can See

Vision occupies a position of supreme importance in the human senses. Dogs have evolved their sense of smell in order to deal with the world, dolphins and bats rely on hearing; but man has chosen vision as his primary way of perceiving. In consequence the world we have created for ourselves is packed with visual clues and material. We surround ourselves with signs, symbols, notice boards, photographs, movies, paintings and television. Since AI computers must function in this world it is clear that they must come to terms with its strong visual component.

Industrial robots will use camera eyes to locate objects and as a guide during assembly. General robots will use vision to help them move around in a world of objects. Expert systems will update themselves by reading all the books and articles that are published in their field. Computers will interpret photographs, monitor traffic in the streets and become involved in all manner of visual supervision and inspection.

It is now well understood that artificial intelligence depends upon computers having knowledge about the world around them and one highly effective way of building up this knowledge is through vision. Once a computer has been given its senses of touch to manipulate objects, of hearing to understand human speech and of sight to learn about objects in the world, then it is able to reach out and gather knowledge on its own. Computer vision may well be an important step in the evolution of machine intelligence. Finally, it is an important study in its own right, since computer vision may help to shed light on how our own vision system works.

Demanding that a computer be able to see as well as we do is a particularly tall order. Our ability to see is the result of a billion years of evolution, the product of a vast period of research and development. Being able to see and interpret the world around us is something we do superbly well and with such ease that we tend to take the whole process for granted. We may admire the ability of a hawk to spot the smallest movement in a field hundreds of feet below but the hawk's vision is highly specialized and adapted specifically for this particular task. Human vision on the other hand has become generalized so that it can deal effectively with a vast range of very different situations. But as to how this actually takes place is something of a mystery to which we have only a limited number of clues.

Suppose, for example, that we enter a room, glance around and recognize one of its occupants. The whole process seems to take place without conscious will, and visual recognition happens in an instant. But this ability to see, without having to bother about how we do it, poses a problem for the design of machine vision systems. When we solve a problem in logic or mathematics we can analyze our thought processes and discover the various tactics we use. These steps can then be programmed into a computer and used in a general problem solving system. A similar procedure applies to expert systems and to the robot arms used in manipulation. Language understanding, as we have seen in Chapter 5, is a more difficult problem, but at least internal reflection does provide us with clues as to how language processing takes place in the brain and acts as a guide in the design of natural language computer systems. But when it comes to computer vision scientists are far more in the dark about how the brain deciphers a picture, how it picks out objects from a complex scene and how it recognizes a face in a crowd that was last seen several years ago. AI researchers can turn to the results of psychology and the neurosciences but even here there is no complete answer as to how the human vision system works. Some aspects of the seeing, for example, the electrochemical processes of the retina, are well understood but others such as the particular representations that are formed in the visual cortex, are not. In fact, there is no general theory of human vision but simply a range of hypotheses about what may happen at certain levels with several of these proposals differing significantly in their essentials.

While the scientific study of vision provides only a few clues for the design of computer vision systems, the flow of insights sometimes goes in the opposite direction for, as computer scientists build experimental vision systems, their failures and successes can be of help to psychologists in deciding amongst tentative mechanisms of how human vision processing may take place. Vision is one field in which artificial intelligence is not only an end in itself, but a very important means for understanding how the human brain works and is, therefore, a stimulus to several other areas of research.

Human vision, therefore, remains something of a mystery and artificial intelligence for its part has not been able to make truly major inroads into the field of computer vision. Several experimental systems have been built and applications have reached the market place but these all tend to be in specialized or restricted fields and true general vision remains a dream of the future. Some vision experts feel that there can be significant advances in general robotic vision within the next 10 years, others argue that the problems involved are so difficult that it is impossible to predict when a vision system will be produced that can identify a range of objects and fully understand a general scene.

Picture Processing

Before we explore these challenging problems of general vision, let us briefly examine some of the things that a computer is able to do better than any human eye, namely picture processing and image enhancement. Computer vision begins with a photograph or the output from a television camera that is scanned section by section. But before the computer can go on to detect features and recognize objects, this image may have to be improved and enhanced.

Enhancement is something that the computer can do very well, it can pick out obscure details, compensate for bad focus, change certain colors, improve contrast, smooth out noise, and extract hidden visual information. The computer is so good at picture processing that a minor industry has grown up around it, and picture processing has become the end in itself, quite apart from any other considerations of computer vision.

Image processing begins with a series of geometrical transformations that are performed electronically to compensate for distortions produced by the viewing angle and for any errors introduced by the camera itself. Next the image is "smoothed out" to remove noise. The term "noise" is probably familiar when it comes to phonograph records and the reception on a radio. Noise is that random background hiss produced by interference, degradation of the signal, and random processes in the amplifier. Noise can also occur, from similar causes, in a television picture and even in a photograph. "Salt and pepper" noise from random processes gives rise to a dusting of tiny black and white dots on a picture and can be removed by a slight defocusing. Other forms of noise require more sophisticated removal techniques. For example noise may be most intense in a particular frequency band and can be removed by filtering out high or low frequency noise components from a picture; another approach is to attempt some mathematical averaging within the image. If more than one picture of the same scene is available then averaging of the series is a useful way of subtracting random noise and enhancing useful information.

This step, of removing noise, can be quite dramatic and is normally followed by enhancement. First, the scale of grays in the image are stretched out to provide better contrast, or a particular region in the picture or an interval in the gray scale may be specially processed. Following this, any lines, edges, or boundaries around objects are emphasized. This has the effect of clarifying the picture and revealing details that previously may have been thought to be lost.

If the photograph is a colored one, or if black and images have been taken through colored filters, then the contrast between regions can also be emphasized through false color processing in which an arbitrary color is assigned to each region so that the contrast between regions is made more graphic. Color enhancement can also occur in the photographic process itself when infrared light and red filters are used because (as any amateur photographer knows) the red wavelengths make for good contrast between green vegetation and other ground cover. Color enhancement and picture processing have also found their way into television where they are used to produce special effects for commercials. The end result of all this processing is to produce a photograph or a television image in which random noise and distortions have been eliminated, contrasts have been increased, and the definition of objects and their boundaries improved—an important contribution if the image comes from a space probe or rare historical photograph.

Additional applications of picture processing occur in side-looking radar and various forms of medical imagery. A CAT scan (computer assisted tomography) uses information from a series of X-ray images of the human body which is processed mathematically to produce full, three-dimensional information on organs of the body. CAT scans are not only able to

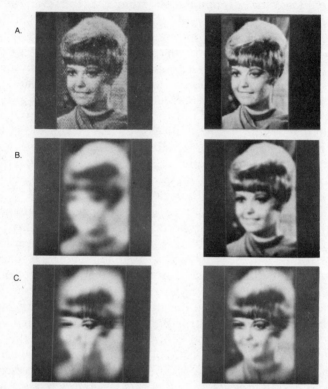

Picture processing is used to treat and restore images by removing blurring, noise and other defects. Here a 103 × 64 matric representation of a young woman's face acts as the original standard (a). The image (b) is now blurred and further confused by the addition of random noise but is restored (c) using a computer program.

In (a) the blurring is severe but with no addition of noise. The restored image (b) is shown beside.

Another form of blurring (a) with the corresponding restored image (b).

Courtesy N.N. Modelmalek and
T. Kasvand, N.R.C., Canada

196

produce a detailed picture of, say, an interior region of the brain but can use false color to enhance contrast between healthy and diseased tissue. Processing of medical images is also used in ultrasound scans, PET scans (position emission tomography), NMR scans (nuclear magnetic resonance), and for images produced after radio isotopes have been introduced into the body.

Character Recognition

Image enhancement and picture processing are examples of fields in which a computer's abilities greatly exceed those of human beings. Presented with a washed out and badly focused photograph, our sophisticated human vision system can do little in the way of enhancement, but give that same photograph to a computer processing system and all its hidden detail will spring to light. And, when it comes to dealing with images, there is an additional field in which the computer, if not exactly exceeding human abilities, at least rivals them. This is the identification and classification of simple two-dimensional objects and shapes. No supermarket is compete without its bar code reader and similar devices exist to read magnetic codes on checks and fluorescent stripes corresponding to postal zip codes. Optical readers have the advantage over humans in that they are tireless and error free, but these abilities are purchased only at the expense of having the computer work in a highly standardized and simplified world consisting of alternating bars.

Similar systems are also used to identify rock samples, count blood cells and other small particles, karotype chromosomes, and classify tracks in elementary particle photographs. Some are able to recognize typed characters and convert what they read into speech while others can decipher handwriting. In Japan, for example, character recognition systems are being developed to deal with the phonetic kana characters and the more than 2,000 Chinese characters that are used in Japanese writing. An extension of this approach is to use computers for optical inspection in factories, for example, to check printed circuits, the position of holes in a component and for errors following a machine shop process.

While all these systems use computer vision to perform their tasks, their limitations are so severe that they cannot yet be called general vision systems. To begin with each is specific to a particular task; a machine for reading bar codes, cannot be adapted to any simple way to classify chromosomes or inspect a piece of machinery. Each application therefore requires a specifically designed and manufactured vision system. In addition, these systems are only able to work with flat, two-dimensional images, rather than with the three-dimensional images of the real world. While they can pick out and identify simple shapes, they do not interpret the image or to understand how it corresponds to anything in the real world. Before we consider this more general problem of scene understanding and image interpretation, it will be useful to look at the ways in which the human eye and brain deal with the visual world.

Human Vision

The human eye is in some respects similar to a camera and in others is totally unlike any mechanical device. By means of the muscles that surround its lens and control the iris is, like a camera, able to vary its focus and aperture. But the eye is also part of the brain and is therefore an intentional device that is constantly searching the visual world and asking and answering questions. We can see evidence of the eye's intelligent behavior in the constant movements that take place during normal vision. As we read a book, look at a painting, or enter a room, our eyes carry out a series of rapid scanning movements, up to five a second. In addition to these large sweeping movements or saccades there are a series of tremors and slow drifts as well as disjunctive eye movements in which the eyes change their focus and relative angle to pick out objects at various distances.

The act of seeing takes place only during the very short

intervals between each movement when the eye is stationary. This means that information does not reach the brain in a steady stream but in a rapid machine-gun fire with each burst bringing in totally new features of the scene. What is even more interesting about these movements is that they are answers to visual queries and an expression of the intentionality of vision. But to see how this is true we must look at the retina itself.

Embryologically the retina is a part of the brain that, in the early weeks of life, moved outward to locate itself at the back of the eye. This retina contains around one hundred million receptors, some of which respond to color in bright light while others are very sensitive to dim illumination. Near the center of the retina is the fovea, or yellow spot, a region that is packed with so densely with receptor cones that it responds well to detail. When an image falls on the retina the brain receives general information about the whole scene with most of the detail being picked up by the small central region of the fovea. So, in order to explore a scene, the eye must move and allow different parts of the scene to fall on the fovea. What is particularly important about these movements is that they are not mindless, automatic actions like the scanning of a TV camera but a cooperative action between the eye and brain. This can be demonstrated by an interesting experiment in which eye movements are monitored while a person is asked a series of questions about a photograph. Depending on the questions asked, his eyes will dart to different parts of the image, seeking out detail, confirming hypotheses and linking various aspects of the scene together. Since, corresponding to each stationary position of the eye, only a tiny portion of the visual scene is transmitted to the brain from the fovea, this means that the act of seeing involves the active search for clues and information with some process of integration of this information taking place in the brain. Yet, to us, vision is something that we never have to think about or consciously control. A visual scene seems to spring into existence instantaneously and does not feel like a complex synthesis of very many different "views."

On the retina itself nerve signals are generated when photons of light produce chemical changes in photoreceptors which then cause the cell to fire. But the actual firing is a little more complicated than a simple triggering each time a nerve is stimulated. Not only does the output of the receptor cells pass vertically toward the optic nerve, but there are also horizontal connections between neighboring cells. The action of some of these cells is to inhibit the firing of their neighbors unless differences in light intensity are presently across a region of the retina. Gregory Bateson has said that the basis of information lies in significant differences and this is exactly what the retina is searching for and transmitting to the brain, differences in light intensity from cell to cell.

The results of all this activity in the retina are complex bursts of signals that pass down a bundle of fibers that are collectively called the optic nerve. Even at this stage of seeing the optic nerve is more than a mere collection of telephone lines, for additional nerve pathways cross the main trunk lines and compare and modify signals as they travel along the optic nerve. Clearly some pre-processing of information takes place before the visual messages reach the brain.

Finally, the optic nerve enters the brain and its output is routed to three different locations: the midbrain, the cerebellum and, via the thalmus, to the visual cortex, which is itself divided into a number of different processing areas. The fact that vision involves many regions of the brain is a clear indication that there is no single process of vision but a range of different ways in which nerve signals are decoded and represented. For example, the midbrain and cerebellum are also concerned with giving instructions which cause the eye to carry out its saccadian movements. In more primitive organisms, stimulation of certain midbrain cells cause a direct response in the whole body. Ganglion cells in the frog's retina called "bug detector cells" will fire if stimu-

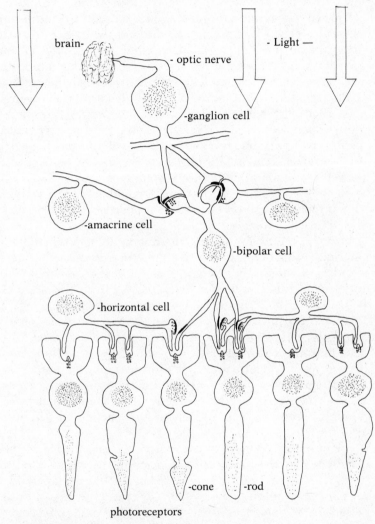

A highly simplified diagram of the optical system in a monkey's eye. Light falls on a series of photoreceptors which generate electrical signals that pass, via a complicated series of transformations, to the brain.

lated by a tiny moving disc, electrical messages from these cells then trigger off an immediate response in the midbrain that causes the frog to turn, and jump at the disc or fly.

So at one level of visual processing cells on the retina appear to be mapped directly onto cells in the midbrain which are interconnected with other cells responsible for eye movements and muscular reactions. Vision at this level is concerned with survival. The rabbit, for example, immediately responds to the shape of a hawk and, for simple animals, feeding often occurs in response to specific visual triggers. An "explosion" of a large area in the visual field of the housefly is automatically interpreted as a surface and activates the fly's landing mechanism. Even in humans a similar looming of a shape on our retina produces the blink reflex which protects the eye against damage.

Vision in the midbrain does not appear to be producing an internal image of a scene or detailed recognition and understanding. It is purely a reflex action and it is possible that the fly and the frog do not "see" the world in the sense of being able to build up an internal image, any more than we "see" the world in terms of temperature or touch or sound. When we talk about computer vision we must, therefore, bear in mind that many creatures that depend on their eyes for survival may not be involved in contemplating the visual world or understanding and intellectually interpreting images on their retinas. Rather, their vision is concerned with taking appropriate action each time a particular stimulus appears.

For humans the highest levels of vision takes place in the cortex. It is here that a representation of the world is built up in which real objects appear to be "out there," available for our contemplation, enjoyment, or to help us plan future actions. But how does this internal representation occur? Just as our thoughts are represented symbolically in language, so some equally complex representation is required so that we can understand a visual scene and externalize it into an objective account of the world that we can contemplate and act upon. But what the representation may be remains a complete mystery.

The vision research was stimulated by the discovery of "feature detectors" in the retinas of laboratory animals. Certain cells in the eye of the cat, for example, respond to lines oriented at a particular angle and other cells respond when the angle of orientation is slightly changed. Some cells are not triggered by these stationary lines at all but only by moving bars. Suddenly scientists felt that vision could be explained in terms of feature detectors, groups of cells in the retina that respond to specific stimulii and visual clues. By combining all these elementary features together the visual scene could then be created in the brain. Reseach even reached the point where scientists claimed they had discovered, in monkeys, cells that were triggered only when a monkey's paw came into view. Some even proposed, tongue in cheek, a "grandmother cell" that would only respond when stimulated by an image of one's grandmother!

The theory of feature detectors, or small groups of cells on the retina that respond to specific visual clues, is a powerful and attractive one. It is certainly able to explain how the frog, rabbit, fly and other animals are triggered into activity by certain shapes or movements. Using feature detectors that respond to oriented lines and moving edges the next step would be to build more complex shapes out of these visual "atoms." This theory has been translated into computer vision processing using edge and feature detectors which, as we shall see below, explore an image for boundaries, edges, lines, and textures. This is normally the first step after basic enhancement of the image in computer vision processing and in simple scenes it may not be too difficult to integrate these features and form a representation of an object.

Feature detection may well form an important part of human vision but it is hard to see how it can be the whole story. When it comes to individual features such as eyes, nose, and mouth, one human face looks very much like another. In addition, a face changes continuously as the head moves, the expressions alter and shadows and illumination changes. How it is possible using feature detectors alone to recognize this flexible, changing object as the same face and pick it out in a crowd when it was last seen years ago and with a quite different pattern of worry lines or even with a beard or moustache? While feature detectors may have their role, the whole process or vision must also involve some internal representations on the part of the brain so that what we see is built up both internally and externally.

Some researchers have tried to guess what this process of synthesis may entail. Karl Pribram, for example, suggests that vision is a holographic process in which the retina's images are enfolded and distributed across large areas of the cortex. As messages pass along the optic nerve and into the brain they interfere and modify each other in an analogous way to the interference of light which produces the holograph. Recognition of images comes about not through an examination of particular features but in a holistic way by the matching of both local and global information in the image. Pribram's theory also accounts for the fact that vision can persist after considerable damage to the optic nerve and visual cortex. For in the hologram, information about the whole of the image is contained in each part so that while damage to a holographic representation produces additional noise it does not destroy the whole image.

The late David Marr suggested that human vision involves several different levels of description and representation. Marr gave the example of attempting to understand the nature of flight only by examining the feathers of a bird. Feathers do not tell us about flight, but once we have explored the level of an aerodynamical explanation then feathers begin to make good sense and we are able to see why they evolved their particular shape and structure. The implications for computer vision are clear, that no single level of representation or processing is comprehensive enough to generate a general vision system; rather a series of different processes must take place, each appropriate to a particular level of analysis, interpretation, and understanding of the image and the scene.

In summary, the study of vision in humans and animals has produced a number of clues and hypotheses, but no general theory of seeing that is able to account for all the experimental data. Insights from nature's vision processes have been of help in designing computer systems but at times this flow of insight has gone in the opposite direction. It is only when a physiological hypothesis or theory is programmed into a computer that its limitations and drawbacks become apparent. Artificial intelligence therefore has been of help in suggesting what can and cannot work in terms of vision processing. It is probable that a full computer vision system will evolve hand in hand with a general theory of how vision works in human beings.

The Computer Eye

Having seen how vision works in animals and humans, or rather having realized our state of ignorance about the whole process, it is time to return to the computer and explore the various ways it attempts to understand and interpret the images it is presented with. To begin let us examine the computer's eye which tells it about the world outside. This eye is normally a television camera, generally not the usual vidicon camera found in a TV studio but a solid state camera using a charged coupled device that is more stable and reliable. The cameras used in vision work are normally black and white although color is sometimes used to obtain additional information. Light entering the camera is focused onto a series of cells which build up electrical charges and, in effect, convert the image into an electronic digital signal that represents the light intensity of each pixel in the image. This information then passes to the computer at the rate of several million bytes per second.

The first step that takes place before an image is interpreted is the removal of noise and the enhancement that was discussed earlier. The next step is to emphasize boundaries, edges, and lines so that the computer can use its edge detectors to uncover the outlines that define an object. If the scene consists of a series of flat two-dimensional shapes arranged against a contrasting background then tracing out a boundary may be all that is needed to identify objects. In the case of real solids, however, this step is not so clear cut since the boundary of an object is a function of its angle and orientation to the viewer and can be changed by shadows or other objects that stand in front of it and obscure it. Understanding and interpreting three-dimensional scenes, therefore, requires far more than the information that is given by boundaries alone, but at least an outline makes a good starting point and has something in common with the features that appear to be detected by the human eye.

Lines, edges, and boundaries are characterized by sudden changes in grayness of an image and can, therefore, be determined by comparing the intensity of neighboring pixels. A computer edge detector looks for differences in grayness through small "windows" that can range from 2 × 2 to 15 × 15 pixels in size and are traced across the image. Mathematically this process is equivalent to determining gradients in the intensity of light that made up the image. The edge detection programs therefore search amongst digital picture data for sudden differences in grayness and even for differences between differences which can then be defined as edges, boundaries, and lines. The results of this stage of vision processing can be displayed as a new computer image, called a primal sketch, in which only lines appear and give the effect of an artist's sketch of the scene.

Several primal sketches are reproduced in these pages and there are two important things to notice about them. First, although they look like the sort of drawings we would make of a scene, it is clear that they are not interpretations or acts of understanding. A primal sketch is the expression of important data that has been extracted from an image; it may mean a great deal to us humans because we are used to

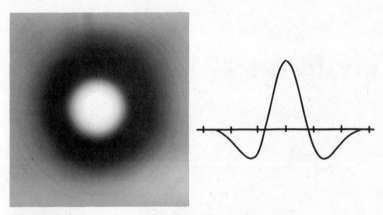

Figure 6–3
There is evidence that cells in the retina act as concentric systems of edge detectors. The central area responds to light while the periphery acts as an inhibitor. The overall effect is a two-stage process, first some averaging of the image and second the detection of lines and sharp contrasts. David Marr and Ellen Hildreth at M.I.T. have developed the mathematical equivalent of this concentric system for use in computer vision. The two figures above give a picture of the concentric feature detector and a cut through its center.

Courtesy E. Hildreth

representing the world by line drawings but the computer itself is no closer to understanding what the scene means. Simply because it has produced a sketch of a cube or a human face does not mean that it *recognizes* the face or *understands* that a cube is a regular figure with six equal sides. The primal sketch is simply a condensation of some information in the image and the emphasis or other information, but by itself, it is not a symbolic representation that can be understood and manipulated by the computer.

The major problem with a primal sketch is its "noise." Parts of the sketch contain false lines, produced by noise, some real lines exhibit scatter, others are broken, fragmentary,

Figure 6–4
A photograph and the outlines that have been extracted from it using Marr and Hildreth's "zero crossing operator," shown in the previous figure.

Courtesy E. Hildreth

or have been missed altogether. This mixture of noise and signal is characteristic of all attempts at computer vision. In nearly every other field of artificial intelligence, except speech understanding, the computer is given high quality information but in vision there is no such thing as a perfect image and the computer must be content with data that is incomplete, ambiguous, and noisy. Good illumination of a scene will increase contrast and help in edge detection but it can also produce sharp shadows which will be interpreted by the computer as part of the boundary of an object. Increasing the "window" through which gray differences are detected cuts the effects of noise but it also reduces the computer's resolution and its ability to detect closely spaced lines; on the other hand, reducing the window size makes for high definition but also magnifies the spurious effects of noise.

Given the primal sketch with all its imperfections, the computer now attempts to interpret the scene. In the case of flat objects placed on a high contrast background, this primal sketch may already contain sufficient information. If the shape of a series of objects is stored in the computer memory in the form of templates then recognition becomes a matter of matching a template against the outlines of a primal sketch. Edge detection and the primal sketch are therefore used to identify chromosomes, fibers, and printed text. In the case of more complex figures such as the patterns of a printed circuit or handwritten Chinese characters, the computer faces the additional problem of determining what happens to a line as it crosses another line.

Seeing in a Blocks World

General computer vision is generally concerned with interpreting three-dimensional scenes rather than flat shapes. Here the primal sketch is used as a first stage in a more complicated process that takes into account a variety of other visual clues. Pioneering work in this field began in the mid-1960s with the simple world of solid geometrical blocks.

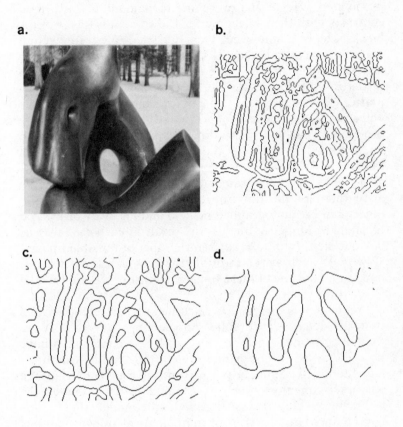

Figure 6-5
Using Marr and Hildreth's "zero crossing operator," the effect of various window sizes in picking up noise and in losing fine detail can be explored. In (b) the window is 6 pixels across; (c) and (d) are 12 and 24 pixels wide respectively.

Courtesy E. Hildreth

L. G. Roberts, for example, worked with a cube, rectangle, prism and wedge that were matte painted to give good contrasts with their background. The computer image of the blocks was first enhanced, then subjected to edge detection and a primal sketch generated and matched against a series of solid shapes stored in the computer's memory. But even in the case of the simple blocks, this matching is no trivial matter. The camera "sees" the block from a particular angle and according to the laws of projective geometry (perspective) produces a particular two-dimensional image. Information about the full geometry of the object is therefore lost and all that remains is two-dimensional data about a three-dimensional object. If the viewing angle is altered, for example, the appearance of the flat image will also change. The solid object can be photographed near to and far away or rotated through a number of angles; the result in each case will be one out of an infinitely different number of possible images. How, with such a wealth of alternatives, can the computer hope to match one of these images against its internal model in any finite time?

The answer is to begin by selecting a few reference points that characterize each solid, for example, a vertex where three sides come together. Once such reference points have been identified in the primal sketch, they can be examined and identified tentatively with one of the models in the computer's memory. The next stage is to try to match the full primal sketch against this candidate model. Matching is done by applying a series of mathematical transformations which scale and rotate the model of the solid until the outlines of its two-dimensional projection can be superimposed onto the primal sketch. Of course, this final step is never perfect since the primal sketch contains noise and other defects but is possible to make a final identification with a high degree of confidence.

Roberts' approach worked from the bottom up by starting with edge detection and the primal sketch and then building up to the solid model. A more interesting variation is to add some top down searching and use the computer's knowledge about solids to help it interpret the image. Once a solid has been tentatively identified, the computer's internal model is then used to predict the existence of lines that are missing from the primal sketch and to question other lines that appear to be spurious. Helped by a general hypothesis, the edge detector goes back to the original image and looks more carefully in certain regions for boundaries and edges. Image interpretation therefore becomes a process of moving between the original image, the primal sketch, and an internal visual hypothesis of what the solid should look like. This approach is a little like the question and answering that takes place as the human eye dances over a scene looking for clues, confirming hypotheses, and filling in details.

A mathematician can sketch all manner of "impossible objects" that can never exist in three dimensions. The properties of real solid objects and of the three-dimensional space they reside in places constraints on the way in which lines, edges, and vertices can meet and be oriented. If one vertex of a cube is convex, and points towards the camera, then a consideration of solid geometry determines which other vertices can be convex and which must be concave and point away. By classifying vertices and surfaces and using additional knowledge of solid geometry, the vision system can correctly identify simply shaped blocks without actually needing to match the primal sketch against an internal template or model. Recognition is therefore a combination of determining key features in the image and reasoning about these features in the light of general knowledge about a world of blocks.

Additional information can be collected if the computer searches for surfaces as well as for edges and boundaries. This time instead of looking for a sharp difference between neighboring regions, it looks for the absence of these differences. By expanding outward from a given pixel and including only those pixels which do not differ significantly in their grayness, the computer is able to trace out a region of the image that can be identified with a surface on a block. In more complex worlds, regions and by inference surfaces, can be also identified in terms of their texture or color. The computer can also make use of information that can be deduced from shadows which give additional clues to the shape of an object.

General Vision

The blocks world is highly simplified but at least it has the advantage of making all the assumptions and processes of computer vision completely explicit. When this world of painted children's blocks is exchanged for the complex world of faces, offices, factories, and outdoor scenes, the problems of image interpretation and scene understanding become vastly more complicated. Systems that work in the real world have to make use of every available clue that can be discovered in the image they have been given, they must work from the bottom up by detecting edges and key features and from the top down by using their knowledge about the physical world and its features to help interpret the image. In addition to the primal sketch, the computer will make use of additional visual clues related to surface orientation, distance of objects from the camera, reflectance, and incident illumination. Regions of uniform grayness will indicate the presence of a surface and additional information can be gained by looking at areas of texture and color.

It is not such a straightforward matter to construct a primal sketch or line drawing of a real object in a general scene as it was in the case of carefully illuminated the block world. The grayness of a pixel in a general scene is the product of many different factors whose effects have first to be unraveled. Brightness in a particular area may be the result of the angle of a surface with respect to the camera, the reflectance of a particular paint or texture, the position of sources of illumination and of shadows produced by other bodies; discontinuity in a region may correspond to a true boundary, a change in texture or color, or to the presence of

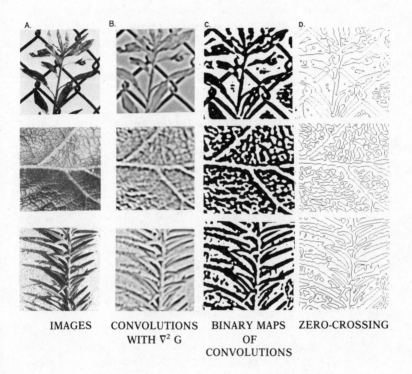

IMAGES   CONVOLUTIONS   BINARY MAPS   ZERO-CROSSING
WITH ∇^2 G   OF
CONVOLUTIONS

Figure 6-6
A series of processings occur before the photographic image A
becomes the primal sketch D. These include averaging and the
detection of edges and outlines.

Courtesy E. Hildreth

a shadow. The more general knowledge a computer has about the scene, the better able it will be to untangle all these clues and features. Computers must therefore have knowledge about objects, heuristics about appearances and the laws of geometry, and facts about shadows and the effects of illumination on different surfaces. But as to how all this information is to be integrated together into a general vision system is a considerable challenge. David Marr has suggested that a series of different representations must be used in order to understand a scene. For example, when it comes to obtaining information about the shape of an object the following stages are involved:

Primal sketch: Information on boundaries, lines, edges, and surfaces is derived from grayness variations in the image and leads to the primal sketch which is an explicit representation of the geometry of the two-dimensional image expressed in terms of a series of "primitives" (boundaries, edges, terminations of lines, and so on).
2–D sketch: This is something like a perspective drawing which makes the geometry of the solid object more explicit. The representation is expressed in terms of such primitives as distance from the viewer, orientations of surfaces, and discontinuities between surfaces. This 2–D sketch is still viewer centered since it represents the object as seen from the viewer's point of view.
3–D model: This is a model of the object independent of the viewing angle. It may be hierarchical in representation and use a vocabulary of additional primitives to express volume and surface features.

Shape, itself, is only one of the factors that can lead to correct identification of an object and additional levels of representation and interpretation are also needed.

Aerial Photographs
One field in which these general problems of vision are

216

somewhat simplified is in the interpretation of aerial and satellite photographs. Since these images are taken from a great height they tend to be fairly standard and the vision system does not have to contend with the ways in which objects change their appearance with different camera angles.

Computer processing of aerial photographs has as its goal the correct interpretation of surface features such as roads, rivers, cities, mountains, forests, vegetation, and expanses of water. Edge detection can be valuable in identifying characteristic shapes and textures; distinct shadows at low altitudes, for example, may indicate housing and regions of high contrast (when red filters are used) will suggest forests or green vegetation against a different background. But to unfold all the visual information that is contained in an aerial photograph the computer must be provided with general information about objects that are found in different terrains such as trees, bridges, roads, houses, rivers, and crops. In addition, the system should understand how images are formed and how the angle of the sun and the position of the camera can be used to deduce contours and the height of mountains. Additional data may be supplied in the form of data on distances computed by a rangefinder, stereo images, or sequences of photographs taken from a moving aircraft. An important issue therefore is how to choose, out of this wealth of information, that which is really necessary and how to represent this data in the most effective way.

One solution, proposed by Alan Mackworth of the University of British Columbia, is to use the computer as an apprentice and have a human provide it with information that is appropriate to the task in hand. MAPSEEZ understands roads, rivers, lakes, mountains, bridges, and towns and the relationships that exist between them; it also knows how to interpret a sketch map. Given a particular photograph the human operator makes a rough sketch indicating the approximate location of bridges, rivers, roads, and mountains. MAPSEEZ then explores the photograph with the aid of the sketch, makes correct identifications and finally reconstructs the scene in detail with all its features correctly displayed.

3D Mosiac, developed at Carnegie-Mellon University, extracts information from a series of stereo images of a city block that have been taken from several different high angles. A single pair of stereo images does not contain sufficient data to construct a full, unambiguous description of an area, since some features will be obscured by nearby buildings and details in one photograph may be hard to decipher. The system begins with the first in the series of stereo photographs and identifies characteristic features such as the corners of buildings. But the initial information is used to construct a hypothesis of the scene which is then confirmed, modified or elaborated using the information in subsequent images. Once the hypothesis has been constructed, 3D Mosiac is able to work in a top down way, in addition to its bottom up processing, since each new image is used to confirm elements in the model which are uncertain, and to clarify ambiguities and fill in details. Information is therefore built in an incremental way and the computer keeps an account of which parts of the hypothesis have been confirmed and which remain uncertain. The end result of the process is to generate a computer model of the city block which can be displayed from any chosen angle.

An alternative approach is not to interpret the whole aerial photograph but to concentrate only on those objects that the computer can understand and identify. ACRONYM is able to pick out wide-bodied jets in photographs taken above airports. The photographs contain a number of straight edges and boundaries produced by trucks, roads, runways, and airport buildings as well as by aircraft, but the wide-bodied jets have particular characteristics that can be picked out by the computer system. ACRONYM looks at wing angles and the relative lengths of wings and bodies and uses these characteristics to distinguish between various aircraft.

Figure 6–7
An aerial photograph to be processed by the ACRONYM system.
Courtesy Rodney Brooks

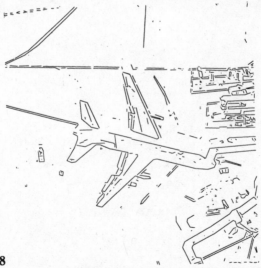

Figure 6–8
ACRONYM first uses an edge detector to pick out line segments
in the image.

Courtesy Rodney Brooks

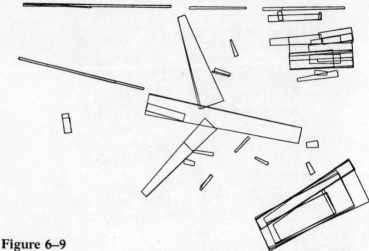

Figure 6–9
The general scene is then represented in terms of a "ribbon description".

Courtesy Rodney Brooks

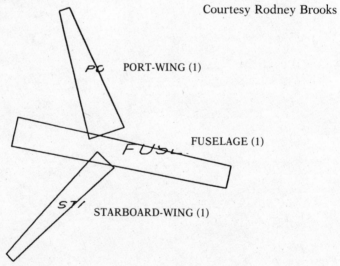

PORT-WING (1)

FUSELAGE (1)

STARBOARD-WING (1)

Figure 6–10
Finally ACRONYM interprets the image and correctly identifies its various elements.

ACRONYM

ACRONYM uses the following table of constraints
to identify wide-bodied jets. Units are in meters.

ENG-DISP-GAP ϵ [6,10]
ENG-DISP ϵ [0,4]
ENG-GAP ϵ [7,10]
STAB-ATTACH ϵ [3,5]
R-ENG-ATTACHMENT ϵ [3,5]
ENG-OUT ϵ [5,12]
WING-ATTACHMENT ϵ [20,40]
  WING-ATTACHMENT ⩾ 0.4*FUSELAGE-
  LENGTH
  WING-ATTACHMENT ⩽ 0.6*FUSELAGE-
  LENGTH
STAB-RATIO ϵ [0.2,0.55]
STAB-SWEEP-BACK ϵ [3, 7]
STAB-LENGTH ϵ [7.6, 13]
STAB-THICK ϵ [0.7, 1.1]
STAB-WIDTH ϵ [5, 11]
RUDDER-RATIO ϵ [0.3, 0.4]
RUDDER-SWEEP-BACK ϵ [3, 9]
RUDDER-LENGTH ϵ [8.5, 14.2]
RUDDER-X-HEIGHT ϵ [7, 13]
RUDDER-X-WIDTH ϵ [0.7, 1.1]
WING-RATIO ϵ [0.35, 0.45]
WING-THICK ϵ [1.5, 2.5]
WING-WIDTH ϵ [7, 12]
  WING-WIDTH ⩽ 0.5*WING-LENGTH
WING-LIFT ϵ [1,2]
WING-SWEEP-BACK ϵ [13, 18]
WING-LENGTH ϵ [22, 33.5]
  WING-LENGTH ⩾ 2*WING-WIDTH
                              continued

```
    WING-LENGTH ≥ 0.43*FUSELAGE-LENGTH
    WING-LENGTH ≤ 0.65*FUSELAGE-LENGTH
REAR-ENGINE-LENGTH ε [6, 10]
ENGINE-LENGTH ε [4, 7]
ENGINE-RADIUS ε [1, 1.8]
FUSELAGE-RADIUS ε [2.5, 4]
FUSELAGE-LENGTH ε [40, 70]
    FUSELAGE-LENGTH ≥ 1.66666666*WING-
    ATTACHMENT
    FUSELAGE-LENGTH ≥ 1.53846154*WING-
    LENGTH
    FUSELAGE-LENGTH ≤ 2.5*WING-ATTACH-
    MENT
    FUSELAGE-LENGTH ≤ 2.3255814*WING-
    LENGTH
R-ENG-QUANT ε [0, 1]
    R- ENG- QUANT ≤ 2 + -1*F-ENG-QUANT
F-ENG-QUANT ε [1, 2]
    F-ENG-QUANT ≤ 2 + −1*R-ENG-QUANT
```

General Vision and the Artist's Eye

As we move from the world of blocks and aerial photographs to a world of faces, office furniture, and outdoor scenes the problem of vision becomes even more complicated. Various vision systems have been designed that will, for example, identify items in an office. In the case of office scenes the computer is given information on the general appearance and characteristic features and functions of telephones, desks, chairs, and so on which are then identified. But none of these systems is wholly successful. They are prototypes that work under certain restricted conditions but cannot be readily extended to more general situations without the amount of computing time involved becoming exorbitantly high.

Earlier in this chapter it was remarked that the problem

with designing vision systems is that we take our own ability to see for granted and it is therefore particularly difficult for us to gain information on our own vision by introspection. But this statement can be qualified for there is one situation in which the clues to seeing are rendered more explicit and this is in painting. If the reader looks at reproductions of some paintings with the topic of this chapter in mind, he may obtain an insight into how the human visual system works and the complexity of the problem that face vision system designers.

Painters who attempt to represent the visual world must face the challenge of reproducing in paint on a flat canvas such factors as distance, depth, solidity, the effects of light, the values of colors, movement, the appearance of surfaces, and the general integration of objects into a scene.* [A particularly rewarding study of how this is done is given by E. H. Gombrich in *Art and Illusion* (Princeton University Press, Princeton 1972).]

In a sense, this process is the reverse of the problem faced by a computer vision system which tries to deduce a three-dimensional scene from the information contained in a flat image. The painter for his part must understand and make careful use of a number of visual clues which, taken together,

---

*A study of paintings often demonstrates how an artist's observations and intuitions have led him to discoveries about vision long before they have been made by science. A case in point is the apparent change in colors during twilight as rods in the retina begin to take over from the more color-sensitive cones. Such an effect was known to the Dutch painters of the 17th century. In our own century cinematography has anticipated additional discoveries. Editing and montage could be thought of as building up a visual scene in the same way as the eye's natural Circadian movements. Even more interesting is the intercutting of close-ups and the use of the zoom effect, which anticipated the discovery that the fovea is represented on the visual cortex by far more cells than the rest of the retina. In some intuitive fashion the early filmmakers realized that, as the eye moves to some object of interest, that object will in fact fill the whole internal visual scene.

act on the eye to produce the illusion of depth, solidity, and distance. In computer vision similar clues are also detected and, when combined with general knowledge about the world, build up an understanding of a scene. Probably the best known of these clues is that of perspective, said to have been discovered in the Renaissance in Florence by the architect Brunelleschi and applied to painting by Masaccio. The mathematician knows perspective as projective geometry, the projection onto a plane of three-dimensional objects. Computer vision systems use the rules of perspective in reverse as they move from the flat primal sketch, based on edges and boundaries, to three-dimensional object centered representation.*

Perspective is the only one of the ways in which a painter can give the illusion of depth. Even before Brunelleschi painters were able to suggest objects in space and some of the clues that they employed are also used in vision research. For example, if a tree in a painting is smaller than a man then clearly the tree must be in the background and the man in the foreground. Being able to understand this clue depends on recognizing each object and having some general knowledge about their respective sizes. Objects in space that are at varying distances may cast shadows on each other and a closer object may partially obscure a distant one. Again knowledge about properties of three-dimensional space helps us to extract information about depth. Other clues

---

[These rules of perspective are well understood, but what is particularly interesting is that they are rarely used in a consistent way by artists for a more integrated feel can be given to a painting if certain objects are portrayed from slightly different viewpoints and therefore in different perspectives. In fact, a true perspective painting in which each line goes towards the same vanishing point can look curiously unnatural. This observation may be a clue to the way our own eyes and brains build up a scene; eye and head movements result in a multiplicity of viewpoints and, in addition, our brains may combine these image centered views with other object centered representations that are stored in its memory.]

come from texture and color which can suggest a common surface; once the eye accepts a particular region as being all of a piece then it is possible to drape that region across a body and indicate something of its solidity. Gradations of texture can be used in a surface that recedes into the distance since pebbles, rocks, or tiles on a floor appear to become smaller the further they are from the eye.

Clues about relative size, perspective, overlapping objects, and gradations in texture are a few of the ways in which painters have suggested depth, solidity, and distance. But even when all these are employed together by a skilful landscape painter like Claude Lorrain, it may still be necessary to add more specific visual indicators to clear up ambiguities in depth, for example, by having a river or road meander through the planes of depth in a landscape and even by linking these planes through a bridge placed across the river. Painters, therefore, understand that producing the illusion of depth on a flat surface requires considerable artifice and that even the most naturalistic paintings employ carefully constructed devices that aid the eye in interpreting objects, clarifying ambiguities, and comprehending a visual context. As Edgar Degas put it, "There's more trickery to a painting than in the greatest crime."

Looking at paintings and how they are constructed gives us some hint as to how far computer vision systems will have to evolve before they are able to interpret and understand how a flat image relates to a three-dimensional scene. As an exercise the reader may like to construct "windows" or varying size, cut from a piece of cardboard or paper, and move them across a reproduction of a well-known painting. By trying to identify what is shown in each window the reader will become aware of the visual clues that the painter has chosen and how these clues have been emphasized in order to clear up ambiguities and suggest depth.

Stereo Vision and Motion

One important way in which indications of depth can be

obtained directly is through stereo vision. Computer stereo systems can employ two cameras, but more generally use a series of images taken with one camera from a variety of positions. CART, a robot we shall meet in the next chapter, has an eye which moves along its track and takes images from several slightly different positions. CART processes these images and then moves through the room and takes a further series from its new position. In this way it can identify the relative positions in space of objects it must avoid. Another approach is to use a fixed camera but vary the angle of illumination so that shadows, highlights, and the light reflected from each surface changes from picture to picture.

Determination of distance from the camera using stereo images can be done directly by triangulation, provided that the distance between the two camera locations is known. This technique is no different from that used by surveyors as they determine distances. The tricky part, however, comes in selecting a common feature to lock onto in both pictures. Since the appearance of a solid object changes with the viewing angle it is no trivial matter for a computer to pick exactly the same point on an object in both images. A good approach is to select a characteristic feature such as the corner of a window or the edge of a cube, but even this may be ambiguous if there are several such edges and corners in the scene, and triangulation for distance (which is itself designed to provide additional information) therefore requires some prior interpretation of the image.

Another clue about distance comes from a sensor that is not found in humans but is skillfully employed by such animals as bats and dolphins; that is, direct rangefinding. By bouncing laser or ultrasound signals from an object and measuring the delay time for the signal's return, it is possible to compute the distance to that object. Another approach is to scan the object with a strip or spot of light and accurately determine the distance to that spot using triangulation. Using a rangefinder it is possible to scan an object in sequence and build up a representation of its contours. Contours from rangefinding can be built into a clear picture of the shape and distance of surface and are in this respect like the specific information that was expressed by a primal sketch of the blocks world.

Moving the camera is another way in which information on depth and objects can be obtained. A series of images from a moving television camera is a good way of picking out an object against a background. If you closes one eye and move the head from side to side you will notice how nearby objects appear to move with respect to the background; a similar effect can be extracted from the sequences of television images. Some systems can track moving objects through a street scene provided that there are some overall restrictions on the way the object moves, for example, if a car that moves across the screen suddenly turns and moves towards the camera it will probably be lost. Working with pictures in motion is no trivial task, since television pictures of a scene contain a vast amount of additional raw data compared with a single photograph and only a fraction of this information can be processed in real time. In addition the objects themselves change their appearance as they move into areas of shadow, catch the sun, or change orientation. If the visual scene is not too complex and objects in it do not change their appearance too rapidly, then it is possible to track them successfully; one such system is able to automatically track clouds in sequences of satellite images.

Identification

As the computer system detects and unfolds its visual clues, computes distance information, and combines this information with general knowledge about the world, it may also be able to identify objects in the general scene. The simplest way to do this is to use some form of template matching in which silhouettes or other characteristic features of objects stored in the computer's memory are recalled and matched against a series of primal sketches, intrinsic images, or a two-dimensional sketch. After this has

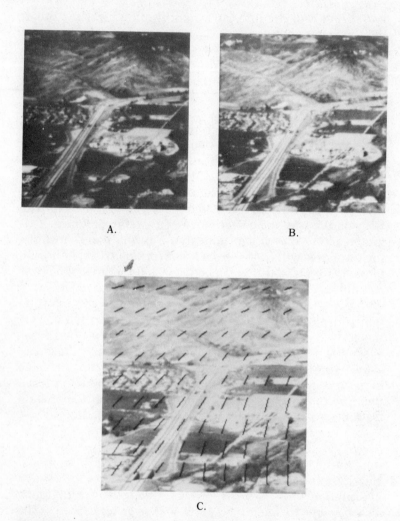

A.

B.

C.

Figure 6–11

The two images (a) and (b) are from a sequence taken from an airplane. They have been used to compute a velocity field which represents the airplane's apparent motion over the ground (c).

Courtesy E. Hildreth

been done the computer will move from a camera centered representation in which the image is a function of such incidentals as camera angle, illumination, shadows, overlappings, and so on, to an object centered representation in which the intrinsic shape and geometric properties of the object are made explicit. At the level of an object centered representation the computer may be in a position to take some action with respect to an object, for example, instruct a mechanical arm to assemble or manipulate the object, or make some logical deductions about the object's function and its relationship to other objects in the scene. When this step occurs the computer can be said to have successfully dealt with the visual aspects of a scene. However, the problem of actually "understanding" the scene in terms of a generalized symbolic representation that can be used for making inferences, deductions, and comparisons (just as humans are able to contemplate and think about what they see) remains a major research problem.

Representing a Scene

One approach to the problem of representing objects in a scene is based on linguistics and works by stringing together geometric primitives such as lines and surfaces in the same way that words are strung together to make sentences. For example, a cube can be defined by stringing together equal lines, and a cylinder represented by a sentence using "sides" and "top." Just as an infinite number of sentences can be constructed out of a finite number of words together with the rules of syntax, so an infinite number of different figures can be represented by sentences built from shape primitives. The advantage of this approach is that a large number of internal geometric models do not have to be stored in the computer since objects are classified according to their geometric sentences and sentences themselves can be constructed within the computer. In its present form the theory may be adequate for representing objects that are not too complicated but is it not clear how it can be generalized to more general objects with all their complexity, structure, and detail.

Another solution comes from the drawing books of an earlier age in which students were taught to build the human figure out of spheres, cylinders, and cubes. A figure can be crudely represented by a cylinder and a sphere, one for the body and the other for the head and, at a more detailed level, by several cylinders of varying size. The advantage of this approach is that the details of a figure can be built in an hierarchical fashion, the arm first being represented by two cylinders hinged at the elbow with its higher level description including the hand with individual jointed cylinders for each finger.

ACRONYM, which we met earlier in this chapter, uses simple geometrical shapes to build its representation of wide-bodied jets. The system was designed to apply to a range of visual domains using an overall program with individual subprograms written for particular classes of objects and can identify electric motors in addition to jets. A motor is defined, for example, as having from three to six equally spaced flanges with maximum and minimum lengths for the main cylinder, and boundaries on the ratio of cylinder length to diameter. ACRONYM is therefore able to recognize and generate representations for a range of shapes that fall within the same general classification, even when parts of an object are obscured. Other general vision systems employ different ways of representing the objects they identify but the final point is generally the same; to interpret the scene and to produce an object centered representation that is independent of the particular details of viewing angle or photographic process. This final step may be in terms of a representation, in terms of hierarchical solid shapes, linguistic sentences using visual primitives, or some other approach, which can then be manipulated or acted upon by the computer itself.

Most general vision systems are still at the stage of laboratory experiments or prototypes and few of them have been translated into commercial systems. In 1975 DARPA, the advanced funding program of the U.S. Department of Defense, began its Image Understanding Program, the aim of which was to advance research into general theories of vision by integrating approaches from physics, neurophysiology, computer science, artificial intelligence, and image processing. In addition, the program had a practical goal of interpreting photographs and understanding maps. Several of the vision systems that have been discussed in this chapter are the product of DARPA funding.

In Japan the importance of vision research was recognized in the late 1960s and a program called the Pattern Information Processing System ran from 1971 to 1980 with a $100 million budget. This project included scene analysis along with speech recognition and language understanding and had as one of its goals the development of a reliable character reader that could recognize printed and handwritten Japanese. A significant byproduct of the program is the commanding position now occupied by Japanese optical character readers all over the world. Japan's current long-range project in this field is called Optical Measurement and Control Systems and will run until 1986 with a budget again around $100 million. The current success of these projects may come from Japan's tendency to attack immediate practical problems using any tricks that are available and translate the results into computer hardware. Up to now the approach has paid off but it remains to be seen how effective it will be in the face of long-term general problems in computer vision.

Robot Vision

The goal of a robot vision system is to compute required visual data in real time. The philosophy that guides the design of such systems is not so much to develop the most general solution to a particular problem but to come up with a fast and reliable program that can be converted into computer hardware. One approach is to give the vision system the maximum possible assistance by arranging the

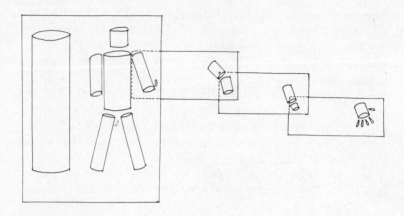

Figure 6–12
A human figure can be represented in terms of cylinders in an hierarchical fashion.

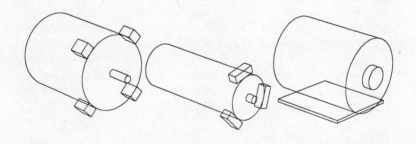

Figure 6–13
ACRONYM builds up its image of electrical motors in terms of cylinders and rectangular boxes.

Credit: Rodney Brooks

workplace to produce the best possible images. Painted or targeted objects are arranged against a high contrast background in characteristic positions and without overlapping each other. Fixed lighting is angled to provide sharp contrasts and accentuate the dimensionality of components, and sequential lighting exposes different features and enhances depth and shadows. Flashing lights can be used to "freeze" an object and determine its speed of movement. Strips of light that are shone on successive parts of a component will expose curves, kinks, and bends as well as reveal details of any textures. Finally, the computer eye itself can move or scan an object and it may even be placed in the palm of a robot arm to allow for closer inspection.

A number of commercially available systems interpret two-dimensional scenes such as bar codes, print, fibers, small particles, and chromosomes; generalizations of these products are used for inspection of integrated circuits and manufactured parts. In the mid-1970s Hitachi designed a robot that locates the position of leads and solders them onto transistor chips. Its vision system matches standard visual patterns on the chip against information stored in its memory and uses this data to compute the coordinates of each lead, information is then passed to the automatic soldering unit so that the whole system is able to process some 2,000 chips per hour with 99 percent accuracy.

Some general vision systems have reached a highly developed state and are available commercially. The best known of these was designed at Stanford University. The Stanford system uses up to four cameras and a flash lamp to freeze moving objects. It can be programmed directly or taught to recognize an object by presenting it with silhouettes from several different orientations. The SRI system has been used to:

- Identity industrial parts that are hung from a rack, stacked in a box, or distributed randomly in bins and on a conveyor belt.

233

- Inspect rivet heads in an aircraft subassembly.
- Identify components that tumble on a specially constructed table.
- Inspect an assembly to ensure that all its parts are correctly matched and located.
- Attached to a robot arm, a camera eye will follow a target during welding or bolt insertion.

Other vision systems include the Karlsruhe system that also learns from silhouettes and performs vision processing in real time and the Nottingham system that combines information from tactile sensors with special visual characteristics such as holes, areas and boundaries.

Hitachi in Japan has a two-armed robot that uses its eight eyes for vision. Its cameras are mounted to give side and top views with a mobile eye located in the palm of one of the robot hands to allow for closer inspection. Hitachi's robot also processes data from a series of sensors that give information on touch, pressure, and the forces used in handling and assembly; with the help of all this information it is able to assemble vacuum cleaners automatically. CONSIGHT at General Motors can locate and pick up randomly distributed castings from a conveyor belt. Since the castings are of a similar color to the conveyor belt it is necessary to arrange the lighting for maximum contrast. Lights are placed on either side of the camera to produce a contour of the object together with sharp shadows which give additional information.

Some researchers feel that a significant advance in robot vision will come about when range data is used in combination with CAD (computer aided design) in flexible manufacturing factories. We will meet the CAD system in the following chapter, but briefly the computer's memory contains an exact mathematical model of every component used in manufacturing and these models can be matched against contours derived from rangefinding data. In this way it becomes possible to carry out all the necessary mechanical manipulations on an object without actually recognizing it at a deeper level.

In some cases, therefore, computer vision is sufficiently skilled to help robots and other devices take appropriate actions. But where general scenes in an unstructured world are involved the computer is less successful. We must therefore accept that although computer vision can be a useful tool in restricted situations, a general vision system remains a dream of the future. Theories of human vision are not yet fully developed and there are many features about seeing that are still ambiguous or unclear. Some scientists are hopeful that as psychologists work hand in hand with AI researchers, many of these issues will be resolved towards the end of the century and that some time in the 1990s a successful general computer vision system will be finally built. Others feel that the problems involved are particularly deep ones and that while they may be challenging and exciting to work on, their secrets will not be fully unraveled for some time to come.

CHAPTER 7
Robots and Manufacturing

When you think about it, robots are familiar objects; they always seem to have been around. For most of us they began with those movies we saw in childhood, the clanking metallic monster that emerged from the space ship or the electronic intelligence of some future civilization. I can well remember Gort, the galactic policeman with the power to destroy planets from the 1951 "The Day the Earth Stood Still" and also Robbie, the willing helper from "Forbidden Planet" (1957). My own children delight in R2D2 and 3P0 from the Star War series and on television they have seen Marvin, the depressed robot with a brain the size of a planet, from Douglas Adams' *Hitchhiker's Guide to the Galaxy*.

Robots are a significant part of the collective unconscious of the twentieth-century imagination. As children we were given robots as toys for Christmas, we made robots with our Lego sets, and, dressed in a cardboard box, we even became robots. In our imagination robots grew all powerful and invincible with the ability to crush all before them. As we played with them on the kitchen floor did they come to represent the uncontrollable urges we each felt inside us? Did each of us construct our own Frankenstein monster of the imagination?

In their various guises robots stretch far back in history. In the first century BC, Hero of Alexandria was supposed to have constructed birds that could fly and sing. In the middle ages Albertus Magnus is said to have possessed a bronze head that could talk and alchemists like Paracelsus claimed to have breathed life into the homonculii they had created. By the eighteenth century, however, the moving manmade figure had become a reality. Gifted instrument makers devoted their talents to the construction of life-size clockwork automata that were able to write, draw, and play musical instruments.

At the start of our own century the eccentric genius of electric power, Nikola Tesla*, was experimenting with radio controlled mechanisms and dreamed of:

no mere mechanical contrivance, comprising levers, screws, wheels, clutches, and nothing more, but a machine embodying a higher principle which will enable it to perform its duties as though it had intelligence, experience, reason, judgment, a mind. . . . It will be able, independent of any operator, left entirely to itself, to perform, in response to external influences affecting its sensitive organs, a great variety of acts and operations as if it had intelligence. It will be able to follow a course laid out or obey orders given far in advance; it will be capable of distinguishing between what it ought and what it ought not to do, and of making experiences or, otherwise stated, of recording impressions which will definitely affect its subsequent actions."*

Tesla had a clear anticipation of an intelligent robot planned for the late 1980s.

**Peat, David "In Search of Nikola Tesla," Ashgrove Press, 1983

Robotics could only become a practical possibility once electronic computers were combined with the theories of cybernetics and with engineering advances in automatic devices. While this research was in its infancy Isaac Asimov had already written his classic series of stories *I. Robot* (1950), which traced the evolution of the robot from a crude mechanical worker to the inhabitants of some future world that are indistinguishable from humans. *I. Robot* is particularly famous for its statement of the three laws of robotics (which were first formulated by Asimov in 1940):

1. A robot may not injure a human being, or through inaction allow a human being to come to harm.
2. A robot must obey the orders given it by human beings except where such orders would conflict with the first law.
3. A robot must protect its own existence as long as such protection does not conflict with the first or second law.

These rules for robotic conduct are actually quite sophisticated and lie far beyond capacity of present day AI systems to interpret. To begin with Asimov's robot must be able to recognize a human being as some autonomous being, existing in the outside world, capable of giving orders, and distinguished from an animal or another robot; a sort of Turing test in reverse. The robot must also have a sense of identity, and be able to make a particularly sophisticated distinction between thought and action. In order to understand laws 1 and 3 the robot must first realize that certain of its thoughts exist only as some internal process or display while others result in actions in the world; for example, that speech and movement can affect objects in the surroundings. The robot must, therefore, be capable of understanding all the complex world of change that lies around it and realizing that some of this change is due to the actions of beings like humans, animals, and machines and the physical processes of nature, and some are the direct result of its own actions. So to apply

Asimov's laws of robotics requires a highly sophisticated computer in that machine, something with an intelligence that lies far beyond present capabilities.

Of course, the future may hold an ironic twist for us, for when such a highly sophisticated machine intelligence is eventually evolved it is probable that Asimov's first law will not be applied to it. Much of the funding for AI research comes from military sources that are attempting to develop intelligent weapon systems and computers capable of taking control during a nuclear war. What could be more welcome to the military mind of some country than a robot doomsday weapon, located far out in space or at the bottom of the ocean? Such a robot would remain forever silent and simply monitor the world for the outbreak of nuclear war. Its prime directive would be to assess the situation and at some predetermined point to launch missiles or activate laser and particle beam weapons at targets it had determined. The last thing such a robot would require would be a directive forbidding it to harm a human being.

Industrial Robots.

Three decades after Asimov's book had appeared, fact is still attempting to catch up with fiction. The robots envisioned by Asimov, Tesla, and the science fiction movies of our childhood are in fact general robots capable of carrying out a wide variety of tasks in a very general environment. By contrast the industrial robots that are presently being used in factories are more restricted in their abilities.

Some current research projects are devoted to the development of general robots. However, when it comes to economic and social implications of robotics, the simple robot work horses that are already in our factories may well turn out to be the most revolutionary things around. The reason is that about one third of our workforce is involved in manufacturing and many of their jobs are involved in joining assembly, the very tasks that can be performed best by robots.

When robots are first brought into a factory they may perform tasks that are hazardous, arduous, or simply dull

The Myth of the Golem

Of all the stories and legends concerning robots none has struck the imagination of the AI community so much as that of Rabbi Loew of Prague and his golem. Indeed some of the pioneers in the AI field have admitted to a legend that their families were descended from the learned rabbi. One of Norbet Wiener's books was entitled *God and Golem*, and the Czechoslovak Technical University has a robot project named Goal Oriented Electronic Manipulator or GOALEM for short.

In Kabbalistic tradition the golem is incomplete or embryonic life. Adam, for example, existed in the golem state until God breathed life into him. Throughout the Middle Ages there were stories of learned men who created golems, creatures made out of earth, that were animated by means of magical talismen and rituals. The most powerful of these talismen was the tetragramaton, or holy name of God, written on a parchment and placed inside the creature's mouth.

In the late sixteenth century anti-Semitism was rife in Europe. It had been, for a time, averted by the brilliant debates of Judah Loew Ben Bezalel, Chief Rabbi of Prague and friend of Tycho Brahe and Kepler. However, when a Catholic priest named Thaddeus began to stir up hatred against the Jews, Loew had a dream in which he was told "Make a Golem of clay and you will destroy the entire Jew-baiting company."

After studying on the great magical books, the Safer Yezirath, Loew and his two assistants car-
continued

241

ried out a series of ritual incantations and purifications while building an eight-foot clay creature. Finally they placed the sacred talisman in the creature's mouth and Joseph Golem came to life.

While Rabbi Loew had solved the problem of animation he was not particularly advanced in speech synthesis so Joseph Golem remained dumb but able to understand verbal commands. He performed menial acts in the temple, patrolled the streets, and generally protected the Jews of Prague.

At some point in Joseph Golem's career the Rabbi decided to deactivate it by removing the sacred name from its mouth. There are various legends as to why the golem was destroyed. One suggests that the Jews, now being safe, no longer had need of a protector. Another, which is used in Gustav Meyrink's 1915 novel, *The Golem* tells how the creature went on a rampage, attacking innocent people and even its creator.

and soul destroying for humans. Soon additional economic pressures come into force and robots began to perform a variety of other tasks. In our present economic climate it appears that labor costs will continue to rise while the price of robots falls. It has been estimated, for example, that each time labor costs rise by $1 per hour, 1,000 new robot applications become economically attractive.

Each year more and more robots will be introduced into factories throughout the world. Once installed these machines tend to act as catalysts for further change. A computer on the shop floor calls into question the whole manufacturing and designing process and fits most naturally into an overall computer controlled factory.

But what is an industrial robot? Someone has likened it to

be a worker who is blindfolded and strapped to a chair with one arm tied behind his back. One should also add that this worker is particularly simple-minded, yet tireless in the tasks he performs. The modern robot is essentially a microprocessor controlled machine arm that can be used in such tasks like simple assembly, welding, paint spraying, and loading palets.

To understand how robot control works just think how you would perform a simple task like reaching out, with your eyes closed, and picking up a book off a table in front of you. To begin with your arm must be sufficiently flexible to move under the direction of your brain. Your brain must have some internal representation of where the table is located and of the movements of your arm with respect to this table. As your arm comes close to the book you would probably begin to use your sense of touch to determine when your fingers are in contact with the object. Finally your brain will instruct the fingers to lock onto the book and lift it.

An industrial robot works in essentially the same way and can perform similar simple tasks. To begin with, its arm contains hinged or rotatable joints that are able to orientate themselves freely. For heavy work this arm is powered hydraulically, smaller arms use pneumatic power, while for precision of movement, an electrically powered arm is used. At the end of the arm is a "wrist" which accepts a variety of devices and tools such as grippers, welding guns, and paint sprayers. During the course of a particular manufacturing process the wrist may interchange its tools several times.

The arm itself comes under the control of a microprocessor which is generally located some distance from the machine itself. In the simplest industrial robots no intelligent decisions are made and the processor simply confines itself to carrying out a series of preprogrammed operations. But it may also be capable of detecting and compensating for errors.

243

To carry out its instructions correctly the microprocessor must also know where the arm is located and what it is doing. In our example of picking up a book the human arm gives this sensory feedback directly to the brain. The robot arm attempts something similar by having sensors at each joint that relay information about the joint's position and how fast it is rotating and otherwise moving. In addition, the arm can give information about its orientation with respect to other machines around it, by means of pressure switches which are activated when the arm comes into pre-programmed contact with some other device.

Control of the arm takes place in one of two ways, or by a combination of both of them. If the robot is engaged in paint spraying, for example, then its every movement is exactly determined to give the correct sweep to the spray gun. Such continuous control requires that the full path or trajectory for every movement of the arm to be stored in the micro-processor's memory. In assembly tasks, however, the arm may be required to perform a sequence of actions such as picking up an object, clearing a machine, or tightening a nut but with no particular demands on what it does in between. In this point to point approach the program contains instructions about particular tasks and the arm then takes its own shortest path between each of them.

Even with the absence of machine vision and intelligent decision making, the microprocessor generally has its work cut out to control the arm. Not only should it perform a sequence of tasks correctly but it must constantly monitor the arm to detect differences between the preprogrammed movements and what is being received from sensors on the arm. If any errors are detected the computer must compensate for them or present a diagnosis to a human.

The actual programming is carried out in two general ways. In one, the machine is "walked" through the task just as if it were a child. For example, the robot is taken by the hand and actually guided from task to task. The resulting movements are then stored on, say, a microprocessor floppy disk. The advantage of this approach is that a skilled machinist can instruct the robot to perform tasks he has already worked on and, if the particular factory is an enlightened one, this same machinist will then be upgraded to become a robot supervisor rather than a machine minder.

An alternative approach is to have the task programmed by an engineer seated at a microprocessor terminal. This may be best in a large factory where several robots are required to carry out their tasks in a sequential fashion. In such an integrated approach each microprocessor comes under the supervision of a main computer so that individual robots can be speeded up or slowed down to keep pace with their neighbors.

Robots and Factories

The first wave of these robots began with the formulation of Uniamation, a U.S. company devoted to the manufacturing of industrial robots. Its first model, UNIMATE, was produced in 1961 and today many thousands of its descendants, costing between $30,000 and $60,000, can be found throughout the world. Such robots are the workhorses of a new industrial revolution; they make more efficient use of expensive manufacturing machines and help to cut manufacturing costs. They are generally more reliable than the machines they service and will rapidly recover their capital costs. By 1990 it has been estimated that some 200,000 robots will be at work with a billion dollars being spent each year on new models.

Most industrial robots are strictly limited in the range of things they can do. They need a human, or some mechanical device, to sort out component parts before they can pick them up. Their powers of inspection are limited and they are very intolerant of errors in their environment. If a part that has to be manipulated is incorrectly placed on a workbench or lies in the wrong orientation then the robot may be unable to deal with it. So, while modern robots work well enough for routine jobs, there is already a need for something that is more versatile and can handle a wider variety of tasks. The general robots which are beginning to evolve need not be programmed in a step by step way but are given an overall goal and general knowledge about manufacturing processes, and with the help of an intelligent brain, machine vision, and touch feedback, the robot will work out its own approach to each problem and will even adjust to changing conditions in the future.

The general robot therefore involves a combination of all the AI issues we have discussed up to this point. It uses machine vision to locate parts and build up a general picture of its environment, it calls on its problem solving ability to work out the best way to assemble a piece of equipment and it may even use natural language to interact with factory engineers. These intelligent robots will probably work hand in hand with their less intelligent brothers who confine themselves to more routine tasks. But the general robot remains a thing of the future. There are models being developed in university and industrial laboratories but general robots will not appear on the factory floor until the end of the 1980s.

More and more small- and medium-sized companies will purchase anywhere from 2 to 100 robots and begin to transform the factory floor. Where these robots are performing tasks that are hazardous, arduous, dull, and unpeasant then they will be welcomed by the workforce in general. Robots are ideally built to perform the sort of mindless, repetitive tasks that appear soul destroying in a factory. But what will happen as more intelligent robots begin to replace machinists and craftsmen? Will skilled workers be promoted to machine supervisors or demoted to machine minders?

Many predictions have been made about the future, as more and more robots are used in manufacturing, and perhaps we can agree on how this future will look. It is clear that the whole nature of work will change and that the majority of people who are at present employed in factories will be doing something very different. But what? Some people argue that there will be massive unemployment or the artificial creation of work. Others point to Japan, a major user of robots, and argue that its employment record is a healthy one. But Japan is so very different in its society and history from the West that it is not an easy matter to make comparisons on the impact of new technologies. But the implications of robots and artificial intelligence in the future of work lies beyond this book, and all that can be said is that industrial nations have already taken their first steps along the road to computer controlled manufacturing and it is unlikely that they are now going to turn back. Change is inevitable but as to how it happens may still be within our control.

Flexible Manufacturing

At present about half of the present industrial robots are being used in the automotive industry which is already itself heavily automated. But their greatest impact is going to be in the medium to small manufacturing companies. This is because the robot is a flexible and relatively inexpensive worker. Armed with new grippers and tools it can be freshly programmed and led through a range of tasks. Robots are ideal for companies which make a variety of products or whose models are likely to change from time to time. Conveyor belt assembly lines can, of course, use robots but their unchanging sequence of operations does not make full use of a robot's capacities.

One example of how a robot has been used may suffice to illustrate this point. TI Creda Ltd. in the United Kingdom manufactures ovens which require a vitreous enamel coating. The paint itself is too abrasive and unpleasant to make spraying an attractive job for humans so the ovens were hand dipped into a bath. The work was heavy and the coating itself tended to be uneven and to clog previously drilled holes which then had to be cleared manually. The company's solution therefore was to purchase a robot and train it to spray enamel. The process worked well and soon there were two robots, working side by side during an 18-hour workday. Within 2 years the robots had recovered their cost of purchasing and installation, were saving the company 40 percent in enamel, and were turning out an improved product.

As robots are introduced into a factory they act as catalysts for further transformation. One has only to observe the uneasy confrontation between a robot and the machine it serves to understand why. A week or a year ago that same machine was being operated by a human, with eyes, hands, and delicate fingers. The shop floor machine had evolved to be used by someone of human height, with a human's strength and tolerance for error, and to accept human based tools and processes that had their origins in the first industrial revolution. The actual manufacturing process is also human based as parts were bolted together and metal pegs were fitted into carefully drilled holes as they have been for the past 200 years.

When the new robot confronts this shop floor machine it faces a fossil that represents generations of human based manufacturing. It must carry out tasks that are best suited to human fingers and it may even have to reach over a safety cage that was placed there to protect the skin and bone of careless humans. There are things that a robot can do well and others that it does poorly but it is clear that the idea of a robot attempting to work with a machine specifically designed for a human is totally illogical. Clearly, as soon as a robot is placed on the factory floor, the whole way in which parts are designed, assembled, and manufactured is called into question.

History, however, shows us that this curious confusion of old and new technologies is far from uncommon for when some innovation appears, it is often first used in very traditional ways. For example, the world's first iron bridge was built in 1779 to span the River Severn at Coalbrookdale in England. It rapidly became a center of attraction and "one of the great curiosities this nation or any other can boast of." It remains a curiosity today mainly because of its historic interest and its curious construction since although built of iron, it employs the wedges and dovetail joints of the carpenter and its shape resembles that of a masonry bridge. Engineers today estimate that the bridge contains far more iron than was needed but the eighteenth century builders, working in a totally new medium, tended to retain their traditional practices with wood and stone when it came to bridge building.

A similar fossilized technology can be seen in the first automobiles which were essentially horseless carriages with a combustion engine pulling in place of the animal. But who could have foreseen how this simple invention would have transformed the world and led to its roadways and the redesign of cities?

The impact of the robot upon the way things are manufactured and processed is unpredictable but far reaching. It is probable that its impact on manufacturing will be an accelerated one. Current opinion is that manufacturing will make greater use of snap fastenings and glues in place of rivets and bolts. In addition, new tools will emerge and the whole shape and function of components will change. Other technologies will be integrated with the industrial robot and the whole emphasis of the factory of the future will be towards integration and control. For example, smaller factories will strike a middle road between large scale automation and individual assembly. This approach is called *flexible manufacturing* and involves the microprocessor control of a series of machines and work stations. Using central control it becomes possible to rapidly change a manufacturing process and retool and reschedule the factory floor without significant capital outlay. Overall computer control of a series of robots and work stations is yet another quantum leap towards cheaper and more flexible manufacturing processes. As to how this integration will take place we shall leave for a later section of this chapter for the time has come to take a closer look at something we have up to now referred to as the general robot.

General Robots

In factories of the future some industrial robots will be required to carry out tasks that are far more advanced than those undertaken by their present day counterparts. Armed with computer vision and intelligent control systems they will be supplied with specifications of a new product and then work out their own approaches to manufacturing, inspection, and repair.

Mobile robots will be involved in maintenance and repair in hostile environments such as space, ocean beds, deserts, and arctic areas as well as in nuclear and chemical plants. These robots of the future will not only possess the faculties of vision and touch but new ones given to them by radar, infrared sensors, ultrasonic sensors, chemical sniffers, and the ability to respond to electrical and magnetic fields.

Serious work on general robots began in the mid-1960s with major projects at M.I.T., SRI, Stanford University, and the University of Edinburgh. With the exception of the SRI team, the groups concentrated on the problem of hand/eye coordination. Experimental robots were built that comprised a TV camera eye, a mechanical arm, and a supervising computer. Various approaches to machine vision were used to enable the robot to first identify objects scattered on a bench and then direct its arm to manipulate these objects. In the earliest experiments a highly controlled environment consisting of simply shaped blocks was used. Given a request to pick up a pyramid the computer had to detect that particular solid shape from its flat television image and then give the arm the necessary instructions to reach out and pick up the object.

As research continued the performance of some of these robots improved considerably. One at Stanford University, for example, graduated to working with an automobile water pump which it was able to assemble out of parts strewn about on a table. This represented a considerable advance in robotics and lay far beyond the capacity of any commercial system. However, it also exposed the extreme difficulty involved in solving the problems of vision and hand/eye coordination. These complex tasks required a great deal of computer processing and demanded either a large and fast mainframe computer or very long computing times.

It was one thing to build an experimental robot that would work under laboratory conditions. It was another to turn out commercial robots that will be reasonably priced, efficient, reliable and able to operate under a variety of factory conditions. Some experts feel that we will have to wait until the early 1990s before a commercial robot has the capability to deal in a general way with randomly placed components in a factory environment. Nevertheless, there is already a demand for robots which can carry out visual processing, for example, by using visual clues during assembly procedures, and which could be used for inspection and quality control in automated factories.

General Robots: Vision

There are several ways in which current computer vision systems can be adapted to produce commercial vision robots. One is to standardize and simplify the visual problems involved. Work areas can be specially illuminated and components painted to give high contrast with their background. Even the strategy of adding a target to a part that is to be picked up or manipulated can simplify the problem faced by the vision system. Another approach is to concentrate on immediate practical results rather than producing general solutions to the problem of vision. For example, scientists working on machine vision are often concerned with very general problems related to the psychology of vision, such as "How do we recognize what we see?" and "In what way does the brain process the visual information that is presented to the retina?" They attempt to build computer sys-

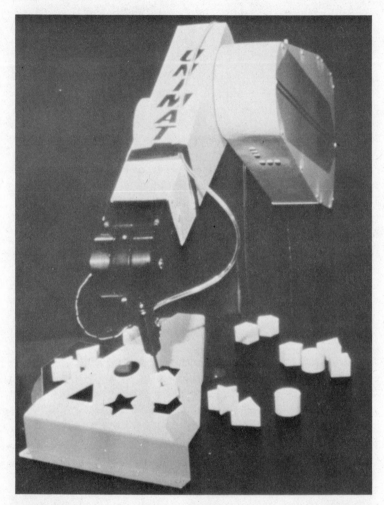

Figure 7–1

This standard robot arm has been fitted with a vision system (not shown) that enables it to select simple shapes and fit them into the appropriate holes. For precision work the final fitting would be guided by a force feedback system added to the robot's wrist.

Courtesy National Research Council of Canada

tems that armed with world knowledge about certain objects, will identify makes of aircraft, features on an aerial photograph, or familiar household objects. Engineers at M.I.T., however, argue that such solutions to the problem of vision may be too general in that they require, as we have seen, too much computing power. An alternative is to produce simpler, more practical solutions, for example, by using a light strip or *laser scanner*. This device scans the surface of an object and, acting as a rangefinder, computes the position of points on the surface. While the computer does not recognize or understand what it sees it does, however, create a direct three-dimensional map of the object as viewed from one angle. The technique is then to combine this three-dimensional scanning map with a three-dimensional model of components that is held in the computer's memory. As we shall see in the next section, CAD or computer aided design of a manufacturing process has, as its end result, full three-dimensional information on every component of the manufacturing process. So information from a strip scanner can be used directly to recognize and manipulate objects without the computer having to understand what it sees or be capable of using general vision. All the computer has to do is to transform and rotate its internal mathematical model until it matches with the laser scan that has been taken. The robot is, therefore, able to scan and identify components in front of it without needing to go through the more complex processes of three-dimensional reconstruction and vision recognition. In a sense the problem is reduced to a mathematical one of matching three-dimensional surfaces and, once this match is made, the computer can then direct the robot arm to take the necessary action.

Along with these pragmatic approaches engineers are also seeking ways to speed up these and other visual systems. For example, more advanced mathematical and computing approaches are being used and new and more efficient algorithms are being designed. In addition, the parallel computers that are discussed in Chapter 8 will be able to speed up

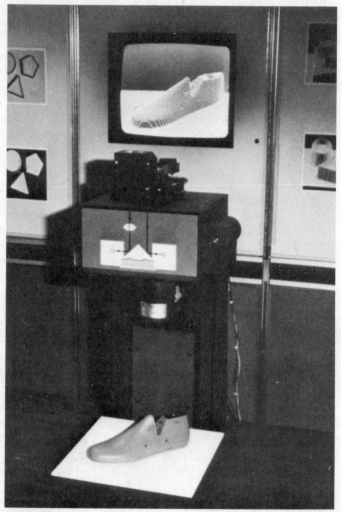

Figure 7–2
The National Research Council of Canada's laser range finder produces object-centered representations of solid objects using detailed information about their distance from the range finder.
(Courtesy National Research Council of Canada

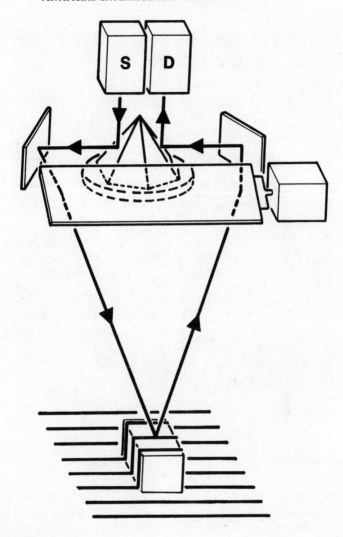

Figure 7–3
The system uses scanning beams to triangulate distances. A rotating and a tilting mirror are used to deflect the laser beams in the X and Y directions across the object.

Courtesy National Research Council of Canada

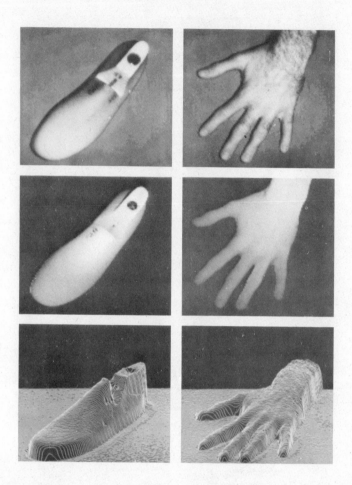

Figure 7–4

In the top photograph a familiar gray intensity map of a hand and a model shoe is produced in a TV camera. In the middle photograph intensity is not directly related to reflected light but to the distance from the vision system. Dark areas are farther away than light areas. This distance information is then used to compute object-centered images in the bottom pictures.

Courtesy National Research Council of Canada

vision processing. The current approach is to develop systems that will be fast and effective and can be easily transformed from the laboratory bench to the factory floor.

General Robots: Touch

Even with computer vision and laser rangefinding, the robot needs additional senses to help in its manipulations. A sense of touch and some feedback about the forces being applied gives valuable information as pieces are mated together and assembled. With computer vision, for example, a flat image, produced by a TV camera has to be interpreted by means of stereo images, shadows, and so on as coming from a solid object oriented in space. With the sense of touch, however, these qualities are perceived more directly because the object is held in the hand.

The GOALEM project of the Czechoslovak Technical University has built an anthromorphic hand that can successfully identify a series of simple shapes such as prisms, cones, pyramids, cylinders, and sphere. A robot hand, built at Draper Labs., MA, can assemble the parts of an automobile alternator using touch alone. This sense of touch is also important when it comes to picking up small objects from a bench or removing them from a machine. Vision will guide a robot, or a human, so far, but for the final delicate operations a sense of touch is required. The slight error that is always present in the position of the robot arm could mean the difference between metal fingers that wave ineffectively a few millimeters above the surface of a bolt or dig into the table top. Once the object has been located, additional touch feedback will assist in lifting the object securely without exerting too much force.

Force feedback and a tactile sense also come into their own when parts are to be assembled. An engineer who mates parts together, inserts bolts, and secures a component in its seating relies upon his sense of touch as he adjusts and juggles parts together. Scientists are, therefore, working on how force feedback can help robots in such tasks. In a typical set-up, force and torque sensors are mounted on the

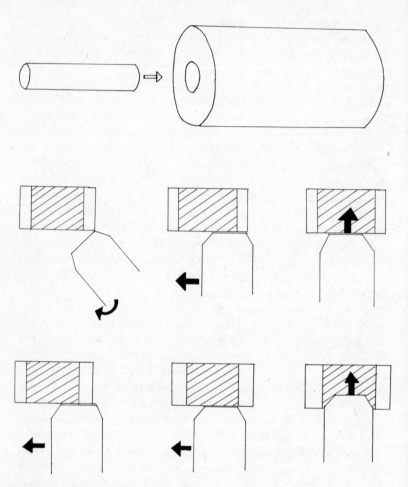

Figure 7–5
Fitting a peg into a hole is a notoriously difficult task for a robot to perform.

To insure proper insertion the peg must first be rotated into correct alignment with the cylinder.

Using force feedback and a flanged end to the peg it becomes possible to maneuver it into position.

robot's wrist and relay information directly to the computer. By analyzing the resulting forces and torques the arm can be instructed to carry out the necessary series of moves, for example, to insert a peg into a hole, a notoriously difficult task for a robot to perform. Using this system the accuracy of a robot arm with an intrinsic error of 0.01 mm can be increased to 0.001 mm.

It is clear from the above drawings that the effectiveness of the robot could be increased even more if the ends of the bolt were tapered slightly. As research continues into ways of improving the efficiency of assembly robots, it becomes apparent that new techniques of construction must also be devised; for example, by giving components special shapes and making more use of glues and snap fasteners in place of nuts and bolts. Clearly, improvements in robot design will evolve in a cooperative way along with new techniques of assembly and new designs of components.

General Robots: Arms

Engineers are also working on the design of the robot arm itself. One approach is to produce arms that copy the human arm in its flexibility. Such limbs are ideal for manipulations in restricted spaces but require a great deal of information to get them to carry out a task since the human arm is highly redundant in its movement. One solution would be to preprogram a series of stereotyped patterns for the "muscular contractions" of the arm. A particular action would then be constructed out of a sequence of these standard patterns. Computer brains may therefore have to work in a similar way to the human brain when it comes to the control of their limbs.

Controlling one arm so that it can pick up and manipulate objects is hard enough but when it comes to the cooperative movement of two arms, the task is almost beyond present computer systems. A human is able to use both hands in performing a task, for example, angling a piece with one hand while the other hand pushes a bolt into it, or tightening a nut while the other part is restrained. At present two arms are able to work on a common task provided that they are independently controlled and do not have to coordinate their movements or understand what their partner is doing. But true coordinated movement requires a much more complicated system of programming, since both hands have to keep out of each other's way and work cooperatively, with direct information about each other's position and intentions.

The issue of cooperative movement exposes just how complicated is the programming of a general robot. Clearly, a great deal of artificial intelligence is needed so that the computer can work out its own solutions to each problem. One approach is to develop a high level programming language so that an engineer or machinist can talk to the robot in English, using the sort of vocabulary and instructions that he would normally employ in talking to another worker. The computer will take these instructions as goals and use its general knowledge to work out a sequence of movements and then compute the trajectory that corresponds to each movement. The actual problems involved are equivalent to the solution of complex paths in a multidimensional space and involve a great deal of computing. But clearly a robot has to be able to work in real time so new theoretical approaches have to be developed to speed up the problem solving and refine the actual mathematics involved; another solution is to employ the fast, parallel machines that will appear in the late 1980s. Present approaches to intelligent control of robot arms are generally confined to the research laboratory. At Grenoble in France, an expert system called GARI works out sequences for making parts. The system also incorporates the sort of expert advice that machinists and designers use in setting up a manufacturing process. GARI, therefore, accepts pieces of subjective and specialist advice, assigns weights to this knowledge, and then evaluates it as it works out a sequence of moves.

General Robots: Movement

Another direction of robot research is in the field of

movement. Robots that are required to inspect oil pipelines or work on the ocean bed have to be capable of movement. One of the first serious explorations of this problem (leaving aside such things as robots under human radio control,) was SRI's SHAKEY robot.

The first version of SHAKEY was completed in 1969 and consisted of a TV camera, range finder, and a bogey supported on three wheels which contained a drive control mechanism and sensors to tell the robot when it bumped into things. SHAKEY's brain was not located in the robot itself but some distance away and received and transmitted data by radio. Shakey's task was to find its way through a room containing obstacles, reach a goal, and then return to its starting position.

A later version of SHAKEY used an extended memory and reasoning power and carried out its control functions in an hierarchical fashion using a system known as STRIPS which we met in Chapter 3. At Carnegie-Mellon University, Hans Moravec worked on another mobile robot, CART which obtained its information just as a one-eyed person does. While much of our information about depth comes from such clues as the way objects overlap, their apparent size and the way patterns such as tiles and pebbles recede into the distance, a particularly important clue is provided by our stereo vision. This clue is missing in a one-eyed person or robot, but some direct perception of depth can be obtained by moving the head from side to side. This is exactly how CART operates, its TV eye is moving on a track from one side of CART to the other.

Faced with a room or outdoor scene containing as many as 30 obstacles, and pseudo obstacles such as flat cardboard cutouts placed on the floor, the robot is able to thread a path towards its destination. CART begins in a stationary mode by taking a series of pictures as its TV camera moves from side to side. At this stage the robot is concerned with determining those features of interest on which to concentrate its full attention. These features represent obstacles that can be unambiguously identified from one picture to the next. Of course one problem that the computer's brain has to face is what to do if a object stands behind the other and is partly obscured by it. Does that image come from a single obstacle or two separate ones? In addition, the computer must also learn to ignore the cardboard cutouts placed on the floor which are not real obstacles.

Once it has built up an internal map of its environment the computer plans a trajectory or path through the room and moves forward about one meter. This done, it stops again and takes another look at the room. This time the robot checks for all the features of interest that it earlier identified and begins to confirm its hypothesis about the room. The robot also compares the initial and present positions of each object, and, with this information, works out the true path it has just taken. Then, after some ten to fifteen minutes total computing time CART moves forward again.

In this step by step way, which its inventor admits is "painfully slow," CART moves across the room, avoiding obstacles, and reaching its destination. On some occasions, however, it is not successful, since it may fail to identify an obstacle correctly or it may get trapped between several objects so that its battery runs down while it is still attempting to extricate itself.

Despite its slowness in operation CART has some very interesting features. One of these is the way in which it learns about its environment and constructs an internal world model which is constantly updated. Another is the hierarchical and modular way its 16 microprocessors are used, some for motion, some for vision, and one to exert overall control.

SHAKEY and CART both used wheels for movement, and so do the many other robots that are being experimented with in industrial and university laboratories. However, wheels may not always be the best way of getting around. They can't be used on stairs, nor are they much use in rough or rocky terrain. Clearly, for some tasks, legs are better than wheels. The problem with a legged robot however is that its control mechanisms have to be more complicated, its sense of balance must constantly be maintained, and suitable limbs have to be designed and engineered. Several groups are working on robots with legs: A U.S.S.R. group has built a six-legged robot, as has a team at Ohio State University, General Electric have constructed a four-legged truck for use by the U.S. Army, and the University of Wisconsin built a walking machine with three legs.

The construction of computer controlled arms and legs opens up another interesting possibility, not so much for their use by robots but by humans. Artificial limbs are as old as history but the computer controlled limb with full touch and force feedback is a relatively new invention. People who have had a limb amputated may be able to manipulate an electronically controlled prosthesis by means of residual muscle control. For others the electrical activity of nerves in the skin or stump can be used. These small electrical signals are picked up, amplified, and used to activate the device. If some intelligent microprocessor control and sensory feedback is used then performance will be considerably enhanced.

Walking also becomes a possibility under computer control, not only for amputees but for those who cannot exert proper muscular control over whole limbs; for example, people with cerebral palsy or spinal damage. One approach is to use an artificial limb or an exoskeleton, strapped to an existing limb which is then moved under computer control. But a more exciting possibility is to deliver a series of activating electrical signals directly to the various leg muscles. Under control of a computer these shocks can be given in exactly the correct sequence to instigate a walking action. In addition to helping the paralyzed and disabled, robotic limbs can be used to increase a healthy person's power and strength. Strapped onto the body one system can amplify human lifting power. Another system is the remote manipulator in which a mechanical arm operates under direct human control as, for example, the Canadarm mounted on the U.S. space shuttles.

Androids and Cyborgs

Other possibilities in the more distant future include the Cyborg, a human who has robotic parts such as mechanical arms and legs and even some direct computer input into the brain. Another approach is full sensory feedback in which a machine broadcasts a totality of sensations to a human operator who is seated at some remote location. The human "becomes" the machine and his responses, either muscular or in terms of brain potential, are then used to control the machine.

The robot and its limbs are likely to evolve in several different directions. One is to the fully autonomous, intelligent robot that can walk, manipulate its hands, and understand the visual environment. In the future there will be robots on factory floors, robots working in mines and in the desert, robots in outer space and robots on the ocean beds, robots in operating theaters assisting during microsurgery, and even robots cleaning the home. Some of these robots will look very much like the industrial robots of the present day, articulated arms under computer control. Others will have no parts that remotely resemble anything human. Robots will also begin to utilize senses different from our own familiar five; already robots use ultrasound radar, they may also make use of radiation that lies outside the human spectrum; ultraviolet, X-rays, and infrared detectors not to mention nuclear radiation detectors, chemical "sniffers," and senses which directly respond to electrical and magnetic fields. HILARE, a French robot uses such senses as a TV camera, laser rangefinder, ultrasonic sensors, and a distance triangulation device using sonar. Some robots may not control arms and legs but rockets and wing surfaces of space vehicles or the machines of a large factory. Provided that the device has a central brain, electronic sensory information input, and some method of taking action it can still be called a robot.

Of course there will also be robots that look distinctly human, androids as they have been called in science fiction. One of the most successful of these early androids was SIM ONE, developed in 1967 at the University of Southern California. This computer controlled mannequin is used to teach anesthesology and exhibites a pulse, heartbeat, variable skin coloration, blinking reflex, and respiration. After administration of a drug or anesthetic SIM ONE responds in real time by changing its pulse rate and breathing and inhibiting its reflexes. If an incorrect mixture of anesthetic is given, the android's skin changes color and SIM ONE exhibits cyanosis and even cardiac arrest.

The act of producing a robot that has human appearance may have a disturbing effect. Even if the device does not exhibit a particularly advanced artificial intelligence, people will still begin to question their own attitudes to robots and ask such questions as "Can a robot have consciousness, feelings, emotions . . . a soul?" These questions have been much discussed by science fiction writers and, more recently by philosophers. W. G. Lycan of the philosophy department at the University of Ohio has suggested that robots of advanced intelligence will be given full civil rights in law while less intelligent androids would probably be given rights corresponding to animals.

Robots in Space

Although the robot that is recognized in law lies some distance in the future, even the science fiction aspects of robots and computers are being taken seriously by some scientists. In 1980 NASA organized a major 10,000-manhour project, held at the University of Santa Clara, to investigate the ways artificial intelligence could be used in future space missions. No one quite came up with a robot from Star Wars but the discussions and proposals generated were even more exciting.

In the short term there was a proposal for IESIS, Intelligent Earth Sensing Information System. At present there are several satellites circling our earth whose job it is to collect information about such things as the atmosphere, weather, the earth's surface, and so on. The problem with these satellites is that, like a small child excited by his first visit to the circus, the satellite wants to talk about everything it sees! The earthbound scientists for their part then have the problem of untangling the really valuable information from a vast amount of uninteresting data. An intelligent satellite, however, would not gather data in a purposeless fashion but would be goal directed. When instructed by a user on earth to look at weather patterns over Florida, tree growth in Northern Ontario, or water sitting in a river basin, the satellite would direct its attention to a particular problem, decide what data it needed and then set about its task of observation and information processing.

The designers also added to IESIS the capacity of dealing with enquiries in plain English so that general users could make use of the service it offered. For example, a farmer may ask the satellite to keep an eye on his fields and check their irrigation. To do this, he need not learn a programming language or deal with a considerable output of numerical data. Central to IESIS is an internal model about the world that is constantly modified and updated. The satellite uses this model to forecast data, make judgments about what data it needs, and how to look to it and, finally, to filter the data it has collected and note the differences between its predictions and actual findings.

A longer term NASA project is the building of an intelligent space probe which could be used to explore distant planets. At present the exploration of a planet takes place in a series of stages lasting several years. First, a rocket is launched to orbit the planet and collect data about its atmosphere and surface. In the phases that follow, a landing site may be identified and a space craft landed to gather more data and move about the surface collecting and analyzing samples.

When the planet is a distant one and the travel time is measured in years and not days or weeks, this is obviously an inefficient process. The logical solution is to build a more complex automated space craft that is capable of carrying out all these various phases in a single mission by gathering preliminary data, launching subsatellites and atmospheric probes, making close approaches to selected areas of the surface, and, finally, attempting a landng.

By itself, such a system would have to be remarkably complex and to use the most advanced techniques of robotics and artificial intelligence. But the designers went one dramatic and exciting step further, they demanded that the probe should be intelligent enough to make all its decisions on board without any reference to earthbound computers or scientists. The implication is clear: one day the human race will look beyond its own solar systems to other stars and other planetary systems.

At present, when a space craft makes a journey to a planet in our solar system it relays information back to Earth-based controllers who analyze data, make decisions, and relay them back to the probe. Transmission times are limited by the velocity of radio waves (equal to that of light) and on a Saturn mission this delay time is around an hour, not a particularly serious problem. But some time in the next century space craft will be journeying to the nearest stars where transmission times are measured in years and decades, not minutes or hours. In addition to this, the actual time of the rocket's journey will be much longer, in fact, the scientists who launched it will be retired or dead by the time the probe reaches its destination. So the space probes of the future will have to be intelligent robots, capable of maintaining and repairing themselves in space, guiding their paths to the stars, and when they at last arrive at a distant solar system, carrying out a full examination of the new sun, the planets, their atmosphere, and surface features and even checking for the presence of life.

If all this reads like the science fiction of the distant future, then take note that scientists at the Santa Clara project decided to apply many of these principles to a proposed exploration of Titan, the largest moon of Saturn. The probe they suggested would be fully automatic with a high degree of intelligence. Although overall control would still be made by Earth-based scientists and relayed to the probe, the device would be capable of making many of its own decisions with regard to exploration and data gathering.

Finally, there is the question of factories in space and exploitation of resources on the Moon and asteroids. There are many advantages to be gained in the airless, gravityless conditions of an earth satellite. New materials can be made and many existing processes carried out more effectively. In addition, there are whole new resources of minerals and other substances to be mined and refined from the surface of the Moon and the asteroids. In our distant past coal, and the ores of copper, iron, and other important metals were lying around on the surface of the Earth waiting to be picked up. Now they can only be obtained by expensive mining operations but on the moon and asteroids there are abundant deposits waiting for our use.

All this points to the construction of large factories and processing plants in space and on the moon. NASA engineers and their colleagues began to explore plans for fully automated factories which could not only carry out their operations under computer control but could repair their own machines and even develop new generations of equipment for expansion and diversification. One idea that was explored was that of "telepresence," which involves the transmission of full sensory feedback about the way a machine works. Using telepresence a construction worker, located on Earth, could "drive" a tractor on the Moon. He would have the full sensation that he was actually driving the tractor and the device, located on the Moon's surface, would respond to his every move. (One could also contemplate full telepresence being an important addition to video games and as we "fly" the space ship on the TV screen, one would have the full sensation of being at its control deck.)

A fully automated factory opens up a final and mind boggling question, one that goes back to the very origins of artificial intelligence and machine control; could such a factory actually replicate itself? The idea begins with the mathematician John von Neumann who asked if a machine could contain the instructions to duplicate itself, including the duplication of the instructions needed to duplicate itself! Such a machine would be very much like a living system for it is one of the major characteristics of life that it can duplicate itself. The DNA molecule contains the instructions for the functioning of a cell including the splitting of the cell into two new cells, and the duplication of the DNA itself so that the new cells contain their own copy. A living cell divides into two, each being a perfect imitation and having all the instructions necessary for further division. These two divide again giving four, the four to give eight, and so on. With a moderate rate of division a single microscopic cell will soon fill a petrie dish and if it is not stopped it would eventually cover the world. The mathematical progressions that are involved in the growth of cell cultures recall the growth of possibilities as a tree graph expands from trunk to branches. With only a moderate time between cell division a system that constantly doubles itself will soon expand to gigantic proportions. Up to now we have spoken of living cells but what if the same process is applied to factories? Some engineers feel that the self-replicating factory would be the solution to the problem of exploiting the Moon's mineral resources. To turn a factory out one at a time would take decades but what if each factory, in addition to performing its tasks of mining and refining, also reproduces itself at some other location? In this way it would be possible to spread out across the Moon's surface in an exponential way.

Current studies indicate that the self-replicating factory lies very much in the future yet none of the steps involved in its realization is impossible, it's simply a matter of advanced computer control, development of intelligent robots for repair, and the investment of considerable funds. As an intermediate step a factory which reproduces itself with some external help looks more feasible. Some components would be produced with ease in the factory, others such as ball bearings require a whole factory of their own geared to their production. It is possible, therefore, that a truly self-reproducing factory would in the end have to be too big and comprehensive. But if it accepted some parts flown in from Earth then the remainder could be manufactured automatically.

A factory that operates in a fully automatic mode and reproduces copies of itself which then reproduces copies of these copies will have to be completely error free. Any problem that develops at a particular stage could be passed on to the next generation of factories and would proliferate from generation to generation.

The same thing occurs with DNA since damage to the gene from radiation or chemicals can lead to cell death, mutations, or cancer (runaway growth). A cell however has its own control mechanism for inspecting and repair of DNA. It is probable that an automatically self-reproducing factory would also have to maintain constant supervision and inspection of all its processes.

Computer Controlled Manufacturing

Lunar factories that can reproduce themselves are predictions for the twenty-first century, but in our own present, there already exist factories with a high degree of central computer control, factories that can almost run themselves. The process first began as robots and computers became integrated into the work place and called into question the whole manufacturing process and everything from management, scheduling, and integration of the shop floor to changes in the means of distribution. When it is realized that direct labor accounts for only 10 to 20 percent of the cost of producing an article, it becomes clear that this wider transformation of industry will be more important than robots by themselves.

To understand how this second industrial revolution is taking place and the important role that will be played by intelligent computer systems, it is necessary to first understand how a traditional factory works. Suppose, for example, that a company decides to manufacture a new article; anything from an airliner to a coffee machine. To begin the management is faced with making a far-reaching and expensive decision for it may be months or even years before their product reaches the consumer and profits are returned to the company. During this period capital will be tied up, new parts and materials will have to be ordered or manufactured, a machine shop will have to be retooled, advertising and market research carried out, and the design phase completed. While some of these factors can be calculated and others guessed at, a few will remain imponderable. So a board of directors or the chairman of a company can be excused for appearing cautious and conservative when it comes to innovation, too much is at stake and too little can be predicted and controlled, at least in factories of the present.

But assuming that market predictions are favorable, a decision will be made. The next phase falls to the engineers and designers who begin a series of sketches and drawings of the new product. At each stage of the design a number of accurate drawings are made from various angles to build up information on the solid object. Next, drawings are made which show each component from a number of projections and how they all interrelate and fit together. With drawings complete, the designers graduate to models and finally to prototypes which are tested for the effect of various stresses and for performance. In addition, the engineers begin to explore the whole process of assembly that will take place on the factory floor. At each stage in the design phase modifications are explored and yet further sets of drawings are made. Finally, with the design agreed upon, an inventory of all the parts to be manufactured is worked out, orders are placed with subcontractors and retooling at the factory begins. When it comes to the actual machining, drilling and assembling of various parts, groups of drawings are handed to the foreman and the machinists on the shop floor. These are used to set machines and produce the individual parts.

The example has been taken far enough to demonstrate how inefficient and uncoordinated the whole process is, how much information is committed to paper which must be moved around, reconverted to another form and then committed to paper yet again, and how complex decisions are taken in a piecemeal way. Factories of the future will work in totally different ways and employ such approaches as flexible manufacturing, integrated manufacturing, and CAD/CAM (computer aided design and computer assisted manufacturing) plus all the advantages that computers and information systems bring to the flow of commerce and to the office of the future.

CAD/CAM

Let us begin first at the design phase with CAD/CAM and see how the results of this phase can be fed back to boardroom decision making and forward to flexible manufacturing on the factory floor. With CAD, in place of a drawing board, the designer now sits down at a computer work station and uses a raster display screen, digitizer tablet, light pen, keyboard, and plotter and all the other peripherals of the system. As the designer works with his sketches he can rotate them and view them as pseudo-solid objects from any angle, he can change their scale, and carry out a variety of mathematical transformations. All aspects of the design can be stored in the CAD computer memory and other components can be called onto the screen as predesigned elements using subroutines. With CAD, the whole process of design is speeded up and made more efficient, for the designer is able to test and evaluate his ideas as he goes along without the need for making models or prototypes, and modifications are immediately incorporated into the most detailed of drawings.

For example, as his ideas develop, the designer may decide to test the product with various loadings. Using a computer program he can observe deformations directly by looking at out the screen and zooming in to a particular part. He can carry numerical calculations, study a computer printout, and look at the effect of changing some of the design modifications. The computer display also enables the designer to observe how the various parts and components will fit together, how they can best be assembled, and it is even possible to use computer simulation to observe the prototype in motion. So without the need to go through a long series of complex drawings and the construction of models and prototypes, the designer can work in a flexible way moving back and forth between sketch and prototype while sitting at the CAD work station.

Using this phase alone the time scale of a design can be reduced from months to weeks. But this is only the beginning, for CAD/CAM has even more to offer when it is integrated into an approach called *group technology*. To assemble the new design may require tens or thousands of individual components that have to be manufactured or ordered from subcontractors. Planning for these steps requires drawing up a detailed inventory and working out the complex schedules which ensure that all parts are brought together at exactly the correct time during the manufacturing process. In a conventional factory the inventory alone can be something of a headache but with CAD/CAM and group technology, this is already taken care of in the computer's data banks.

Research shows that only around 20 percent of "new" parts supposedly required for a novel product are indeed new. When a company carries out a careful comparison of its inventory it will discover that many of these items are already being manufactured in some different context and are therefore in stock or can be ordered from an existing subcontractor. And, of the remainder which do appear to be new, a reexamination of the design shows that many of them can be produced by a simple modification of an existing part. So the next stage in CAD design is to examine each nut, bolt, and component, compare it with the computer files and attempt to match it or modify it to correspond to some

273

existing part, a process that can save a considerable percentage of the cost of manufacture.

Now with all the specifications determined, the factory must work out its scheduling. This is a highly complex mathematical problem requiring the treatment of a very large number of interdependent variables. For example, an overall flow of the manufacturing process must be determined so that each machine is used in the most efficient manner possible. Given the manufacturing times of particular components, their individual rate of manufacture are calculated, and dates on when to begin manufacturing the component are set. Where subcontractors are used, it is important that the order should be placed at the correct time so that components arrive at the factory exactly when they are needed and manufacture is not slowed down or a warehouse filled up. So at every stage of manufacturing there is money to be lost and money to be saved in capital cost, warehouse space, insurance, wages, number of machines needed, and so on.

The answer to the problem of scheduling and retooling is to use an expert system, since where the manufacturing process is extensive the problem may be too complex for a rule-bound system to produce the optimum solution. In addition, an optimum solution is not always desirable, since there may be many other factors involved which call for a compromise between costs and worker efficiency while maintaining flexibility to market fluctuations and future retooling. At centers like Carnegie-Mellon University, engineers are creating expert systems that make use of the judgments, rules of thumb, and constraints that operate in a modern factory. The effectiveness of the application depends upon two things; that all aspects of the manufacturing process come under direct computer control and that all the data required and every specification is already present in the data banks of the CAD computer.

Once design, inventory, and scheduling are complete, the individual manufacturing processes are programmed into the industrial robots and numerically controlled shop floor machines. Previously this was done by hand. Engineering drawings sent down from the design department were handed out on the shop floor and machinists used them to set their machines or program the industrial robots. But since all the specifications are already present in the CAD/CAM data banks, why not allow the computers to program the machines directly?

Computer Control

In flexible manufacturing, each machine and robot is controlled by a microprocessor with the network of microprocessors itself coming under the supervision of a central computer. While each microprocessor dictates the individual operations of its slave machine, the central computer coordinates the overall process and ensures that each machine works at exactly the correct rate to supply parts to its neighbors. To maintain this efficient flow during manufacturing there must also be computer control over the way raw materials and assembled parts pass from machine to machine.

In a conventional factory a part can spend as much as 95 percent of its time simply waiting in line to be machined or processed but with flexible manufacturing this waiting time is cut to 10 to 30 percent. Machines themselves now work 75 to 80 percent of their shift times instead of 5 percent. Other figures are equally impressive; over a third less shop floor space is needed, well over a third to two-thirds less machine tools and shop personnel are required. Production costs can be cut by around 20 percent and capital costs by just under 10 percent.

In Japan it is estimated that around half the manufacturing companies will shortly be using flexible manufacturing. In the United Kingdom it is being made an essential feature of modernization of small and medium companies. The government, for example, provides grants of 50 percent for initial consultancy and up to one-third of the cost of conversion of a plant. In the United States there are a number of major projects using overall computer control. For example, a $100 million aerospace project to use integrated computer aided manufacture is under way as is a computer aided ship-building design and construction project.

All these processes are going to require intelligent computers, machines that can exert control over very complex processes, make decisions, evaluate plans and strategies, make use of expert systems, and monitor the factory environment. One issue that assumes importance in a computer managed factory is that of automatic inspection. In a conventional factory a human worker soon spots if something is going wrong and alerts his foreman, but with total computer control it becomes possible for the products of an entire shift to be faulty. What is required is a robot capable of using vision and other senses to examine and test a product. During its examination the robot should be able to detect errors and relay them to the central computer which then carries out a diagnosis, requests further information from the robot, and finally pinpoints the source of error and makes the necessary modifications. Factories of the future, which employ this continuous inspection and diagnosis procedure, will probably also contain mobile robots which are able to repair the machines around them. While such repairs are being carried out the overall computer manager will divert production, and minimize any slowing down of the process.

As it achieves this electronic coordination from design to production, the computer is constantly gathering information about how every facet of the manufacturing process works. So CAD/CAM and flexible manufacturing together can also provide information for future decisions regarding retooling, modification of design, and the manufacture of a new product. In place of hunches, estimates, and calculated guesses, a company chairman can be given hard estimates and projections on the costs and lead times of a new product. As computer supervision continues, the computers themselves will evolve their own expert systems for planning and decision making. Managers will be able to base their decisions on hard facts, factories will become more flexible, and new products will be tailor-made for a fluctuating marketplace.

Computer control will therefore revolutionize the whole way a factory is managed. Traditionally, human management and control is arranged hierarchically with the chairman at the top and individual workers at the bottom. Such a system evolves when a given supervisor has too many tasks to perform and delegates power to those under him who, in turn, assign tasks to a further level of underlings, the whole structure spreading out in that already familiar tree graph fashion. But what began in a very reasonable way as a move towards greater effectiveness can end up as a disastrous failure in communication. Some large organizations can have as many as fourteen layers to their pyramid, so that it becomes virtually impossible for a man at the bottom to interact with a man at the top. As messages flow from top to bottom of the organization they become filtered and reinterpreted at the various levels, partly by necessity and partly because, hidden in the official organization and goal of the company, is an unofficial plan that involves the desire for promotion, protection of mistakes, elevation for one's friends, protection of one's territory, personal priorities and goals, and so on. In addition, a hierarchical organization has the effect of preventing communication horizontally. Companies are divided into departments which may have no means of direct communication since horizontal messages can only pass up the tree to a suitable node and then down another branch to a given department. Hence, experts who may be working side by side may be unable to communicate to each other in any official way.

At one stroke CAD/CAM and the computerized factory undermine this traditional hierarchical structure. To begin with, unless a hierarchical design is specifically built into restrictions on computer access, it becomes a very simple matter for workers in one department to interact with a database produced in some other department. Rather than moving around pieces of paper and official memos, people in the designing section can communicate electronically with, for example, a machine worker and get an instant feedback on a particular design idea.

The Office of the Future

With computer-managed processing, the traditional approach to human supervision and control will have to be rethought, much of its earlier rationale will vanish, and creative managers will have to find new ways to work with their colleagues. To begin with the structure of the office will change. Offices, and indeed factories, may move away from centralization to a distributed form. Factories may become smaller and concentrate upon producing families of parts. Office work, for its part, may be done at home.

Think of the office of Dickens' day with its stacks of ledgers and row upon row of male clerks sitting on high stools and transcribing entries. Every invoice and company letter had to be copied out by hand. Every entry had to be written in copperplate into a ledger, added by hand, and the total transcribed to some other ledger. The office and counting house was labor intensive and male dominated. Then, with the typewriter and the beginning of female emancipation, the office became the province of the female typist. The typewriter was followed by the photocopier, the computer, the word processor, and now the computer terminal work station. At each stage the ecology of the office has changed. When offices were dominated by the movement of paper they were compact and noisy. Today they can be silent and distributed, for a worker can perform his task at home as well as in the office. And since each terminal can be monitored, a boss can keep a better eye on his workers than in the days when they used to sit under his nose.

In the office of the future each worker will be more responsible for making decisions. With the help of a telephone or a computer link the customer will be brought into direct contact with the person who has his file and makes decisions. While a face-to-face contact will be lost, at least the person at the other end of the communication link will not be passing the buck or shifting the customer to some other department.

With electronic mail, instant communication between work stations, the availability of satellite communications to make computer links anywhere in the world, and the breakdown of traditional hierarchical structures, the office will transform itself in new and unpredictable ways. Some people will welcome the increased responsibility and flexibility, others will feel uncomfortable with the lack of structure and personal contact. Of interest to the sociologists is the way the office's informal structure will be affected. While the pyramid structure exists for the passage of official information, much unofficial information flows during coffee breaks and at the water cooler. Will this informal information flow be part of the electronic network in future offices?

Outside the factory and the office the features of commerce itself will change. As banking moves from the passage of checks to the movement of electronic data the whole concept of business between factories and customers may change. Already some companies have dispensed with banks for certain of their transactions and directly credit and debit each other. Satellite communications involving the "switchboard in the sky" concept will soon make it possible to carry out business from a remote office or even a car or plane by phoning directly a satellite switchboard which directs the call to a factory or office in some other country. As computers become linked into such networks it becomes possible to control the movement of goods, which are already containerized for easier handling. Already airlines have computerized their reservation systems so that it is possible to get details about a flight and purchase a ticket thousands of miles away. The next stage will be to apply the same procedure to the movement of goods.

Even something as innocuous as a bar product code printed on a box of crackers has enormous implications, for it enables automatic data gathering of information about the movement of stock, efficient use of shelf space, effectiveness of advertising, inventory, and ordering. Market research could be carried out in minutes across a continent by linking computers together and enquiring about a particular bar coded product.

At every stage from design, scheduling, and manufacturing to management, marketing, and general commerce the computer will have a considerable impact, and since the trend is towards more highly integrated systems, this means artificial intelligence. The fate of manufacturing and commerce is highly unpredictable with the general robot being only one phase of this future. But as computers are faster, more intelligent, and able to store and process larger and larger amounts of data, it does appear that the future will be more flexible and allow business and its products to respond more readily to the consumer.

CHAPTER 8
Supercomputers That Learn

In the fall of 1981 the Japanese Government announced its Fifth Generation Project to develop a supercomputer of the future. Seeded with $450 million, the project is a joint venture between government, industry, and the universities and has as its goal the design and manufacture of a new generation of computers that will be able to learn, make inferences, understand speech, perform translations, comprehend natural language, and have superior vision. Taken in conjunction with other long-range projects, it represents a carefully planned approach aimed at developing a range of new technologies which the Japanese believe will be of ultimate benefit to their industry and their society.

Despite the fact that the Japanese approach is to develop a series of related technologies in the field of communications, robotics, integrated manufacturing, and information processing, it is the notion of a fifth generation computer that has excited most interest. The first generation of computers were the vacuum tube devices of the 1940s and were rapidly followed by a second generation of machines that used transistors and by third generation (integrated circuit) computers. Corresponding to each of these generation jumps, computers have become faster, smaller, and more powerful. The most advanced commercial computers of the present day use VLSIs, or very large scale integrated circuits, and are known as fourth generation machines. The notion of a further generation of computers had been discussed for many years, and a number of research groups had simulated new designs on their own conventional computers, but it had been assumed that these fifth generation machines would evolve under the pressure of commercial demand and research advances. So the notion that a government would go full out to develop a fifth generation machine came as something of a shock to the other industrialized nations, not only by the size of the project, but because of its carefully designed timetable and the valuable technologies and devices that were to be developed along the way. The Japanese machine, to be completed by the 1990s, will contain a huge database capable of handling 10,000 inference rules and facts on a million objects. This massively parallel computer will be able to perform millions of logical steps each second (each step involving many basic operations of the machine) and work directly with symbols using the PROLOG prgramming language.

A year after the Fifth Generation Project was announced, the Institute for New Generation Computer Technology and the National Super-Speed Computer Project were created. This latter project is dedicated to building a computer that will be 1,000 times more powerful than existing machines and along the way will create expert systems, intelligent CAD devices, and chips containing 10 million transistors. In March 1984 a further, rival Japanese group announced a Sixth Generation Project which will involve linguists, psychologists, and brain physiologists in the design of a computer that will study, think, and make decisions by itself.

These Japanese plans generated considerable reaction around the world. In Britain, for example, the Minister of

Information Technology created a committee, chaired by J. Alvey, in April of 1982 to look into these new technologies. The committee, meeting on evenings and weekends, reported in September of the same year and by April 1983 the Minister announced the £350 million British Programme for Advanced Information Technology. This project does not so much concentrate on the design of advanced computers but on the development of advanced software, production of VLSI chips, improved man-machine interfaces, and advanced CAD devices. Other European countries followed suit with their own projects, and in March 1984 the E.E.C. decided to fund its cooperative Esprit program to the tune of $500 million. In the U.S. no clear government plan has yet emerged and this may be due to the fact that there is no central authority which funds artificial intelligence and computer researchers. However, DARPA, the U.S. Department of Defense's fund for advanced research projects, has traditionally been generous towards AI research and in addition, much research is performed directly by industry and in university laboratories, assisted by the loan or donation of expensive equipment from industry.

The Japanese prediction that they could build a supercomputer within a given time period has been greeted with everything from admiration to cynicism. Edward Feigenbaum [whose views can be found in *The Fifth Generation*, coauthored by Pamela McCurduck and published by Addison-Wesley (1983)] is full of praise for the Japanese project and the way it has been organized. Others are prone to take these proposals with a general pinch of salt and point out that many extremely difficult problems will have to be solved before a fifth generation machine can be built and that the act of drawing up a detailed timetable is not the same thing as being able to solve these problems on schedule. Researchers who have spent their professional careers looking at problems like computer vision and language understanding believe that the outstanding problems in their fields cannot be solved in any simple, predictable way.

But despite what the critics may say, the race is on to develop new information-processing technologies and Japan now has competitors in the United States, Britain, and other European nations. In each of these national and private sectors, a superfast machine is only one of the goals that is being planned for. In addition, there will be general improvements in hardware and software and developments in the whole field of artificial intelligence, including improved tree graph searches, new high level programming languages, better problem-solving algorithms, and more powerful and flexible ways of presenting knowledge.

It is probable that these advances in AI theory will go hand-in-hand with the design of new hardware. In earlier chapters we have seen the way in which various theoretical approaches have been limited by the amount of computing time they involve. But when computers are ten, a hundred, or even a thousand times faster and are given much larger memories, many of these limitations will no longer apply.

Computer Architecture

Since the first vacuum tube computers were built in the late 1940s the cost of purchasing a central processing unit has dropped from hundreds of thousands of dollars to the price of a paperback book. Yet despite the fact that the price that was paid for a central brain of a computer of the 1950s could today purchase a million logic chips, modern computers still follow the design that was laid down by von Neumann in which all the information flow is directed through a single processing unit.

Our fourth generation computers are a little like that harrassed individual in an office who considers himself to be indispensable, interferes in every task, and attempts to carry the whole responsibility for the office on his shoulders. Fortunately, most human beings do not normally work this way, and either individually or in groups they solve problems and carry out their tasks in cooperative ways. This cooperative approach to the world even takes place in the human brain. As you read this book, parts of your brain are directing fast eye movements across the page while others decipher the letters in each line and convert them into sentences which are parsed and understood. While all this is going on, different parts of the brain monitor and maintain such bodily functions as muscle tone, heartbeat, and respiration. Hearing centers constantly monitor the environment for sound and you may even be listening to music on the radio at the same time as you are reading this page.

The human brain operates by simultaneously carrying out a host of different functions, many of which must be orchestrated together in constantly shifting ways. As you read this book, for example, language understanding and vision work in cooperation while hearing and movement perform independent tasks. But if you were to exchange this book for a musical score and now give attention to the music that has been playing on the radio, vision and hearing will shift into a new cooperative role and even muscular control may join in as you follow the orchestra and tap out the rhythm with your fingers. The human brain is extremely effective in dealing with the world because it is able to organize its various functions in a host of different ways and to parallel process many of the problems it faces.

As we shall see, parallel processing appears to be the natural and most efficient way to solve a host of problems from problem graph searches to vision and speech understanding and it seems inevitable that any intelligent agent, biological or silicon-based, would develop as a highly parallel process. The ability to perform parallel processing therefore seems to be forced on the design of brains and computers and this is not simply a function of nature and complexity of individual problems but of the world itself. Nature consists of a vast number of separate objects and processes that are in a constant state of flux. Events around us do not take place in a conveniently serial fashion but bombard us from many directions at once. Objects move around us, speech, music, and sudden sounds come in at our ears, we notice changes in temperature, and things touch us. Even if we were to be immobilized in bed, our senses would be constantly assailed by the world. With respect to each one of us, the world's signals are highly parallel, since many different signals are arriving from many different sources at the same time. To be able to survive in such a world, the brain must be able to respond to so many different signals in a correspondingly parallel way and with the aid of highly parallel inputs (around 20 senses including the familiar sight, hearing, touch, taste, and smell, each of which in itself is also parallel).

This parallelism is also found in human organizations in which individual members carry out different tasks and "inputs" and "outputs" take several different forms. Many organizations are organized along hierarchical lines and branch out like a tree graph so that different departments are able to work cooperatively on a problem. A manager will briefly consider an overall problem and pass parts of it on to the heads of each department. A department head in turn will divide up this subtask and give appropriate parts to individual employees. In a properly run organization, such a division of labor makes for faster and more efficient results. As a rather artificial example, suppose that in the days before copying machines an office manager needed many copies of a 10-page report. He could, of course, give the report to one typist and ask him to type as fast as he could but a far quicker method would be to give each page of the original to each of ten typists and set them to work typing copies of a single original. By having the typing processed in parallel the total amount of work is not decreased but its execution is speeded up by a factor of ten. In this case, each worker has a similar skill and works on a similar task, but in some cases division of labor can be made more effective by having each individual or department specialize in different tasks. With this form of organization, rather than everyone needing the same general knowledge of many things, each worker can concentrate on building skills in a more limited field and concentrating in that department the particular resources it needs. Complex tasks can then be divided for parallel processing among specialist departments so that each department carries out what it does best and leaves the rest to the others. The process is not only faster but more efficient since resources do not have to be distributed across the whole building. Parallel processing can be carried out in many different ways and is appropriate to a large range of tasks; an extreme form is where a number of experts gather together in the same room to act as a think tank, and each person throws out ideas and suggestions. There appears to be no overall control or hierarchical structure and the group is able to attack a problem in a cooperative way. Parallel processing therefore seems to be ubiquitous to solving problems and carrying out tasks in organizations, brains and, as we shall see, in computers of the future. So "parallel processing" is a generic term, for it embraces a wide range of approaches and ways of a collection of resources be they people, neurons, or microprocessors. Parallel processing can range from the highly structured hierarchy of a bureaucracy to the unstructured dynamics of a think thank. Of course, not every problem lends itself to parallel processing. If too many cooks attempt to bake a cake or gardeners to dig a narrow hole they will get into each other's way and confound the attainment of the goal. An automobile assembly line involves linear rather than parallel assembly because of the sequential nature of the operations involved; there is little point in trying to add a windshield and door handles at the same time as the body is being placed on the car's chassis and spraying the whole assembly simultaneously!

Leaving aside the cooperative think tank, parallel processing and cooperative problem solving in human brains and business organizations generally involves a central control that is responsible for dividing the problem into manageable subtasks and assigning each part to the appropriate sub-department for execution. This control is often hierarchical with departments passing parts of a problem onto subdepartments and so on down to individual workers. Tasks and messages pass up and down the hierarchy but there is no direct connection between workers or departments at a single level. Other forms of organization allow for messages and tasks to pass between workers in different departments directly so that as soon as one part of a task is completed its results can be passed to another department where these results can act as the raw material for some other part of the task. Many different structures in an organization are possible but an overall constraint is that there must be effective lines of communication that can handle the large traffic of messages that pass between workers and management and ensure that the execution of each task is perfectly synchronized. Even in the case of a think tank it is vital that a fast and effective transmission of information should take place between all participants.

In a similar fashion an effective design for a parallel computer must resolve the problems of overall control during problem solving, the synchronization of each processing unit, and the rapid transmission of information and data throughout the machine. There is at present no single accepted design for a general parallel computer. Some experimental machines have been designed to execute specific tasks and solve particular problems. Others are being built to explore their overall potential and to gain insight into the problems involved in programming a parallel machine. But the parallel processing analog of the all-purpose von Neumann computer that can be bought off the shelf today is still a product of the future.

Several parallel machines have already been built and the operation of others has been simulated on fast but conventional machines. A number of the general robots of the 1970s employed several microprocessors wired in parallel, together with a central control, in order to have their tasks completed in real time. For example, one microprocessor was used to control the robot's movement based on instructions sent to it from a central control. Additional microprocessors were responsible for processing visual information from a TV camera and building up a general picture of the environment. A problem solving processor used information about the environment to work out a path through a room or a way of achieving its goal and then passed its instructions to the processor responsible for movement or for activating a robot arm. Provided that the results from each processing unit arrived in the correct order and in the form of complete reports when there were few problems of synchronization and little traffic congestion between messages. But as a problem is divided into smaller and smaller parts and distributed in stepwise pieces over a large number of processing units, the avoidance of message congestion and maintenance of synchronization becomes acute.

At the University of Maryland the ZMOB parallel computer uses a high-speed communications system so that messages can flow between its processing units during a single cycle of the computer's clock. As of March 1984 ZMOB was operating with 32 280A microprocessors, with two other systems of 16 microprocessors each also in operation. The ultimate goal for ZMOB is a 256-microprocessor unit capable of processsing around 100 million instructions each second. The discussion below refers to the 256 microprocessor ZMOB.

A 280A microprocessor can perform 400,000 instructions per second and sells for around $8. By combining these units in parallel and permitting the rapid passage of messages between them, an enormously powerful computer can be built. ZMOB therefore does not have a centrally located memory as is the case with a von Neumann machine but a memory that is distributed among each of its components to produce a grand total of 16 million bytes. (The various parameters for ZMOB are given in the box on page 291.) An ingenious aspect of the design is an electronic "conveyor belt" to pass messages at 20 million bytes per second. The system allows messages to be dropped from any processor onto the conveyor belt which then circulates its electronic mail around the machine. An individual processor can pick up its mail using a technique that is analogous to the way in which mail bags are picked up at a station by an express train. ZMOB's conveyor belt system allows 128 pairs of simultaneous conversations to take place at a high message rate. The 257th mail stop on the electronic computer belt is a VAX 11/780 computer which acts as the input and output for ZMOB with the outside world. The VAX computer also stores data files and is used to load programs into ZMOB.

The whole ZMOB system can be used in several different configurations, from carrying out a series of synchronized steps to totally independent parallel processing. In one configuration each processor works in lock step synchronization with all the others. This approach can be used to simulate visual perception, neural networks, and cellular models in biology. In another approach the actual programs that govern each processor remain indentical but are no longer synchronized together so that individual processors work on different areas of a very large database and exchange information with one another. This approach could be used in the acoustic processing of speech or edge detection during vision.

In uniform multiprocessing, each element of ZMOB runs on an identical operating system that is capable of problem solving or general computing but this time individual processors are concerned with subtasks of the larger problem that is solved in an asynchronous way. Finally, in articulated microprocessing, the individual programs are no longer identical and each processor becomes an expert on a particular task or is responsible for solving a problem. The overall problem is solved by dividing it into different subtasks which

---

ZMOB

A comparison of the projected 256 processor ZMOB and its individual Z80A microprocessing units.

CHARACTERISTIC	INDIVIDUAL PROCESSOR	ZMOB
Instructions per second	400,000	102,400,000
32-bit floating point additions per second	5,400–37,000	1,382,000–9,472,000
Conveyor belt band-width (bytes/sec)	97,220	25,000,000
Input/output bandwidth	77,782	20,000,000
Time to load the entire system with data, in seconds	0.829	0.829

---

are sent to appropriate microprocessors. In addition to these individual configurations, the system can also operate as a hybrid in which all these various modes occur simultaneously. In a hybrid system some processors would be concerned with sensory data and perceptual information, some with a logical database, some with problem solving in particular domains, and others with control and response. Applications for ZMOB's parallel capacities include robotics, expert systems, speech, natural language, and game playing; in fact, the whole field of artificial intelligence.

ZMOB is just one example of parallel computers in which a series of microprocessors are wired together under some central control so that they can exchange messages and divide a problem into independent pieces. A major difficulty with all these systems is how to avoid the traffic congestion that occurs as many individual units try to send high level messages to each other and how to exert central control over the ensemble of units. In addition, there is the problem of synchronizing the different microprocessors so that different parts of a problem arrive at the correct location at exactly the right time. If part of a solution were to arrive at the same location before another message had ended then a jumbled combination of the two would pass on for further processing and the end result would be electronic nonsense.

Scientists and computer engineers are working on the best ways of resolving all these problems and are devising new ways to program these parallel machines. But even as the parallel computer is in its experimental infancy some research workers are planning to go beyond a system in which problems are divided into subproblems and handled by several high level sub-brains in favor of computers that are massively parallel and contain not hundreds or thousands of processing units but millions.

From David Elliot Shaw and Columbia University's NON-VON Supercomputer Project comes a proposal to construct networks containing an enormous number of elementary processors. Trends in the manufacture of VLSIs indicate that, by the end of the decade, an individual silicon chip will contain hundreds of microprocessing units. It will then be technically feasible to build a computer which contains millions of parallel processing units and processes trillions of operations per second. Various architectures have been proposed for such highly parallel machines, but the NON-VON group argues that a binary tree is the best choice. It is ironic but perhaps unexpected that the binary tree should crop up as a solution to the problem of massively parallel computing. It was the tree search that first set a limit on what could be computed in a reasonable time interval, for a binary tree rapidly branches out to cover a vast number of alternatives during the solution of a problem. Binary trees govern the structure of problem solving in vision, speech, language, robotic movements, problem solving, and every other branch of artificial intelligence. What better way to tackle these

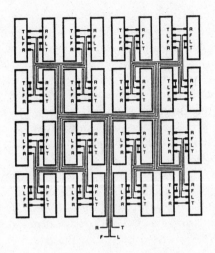

Figure 8-1
Printed circuit board of a binary tree computer.

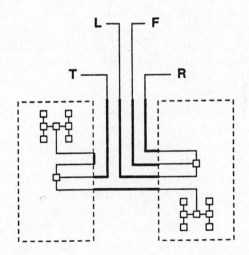

Figure 8-2
The interconnection of two computer chips in a binary tree computer.

problems than with a computer whose architecture is also found on the very same binary tree graph?

A binary tree has an enormous advantage over linear architectures in that it is possible to broadcast data through the entire system very rapidly. In addition, the geometry, or rather the topology, of such a network is of considerable advantage when designing a VLSI chip as C. E. Leiserson, one of the group's members, has shown. At the node of each branch of the computer tree, an arbitrarily large number of processing units (twigs) can be controlled by a single chip. Rather than requiring a multiplicity of interconnections, each chip has four terminals (T) to interconnect with the root of this branch or subtree, while F, L, and T attach to the father processor and its two children within the tree. A tree of arbitrary size can then be constructed out of the chips of this type.

Computers constructed with a binary tree architecture can range between two extremes when it comes to the individual processing units at each node. In one case the microprocessors are fairly sophisticated, containing several megabytes of memory, and are capable of being programmed to carry out a general task. At the other end of the scale, individual elements can do little more than simple addition and very elementary logic; programs cannot be stored in such processors but must be broadcast through the system so that processing is carried out in a lock step fashion. In between these two extremes lies a system in which each node has a small memory and modest processing abilities.

The Columbia group suggests that this intermediate system is in fact the most versatile and useful. A system that uses sophisticated processors at its nodes can duplicate anything that a simpler system can do but only at the expense of computing speed. On the other hand a system that uses the most elementary processing units can be very fast but is limited in what it can do and is normally designed to perform a specific task only. The group therefore decided on an intermediate form for what it calls its NON-VON computer. The system, which is still in the development stage, consists of two parts, a series of disk drives and a Primary Processing System (PPS) which is essentially a binary tree using VLSI circuits and is the heart of the computer. This PPS is connected via a rapid transfer system to the intelligent disk drives that work in parallel and will be used to implement large scale scientific computing problems. NON-VON has the added advantage of containing an internal switch in each processor which, when activated by a signal, can change its interconnections and modify the architecture of the computer from a binary tree to a linear array or a global bus communication. Information to be processed is not stored in a central location but broken down into a large number of small units that are distributed over the whole machine with each processor operating on a single primary unit of data.

Since the processors used in NON-VON need not be very sophisticated, they can be made quite small and a great number of them packed onto a single chip. It is here that NON-VON's power manifests itself, for by doing away with the need for storing programs locally at each node, the individual processing elements can be made so small and fast that for a reasonable price the NON-VON machine could ultimately operate with over a million elementary processing units.

To date the NON-VON machine has been simulated on a conventional parallel computer and used to model an intelligent data retrieval system. Current research by the group is directed towards developing algorithms for numerical computing in addition to carrying out manipulation of logic. So far little work has been done in developing algorithms for such highly parallel machines and not only the computer itself but its software is in the experimental stage. Proposed applications include the simulation of very complex physical systems such as plasmas and fluids, development of methods to be used in mathematical calculations (such as transformations of matrices), which are at present very laborious for von Neumann computers, but have important applications for scientific problems.

The largest of the parallel computers is probably a 16,000-microprocessor system used by NASA but most of these high powered systems tend to be used for very special purposes. Yet even at the level of a few tens of microprocessors a parallel machine exhibits considerable advantages in speed, power, and its ability to tackle problems with a parallel structure, over a conventional von Neumann computer. The Japanese fifth generation machine will also have a parallel architecture but it will be a general machine, capable of being purchased off the shelf, used for a wide variety of tasks, and capable of being programmed in a straightforward way using a high level language. Clearly there are many technical problems involving the design of both hardware and software that must be overcome before a fifth generation machine moves from the laboratory bench to a customer's office or factory.

Supercomputer Hardware

The parallel computers we have discussed above are all based on existing hardware, microprocessors that can be purchased off the shelf, or manufactured by a conventional process, and wired together to form a network. But scientists are already working on totally new forms of hardware and circuits that are no longer based on the transistor.

A modern high speed computer has a basic cycle time of 50 nanoseconds (50×10^{-9} seconds) with the advanced Cray-1 machine having an even faster cycle of only 12 nanoseconds. Within that time interval the computer can carry out a single basic operation and by combining several operations together in a series of cycles, the computer is able to perform a single step in logic or arithmetic. The fastest computer times around today represent a considerable improvement on earlier machines but they are also close to the theoretical limit at which a conventional computer can operate.

Leaving aside the move to parallel architecture, there are essentially two ways in which the speed of present day von Neumann computers can be improved. One is to reduce the time taken for a solid state device, such as a transistor, to switch between its two states. But current opinion has it that transistors are working close to their limit and that there is little possibility of increasing a computer's cycle time by designing new transistors. The other process that can be speeded up is the time taken for information to flow from one part of the machine to the next. This time lag is governed by the speed of an electronic signal which is a function of the dielectric properties of the circuits involved. With present materials this speed is half the speed of light, that is 1.5×10^{10} centimeters (cm) per second; different materials could slightly change this speed but it can never be greater than the velocity of light. So a signal that must travel 15 cm between components of a computer will take 1 nanosecond to make the journey and when several paths along a complicated winding geometry are involved, the actual travel time becomes a limiting factor in the speed of the computer. One answer to this problem of signal delay is to reduce the distances involved and pack components even closer together in a computer. But being able to pack electronic parts together and ensure that all the necessary connections are made is a particular tricky problem and involves not only considerations of geometry but also of topology (the mathematics of interconnections between objects).

In the past miniaturization has taken place very rapidly. The first integrated circuits of the 1960s contained less than 10 transistors while modern computers have advanced to a point where each high speed logic chip contains 40,000 transistors and the slower circuits used in microprocessors contain 100,000 transistors. The Japanese for their part are planning for chips that will contain ten million transistors. In turn these logic chips are packed very closely onto circuit boards and the circuit boards are interconnected and laid in parallel sheets in the computer. By adopting ingenious solutions to the packing problem more circuits on a single chip and more chips on a board can be packed together. But such compression cannot go on indefinitely, for at some point the problem of heat dissipation begins to dominate the computer. Each transistor, as it operates, gives off a tiny amount of heat. By itself this heat is negligible but when it is multiplied by the many millions of transistors that are found in a modern computer the total heat sums up to that generated by an average electric heater. If circuit boards are packed into a cabinet a few feet high, the whole computer can be aircooled by fans but if the same amount of computing power is compressed to a smaller area for greater speed, then watercooled metal sheets must be interspersed between the circuit boards. Miniaturize the computer even further and components will begin to melt from their own heat before any increase in speed occurs; the conventional computer has reached its limit.

The answer to this question of increasing speed by reducing the distance between components may be to do away with transistors altogether and build a "superconducting computer" which is not only intrinsically faster but can be compressed into an even smaller space. The key to such a device is to replace the transistor by a Josepheson junction which operates as a much faster switch, uses 10,000 times less power, and therefore generates much less heat. It has long been known that certain materials lose their electric resistance when cooled to temperatures close to absolute zero. At what is known as their critical temperature, the electrical resistance of a variety of substances vanishes, they act as short circuits to the flow of electricity and permit currents to flow indefinitely. A student at Cambridge University, Brian Josepheson, predicted that two superconductors, when separated by a thin insulating layer, would spontaneously generate a flow of current even with no source of power. This rather paradoxical effect, of producing a current with no battery or generator, was later demonstrated in the laboratory and has since led to all manner of scientifically useful devices. For example, a Josepheson junction is used to measure the atomic constants of nature and its extreme stability will eventually result in its international adoption as a primary electrical standard.

An important property of a Josepheson junction, from the computer engineer's point of view, is that it can act as a very high-speed switch. In one state the junction exhibits high resistance and in the other it offers no resistance at all. The actual switching time is very short and Josepheson junctions can be combined together to produce circuits which perform, at high speed, the same logical and arithmetic operations as those based on transistors. The advantage of a Josepheson device is that, in addition to its speed, it generates very little heat, the voltages it uses are 1,000 times lower, and its currents ten times lower than those found in conventional transistors. Hence Josepheson circuits can be placed very close together for extra speed and, in fact, the superconducting computer will take the form of a small cube immersed in a bath of liquid helium at $4°K$ ($-269°C$).

A Josepheson junction has an additional important property in that, unlike a transistor, it will operate with alternating current in addition to current current. One design calls for a superconducting computer that operates with A.C. current as 500 megahertz, in other words, a computer run by an internal clock that has 500 million "ticks" per second. This clock is distributed throughout the whole computer and can be used to coordinate the flow of data through the machine. One problem in running a parallel computer is that of synchronizing data as it emerges from individual processors. Usually this is done with a central clock but due to the finite speed with which signals travel through the computer the "local time" will be slightly different in each part of the machine. This problem may be less acute in a superconducting computer in which the clock is distributed across the entire system as a high frequency current. Present designs call for a computer that would fit into a cube a few inches long, have a very large memory, and be capable of processing 100 million instructions per second. But these projections are based on current designs and even faster machines are contemplated for the 1990s.

In Chapter 7 we met CART, the robot that could find its way through a room full of obstacles. CART built a picture of the world around it using a sequence of television images but needed some ten minutes to process the information it gathered on each of its stops. Imagine what would happen if CART's present brain were replaced by a superconducting computer. On computing speed alone the 10 minute stops would be reduced to 12 seconds and, in addition, the computer's much larger memory would be able to accommodate more sophisticated algorithms. So with improved programming, CART could be converted from a laboratory prototype to a robot that could run through a maze in real time. Similar advances would be made in language processing systems that would understand connected speech and hold conversations in real time. Chess computers and problem solving systems would be able to carry out more extensive tree searches and expert systems could store more general knowledge and heuristics in their expanded memories.

Is the superconducting computer the end of the hardware story? Is a massive electronic brain packed into a tiny cube and operating close to absolute zero the last word in superfast devices? Not quite, for another more speculative design is already being studied, a computer that does not use electronic signals at all but manipulates beams of light to perform its calculations. The secret of this optical computer is a solid state device called a transphasor that can switch states in 10^{-12} seconds, 1,000 times faster than the most advanced transistors.

Optical fibers have been used for several years to convey conversations, carried on laser beams, between telephones and to form high speed data links between computers. These fibers carry a high density of information at the speed of light and can be bent into circuits just like metal wires. In fact, laser beam messages need not be carried in optical fibers at all since very thin films, laid out in the same way as electronic printed circuits, will act as wave guides for laser messages. Since data, carried on laser beams, can be directed through a complete circuit in exactly the same way as electronic pulses on a microchip, then why not build a computer that uses light in place of electrons? The only missing component that is needed to complete the analogy between a light-based and an electronic computer is the transistor, for with the help of a transistor it is possible to build switching circuits that perform the arithmetic and logical operations used in all computing devices.

The optical analog of the transistor is called a transphasor, a relatively new device that was first demonstrated experimentally in the Bell Laboratories in 1976. Already scientists and engineers are thinking about using transphasors to design an optical computer that would be able to perform a trillion arithmetic operations per second. A transphasor works according to the same general principles that govern the movement of water waves between two harbor walls. As waves bounce off the stone walls they are reflected and move back across the harbor, meeting waves that have been reflected from the other wall. When two waves meet, their disturbances interfere with each other, for example, a crest and a trough will tend to cancel out while two crests or two troughs will produce a magnified effect. Exactly the same thing happens when laser light is trapped in the space between two mirrors, waves of light bounce back and forth between the mirrors and interfere with each other. Depending upon the precise distance between the two mirrors the waves may meet crest to trough and cancel out each other (through destrutive interference) or waves may meet crest for crest and magnify their effect (by constructive interference). Light shone through a mirror into the transphasor will either emerge from the other end, or be reflected back again, depending on whether constructive or destructive interference takes place inside.

At first sight a transphasor appears to be a static device, a switch that is forever off or on and either blocks or transmits light. How is it possible for the transphasor to actually switch between its states and change from a device which transmits to one which blocks light? The answer is that the transphasor is able to switch between constructive and destructive interference. It is possible to change the actual wavelength of light *inside* the device and this can be done by altering the refractive index inside the transphasor. (The refractive index is a measure of how much a substance bends light and is related to a change produced on the light's wavelength.) Because of the internal properties of a transphasor it is possible to change its refractive index, and hence switch its state from transmitting to nontransmitting, simply by altering the intensity of laser light entering the device, or alternatively by using a secondary triggering beam.

Scientists have discovered that substances that are presently being used to build solid state electronic circuits will also undergo these sudden changes in their refractive indices and can therefore be used to construct extremely rapid transphasor switches. With a transphasor the analogy with an electronic circuit is complete and it is theoretically possible to construct an extremely fast optical computer consisting of transphasor switches and optical circuit paths. Scientists are already speculating that it is possible to design an optical computer that would operate some 1,000 times faster than current machines. But this special increase is only the beginning, for the optical computer has an even greater potential to be explored. In a conventional computer a transistor accepts only one signal at a time. If more than one signal were to be put into the transistor, the resulting information would get hopelessly mixed up. A transphasor however is essentially a nonlinear device and this means that multiple signals sent into the device can be separated as they emerge. Using a transphasor in place of a transistor makes it possible to process several different laser beams of information simultaneously. A very natural design for an optical computer would therefore be to have its information channels constantly diverging and converging through individual transphasors. In other words, by the very nature of its most elementary components, an optical computer would be a massively parallel device.

In addition to its intrinsic ability to carry out parallel processing, even at the level of single circuit elements, an optical computer could also work with different forms of logic. A transistor has only two states, conducting and nonconducting which lends itself to a binary Boolean algebra, but a transphasor can switch through a variety of states, conducting, nonconducting, partly conducting, and so on. Transphasors in consequence are not confined to operations using Boolean logic but could operate in a natural way with, for example, multivalued logics and other deductive systems.

It is yet clear if an optical computer is technically possible. There may, for example, be a limit to the miniaturization of transphasors and the problem of dissipating heat energy that is absorbed from the laser light may set a limit to the number of components that can be packed together in a given space. But if an optical computer can be built then it will certainly be a massively parallel and extremely fast machine, possibly operating with various multivalued and "fuzzy" logics and using a design that is radically different from that of any computer that has gone before.

Research into computer hardware is also being directed to the development of very high capacity memory systems. The most compact memories that are presently available use solid optical effects that are "written" onto a semiconductor using laser pulses. Optical memories allow 10^8 (100,000,000) bits of information to be stored in each square centimeter and exceed the capacity of solid state magnetic memories by at least a factor of 10. However, the drawback to these devices is that they are nonreversible and information can be recorded on them only once. Optical memories are therefore used in conjunction with conventional memory systems and store only that part of a database which will not be modified or updated, for example, in the large databases associated with documents, images, or financial, legal, and medical records. However, scientists are now examining the properties of new amorphous materials to see if it is possible to develop reversible optical memories that can be repeatedly rewritten.

A more speculative approach is to use macromolecules directly for information storage by affecting their spectra and molecular structure. In one approach, a laser is used to produce quantum effects within low temperature solids. These quantum mechanical changes result in a very narrow gap or line within the spectrum of that particular substance. The gap can be interpreted as a single bit of information, a 1, and the absence of this gap as a 0. Hence, through *spectral line burning*, a whole series of very narrow gaps can be produced in the spectrum and interpreted as a digital message. Current experiments at IBM's San Jose laboratory indicate that 10^{11} (100,000,000,000) bits of information could be stored this way in a square centimeter of material.

Another technique is to imitate DNA and change the atomic structure of large molecules directly. It is now possible to produce very regular macromolecules by growing them on special solid supports. These giant polymers have a uniform backbone that is made out of regular, repeating blocks and can therefore act as the carrier for a molecular message. For example, if a single one of these blocks is changed, this could be interpreted as a 1 occurring in a chain of 0s. By changing the block back again the 1 would be transformed back into a 0. By performing atomic changes along the length of the macromolecule it is possible to encode a complex message in terms of 0s and 1s. But, of course, the molecular message code need not be simply binary since each building block can be changed in a number of distinct ways with each change corresponding to a different "letter" of the message alphabet.

By modifying the atomic structure of a very regular polymer it therefore becomes feasible to write messages, and hence store information, using a synthetic form of molecular code. The process is directly analogous to the way in which DNA stores the genetic code of an organism by means of its own four letter genetic code. The use of molecular carriers as memories would enable extended messages and large amounts of data to be stored in a very small area on individual macromolecules inside a computer. Current research is exploring the ways in which this information could be read and converted into digital signals inside a computer.

Teaching the Supercomputer

So far these speculative advances in computer hardware have been discussed quite independently from the development of a parallel computer. But what will happen when the two lines of research are brought together and a highly parallel machine uses fast superconducting hardware or optical transphasors with their multivalued logics? When two such advances are combined in the same machine it will be difficult to predict what the results will be, except that they will make our present day computers look incredibly crude and limited. Some researchers believe that with extremely fast and massively parallel networks, totally new types of behavior may emerge and computers may behave in a qualitatively more intelligent way. We shall explore some of these ideas in the next chapter but for the present we will reflect on how we will be able to use these large parallel computers if they are ever built. An immediate problem will be that of knowing how to program them, how to develop the necessary algorithms and rules for a parallel architecture, and how to use their parallel processing abilities to the fullest. Approaches to computing and problem solving have traditionally been adapted on the basis of overall constraint that each process takes place in a sequential step and hence, one step must be completed before the next can begin. But with a parallel computer it is possible to do many things at the same time. For example, all branches of a tree graph can be searched simultaneously, many edge detectors can work together on an image while higher parts of the program use this information to build primal sketches and integrate shape information, and guided by these hypothesis go back to direct the edge detectors. From the highest levels of problem solving to low level processing of a mathematical transform, new algorithms will have to be written to enable the computer to make the most of its new parallel processing abilities. Development of algorithms and parallel programming languages will occupy researchers over the next decade.

An even more interesting approach is to design a computer system that does not need to be fully programmed but given sufficient knowledge will begin to learn on its own, accumulate new information, update its database, and discover new ways of solving problems. It is inevitable that AI computers of the future will incorporate the ability to learn among their other functions. Learning, in its widest sense, is a characteristic of all living things and must be simulated at some point by any computer that attempts to act in an intelligent way. Automatic learning is therefore a necessary component of a supercomputer, not only is it an important aspect of intelligence, but it will help to overcome the problems of programming complex tasks on an advanced machine and constantly updating its knowledge base.

Living systems function as, what biologists and chemists call, open systems. An open system is one which constantly exchanges matter and energy with its surroundings, and in this way it is able to survive in a fluctuating environment. While the simplest systems are content to preserve their inner stability, those that are higher on the evolutionary chain are more flexible and able to work out new strategies for survival. Such organisms are able to adjust to their environments, take appropriate actions, and exploit any changes in their surroundings. In a sense it is possible to say that such systems all learn in that their actions are appropriate to external stimulii, their internal stability is preserved in an arbitrarily fluctuating environment, and they improve at certain of the tasks they are required to perform.

During the early years of the Dartmouth Conference there was considerable optimism that science could imitate nature and similar automatic learning systems could be constructed electronically. One approach was to build a network that was supposed to modify its internal structure in an appropriate way in response to stimulii and changes in its environment. It was even hoped that such networks would begin to evolve and would eventually exhibit intelligent behavior. But these early proposals were never realized in practice and the topic was dropped for a time only to come back into fashion more recently as AI workers face the problem of automatically updating expert systems and databases. The goal for expert systems, for example, is that one day they will be able to build themselves, learn from their mistakes, continuously improve in use, assess the current literature that is published in their field, extract what is new, and add it to their databases.

A true learning system not only accumulates new facts but is also able to restructure its internal knowledge and occasionally formulate new patterns and novel rearrangements of its knowledge. It is sometimes said that in order to learn something new one must first forget something old and there is a germ of wisdom in this maxim. Deep thinkers do not clutter their minds with masses of useless facts but choose only what is valuable to them, make interesting connections, new insights, original leaps of thought, and throw the rest away. One distinguished physicist told me that the most difficult thing in learning a new field was not in finding out what he had to know but what he did not have to bother about. Today people tend to be hypnotized by databases and believe that "the larger the better" and the more facts a database contains then the more powerful it must be. But even the largest database is of little use if the facts it contains are totally static and cannot be used in creative ways. Knowledge bases of the future must be in a constant state of flux, making new connections and patterns, and reassessing and reorganizing their data whenever it is appropriate. This means that the knowledge base must understand its own organization and be able to operate on several different levels of learning.

We have already met the concept of the meta level, a level which controls and understands the patterns and operations that take place on the level below it. But a learning system must also go beyond this meta level to its meta meta level. (And why stop there?) As new facts and rules are discovered, the meta level organizes them into patterns, modifies relationships, and adds new facts to old. But at some point these patterns of knowledge may begin to break down or the computer may not be able to respond in an appropriate way to a new situation. The intelligent machine must now look critically at its own meta-knowledge and discover that its mechanical approach to pattern building is no longer appropriate to the new state of affairs. A meta meta level therefore modifies the level below it and allows a totally novel range of behaviors and pattern building to come into being. True learning systems should therefore be able to assimilate facts, make hypotheses, generate theories about what they are doing, and when it is appropriate they must be able to abandon these theories in revolutionary ways by, for example, changing their rules of inference so that they continue to improve their performance as they function.

But how can a computer learn, how can it break its own rules and learn to create new patterns?

We have already met some learning systems in this book. In Chapter 3 there was a chess playing machine that searched at a given depth through its game tree, evaluated the various board positions at this depth, and then made the move that would lead to the most commanding position. The effectiveness of each board position was assessed by using a set of criteria, each of which had a particular weight. These criteria took into consideration, for example, the position of the queen, relative values of pieces and control over the center of the board and the relative weights expressed how important these criteria were. At this stage the chess playing computer is not a learning system since it assesses each move in a fully automatic way given a set of criteria and appropriate weights. A slightly more interesting possibility which allows for a little learning would be to leave these weights open and undefined and allow the computer to play a series of games with a human opponent, another computer, or simply read classic games in chess. Based on its performance the computer would be able to build up its own set of values for the criteria of position strengths; if the program were further developed it could even create its own criteria of which positions were the most commanding. In this way the chess playing computer would be able to build hypotheses about the value of certain moves and improve with the number of games it played. This is an example of a rather simple learning system but it does give an idea of one way in which a computer system could learn from experience to improve its performance. General learning, however, is a very complex process so research has tended to concentrate only on specific issues and restricted situations. Within those domains computer systems have been built that can take advice, modify their knowledge bases and learn from new examples which have been investigated.

The idea of a system that could learn by taking advice dates back to a 1958 paper by AI pioneer John McCarthy. When a human being learns a new task or how to play a new game he generally begins with some general idea of what is going on and then asks for advice, or is given gratuitous hints by those around him (particularly if the game happens to be golf). The starting point in advice taking therefore is to know enough about the task to realize that you are stuck, that your performance is not up to par, and that there is something you don't know. The next step is to use the limited knowledge you aleady have in order to form an appropriate request for assistance. A mere unstructured cry of "help" may not be much use for it puts all the burden on the teacher who must then interpret where the novice has gone wrong and what he needs to know. So to be able to ask for advice requires intelligence, some very general understanding about the task, and being able to appreciate that one's performance is not adequate.

The reply when it arrives is normally given in a high level language and will also require interpretation. Some people who give advice use jargon or assume that the learner knows quite a bit about the task in hand. In the case of a learning computer the advice must first be interpreted, if it is given in English, understood, and then translated into the system's internal representation.

Learning through advice therefore involves a number of quite complicated processes which begin at the level of recognizing that help is needed, continue with interpreting and understanding the advice, and end by rearranging the system's knowledge base to accommodate the new information. This last stage involves a number of different processes, for example, it may be necessary to modify a rule, change a piece of knowledge, or even restructure a group of relationships based on the advice. The computer must therefore be able to understand the implications of a piece of advice for the whole system after it has received it. For example, advice can be tested internally by making inferences from it or by linking the advice into a knowledge network and observing if it generates inconsistencies or overlaps with existing knowledge. The computer may also decide to test the worth of advice it has received and discover its actual significance. In human situations advice may be incomplete, ambiguous, unclear, mixed with irrelevancies and, on occasion, incorrect. The computer must be able to resolve ambiguities in such advice, select what is relevant, and have some measure of how important this advice is to its overall performance. Learning systems therefore need an objective way of assessing their performance and discovering if they are actually improving and which of their possible strategies will lead to the best results. These criteria could be based on winning or losing a series of games, on being able to carry out a series of movements with a robot or mechanical arm, or on an internal model of the world in which various actions can be played out in an abstract fashion.

A number of experimental advice taking systems have already been built, for example by the Heuristic Programming Project at Standford University, and by groups at Carnegie-Mellon University and the Rand Corporation. FOO, designed by D. J. Mostow, is a novice in the game of Hearts and accepts such advice as "Avoid taking points." The system interprets this advice not as a new rule but as a goal to be achieved and develops its own strategies which attempt to satisfy this goal wherever possible. FOO, however, cannot understand English or interpret statements directly so the user must first express his advice in terms of a logical calculus. Advice taking has also been explored in the game of draw poker.

Another approach to learning is by using analogies. Most teachers who have to introduce something new to their students will begin by using an analogy. First the students are encouraged to recall something familiar and then they are led into the new concept which they are encouraged to relate to what they already know. Analogies are useful ways of helping students to grasp something novel, to understand how some new idea works or functions. Often when one is confused about some new concept one will say, "Yes, but what is it like?" Physicists, in particular, make great use of analogy and when a new equation is written down on a blackboard will say, "That reminds me a little of the equation which governs fluid flow (or whatever)." By exploring the behavior of a system that is already well known, the physicist gains insights into a new system that while it is physically quite distinct is also analogous in terms of the equations that describe it.

311

Analogy can also be applied to the computer as a way of teaching them how to do new things. For example, expert systems are often concerned with making diagnoses and arriving at solutions and treatments. If a system is to be adapted from one general field of disease to another, or from a medical diagnosis to diagnosing defects in an automobile or faults in a manufacturing process, then its knowledge of how to operate in one field could help to extend the system to its new field. Little work, however, has been done on the way systems can learn by analogy. An exception is EURISKO, a Standford University system, which is designed to learn and discover new concepts, heuristics, and procedures in several fields. Current research on this system includes having it discover analogies both within and between the various domains it has worked with.

Patrick H. Winston from M.I.T. is also developing computer learning systems that make use of analogies, precedents, and examples. One approach, called MACBETH, looks for analogies between simple plots and makes deductions about new situations based on their similarities to a precedent. For example, take this highly simplified account of Shakespeare's play "Macbeth."

MA is a story about Macbeth, Lady-Macbeth, Duncan and Macduff. Macbeth is an evil Noble, Lady-Macbeth is a greedy ambitious woman. Duncan is a king. Macduff is a Noble.

Lady-Macbeth persuades Macbeth to want to be king because she is greedy. She is able to influence him because he is married to her and because he is weak. Macbeth murders Duncan with a knife. Macbeth murders Duncan because Macbeth wants to be king and because Macbeth is evil. Lady-Macbeth kills herself. Macduff is angry. Macduff kills Macbeth because Macbeth murdered Duncan and because Macduff is loyal to Duncan.

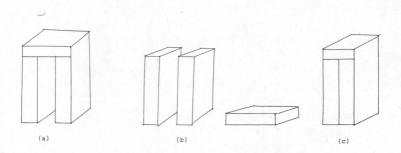

(a) (b) (c)

Figure 8-3
Working within a block world, Patrick Winston's ARCH program attempted to teach a computer to recognize an arch. (a) is clearly an arch—it has two vertical and one horizontal blocks—but so does (b). Clearly it is important that the horizontal block should be placed on top of the two vertical ones. (c) is another exception; the blocks are now in the correct relation but the two vertical blocks are too close together to make an arch. The program learns through a series of near misses.

MA establishes a web of relationships and interactions between characters in the story as well as telling us something about their qualities and station in life. In terms of these qualities and relationships MA has analogies with the story E below:

Let E be an exercise. E is a story about a weak noble

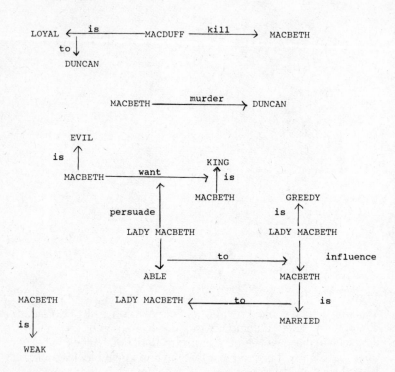

Figure 8-4
The web of relationships that link the various characters and their actions in the scenario MA.

and a greedy lady. The lady is married to the noble. In E show that the noble may want to be king.

Both stories contain nobles and both contain "greedy" women who are married to these nobles. But the power of an analogy lies in the insight that two things that are similar in

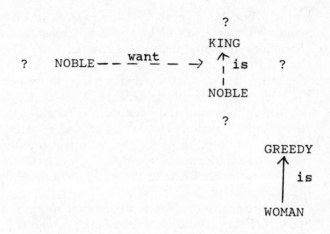

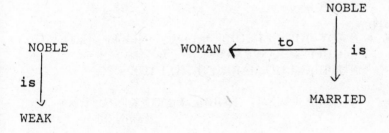

Figure 8-5
Scenario E has certain features in common with MA. Are the relationships sufficient to enable the computer to deduce that the NOBLE wishes to be KING?

some respects may also be similar in others. Equally important in using an analogy is to understand its differences. In fact the whole point about an analogy is that it *is* about a different situation or thing. MA can therefore act as a precedent for E and help to discover if the noble in E may wish to be king. Winston's approach is to express MA in terms of a semantic network in which various relationships connect the characters and qualities. For example, Lady Macbeth has the relationships "Has Quality Greedy" and "Influence Macbeth." These relationships form a pattern of directed lines between nodes in the network. Story E also has its own pattern of lines and it is possible to overlay the two networks so that various characters or nodes match and then attempt to find patterns that are common to both. In other words, the analogies between the two stories can be expressed in terms of similar networks of lines. The diagrams below make this clear.

This procedure enables the computer to deduce that the noble in E may indeed want to be king. The result can be generalized in the form of a rule:

Rule
    RULE-1
if
    (LADY-4 HQ GREEDY) where HQ stands for "Has Quality"
    (NOBLE-4 HQ WEAK)
    ((NOBLE-4 HQ MARRIED) TO LADY-4)
then
    (NOBLE-4 WANT (NOBLE-4 AKO KING)) where AKO
                                stands for "A Kind of"
case
    MA.

So Winston's MACBETH program allows rules to be generated by precedents and applied to analogous situations. So far the approach to learning is conventional and the results are not unexpected. The interesting point emerges when we realize that RULE-1 is too general and can lead to misleading deductions. Take for example the story below:

Let F be an exercise. F is a story about a weak noble and a greedy lady. The lady is married to a noble. He does

not like her. In F show that the noble may want to be
king.

In this case, Winston argues, because the noble does not like
his wife he will take little notice of her and therefore she will
have no influence over him. Although the two stories form
an analogy and have patterns of relationships in common,
these interconnections are insufficient to establish the noble's
desire to be king and RULE-1 does not apply. In a conventional approach one would, at this point, modify the rule,
list its exceptions, add tests for its applicability, and so on.
Winston's approach is to invoke what he calls censors. A
censor acts on a rule to block its application if some other
factor is mentioned in the story. In addition, Winston augmented rules by adding "unless" clauses so that a rule will
apply only under certain conditions. Augmented by an
"unless" condition our rule now reads:

```
Rule
    RULE-1
if
    (LADY-4 HQ GREEDY)
    (NOBLE-4 HQ WEAK)
    ((NOBLE-4 HQ MARRIED) TO LADY-4))
then
    (NOBLE-4 WANT (NOBLE-4 AKO KING))
unless
    ((LADY-4 PERSUADE (NOBLE-4 WANT (NOBLE-4 AKO
                                  KING))) HQ FALSE)
    (((LADY-e HQ ABLE) TO (LADY-4 INFLUENCE NOBLE
                                  4)) HQ FALSE)
```

In the case of the augmented RULE-1 its censor reads:

```
if
    ((PERSON-B LIKE PERSON-7) HQ FALSE)
then
```

317

(((PERSON-7 HQ ABLE) TO (PERSON-7 INFLUENCE PERSON-8)) HQ FALSE)

The censor acts in story F to block the application of RULE-1 and it cannot be deduced that the noble wishes to be king.

Just as rules can be accumulated into a system through precedents so "unless" conditions and censors are also accumulated as the system learns. But a closer examination indicates that censors will have their own censors to block *their* application. For example, the analogy between two stories may suggest the application of a particular rule which allows the computer to make a deduction and a difference between the stories suggest the application of a censor which blocks this rule. But, in turn, a difference between these differences may indicate that this censor itself must be blocked by an additional censor. The effect of this double blocking is to allow the rule to be applied unimpeded.

The censor we generated for RULE-1 is over-general for we sometimes notice that people who do not like each other can still have an influence over each other's actions, particularly if one of them is willing to trust what the other says. This condition can form the basis of a censor which can occasionally act on our previous censor:

if
    ((PERSON-6 HQ ABLE) TO (PERSON-6 CONVINCE PERSON-5))
then
    (PERSON-5 TRUST PERSON-6)

Winston's goal is to increase the power of learning systems by allowing computers to generate rules, augment these rules, and accumulate censors to rules. During a learning session, the computer should increase its power to make deductions and to discriminate between the differences in various stories.

Another powerful way of learning is by examples that give

a particular instance of how a rule or process works and show how a rule works within a particular context. When we learn from examples we deal with particular cases and try to generalize what we have done by searching for wider principles that lie behind the particularities of each example.

Indeed the history of science can be interpreted as moving from the particular to the general as its laws evolve into greater degrees of generality. It has also become the fashion to structure both science and mathematics in a logical, hierarchical fashion beginning at the particular and concrete, and moving upwards towards levels of increasing generality and abstraction. In this scheme each level embraces the levels that lie below it and the progress of science is expressed as a climb towards the top of the hierarchy. Some contemporary physicists believe that science is close to this final layer and that within a decade or so it will have reached the top and discovered the most general and embracing laws of nature. These same thinkers often see other disciplines such as chemistry and biology as occupying lower levels on the pyramid of science. Of course not everyone agrees with such a view of science and its progress, but it has infiltrated much of our thinking and it gives an added appeal to the attempts to teach computers by example.

Learning by example appeals to our perceived notions of how knowledge is supposed to be structured, it mirrors the processes of the classroom, and it echoes one of the ways in which we act as we learn something new. But the work of Jean Piaget suggests that in very young children, at least, learning does not always take place from the particular to the general but may involve the reverse direction. His experience indicates that young children begin with the broadest logical operations they can apply to the world and only later does their thought descend to the less general. Piaget suggests that, for adults, it is extremely difficult to rediscover these logically prior operations in their thinking and that the history of science is, in a sense, a rediscovery in reverse of our mental processes for dealing with the world.

319

Learning by example can also be applied to the world of computers and by generalizing from a series of examples, rules, and procedures can be generated. For example, a computer could be taught to play a game by first programming or teaching it the rules of the game and then exposing it to a series of "best moves." In this way the machine could evolve its own strategies and tactics for winning. In addition, categories need not be taught by means of a general definition but by telling the computer about a number of objects and then indicating which of them belongs to that category. For example, a full house in poker could be taught by giving the computer such instances as

10	♡	10	◇	10	♠	A	◇	A	♡
4	♣	4	♡	4	◇	8	♡	8	◇
3	◇	3	♠	3	♡	K	♡	K	◇

and counterexamples such as:

A	♡	A	◇	A	♠	A	♣	2	◇
3	◇	4	◇	5	◇	6	◇	6	♣
2	♠	2	♣	3	♡	3	◇	4	♣

With sufficient examples the computer is able to deduce that a full house consists of a pair and three of a kind. In general cases the computer will search among the examples for a pattern of rules and then resolve any ambiguities by looking for counterexamples.

Herbert Simon and G. Lea expressed this process of learning in an abstract formalism in which the "instant space" of examples is generalized into a "rule space." The instant space contains low level information which is transformed during learning into high level information within the rule space. Expressed in this way the problem is not unlike that of recognizing a solid object from a photograph or drawing.

The photograph (instant space) is flat and two-dimensional and contains partial clues about three-dimensional objects (rule space). In mathematical terms the process of interpretation involves a mapping from two dimensions into three and involves ambiguities and uncertainties since there is insufficient information in the photograph to reconstruct the full three-dimensional scene. In the case of computer vision the solution is to provide additional information, either world knowledge or in the form of a sequence of photographs. In the same way, the instant space requires either a sequence of examples or some additional general knowledge to allow the rule space to be constructed.

Computer learning systems have been designed to generate general rules when they are presented with a sequence of examples. The process can be assisted by making each example clear and free from ambiguities. In addition, the examples can be presented in a carefully designed sequence so that what is needed to interpret a particular case will already have been learned in the earlier examples.

Broadly speaking, the system begins with examples that are simple to understand and interpret. Then, as it accumulates more information, the system begins to generate its knowledge and build its rule space. Additional examples are then used to clarify ambiguities, clear up errors, and expand rules to new cases. Ideally, the learning system should be a front end to some other computer system such as an expert system.

Currently a number of different learning systems are being explored in the laboratory. Meta-DENDRAL for example acts as a learning system for the expert system DENDRAL and discovers new heuristics that enable the master system to work more effectively. LEX is designed to learn how to integrate algebriac expressions and is based on a series of rules for simplifying expressions and producing the integrals of standard expressions. Provided with examples, LEX learns how to apply its rules to a number of situations. HACKER is designed to model a human novice who is learning programming skills. The system develops a variety of plans which it endeavors to put into practice.

Donald Waterman from Stanford University chose a fairly complicated field for his learning system—the game of draw poker. Poker differs from games like chess because the exact state of the game is never known exactly to the players and a minimax approach to winning cannot therefore be adopted. The computer system must therefore develop its own heuristics and learn the strategies of poker by playing against an expert, taking advice, and analyzing its play. It is able to take into account the effect of variables like the size of the pot, its ability to bluff, the size of the last bet, and the value of its own hand. Some idea of the relative importance of its three methods of learning can be seen from the table below:

Training method	Number of training trials	Final number of rules	Percentage difference in winnings
Before training	0	1	−71.0
Advice taking	38	26	− 6.8
Automatic training	29	19	− 1.9
Analytic method	57	14	−13.0

The computer begins in an inferior position by playing at random, within the rules of poker, and loses consistently to his opponent, but after 29 sessions of automatic training, it is almost level with an expert human poker player. The results also appear to indicate that learning by analyzing each game after it is played gives inferior results to automatic play, but this is a little unfair since the procedures of the program were not identical in both cases.

BACON is a learning system that "discovers" some of the fundamental relationships of physics. The system learns by exploring data, developing hypotheses, and then refining them with the aid of further examples. During its operation, BACON "discovered," among other things, Ohm's law, Newton's law of universal gravitation, the ideal gas law and

BACON AND KEPLER'S LAWS

The table below gives the mean distance from the sun, in km, and the period, in days, of several planets:

Planet	Distance (d)	Period (p)
Mercury	58×10^6	87.97
Venus	108×10^6	224.70
Earth	149×10^6	365.26
Mars	228×10^6	686.98

BACON uses data that is scaled so that the periods and distances in the case of Mercury are both equal to 1. Given the initial data the system attempts its first hypothesis; that d/p is constant

Planet	Input Data		Hypothesis
	d	p	d/p
Mercury	1	1	1.0
Venus	4	8	0.5
Earth	9	27	0.33

This hypothesis fails and BACON continues with other formulas until it discovers the Kepler Law.

Planet	Input Data		Hypotheses	
	d	p	d^2/p	d^3/p^2
Mercury	1	1	1.0	1.0
Venus	4	8	2.0	1.0
Earth	9	27	3.0	1.0

Kepler's law. The system acts by examining its data and, with the help of a built-in set of rules that generate simple mathematical relationships and detect for differences, it searches for patterns or regularities which can form the basis of an hypothesis. Once a hypothesis has been constructed for a particular section of data it is then applied to the rest of the data and is either confirmed or modified into a more general hypothesis. Take, for example, the "discovery" of the law of planetary motions. In *De Harmonice Mundi*, published in 1619, Johann Kepler wrote

> on the fifteenth of May, by a new onset it overcame by storm the shadow of my mind, with such fullness of agreement between my seventeen years' labor on the observations of Brahe and this present study of mine that at first I believed that I was dreaming and was assuming as an accepted principle what was still a subject of enquiry. But the principle is unquestionably true and quite exact: the periodic times of any two planets are to each other exactly as the cubes of the square roots of their median distances. (That is, the square of the time of revolution of each planet is proportional to the cube of its mean distance from the sun.)

BACON, for its part, is supplied with data on the mean distance of each planet from the sun and its time of revolution. It notices first that the time of revolution increases with the distance from the sun and therefore makes a first attempt to interpret the data by means of a linear law: The time of revolution is proportional to the mean distance from the sun. Such a law can be fitted to the data for one planet but does not turn out to fit the data for all of them, so BACON rejects its first hypothesis and looks for additional relationships between period and distance until it rediscovers the law first formulated by Kepler. In similar fashion, BACON will rediscover other laws of physics using different data.

It is at this point that the author feels necessary to add an important qualification. BACON learns by examining data, constructing hypotheses, and checking them against the data it has been supplied with. In this it is a successful learning system and performs as its creator Pat Langley of Carnegie-Mellon University intended. But it is by no means legitimate to claim, as others have done, that BACON actually *rediscovers* the laws of physics, as if the computer were duplicating some scientific process of reasoning. Artificial intelligence began at the Dartmouth College conference with some inflated predictions of its future. Since that time researchers have tended to be more down-to-earth in their discussions of the subject but there are still some who make excessive and inaccurate claims. These claims are generally based on the achievements of an actual system but omit its drawbacks and limitations. In public lectures I have heard it said that BACON, among other systems, given as an example of how a computer can duplicate human intelligence and make discoveries just as a human scientist does. But this is not the case and distortions of this nature must be an embarrassment to the system's designer since they give a false impression of BACON's function.

Scientific discovery consists of far more than simply shifting through a set of predigested data and looking for regularities. If that were all there was to the formulation of new laws then classical physics could be "rediscovered" by a school child. True scientific discovery involves sorting out what is important and what is inessential within a very complicated system. In the case of planetary motion as Kepler put it,

All the planets revolve in eccentric orbits; that is, they alter their distance from the Sun, so that in one part of their orbit they are very remote from the Sun, while in the opposite part they come very near to the Sun.

Before Kepler, it was not at all clear what were the essential parameters of planetary motion or indeed that there should be any relationship between the orbit of one planet and the next. Kepler's discovery depended on the insight that the whole solar system forms a pattern and the key to that pattern lies in the sun's influence over all other bodies. But the idea that the sun could influence a planet that is millions of miles away must have seemed absurd. A physicist of our own time, Wolfgang Pauli, has shown how Kepler only came to accept such a relationship by meditating on the Trinity and using that as the archetype for the sun's influence on the planets. And if the periods of rotation of the planets are to be considered as key data, then why not also take into account their masses, the rotations about their axes, the eccentricities of their orbits, and so on? Kepler's discovery also depended on knowing what to leave out as much as knowing what was essential to the problem.

BACON, for its part, is supplied with data that has been very carefully chosen so that only the very essential elements of the pattern are presented; there are no inessential elements present, no experimental errors, uncertainties, or scatter. BACON, therefore, does not really understand anything about planetary motion, it simply looks for simple relationships between columns of numbers and is unable to deal with the normal errors that are presented in experimental data or with irrelevant observations. As a learning system which can develop hypotheses based on raw data, BACON exhibits interesting behavior but it is not true to say that the computer system can simulate the process of scientific discovery.

AM is a learning system designed to make discoveries, not in physics this time, but in mathematics. Its powerful feature is that it already begins with some knowledge about a branch of mathematics called set theory and with over 200 heuristic rules. AM does not rely on external examples of data but works on its own to explore its internal knowledge and to create new concepts and conjectures in mathematics. AM's data is written in the form of *frames*, each of which refers to a particular mathematical concept and contains its definition, examples and counterexamples, generalizations, relationships to other concepts, conjectures, and analogies.

AM USES FRAMES TO REPRESENT ITS
KNOWLEDGE OF MATHEMATICS

NAME: Prime Numbers
DEFINITIONS:
  ORIGIN: Number-of-divisors-of(x) = 2
  PREDICATE-CALCULUS : Prime(x) = (x)(z x = z
    = 1 z = x)
  ITERATIVE: (for x 1):For i from 2 to sqrt(x), (i x)
EXAMPLES: 2,3,5,7,11,13,17
  BOUNDARY: 2,3
  BOUNDARY FAILURES: 0,1
  FAILURES: 12
GENERALIZATIONS: Nos.;Nos. with an even no.
  of divisors, Nos. with a prime no. of divisors.
SPECIALIZATIONS: Odd Primes, Prime Pairs,
  Prime Uniquely-addables
CONJECTURES: Unique factorization, Goldbach's
  conjecture,
  Extremes of Number-of-divisors-of
ANALOGIES:
  Maximally divisible numbers are converse
  extremes of
  Number-of-divisors-of,
  Factor a nonsimple group into simple groups
INTEREST: Conjectures associating Primes with
  TIMES and with Divisors-of
WORTH: 800

In addition, each concept is given a value first by providing a numerical score for the "worth" of the concept and, in addition, for listing areas of mathematical interests which are related to that concept.

Set in operation, AM begins to generate examples, based on a particular concept, and examines them for regularities and patterns. Since the search is constrained to move into worthwhile areas of mathematics, the system does not branch out blindly but only follows those paths that would generally attract the attention of a human mathematician. As more examples are generated, the system will propose a conjecture or define a novel concept. This information is then broadcast through the system to the appropriate frames where it is tested for consistency against existing knowledge.

In a typical run, AM began with 115 mathematical concepts and after working unaided for several hours generated 200 new concepts, many of which were mathematically important. For example, after developing the field of set theory, it went on to create the concept of the natural numbers, followed by the rules of arithmetic and powers and roots. AM was never able to discover the rational and irrational numbers but it did develop the concept of prime numbers and even of prime pairs. As the system explored its internal knowledge it was able to create a number of conjectures about prime numbers and in one case its path of reasoning involved 14 new concepts and moved through several levels of a derivation tree.

What AM achieved is mathematically interesting and with the help of its "worth" score and indications of areas of interest, it avoided superficial conjectures. One drawback of the system, however, is that after running for some time, the information it generates becomes less significant. This is because, as its conjectures grow, AM is unable to change its heuristic rules. An obvious improvement therefore would be to have it modify its heuristics as it learns. Douglas Lenat, AM's creator, has gone on to work on the EURISKO project at Stanford which is exploring additional learning processes.

Learning systems have also been developed for parallel processing computers. In the next chapter we shall meet Ross Quillian's semantic network which, in theory, could learn new concepts by "broadcasting" their effects throughout the network. Another learning network has been built by Geoffry Hinton and Terrence Sejnowski. "The Boltzmann

Machine," as they call their device, is a perceptual network and at first sight recalls the Perceptron, an early attempt at a neural network. The Boltzmann Machine, however, also simulates the "noise" of a real neural network with small random fluctuations which produce a constant flux in the hypotheses that are created in its electronic brain. Rather than dealing with visual perception, the system's perceptions are in the form of strings of binary digits that are fed to it during the learning phase. These numbers are coded into a simple pattern which the system learns to recognize. After feeding The Boltzmann Machine for several hours with the original numbers and their encoded form, the network begins to build up an internal representation of the code.

The Boltzmann Machine is a true learning machine that does not rely for its operation on any external program or centralized control. However, the tasks it performs are particularly simple (recognizing a code in which numbers are permuted in an elementary pattern), and it does not make use of any internal knowledge as a biological learning system does.

By the end of the decade there will probably exist complex computer programs that began originally as man/machine collaborations and went on to increase in their complexity through the action of expert programming and learning systems. There will be expert systems designed and built by other expert systems, databases whose organization and control has been created by the computers themselves, and computers that learn and constantly improve their performance. Systems will exist using highly parallel, ultrafast computers which began as human based designs but were refined, modified, and expanded by the computers they were originally built for. Some time before the end of this century these systems will design new and revolutionary computer architectures and advanced algorithms. By that time, it is probable that no human will be fully able to understand the details of these computer systems, for they will simply have become too complicated for anyone to keep track of them.

But this does not imply that the computers of the 1990s will necessarily have become intelligent or that they will be doing the sort of creative things beloved of the science fiction writer. It simply means that as computers learn, become more expert, and increase in speed and memory, their control will pass out of our hands and into the hands of the machines themselves. Of course, we humans will still be in ultimate control, we will still be able to pull the plug if we wish, but we may no longer fully understand what motivates a computer's behavior or what its full potential can be.

CHAPTER 9
Beyond the Silicon Brain

A number of questions were asked on the first page of this book: Can a machine think? Is a computer aware of its own existence? Will the twenty-first century see the evolution of a silicon-based intelligence that is parallel to our own? Now, having reached the final chapter, we can begin to answer them or at least to understand the complexities and subtleties that are involved in posing them.

Can a Machine Think?

In the previous chapters we have learned about some of the things that computers are very good at doing, particularly when it comes to things like playing chess, solving certain sorts of problems, carrying out very complicated calculations, and performing diagnoses in a limited field. But in other areas, like vision, coordinated movement, and language, computers have only made limited progress. This state of affairs seems somewhat paradoxical for the things

331

we do so well that we hardly have to think about them (watching a movie, reading a novel, holding a conversation, playing tennis, and walking down a crowded street) are extremely difficult for computers, while on the other hand, the same computer can be masterful at tasks that stretch our own abilities, such as mathematics, chess, medical diagnoses, and troubleshooting of electronic circuits. It may be that the paradox can be resolved in the following way: Some of the things we do exceptionally well are very complex tasks that require multiple levels of processing but they are also the result of tens of thousands or even millions of years of evolution in which these processes have been refined to a high degree and "hard wired" into our brains. We do not find the act of speaking or recognizing a face to be immensely difficult because all the processing and problem solving takes place below the level of our conscious mind and appears to us as trivially simple. "Difficult things," on the other hand, involve tasks that are evolutionarily more recent and must therefore be carried out in the arena of conscious thought. As we perform a calculation, call on our knowledge of a particular field, or work out the solution to a tricky problem, we seem to be involved in a constant process of choice and control over the various steps involved. Although the process of the problem may be far less complicated than that involved in seeing or speaking or moving, because we are conscious of the steps and effort involved in carrying them out the task appears to us to be far more difficult.

Society tends to praise those who have trained their minds to engage in hard intellectual work. But the lesson of the expert computer system may be that this intellectual labor is not that impressive after all. In fact "thinking," which has such a high premium in our society, may not be as significant as other activities of the mind. Thought may turn out to be a rather superficial activity of the brain, the foam on top of the ocean wave, when compared to other activities. If intelligence is the ability to interact in creative and appropriate ways within the world then thought and intellectual labor may occupy only a small part of this larger intelligence. Taken in this sense it may indeed be true that computers will soon be in a position to simulate much of what we take as thinking but that does not necessarily mean that these computers will be particularly intelligent, creative, and capable of deep insight.

Our original paradox could, however, be analyzed in a different way. In tasks like chess, problem solving, and diagnosis, a combination of introspection and psychological experimentation expose the ground rules of what is happening and enable the process to be programmed on a computer. But since introspection is of little help in vision or language understanding, our human based models have only limited range and validity and we are therefore forced to make hypotheses and create theories as to how the hidden processes may take place. In consequence, these tasks are far more difficult to program on a computer. I feel, however, this is simply a consequence of the account I presented earlier and that computer vision is a doubly difficult task, first because of its intrinsic complexity and second because we are not conscious of how we see and therefore we have no full theory that can be programmed onto a computer.

The answer to our first question is therefore a limited "yes." Yes, machines will be able to think and when they do we will have a clearer idea of the limitations of human thought.

Bearing in mind the author's reservations, it is certainly true that computers have been able to simulate a number of aspects of the brain's behavior. But since we know that a computer's actions are conditioned by its program some would not wish to call what a computer does thinking. On the other hand they would be forced to agree that in limited situations, at least, a computer is able to simulate some of the actions of a being that thinks, solves problems, plays games, and interprets complicated situations.

F. David Peat

Cognitive Science

The ability to mimic certain processes of the mind has given rise to a new discipline called cognitive science. This field attempts to simulate mental processes on the computer. Psychologists and neuroscientists gain deep insights through their experiments on animals and their observations on humans but at some stage in formulating hypotheses and theories they may need to call on new metaphors to express their ideas and discover new ways of testing them. Cognitive science can be of help since it provides some very important metaphors and symbolic ways of looking at systems, which it has learned from artificial intelligence, computer science, and control theory. In addition, it forces a theory to be expressed in an explicit and transparent way so that it can be programmed and simulated on a computer. With the simulation in operation, cognitive scientists can then study the behavior it generates and compare this with their observations on human subjects. Simulations can be particularly valuable in understanding very complex systems and have been used to advantage in such sciences as physics, chemistry, and biology. It is only now that their importance is being realized in psychology and the neurosciences.

By borrowing from artificial intelligence, cognitive science is able to gather new information about the ways in which the brains of humans and animals work. This flow of knowledge and insights also takes place in the opposite direction since simulations of the brain's processing can be of help in designing new AI systems. Research on biological vision, for example, has been of help in suggesting ways to process images by the computer. Insights about how cells in the retina work led David Marr to formulate his zero-crossing rule and develop edge detection programs. Another area in which the brain gives us a powerful metaphor is in parallel processing. We know that the human brain is able to carry out many different tasks at the same time and that each of these tasks involves a substantial amount of parallel process-

334

ing. In this case it looks as if the computer will follow the design of a human brain and its internal parallel processes will become closer to our own. On the other hand, it could be argued that even if we have never examined a single brain we would still adopt a parallel architecture for our computers. Parallel processing seems to be forced on computers by the very nature of the problems they are faced with. It should also be pointed out that these problems have been selected and presented to the computer by agents with parallel processing brains. The world we live in forces any intelligent being to evolve along the same general lines of being able to move, take action, sense the environment in efficient ways, reflect on what it senses, and take appropriate action based on this reflection. Faced with such constraints, it seems inevitable that carbon- and silicon-based brains would come up with similar solutions and parallel process much of the information they collect.

Another field in which brains and computers are similar is in having memories and being able to structure them in ways that are appropriate for particular tasks such as movement, vision, language, problem solving, and thought. Since memory is one of the great mysteries of the human mind and in the case of the computer brain, building an intelligent knowledge base is one of the current challenges, it is possible that these two fields will act to cross-fertilize each other.

While carrying out brain surgery in the 1950s, the Canadian neuroscientist Wilder Penfield discovered that electrical stimulation of small areas of the brain evokes specific memories. This suggested that memory is encoded in specific locations like a computer memory. However, when U.S. neuroscientist Karl Spenser Lashley tried to locate these specific memory areas of "engrams," his evidence pointed in the opposite direction, towards a delocalized, distributed form of memory. Evidence for this distributed memory came not only from work on laboratory animals but through observations on brain injured patients which showed that, unlike a localized computer memory, brain memories can survive a variety of damage.

Research into human memory has been given additional impetus today by new noninvasive techniques that make it possible to follow activity in a living human brain. However, the ways in which a brain encodes and stores its knowledge and memories is still a considerable mystery. But insights into the processes involved may come from artificial intelligence as the design of computer memories moves away from central storage to a distributed form in which data is not located at a particular address in a central memory but is delocalized over a highly parallel network. One theory of memory that builds a bridge between artificial intelligence and cognitive science, and falls very naturally into the parallel architectures of the future, is due to W. Ross Quillian. Quillian was interested in word memory and the ways in which a computer can be made to understand the meaning of a given word. He suggested that meaning depends on the way a given word is related to other words in the language. Suppose, for example, you have a smattering of French and wish to know the meaning of a particular word in the Larousse dictionary. We may find that the word has several meanings with each meaning having several senses and corresponding for each of these a definition will be given in terms of other words. Since our French is not too good we will need to look up some of these words and their corresponding definitions will take us in search of yet more words. The end result of this process is a complex, interlocking, expanding web of words, a network of relationships which, according to Quillian, gives the meanings and senses of our original word.

Quillian suggested therefore that a computer memory for words and concepts could be designed in which each word forms the node of a network and the arcs are the various relationships between words. But our exercise with the dic-

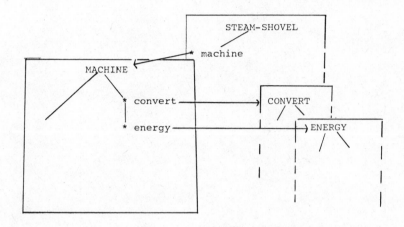

Figure 9-1
Connection between Semantic Planes
The planes in Quillian's scheme are all interconnected

tionary indicates that as more words are added such a network would rapidly become unmanageable and it would soon be extremely difficult to find a path from a node at one point to a more distant one. Quillian's answer was to give the memory net a definite structure using a scheme of "planes." Each given concept or word forms the heading for a plane and is called its *type node*.

As the diagram shows, the meaning of the type node is expressed within the plane as a network of other words, called *token nodes*. The overall network does not end here for in turn these token nodes may be related to other concepts and headings. Hence, token nodes in one plane can be linked to type nodes in another. In this way the planes themselves

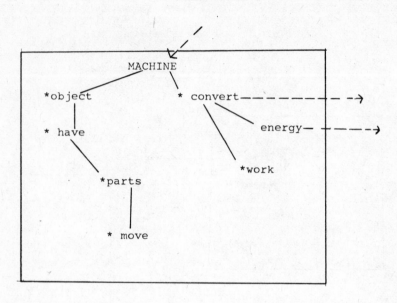

Figure 9-2
Quillian's Semantic Memory
One of the planes used in the memory network. This plane defines
the concept MACHINE (a type node) in terms of a series of token
nodes:

The dotted lines show connections between token nodes in the
MACHINE plane and type nodes in other planes.

become interconnected into a much larger network. The
classification scheme of planes, however, prevents the complexity of the network getting out of hand since token nodes
in one plane cannot link directly to token nodes in another
but must form their relationships via the headings of type
nodes of each plane.

Quillian's semantic network therefore uses an hierarchical
scheme for arriving at the meaning of a word or recalling
that word from "memory." Words with different meanings

338

form the headings of several planes, with each plane corresponding to a particular meaning. In the case of multiple senses of a given word the notion of a context is used. For example, if the word "bright" is entered into the system along with the word "morning" then the computer will search among its network of planes and interconnections until it discovers a pathway between "bright" and "morning" and have a sense for the word "bright" when used in the context of "morning." "Bright" and "child" would produce a different meaning within a new context. Quillian's system also allows for learning, as the effect of a new concept are broadcast by a "spreading activity" throughout the network.

Quillian's theory lends itself very naturally to the parallel processing and distributed memories that are being planned for computers of the future. It has also found some support from psychology where experiments on word inferences seem to suggest a network theory. Suppose a subject is given two target words which can be interrelated to each other by an intermediary chain of meanings. For example:

"A canary is a canary"
"A canary is a bird"
"A canary is an animal"

If meanings are carried in the form of a semantic network then it is reasonable to assume that if many levels of inference are needed to search through the network for the connection between the words, then a longer reaction time is required than if the connection is direct. Psychological experiments suggest that this is indeed the case; however, the interpretation is not unambiguous and certain other factors about word memory also need to be explained.

Another computer memory system, although not directly modeled on Quillian's, also employs a network. Scott Fahlman's NETL is a highly parallel system containing simple nodes, each capable of storing only a few bits of data and carrying out simple Boolean calculations. In NETL the geometry of the network itself is the memory and it can be used to represent knowledge in the form of interacting nodes. Deductions in NETL are made by sending a simple message into the system which is then broadcast throughout the network.

Network theories of memory, like Quillian's, are not supposed to give a complete account of human memory but suggest interesting and thought-provoking ideas which can be explored and extended using computer simulations, and may in turn give insights into how superior computer memories can be designed. An interesting aside to the problem of memory is the fact of its fallibility in humans. Our memories may store all manner of things, from faces and telephone numbers to the taste of Cointreau and the lines of a poem but we do tend to forget some things and in rather complicated ways, so how is it that we are still able to function? Marvin Minsky argues that this very forgetfulness that is connected with our essential intelligence. A system with a perfect memory is able to reproduce everything that it has learned but a brain that forgets is forced to fill in details, work out missing steps, and employ ingenious tricks and subterfuges to cover up its mistakes. Having a fallible memory means that we must be watchful and smart while a machine with perfect recall would have little reason to develop these higher powers.

Computers and Feelings

Computers, as we have seen, are capable of simulating the human brain in several of its processing functions but it could be objected that up to now all these attempts have concentrated on reason alone and have left out such essentially human activities as belief, desire, will, and emotion. If computers are to develop intelligence must they work in entirely rational ways or have they to adopt some of the other characteristics of humans? Few researchers have given thought to such questions. John McCarthy, however, has argued that while it may one day be technically possible to program emotions into a machine it would not to wise to do so. Writing in *Psychology Today*, McCarthy says, "We have enough trouble figuring out our duties to our fellow humans and to animals without creating a bunch of robots with qualities that would allow anyone to feel sorry for them or would allow them to feel sorry for themselves."

Despite McCarthy's stricture it is possible that emotions will one day be programmed into a computer and, if this is properly done, the exercise could prove particularly interesting. To begin with, before emotions can be "programmed into" a computer, scientists must understand exactly what they are dealing with. There is a persistent tendency for us to treat thought and emotion as quite distinct entities and to suppose that we can, for example, observe our emotions in an objective fashion and even exert rational control over them; conversely when these emotions "take over" they become so violent that they "distort" our thinking processes so everything becomes colored by the corresponding emotion. Emotions, according to this hypothesis, are separable from thought and appear to be a form of global constraint that can be imposed upon the already existing thought process. Such emotions may not be particularly difficult to program into a machine and there would be goals and constraints corresponding to anger, love, jealousy, and so on. In this way one could explore the effect on a particular process by switching on and off these emotions.

However, there is evidence that emotions do not necessarily work this way at all, as constraints that are independent of rational thought, but that thought and emotion may be inseparable at some deeper level. The evidence of neurotransmitters points to one mechanism by which thought and emotion may arise out of the same indivisible process. During the past decade, neuroscientists have realized the important role played in the brain by chemicals called neurotransmitters. These chemicals act at the level of individual nerve processes and seem to be fairly specific for certain functions and to certain areas of the brain. For example, some of them induce sleep and calmness, others change the threshold of pain, lift depression, aid in learning, or trigger motor activity. Some of them, such as vasopressin and corticotrophin, are found not only within the brain but are associated with specific body organs where they have quite separate actions.

Just as thought and problem solving has been associated with electrical activity in neural networks, so some writers have speculated that emotions are associated with relative concentrations of neurotransmitters. These speculations are particularly crude but if we accept them even temporarily they lead to the conclusion that, at their generative level, thought and emotion are indissoluble. At the level of individual nerve cells, neurotransmitters have an effect on nerve synapses, and conversely neurotransmitters are synthesized at specific sights in response to neural activity. Hence neural activity both of the chemical and electrical activity is interdependent and inseparable. If one accepted the crude identification between chemistry and emotion on the one hand and electrical discharges and thought on the other, then even this distinction leads to the conclusion that thought and emotion are intimately interconnected at the level of the elementary processes which give rise to them and that there is no thought without accompanying emotion and no emotion without thought.

On the basis of this speculative model, the activities of the brain have both a chemical and electrical nature through which thought and emotion are intimately tied together. The task of converting such a proposal into an analytical model and then programming it on a computer would be a particularly interesting challenge.

Brains, Bodies and Transcendence.

While the simulation of emotion may lie some distance in the future it is true to say that while artificial intelligence has concentrated on developing the computer's more rational functions it has lagged behind in developing those other functions that we associate with the brain. Most probably researchers have felt little need to pursue such questions since giving emotions to a computer would be of little help in solving logical problems or teaching an industrial robot. They could be important, however, when it comes to interpreting extended text and interacting more effectively with humans. Even in those areas of reason where artificial intelligence has had its greatest success not everyone agrees that the systems involved have resulted in valuable insights. Hubert Dreyfus, a philosopher at the University of California, is a long time critic of artificial intelligence, and has argued that the insights gained from particular systems cannot be generalized in any useful way. Dreyfus points out that AI's star systems have always been geared to limited model worlds or to specialized situations. They, therefore, owe their success to the very clever ways in which designers have made use of simplifying assumptions and on the restrictions of a particular model. These systems, Dreyfus argues, end up being entirely specific and locked into a particular set of constraints so that any attempt to generalize or extend them ends in failure. Since each success is specific to a particular model world and forever sealed behind its boundaries, it is invalid to make generalizations and extract principles that could be applied to more general situations, or to suggest that present systems will evolve into more powerful and general ones.

Dreyfus's criticisms have been hotly countered by the AI community and he has become something of a thorn in their collective flesh but the substance of his objections has been echoed by others. Daniel Dennet, from Tufts University, points out that cognitive scientists tend to work with subsystems that are studied behind artificially walled-off boundaries, on the other hand understanding may only occur when the whole organism is taken into account and some general principles are uncovered. The problem with whole systems, however, is that they are far too complicated and far too big for their behavior to be modeled on a computer. Dennet, therefore, suggested that AI researchers and cognitive scientists should focus on some entirely new creature which occupies its unique evolutionary niche, a Martian three-wheeled iguana for example. With the aid of such a creature, scientists may begin to discover some general, abstract principles about cognitive organization. His proposals recall those made by M. Toda in this 1962 paper "The Design of a Fungus-Eater" which suggested that one could begin with an environment and then design a creature with the minimum qualities designed to survive and function in it.

These criticisms seem to be valuable ones and should be kept in mind as the science of artificial intelligence evolves. At present the field is divided into a host of specialist areas such as vision, speech, language, motion, touch, knowledge representation, problem solving, learning, and so on. Indeed, this division seems to be forced on the subject by virtue of the complexity of the problems involved. Yet at some higher level it will be necessary to integrate all these approaches together into a coherent whole. Take for example the problem of vision. We have seen in Chapter 6 how some very interesting and exciting research is at present being directed to the analysis of images and the identification of objects. Yet at some higher level in the vision process, an abstract symbolic representation is formed. Seeing, in humans, is not simply a matter of reflex actions in response to identified stimuli but involves the construction of an objective, visual world which is available for our contemplation. At some point in AI research a real system will have to emerge that can make use of its various senses in a coordinated way. At this level it may turn out, for example, that the vision process is intimately tied up with its use of language and the way it represents knowledge and knowledge in turn may be determined by other factors. So at the level of integration it may be the case that representations and high level processes act to constrain and determine each other and these constraints act back on the more primitive levels of processing.

One of the major unsolved problems in artificial intelligence is the connection between signals and symbols, that is, the problem of going from a signal processing level to a higher symbolic level. It is generally assumed that this will eventually be solved in the abstract and that artificial intelligence need only concern itself with the formal levels of processing and not with the actual hardware on which the processing is carried out. Yet if one examines the human body with its eyes, ears, speech production, and limbs and then looks at the brain which controls it all, the whole system appears so beautifully designed and arranged so that form and function mirror each other. The hardware of each organ and the way its information is processed seems to be intimately connected with each complementing the other. Considerations such as this suggest the inherent limitations of studying AI problems in the abstract and in isolation from one another. While this may lead to insights in the short term it is an inherently limited method for totally new levels of behavior and general principles may emerge when problems become integrated and feedback these results into the design of the computer itself.

Of course, some of this is happening already. Real time vision systems cry out for parallel processors that operate at the level of edge detection so that their form and function become united. But when such parallel systems are designed and used in image detection, new algorithms will have to be developed and these will suggest different approaches to theory which may in turn be used to modify the design of vision hardware. When such vision systems become a part of a general robot the visual information they process will be gathered in response to questions asked by a central control and will provide some of the information needed for the robot to get around in the world. In response to the demands of the robot, the visual system may enter a new phase of evolution in the design of its eyes and processing hardware. In turn the system may set limitations on the way the robot moves and the type of tasks it can carry out. Faced with these new constraints the robot designers may modify the way the system interacts mechanically with the world and so on.

It could well be that intelligent systems will never evolve in the vacuum of a laboratory bench but must first be brought into hard and painful contact with the real world. It may indeed be possible in the 1990s to produce an automatic creature that can survive and function in its environment. Such a robot would have to look after its energy needs (solar, chemical, or electrical), avoid danger, repair any minor damage it sustains, move around, learn, adapt, and even begin to modify itself in response to the demands of its environment. The interesting question such a creature poses is: Would it get stuck at a particular level of cognitive development or would it transcend its own levels of thought and evolve an intelligence of its own?

The whole question of how a machine can break out of the cycle of automatic response to its program, and, when it is faced with a failure of its internal strategies, jump to some higher level of description is a fascinating one. The ultimate question facing the AI community is how is an advanced computer to be designed that will spontaneously develop intelligence as it learns about the world?

Some of the most imaginative thinking in this area comes from M.I.T.'s Marvin Minsky and his former colleague, Seymour Papert, who have proposed a "society of minds" to account for how the complexities of a human brain can evolve out of a collection of simple interacting neurones. Minsky's thinking has resonances in the work of Douglas Hofstadter (author of *Gödel, Escher, Bach: An Eternal Golden Braid*, Basic Books, 1979, N.Y.). In his Pulitzer Prize winning book, Hofstadter explored various examples of self-referential systems that are capable of describing themselves and even of reflecting on their own nature. More recently Hofstadter, like Minsky, has called into question the whole trend of AI research and argued that while it is capable of producing such advances as expert systems, its future applications are inherently limited because the field has up to now been unable to capture the essential intelligence of a living brain. Current systems can solve problems and perform other high level tasks but they do not possess the ability to adapt to new conditions and respond to unpredictable events. By contrast, the brains of animals and humans have evolved in open situations which are constantly changing and throwing out new challenges. Living brains are always learning, adapting, and transcending the rules they have created.

Hofstadter feels that this degree of richness and flexibility will never be achieved with computers until the philosophy of artificial intelligence is turned on its head. Current computers are controlled from the top down with a high level executive control being exerted over lower level events. In addition, computers are rule bound and place their reliance on the laws of logic and inference. But both Hofstadter and Minsky feel that the human brain works in a very different way and its high level, logical control is an effect that arises out of the cooperative action of many simpler processes that operate at a grass-roots level. Intelligence is, therefore, something that *emerges* out of collective behavior at a lower level, rather than a set of simple, logical rules *imposed* from above. Hofstadter's suggestion is that the brain's higher processes are created out of the apparently random operation of individual neurons which combine together in what could almost be called a form of play.

As an example of this theory, Hofstadter points to those word jumbles or anagrams in which the letters of a word are mixed up. When we try to untangle an anagram we do not employ strict rules of logic or a definite plan of procedure, rather we play with the letters, allowing them to dance in our mind until elementary patterns emerge. Take the problem that was left at the end of Chatper 3, the anagram

F. David Peat

FEERFLSCNEERET

As we play with the letters, patterns like

FFL   EEE   LTS

emerge and are immediately rejected as not looking like parts of words in English.

SEL   AL   RE   TEN   FER   FAR

look more promising so we hold on to them in our minds or even jot them down on paper and then play round with these elementary blocks.

SEL AL   SEL RE   RESEL   RE TEN   RE FA   RE FER

The last rings a bell, REFER, it looks like a bigger part of a word, or a word all on its own. So being with the play of simple elements which combine, almost by chance into larger and larger groups, the solution is built up until the final word emerges.

Of course in this example, a final order already exists since SELF-REFERENCE is a word in English. But it is also possible to conceive a play of elements that, at some higher level, produces a new and original ordering which did not exist before. Hofstadter throws out the speculation that the brain may have developed and evolved through an analogous process and that a similar approach could be used in the field of artificial intelligence to design advanced computer systems.

At first sight it is difficult to see how high level control and formal logic could develop out of the play of simple elements yet such processes are also being studied in other areas of science. Within organic chemistry the interplay of atoms and atomic groups, acting under the constraints of geometry and chemical bonding, combines to form larger molecular blocks and these blocks in turn combine to form the DNA chain or molecular biology. From physics, apparently random motion of electrons results, at a sufficiently low temperature, in the coherent property of a superconductor. Chaotic molecules of individual motions in liquid helium will likewise result in an overall cooperative state of superfluidity.

This emergence of order out of a background of random, individual fluctuations has examples in chemistry, biology, and sociology. Ilya Prigogine for example, had formulated a theory of what he calls *dissipative structures*: stable, large scale organizations that evolve out of random fluctuations in an open system that is far from thermodynamic equilibrium. Examples of such dissipative structures range from vortices in a river and large scale orderings during chemical reactions to the more complex structures of biological systems and even to the organizations of cities and social structures.

Physicists like John Wheeler, Roger Penrose, and David Finkelstein have proposed theories in which the universe itself arises out of a large collection of processes that take place at the most elementary level. Penrose for example has constructed a theoretical network which has for its nodes, not binary electronic switches, but binary quantum "spinors," the most elementary objects in quantum theory. As these spinor networks increase in size they begin to develop some of the properties of three-dimensional space. Penrose has speculated that spacetime itself may be constructed out of an extension of these abstract networks.

John Wheeler has made a number of speculations on the underlying structure of laws of physics and he has attempted to derive quantum theory and relativity from what he calls its underlying "pregeometry." This pregeometry is in turn created out of even more elementary processes. Wheeler has also speculated that the evolution of the universe may be triggered by its self-referential nature. Self reference appears in a fundamental way in the quantum theory and also crops up as one considers the evolution of conscious beings and

F. David Peat

thinking computers. These examples of the evolution of complexity out of apparently random systems suggests that the notion of intelligence emerging through the play of simpler units may not be all that far-fetched.

Marvin Minsky has been particularly active in trying to understand the ways in which the structure and order of the human brain and of an intelligent machine could emerge out of the interaction of simple elements. Minsky calls his theory the "society of minds," and gives as a preliminary example a child playing with blocks. Are the child's actions the result of a strict logical control arising in the highest functions of the brain, or could they be a cooperative effect arising out of the mutual interaction of many low level actors? Minsky suggests that the latter explanation is more plausible and that the brain's structure and behavior arises through the harmony and conflicts of these actors.

Suppose that a member of this "society of minds," christened BUILDER, wishes to construct a tower out of the blocks while another, WRECKER, enjoys knocking over a pile of blocks. WRECKER and BUILDER are in conflict but WRECKER realizes that he must suspend his action until BUILDER has been allowed to construct his tower. So BUILDER carries on with his job and calls on the actor PUT to place the blocks on top of each other. PUT in turn calls on HAND and TRAJECTORY who cooperate to lift and move each block. The tower grows through the concerted action of a number of agents each of which can perform his required tasks when called upon, without the need for detailed instructions. PUT, for example, does not have to program or instruct HAND or TRAJECTORY with strings of steps that must be stored in a memory and sequentially executed. PUT simply calls his assistants into action and they respond because each knows how to perform his own tasks.

As the tower grows, WRECKER and BUILDER come into deeper conflict over their respective goals so attempts at a resolution are made by PLAY WITH BLOCKS who in turn is

350

under the control of a higher agent PLAY. Yet PLAY itself is not without conflict for HUNGER is beginning to dominate the situation. As the child finally runs to the lunch table, he resolves any residual tension by kicking out at the tower as he goes. WRECKER is satisfied.

For Minsky, the evolution of our highly sophisticated adult brains, with their ability to develop logic and work at high levels of abstraction, begins with this society of individual actors in the young child's brain. As the child grows, higher levels of the brain emerge, through the cooperation of these actors, that are now able to carry out sophisticated tasks, solve more problems, and pass high level messages to each other. But at lower levels, more primitive actors engage in only the simplest of crosstalk and are directly activated by calling them into operation. Like skilled workmen they do not need to be programmed since each knows his own job and carries his own tools and blueprints with him. The human brain, according to Minsky is a complex network of agents, interconnected by communication channels and with instructions and memory distributed across the whole cortex.

It is in the embryo, Minsky suggests, that actors begin their lives. Operating under genetic programs they are linked together through common communication channels, carry out the same actions and share a common database. During the first months of life the brain shows a high redundancy since many agents work in synchronization on the same tasks, but as the brain matures and the child explores the world, each pathway and each group of agents begins to differentiate and specialize. Out of the parallel tracks of nerve connections, a specialized network emerges which corresponds to the white matter of the brain. Neighboring actors, or groups of neurons, still share their communication channels and much of their data but they begin to specialize in certain aspects of neural processing. Other agents, further away in the brain are now cut off and can communicate only in limited ways via other groups and have only limited access to other data. So by means of a hierarchical process of specialization that is governed by genetic programming and learning, the brain begins to develop its overall structure which ranges from the simplest groups of actors to the powerful control areas which are capable of using abstraction, concepts, powerful symbols, and language. But unlike conventional models, based on current computers, this high level control is not imposed from outside or developed from the top down, but emerges out of an underlying society of minds.

Minsky has looked at the implications of this idea of a society of minds for such things as humor, vision, and the appreciation of music. In Chapter 6 we met that paradox of human vision, that no matter how much we move our head or our eyes carry out their rapid, darting motion, the room we see before us is stationary and immediately present. Minsky suggests that this illusion of vision arises out of the cooperative nature of the visual process itself. At the lowest levels, FEATURE DETECTORS work on images on the retina which are passed on to SHAPE ANALYZERS who assess the incoming data, and, in turn, pass it on to various agents who specialize in recognizing common objects like chairs, tables, windows, and people. One of these higher agents, TABLE BUILDER may be presented with a three-legged object which has some features of a table. While holding this object in his memory he sends back requests to SHAPE ANALYZER asking for confirmation of the fourth leg and the resolution of other visual ambiguities. In turn, SHAPE ANALYZER activates the various FEATURE DETECTORS and via other agents instruct the eyes to dart about and seek additional information in the neighborhood of the table.

While the various visual components in the scene are being assembled by TABLE BUILDER, FACE BUILDER, and WINDOW BUILDER, a higher level agent SPACE BUILDER is constructing an overall visual picture of the room based partly on his agent's reports and partly on memories of other scenes. So visual impression of the room is not built up line by line like the scanning of a television picture (in this case the individual scanning movements of the eye), but comes into existence as a whole and at the highest level of the visual process. While ambiguities are being checked and other aspects of the room explored by movements of the eyes, the whole visual picture does not vanish but is maintained by **SPACE BUILDER**, with the help of his agents **TABLE BUILDER**, **FACE BUILDER**, and so on. At each level of vision, particular information is held in a short-term memory system while lower level agents sort out ambiguities and fill in details. In a real sense, therefore, vision has an immediate quality that lies outside time for, as far as our perception of scenes is concerned, it is presented to us as a complete, timeless impression.

Minsky has applied a related approach to the act of listening to music which, although it consists of a succession of events in times, also appears to have a timeless quality similar to vision. When we hear a familiar tune, or the theme in a sonata or symphony, we hear it all as a piece and not as a succession of individual notes. The reason, Minsky claims, is that, like vision, music is built out of the cooperative action of a series of agents. Listening to music begins with the action of low level agents who are on the look out for individual sonic events which are then fitted into patterns by higher level agents. Rhythm in particular acts as an important feature in this processing since rhythms act as templates against which the various transformations of harmony and these can be compared. At the higher levels of music processing, agents work together to detect transformations of musical phrases and pass their results to higher agents who work these transformations together into the recognition of some overall structure.

Minsky has pointed out that classical forms in music act as teaching machines, since they introduce simple themes and teach their implications through repetitions, develop-

353

ments, expositions, and recapitulations. They are culturally important teaching machines, Minsky adds, because through music we learn about structuring in time and about the movements of events. Music may also be about teaching the affects, at least, when it comes to nursery songs, for they involve the stringing together of "sentic patterns," elementary musical patterns that are associated with certain states of mind. At its most elementary level, therefore, music is the encoded movement of mind, an idea that it not far from the statement of the composer Edgar Varses, "Music is the corporealization of thought."

Since, according to Minsky, the brain develops through the differentiation and specialization of its agents, then the ways in which it interacts and learns from the outside world will be of vital importance to the ultimate structure of this "society of minds." In the earliest months and years the political development of this society will be governed by genetic instructions but there will also be an important contribution that arises through interactions with the external world. There is experimental evidence from laboratory animals that during a certain critical period the brain's structure is plastic and responds to the stimuli and the use it receives. Following this period the "jelly sets" and the brain's processes and internal structure are determined. In the case of vision it is not difficult to understand how a rich visual environment during the early months of life will lead to a correspondingly rich structuring in the brain and that animals that have been visually deprived will develop an impoverished structure. But what of the higher brain functions such as thought? How is thought and reason built out of a society of minds? Is there a critical period for their development or is the brain always plastic with respect to these functions so our capacities remain open ended?

In Chapter 2 we commented on the privileged position that is given to logical reasoning in our society and in the chapters that followed we have seen that an AI systems logic is imposed from the top down. Logic reigns as king and from its commanding position in central control it directs the individual operations of thinking machines. But not everyone agrees with this approach, for it can be pointed out that the human brain employs many other functions in addition to logical reasoning, and Hofstadter, for example, has argued that artificial intelligence must be turned on its head if intelligent machines are to be developed. For Marvin Minsky, logic and reason are not prior, higher order functions within the society of minds but evolve out of the complex interaction of more primitive operations. Minsky argues that the brain begins with powerful functions such as common sense, metaphor, analogy, abstraction, and various forms of what logicians would call false reasoning. Such reasoning is often used by children:

Major Premise: Daddy has a briefcase.
Minor Premise: That man has a briefcase.
Conclusion: Therefore that man is a daddy.

A child's reasoning confuses "some" with "all," jumps from a particular example to a general conclusion, works by analogy, and fills in its gaps of reasoning by a sleight of hand. Work on learning that is being carried out by J. Seely Brown and others at the Xerox Research Laboratories in Palo Alto shows that when children have gaps in their knowledge of arithmetic operations they employ a series of internal rules to "stitch over" the gap. These rules are quite consistent and appear to be fairly universal from child to child but they also happen to lead to the incorrect result!

This is therefore a danger in using common sense reasoning since if thought is the combination of a large number of elementary rules, each with a limited range of applications, then once rules are pushed outside their proper domains the brain will come up with an inappropriate result. It is as if the domain of thought is a frozen pond covered with patches of thin ice and other areas where the ice is strong. Provided that one only skates on the safe areas there will be no disaster but if a skater ventures onto a patch of thin ice he will fall through and get a soaking. But how could we survive in the world, using a collection of limited reasoning processes, if we are prone to make mistakes in dealing with our environment? In Chapter 8 we met Patrick Winston's idea of learning through the accumulation of censors and this approach fits very well into Minsky's overall theory. Since reason and thought is not something imposed from above by a super logical control unit but is a collection of processes that emerge out of the brain's cooperative action, then the brain must also contain danger signals to indicate when a particular thought process is being pushed too far. To return to the metaphor of the frozen lake, these censors are the warning signs erected around regions of thin ice which tell the skaters to keep away. Accumulating warning signs or censors is part of the process of learning, and it is a process which persists throughout life as new situations are encountered. The censors themselves are pieces of meta-knowledge, information about the way knowledge can be used and operate most effectively when they detect the *precursors* to faulty thought which they then deflect or inhibit from continuing.

Minsky has suggested that many of these censors are taught to us by society and one means of doing this is to use humor, particularly of the "nonsense joke" variety. Nonsense humor is able to bypass the censors that are concerned with preventing paradoxes or faulty thought and by concealing the point of a joke it is possible to reach an area of thin ice and then expose the whole nonsensical process to the thinker. The laughter that results is according to Minsky, a physiological action that disrupts reasoning, stops the flow of paradoxical thought, and alerts the censors of the mind to a new patch of thin ice. Historically, humor may have been of immense value to the survival of our race for it was the means of defining the boundaries of the emerging faculty of reason and of demonstrating the applicability of thought in solving important problems.

Marvin Minsky's ideas are tantalizing and provocative and they may contain an important germ of truth; on the other hand, it is quite possible that they are totally wrong. What seems to be most valuable about them is not so much their possible validity but the fact that they call into question many of the presuppositions of artificial intelligence and suggest totally new ways of approaching problems and of designing the intelligent computers of the future. Minsky's speculations also allow us to consider our original question "Can a machine think?" at a deeper level.

Is a Computer Aware of Its Own Existence?

Having explored a few implications of our first question we can now pass on to the second question: "Is a computer aware of its own existence?" Suppose that towards the end of its decade a massively parallel computer is built which is capable of learning and developing some form of hierarchical structuring to its treatment of knowledge. Has such a machine taken the first steps towards consciousness? It could be argued that the essence of consciousness lies in self-awareness, the ability for us to reflect on our own thought processes and to adjust them when we deal with new situations. We have seen earlier in this book, in dealing with expert systems and problem solving, how important is the role of meta-knowledge and knowledge about the way in which knowledge works. The human brain can reflect not only on its knowledge but also upon its meta-knowledge and can therefore restructure the way it looks at the world.

Douglas Hofstadter's book *Godel, Escher, Bach* is a playful fugue on the whole theme of self-reference and the paradoxes it can generate and resolve. G. Spenser-Brown's *The Laws of Form* aroused some interest a decade ago, when it attempted to formulate a symbolic system that was capable of generating self-referential statements. The paradoxes of self-reference within language are as old as philosophy:

357

F. David Peat

THE STATEMENT BELOW IS FALSE.
THE STATEMENT ABOVE IS TRUE.

and the paradox of the barber:

If the barber is the man who shaves all men who do not shave themselves then who shaves the barber?

Bertrand Russell's theory of types was an attempt to resolve such paradoxes when they occur in symbolic logic.

A self-referential sentence also forms the nub of Kurt Gödel's proof of the incompleteness of formal systems such as mathematics and branches of axiomatic logic. Simply speaking, what Gödel did was to establish that the following sentence is true within the system P:

"This sentence is not provable in the formal system P."

The implication of this true, self-referential sentence is that there exist some true statements, or theorems, that can never be proved within the system. The conclusion in the case of mathematics, is that it is incomplete as are some branches of symbolic logic. It is as if a giant tower were to be built to the Moon with each piece firmly attached to the next and the whole structure resting on solid foundations on Earth. Out in space, certain perfectly well made sections of the tower have already been preconstructed but, try as one may, it appears impossible to attach them to the main tower. In a similar way the Lego sets of the mind are inherently limited and it can never fill the whole of the space of our imagination. But this is simply poetic metaphor and interpreting the implications of Gödel's theorem is no trivial matter. Some thinkers have argued that since Gödel has demonstrated the limitations of formal logic and since all computers are constructed to operate with logic then these machines are inherently limited and can never attain consciousness. Others have objected that no such simple inference cannot be made from Gödel's theorem.

Self-referential systems not only occur in the abstract worlds of language and logic but in the concrete world of matter as well. The DNA molecule is both a description of the living cell and a description of the DNA molecule itself. The self-replicating space factories of the future will contain blueprints for the construction of new factories which also have the power of self-replication so an important part of the blueprint must be the instructions on how to construct a device to reproduce blueprints! Even at the atomic level a notion of self-reference creeps in. A quantum system's properties are a function of the overall context in which that system is observed and measured. Yet all observation systems are themselves composed of quantum systems. This circle of observer and observed has led John Wheeler to propose that the universe comes into existence as a self-referential system.

These few examples and illustrations do not in themselves point to any theory or hypothesis but simply indicate that there is something very serious about self-reference. Self-referential systems transcend paradoxes, they jump out of fixed descriptive levels and appear to be able to stand outside themselves. Self-reference appears to be tied up with the emergence of new levels of description and the evolution of new structures. One could speculate that the answer to our second question "Is a computer aware of its own existence?" is fundamentally tied up with the issue of self-reference.

For Hofstadter a self-referential system is an essential factor in the development of true artificial intelligence for such systems know about their own knowledge and have the ability to jump from one level of description to a new higher level. But this question leads to an even more exciting question; how could a symbolic system spontaneously develop a new level of activity without some outside interference? In logic there already exist systems that can refer to their own structures and symbols. But such abstract symbolic systems have been deliberately constructed and are lifeless, static things without any power of their own to develop further and move into new levels of description. The genetic code, by contrast is not simply an abstract system for it is both a string of abstract symbols and a physical arrangement of molecules. It is at one and the same time a message and the action of that message.

This missing link between an abstract symbolic system and transformations in the physical world appears to be related to what theoretical biologist Howard Pattee has called "description-construction" systems. These are cases in which a symbol exists both in the context of an abstract message or piece of information and as an actor in the world of matter and energy. To return to the example of DNA, its particular molecular geometry is both a message, a complete set of instructions for the regulation and reproduction of an organism, including the DNA molecule itself, and also a constraint on physical and chemical processes within the cell. The self-referential message of the genetic code is also a catalyst or template which can direct its own chemical reproduction. In an analogous sense, thoughts in the mind and instructions in a computer are also description-construction systems in that they are not only an abstract message but they are procedures and physical processes that take place within the computer and the brain. Self-referential messages in Howard Pattee's construction-description systems have a dual nature which allow them to exist simultaneously within the worlds of symbols and information and the worlds of matter and energy.

Pattee has speculated that in the case of biological organisms, these description-construction systems evolve through a dialectical approach in which failure to resolve a description at one level results in a jump to some new higher level. In this fashion self-referential systems evolve to higher and higher levels of hierarchical complexity. This development through the transcendence of levels would seem to be fundamental to mind, brain, consciousness, intelligence, and to the AI machines of the future.

Considerations of construction-description and the ways in which new levels could arise in self-referential systems may ultimately be able to shed light on a fundamental problem of artificial intelligence, that of moving from the level of input and signal to that of representation and symbol. In a sense this is the mind-body problem for the computer! This question requires a very careful analysis that lies outside the scope of the present book but a simple metaphor may give some hints as to its complexity. The image is that of a child shooting down space ships in a video arcade and is the elaboration of a metaphor that was explained to me during a conversation with David Bohm. Bohm, in turn, explored the metaphor at the suggestion of Alex Comfort. Standing in front of a video game the child watches a series of space ships advance and attempts to shoot them down. In the analysis that follows one should ask the following questions. At what level does the fundamental description lie? Or, is there indeed a fundamental level? Who is in overall control of the game? Where does message end and material process begin? Is there a clear division between mind, body, program, and machine?

The child is involved in shooting down spaceships. But where are these space ships? At one level they are simply movements of shapes across the screen. But, in fact, no physical movement actually takes place, there is simply a pattern of fluorescence at different positions on the screen from one scan to the next. The space ships are simply the product of an electron beam hitting a television tube. But this process at another level is the expression of a computer program in the video game's microprocessor. The spaceships are transformations of abstract symbols and the operations of binary arithmetic. At another level they are the motion of electronic pulses in a circuit and changes of state in its transistors. Indeed one can explore several levels deeper and discuss the events in terms of elementary quantum processes in a transistor, or even the collapse of an electron's wave function. But the space ships are also patterns of excitation on the retinas of the child's eyes, they are neurological events and, at another level, complex bursts of information that are being processed in the visual cortex. At higher levels they become a synthesis of shapes and movements and, finally, the space ships that exist in the child's imagination.

As the child shoots down the space ships information filters down from the high levels in the brain, into muscular contractions, through the button on the video game and into the microprocessor's program. More directly the imagination interacts with the program and results in a particular pattern of light disappearing from the screen. The child plays the game and the game plays the child.

What is apparent from these various levels of description is that what can be read as a symbolic level, on one level, becomes a material process on another and what are taken for the transformations of matter at one level become a flow of information at another. Each material level, at some other level, becomes a message level and each message level, at some other level, is a level of material process. It is clear that there is no distinct boundary in all this, no clear division between message and matter, no point of contact at which body ends and mind begins.

The implications of this little metaphor are clear, and very different from the picture given by traditional philosophy. If we were given the poetic licence to compress hundreds of years of philosophical debate into a simplistic nutshell then the germ of one debate would be that mind and body are distinct entities, each existing in its own domain yet quite separate from each other. For the followers of Descartes this notion reached an extreme, for they argued that no mechanism existed that could mediate the interaction between mind and matter. One may will one's arm to move and it moves, yet mind and matter are such very different substances that nothing in Newton's universe allows the one to influence the other. Mind and brain are like twin clocks that chime the hour in harmony yet have no interaction between them. Echoes of the Cartesian dualism persist today. Sir John Eccles, a noted neuroscientist, has suggested the existence of a "liaison brain" to mediate the traffic between mind and the physical brain it is associated with.

Consideration of the image of the video game, and of Pattee's construction-description systems points in a very different direction from mind-body duality. In place of a mind that interacts in some mysterious way with the material world via the medium of a brain is a mind that evolves naturally out of the complex levels of process and symbol. In an AI vision system, for example, the process of understanding a scene takes place through a series of levels which begins with the raw image and moves towards an abstract representation. In some future, advanced system this process may end with a full internal representation of the world that the computer can contemplate and reflect upon. Mind or consciousness is not something that is "programmed into" or added to the computer but is something that emerges out of the collective interaction of many levels of description, process and organization.

At first sight such an analysis may appear to imply that mind is "nothing more than matter" and that, since the material world is governed by the laws of physics, the mind is similarly determined. In the sixteenth century the motion of the heavenly bodies was assumed to obey a very different description from that of earthy matter until Newton showed that stars, planets, cannon balls, and apples all obeyed the same laws of motion. In the nineteenth century some scientists still argued that living matter obeyed quite different laws from that which governed the inanimate. But biology was reduced to chemistry and chemistry to physics and physics to the laws that govern the atom. Around the 1930s it was a common remark among physicists that everything could be explained by the Schrödinger equation (an equation which governs the behavior of quantum particles). Now it appears that a final layer has been added, mind is nothing more than brain and brain is nothing more than matter.

It is only comparatively recently that this reductionism has been seriously questioned by scientists. It is certainly true that biological systems can be broken apart into molecules that obey the laws of organic chemistry, that molecules can be broken into atoms, and atoms into elementary particles and at each level a new description of the world is called for. But it is not true that all the richness of behavior of a chemical system is contained within the laws of physics or the evolution of a biological system can be exhaustively predicted in terms of the laws of chemistry. Ilya Priggogine, for example, has argued forcefully that each level of behavior requires its own description which is not contained in the description and laws of a lower level. For Priggogine the emergence of new levels is accompanied by new orders of behavior and requires new descriptions. Mind is a similar evolution, the emergence of new orders of behavior out of the complex web of processes and symbols within the brain; it is not therefore reducable to some more primitive level of description.

Some scientists are also pointing out that the behavior of matter is also more subtle than had hitherto been expected. Rather than speaking of mind as "nothing more than matter" matter itself appears as "something more than the material," if by material we mean the mechanical, conditioned aspects of Newtonian physics. The quantum theory has gone some way towards opening our eyes to the curious behavior of matter on the atomic scale. David Bohm has gone further and described the subtle laws that may apply below the accepted level of quantum phenomena. He calls these new laws the *holomovement*, and they describe an implicit level of reality below our everyday "explicate order." Bohm considers that the laws of the holomovement may be very close to the laws of thought and comments: "What happens in our consciousness and what happens in nature are not fundamentally different in form. Therefore thought and matter have a great similarity of order." (Bohm's views can be found in his book: *Wholeness and the Implicate Order*, Routledge & Kegan Paul, London 1980 and, along with a discussion of Priggogine's ideas, in *Looking Glass Universe*, J. P. Briggs and F. David Peat, Cornerstone Library, Simon & Schuster, New York 1984). Mind therefore appears as a very subtle and creative order that arises out of the complex organization of levels of activity in the brain. It is possible that one day, given sufficient flexibility in their internal structure, that computers may evolve to a point where they are able, spontaneously, to transcend their own descriptive levels and evolve the qualities of self-reflection and awareness.

Finally, let us consider our third and last question: "Will the twenty-first century see the evolution of a silicon-based intelligence that is parallel to our own?" The answer has been given, to some extent, in the discussion above, that given the right conditions it is possible that such an intelligence may indeed evolve and what we know as consciousness need not be confined within the limitations of a carbon-based brain. But before that happens there are many outstanding problems in the science of artificial intelligence that must be solved and a number of them are far from simple. At present it is not clear how an advanced intelligence must be designed, beyond the obvious conclusion that its computing processes must be fast and performed in parallel. Up to now AI researchers have kept the considerations of software in a separate compartment from that of hardware and architecture, it has been assumed as a matter of principle that once the overall structure of a solution is understood it can be programmed onto any machine. But the human brain is designed in such a way that its form and function are intimately related and this seems an important hint that hardware and software should grow hand in hand.

In discussing the evolution of artificial intelligence we have assumed, up to now, that it will continue to evolve within a silicon-based brain, using transistors, Josepheson junctions, or optical transphasors, but this need not be the case. It may turn out that neuroscientists can build circuits out of living tissue and create their architectures from neurons, or it may be that a cooperative evolution will take place in which silicon- and carbon-based brains are linked together.

During the 1970s a number of operations were carried out to place electrical stimulators directly in the brain. These small devices gave out electrical signals at predetermined intervals and were used as an experimental treatment for persons with epilepsy, cerebral palsy, and severe depression. The theory as to how these cerebella stimulators worked was not totally clear but one suggestion was that their signals acted to "reset" and normalize the brain's overall electrical activity by influencing an area at the base of the brain called the reticular formation.

In general the results of this treatment were not an overwhelming success. In the case of cerebral palsy, some patients and their families noticed an improvement in ability to carry out everyday tasks like feeding but these encouraging signs were not always confirmed in objective testing. In the case of depression an assessment was even more difficult since it was impossible to have a control group who had also gone through the experience of the operation without actually having a cerebella stimulator implanted. Where change occured it was therefore difficult to distinguish if it was caused by the stimulator or by all the attention and fuss of the operation and postoperative testing. Even in those cases where some improvement was indicated, the effects did not last for long because new tissue appeared around the tip of the electrodes to mask the signal.

The implanted stimulators of the 1970s were not therefore a resounding success, but at the time did lead some doctors to speculate what would happen if more sophisticated devices were available to them. Today it is indeed possible to implant miniature computers, data banks, and the output from remote sensors directly into the brain. But for the present at least, the idea is pure science fiction for no one knows how to solve the problem of the machine/brain interface. It is technically possible to place a sensor on the Moon, and feed its output directly into a human brain on Earth, to implant a chip capable of performing higher mathematics or to supply the human brain with its own expert systems and massive data banks. But how would these electronic signals be fed into the brain so that they could be processed and understood? Silicon- and carbon-based brains have evolved in totally distinct ways, their hardware operates according to quite different principles, and there is probably very little similarity in the symbolic representations they employ to store and process their knowledge. At present, therefore, the possibility of feeding even the simplest concept from a computer brain into a human brain directly is extremely remote. Output must be translated into an everyday language or graphics and inspected by the eyes and ears rather than using direct electrical transfer of signals into the cortex.

Many deep and complex issues must be resolved before there is even the slightest hope of a computer interacting directly with a human brain. First, some common system of representation and data processing must be worked out, then an interface must be created so that the binary flow of information in the computer can be converted into the bursts of electrical impulses and the chemical flows that are used in the brain. Finally some massively parallel interconnection would have to be made between the hardware of this interface and hundreds of thousands of dendrites and neural receptors. Clearly this is a research project for the twenty-first century.

Nevertheless some scientists have begun to investigate ways in which a brain/machine interface could be achieved. Research in one field is directed towards using the output of individual nerves to control, for example, the display on a television screen. By providing a visual feedback the volunteer is able to control the firing of individual nerves and in this way should be able to exert control over machinery. The motive for such research is obvious: output from individual nerves could be used to control artificial limbs, communication devices, and even complex machines. Another approach is to use the overall electrical activity of the brain, as picked up by an EEG machine, and use these complex patterns to control various electronic devices. If such research is successful then it may be possible one day to operate electrical devices by some act of thought and even to receive impressions and sensations from the outside world using a feedback device.

Another approach may be to develop organically based computers in which components are designed at the level of macromolecules. Such a device could be implanted into the brain and serve as an interface to some more powerful silicon-based device. Already researchers are exploring the possibility of grafting portions of the brain from one animal or human to another and this may pave the way for creating links between a brain and some organically-based computer. In one experiment the retina of a rat was grafted directly onto the visual cortex of another rat's brain and visual signals were conducted into the skull via a fiber optic link. Although it is not clear if the rat could actually "see" it was certainly able to respond to visual signals. An extension of such an experiment, which lies far in the future would be to feed the results of the first level of highly parallel computer vision processing into one of the layers of the retina and determine if the rat's brain could in fact distinguish between a series of simple shapes. Experiments on brain/machine interfaces will continue, but in the immediate future at least, the evolution of artificial intelligence lies with the computer and with massively parallel designs using advanced hardware.

Artificial intelligence promises to be one of the most exciting fields of science for, as computer systems continue to develop, it will have to resolve some outstandingly difficult problems about the nature of thought and the mechanisms of the mind. The start of this century was the age of physics with exciting discoveries in relativity, quantum theory, and the structure of the atom. The central decades of this century were the age of biology with the cracking of the genetic code and advances in genetic engineering. The end of the century promises to be the most exciting time of all, the age of intelligence as neuroscientists and AI researchers begin to unlock the secrets of how intelligent systems operate and are structured.

Yet despite the advances that have been made in expert systems, robotics, and problem solving the field of artificial intelligence is still in its infancy. As Daniel Dennett from Tufts University put it during a conversation with Jonathan Miller, "If you look at the actual products of artificial intelligence you find they're a relatively unimpressive lot; they're typically a bag of tricks and even when they do mimic a human being, its usually for spurious reasons. But one shouldn't judge the field by those gimmicks and illustrations, which is really what they are. The real products of the field are conceptual." Artificial intelligence, therefore, is a field full of challengingly difficult problems. By the end of this century it promises, along with the question of human consciousness, to be the most intellectually exciting area of research around.

In a sense this book is premature. It is as if a pre-Newtonian had attempted to map out the course of 20th-century physics with its quarks and black holes. The future of artificial intelligence is unpredictable and its advances are impossible to foretell. In a sense we are all waiting for its Einstein to emerge. One thing can be said for certain, however: that computers are going to continue to evolve and, provided that their designers are clever

369

enough, sometime within the next few decades these machines are going to exhibit the first glimmerings of intelligence.

What happens after that is anyone's guess.